W9-BPL-471

Unanimous acclaim for William C. Dietz's
LEGION OF THE DAMNED

"BUCKLE YOUR SAFETY HARNESS AND ENJOY THE RIDE."
—Steve Perry, author of *The Forever Drug*

"THE UNRELENTING ACTION SWEEPS ALL BEFORE IT." —*Kliatt*

"ROCKETS AND RAY GUNS GALORE . . . and more than enough action to satisfy those who like it hot and heavy." —*The Oregonian*

"ONE THAT I RECOMMEND to enthusiasts of military SF." —*Australian SF News*

And more praise for William C. Dietz's *Drifter* trilogy and the *Sam McCade* series . . .

"SLAM-BANG ACTION!"
—David Drake, author of *Through the Breach*

"ALL-OUT SPACE ACTION!" —*Starlog*

"GOOD SOLID SPACE-OPERA, WELL TOLD."
—*Science Fiction Chronicle*

"A FAST-PACED 'SHOOT-EM-UP' . . . ONCE THE ACTION STARTS, IT NEVER LETS UP." —*SFRA Review*

THE FINAL BATTLE

WILLIAM C. DIETZ

ACE BOOKS, NEW YORK

This book is an Ace original edition,
and has never been previously published.

THE FINAL BATTLE

An Ace Book / published by arrangement with
the author

PRINTING HISTORY
Ace edition / July 1995

The Penguin Putnam Inc. World Wide Web site address is
http://www.penguinputnam.com

ISBN: 0-441-00217-X

ACE®
Ace Books are published by The Berkley Publishing Group,
a division of Penguin Putnam Inc.,
375 Hudson Street, New York, New York 10014.
ACE and the "A" design are trademarks
belonging to Penguin Putnam Inc.

PRINTED IN THE UNITED STATES OF AMERICA

10   9   8   7   6

This book is dedicated to Dr. Sheridan Simon, who designed the Hudathan homeworld, the Hudathans themselves, and the planet Algeron. We miss you, Sheridan, and think of you when we look at the stars.

ACKNOWLEDGMENTS

In order to prepare for this novel I read a number of excellent books, including *March or Die*, by Tony Geraghty; *Mouthful of Rocks*, by Christian Jennings; and *The French Foreign Legion*, by John Robert Young.

Prisoner of war! That is the least unfortunate kind of prisoner to be, but it is nevertheless a melancholy state. You are in the power of your enemy. You owe your life to his humanity, and your daily bread to his compassion. You must obey his orders, go where he tells you, stay where you are bid, await his pleasure, possess your soul in patience. Meanwhile the war is going on, great events are in progress, fine opportunities for action and adventure are slipping away.

Winston Churchill
My Early Life: A Roving Commission
Standard year 1930

Worber's World, the Confederacy of Sentient Beings

General Natalie Norwood stood, stretched, and eyed the empty expanse of the light-blue computer screen built into the top of her desk. The cursor blinked steadily in the lower right-hand corner. It had taken twelve hours of hard work to deal with the seemingly endless stream of orders, requests, reports, inquiries, memos, interrogatories, and just plain bullshit that went along with command of Confederacy *Battle Station Alpha XIV*, better known to her six-thousand-plus inhabitants as the *Old Lady* (plus a host of other less charitable names). And old she was, dating back to before the Human-Hudathan war, having originally been commissioned as a battleship.

"Do you need anything else, General?"

The voice pulled her back. A master sergeant filled most of the hatch. He was huge, and ugly as the pit bull he resembled. Until he smiled, when his face took an expression so pure, so angelic, that it melted the hearts of women everywhere. He took advantage of this fact as frequently as he could. Norwood shook her head. "Thanks, anyway. See you in the morning."

Morning is a relative concept in space, but Master Sergeant Max Meyers knew what she meant and nodded in response. "Yes, ma'am. I can hardly wait."

It was an old joke, one they had shared many times, and Norwood laughed. "Me too. Get some rest."

Meyers looked at the lines etched into her still-pretty face, the fatigue that filled her big brown eyes, and the gray that dominated her once-auburn hair. He wanted to tell her that she lived too close to the edge, that she worked too hard, that she had been aboard the ship about sixteen years too long.

But a chasm existed between generals and sergeants, a chasm so wide it could never be jumped, even if they worked together every day. The sergeant withdrew. The hatch closed behind him.

Norwood checked the computer screen one last time, assured herself that nothing new had appeared, and headed for her cabin. It was only steps away, a clear indication that the engineers who had designed the *Old Lady* knew how commanding officers lived, and had incorporated that knowledge into the ship's design.

Thick carpet cushioned her footsteps, a blast-proof hatch swished out of the way, and a ghostly glow threw heavy black shadows across her private compartment. The source of the reflected light, a blue-brown planet, filled the view port.

Unlike the location of the cabin, Norwood saw the view port as an indulgence of the sort that makes enlisted people justifiably cynical, and had given serious consideration to eliminating it. But that had been in the early days of her command, before the view port had become her secret obsession, claiming what little free time she had.

Norwood stripped off her uniform, threw it toward the usual corner, and stepped in front of the bulkhead-mounted mirror. Her breasts sagged a tiny bit, but the rest of her was firm and reassuringly fit. Still, it had been a long time since anyone else had seen her body or touched it, and she wondered what they would think.

Norwood turned and walked toward the chair. It was big, black, and mounted on a pedestal. She knew the chair was an extension of her obsession, a part of the nightly ritual, but the knowledge did nothing to lessen her need. The leather felt deliciously cool against her naked skin. She wiggled slightly and felt the chair adjust to her form. Her fingers sought the familiar buttons, touched them in the usual order, and caused the machine to tilt backward. Then, with the chair just the way she wanted it, Norwood took a moment to admire Worber's World, to appreciate the familiar outlines of its continents, and the manner in which the clouds marbled its surface.

From miles up in the sky there was no way to see what the Hudathan bombs had done to the surface or to appreciate the mathematical precision with which the swaths of destruction had been etched into the land, or the remains of the millions who had died. And died, and died, until no one was left.

The army, navy, and a pitifully small number of legionnaires had fought back, but when the fighting was over, Norwood's family, friends, and—with the exception of a handful of people like herself—every other person on the planet had perished.

And not just on Worber's World, but on hundreds of human-held planets, until the aliens had been stopped just short of the inner worlds. Been stopped, and soundly defeated, resulting in thousands of alien POWs, every damned one of which was down on the surface of what had been *her* homeworld, living out their miserable lives in the midst of their own tailor-made hell. A hell *she* supervised.

Yes, there were negotiations, but they had been going on for the better part of twenty years, with no end in sight. No end to the days spent in orbit and the nights spent in the black chair.

The idea pleased her and the touch of the keypad brought fifty vid screens to life. They framed the view port and provided the images she craved. Images of Hudathans suffering the way they *should* suffer, paying for what they'd done, and atoning for their sins.

The touch of another button was sufficient to enlarge one of the pictures and superimpose it upon the view port. She recognized the shot as coming from the heavily armored camera positioned near the north end of Black Lake, a lake that had been born when a subsurface torpedo burrowed its way under the planet's capital city, exploded, and created a huge crater. The entire general staff had died that day, leaving a rather junior colonel named Natalie Norwood in command of the surviving military forces. Of which there were damned few.

Norwood had tried to surrender, tried to end the slaughter, only to discover that the Hudathans were bent on nothing less than the total annihilation of any race capable of opposing them, and had no concept of mercy. And so it was that she had fallen into the hands of a Hudathan war commander named Niman Poseen-Ka, who had used her, only to be used himself, and ultimately imprisoned on the planet below.

Norwood selected another camera, a mobile one this time, and watched a radiation-induced lightning storm play across what had been some of Worber World's most productive farmland. The light seemed to strobe on and off, momentarily illuminating the ruins of a church, its steeple pointing accusingly skyward.

Anger boiled up from deep within her just as she had known that it would. Another image was selected and routed to the view screen. The shot came from above this time, and showed the ruins of what had been an industrial city, its once-sprawling factories reduced to little more than isolated walls and piles of randomly heaped rubble.

That's the way it *looked* anyway, but Norwood knew better, and directed the camera down until it skimmed the ground. Now it became obvious that there was life in the ruins, *alien* life, as hundreds of Hudathan POWs shambled about, repairing makeshift shelters, hauling water from the cisterns they had built, or pursuing other less identifiable tasks.

The most amazing part was the fact that thousands of Hudathan troopers had managed to survive the surface conditions for more than twenty years, unaided except for the food they were given, and unharmed insofar as Norwood and her staff could ascertain.

The ambient radiation would have killed a human within a week or so, to say nothing of the never-ending storms, floods, and volcanic activity that played havoc with the planet's surface.

But the Hudathans had evolved on a much different world than humans had, a planet that rotated around a star called Ember, which was twenty-nine percent larger than Earth's sun, and had a Trojan relationship with a Jovian binary. The Jovians' centers were only 280,000 kilometers apart, which, when combined with effects of other planets in the system, caused the Hudathan homeworld to oscillate around the following Trojan point, resulting in a wildly fluctuating climate. A climate that might be blistering one week and frigid the next, leading to some remarkably adaptable bodies.

The average Hudathan male weighed 300 pounds or so and had temperature-sensitive skin. It turned white when exposed to high temperatures, gray when the climate was temperate, and black when it was cold. They had humanoid heads, the vestige of a dorsal fin that ran front to back along the tops of their skulls, funnel-shaped ears, sauroid mouths, and upper lips that remained stationary when they talked. In addition to which they were extremely resistant to the effects of bacterial infection and radiation.

In a word they were tough, something Norwood knew firsthand. She was one of the few humans to kill a Hudathan in hand-to-hand combat.

But no amount of toughness would allow the Hudathans to make themselves comfortable on the surface of Worber's World. So they suffered. And, given the fact that the aliens had no place to hide, Norwood could vicariously enjoy their suffering, something she did with increasing frequency.

Twenty years is a long time for any sentient to spend as a prisoner of war and a more than sufficient time for a multitude of disciplinary problems to surface. Left free to deal with miscreants in whatever way they chose, the Hudathans had implemented a well-regulated system of punishments. The punishments were almost always physical in nature, and took place at the same times and locations each day, making it easy for Norwood to watch.

One such place Norwood thought of as "the dungeon," due to its location in the basement of a bombed-out library. Her camera had no difficulty making its way down the stairwell and into a large room, where it was systematically ignored by the Hudathans.

Although the aliens had destroyed hundreds of similar cameras during the first few years of their imprisonment, they had long since grown weary of the reprisals that such activities brought and had given up. The camera bobbed through a crosscurrent, floated behind three ranks of official witnesses, and gave Norwood a wide shot. She saw an open space backed by rows of old-fashioned books.

The officer's excitement grew as a scaffold of X-shaped beams were dragged into the middle of the room. The prisoner was huge, at least 350 pounds, and carefully impassive. Norwood knew that any sign of distress on the trooper's part would be interpreted as an indication of weakness by his peers and leave him vulnerable to physical attack, a rather cruel practice by human standards but normal within the framework of Hudathan society.

She reveled in the moment when he was tied to the rack. Her hand followed a well-traveled path down across the hard, flat plane of her stomach, through the tuft of wiry pubic hair, and into the moistness between her slightly spread legs.

Countless hours had been spent thinking about the pleasure that followed. What did it mean? Was she sick? Twisted? Perverted? She didn't know. Whatever the condition was, it had manifested itself during the last two years. She wanted to talk to the psych officer about it but was afraid to try. After all, what if she were found unfit for duty and her job went to someone else? A more trusting soul who didn't know what the Hudathans were capable of, and would relax some of her more stringent policies.

And what difference did it make anyway? The pleasure she granted herself came at the enemy's expense and troubled no one else. No, thinking about it, worrying about it, was a waste of time. Reassured, Norwood turned her attention to the dungeon.

The charges had been read and the negative reinforcement began. Denied the high-tech dispensation of pain they normally preferred, the Hudathans had fallen back on older but still effective methods of punishment. The whip was made of hand-braided cord and ended in six knotted tails. Norwood knew that each knot would cut into the alien flesh in a most pleasing manner and produce intense pain.

A ragged-looking noncom withdrew the whip from a scrupulously clean bag, handed it to the master-at-arms, and stepped back. The master-at-arms took his position, planted his feet, and flicked the whip back and to the right. His arm flashed forward. The whip made a swishing sound, followed by the crack of impact, and a grunt of expelled air. The blow left a pattern of crimson lines. The soldier jerked but remained silent.

Yes! Norwood thought to herself. Each and every one of the aliens should be punished for what they'd done, made to suffer as their victims had suffered, then eradicated from the galaxy. Nothing less would make amends, nothing less would ensure safety, and nothing less would bring peace.

The strokes came more quickly now, and Norwood's hand moved to the same rhythm as the whip, her excitement building until a series of short but powerful orgasms racked her body, and she moaned in pleasure. All of the stress, all of the tension seemed to ebb from her body, leaving her adrift on a tingly tide. The crack of the whip took on a monotonous quality. Norwood closed her eyes and felt the heavy hand of sleep pull her down. Darkness wrapped her in its warm embrace and oblivion carried her away.

Hundreds of miles from the room where the punishment took place, in a building that had originally served as a military museum, War Commander Poseen-Ka sat hunched over a makeshift table. It was huge and bore the considerable weight of a relief map made from hand-molded clay. A cone of sickly yellow light came from high above and threw short, stubby shadows across the make-believe land. Naval technicians had rigged the light from materials found in the ruins of cities he had destroyed. Power came from batteries and the occasional sunlight the humans were powerless to deny him.

Long, hard years of imprisonment had trimmed a hundred pounds from the Hudathan's frame and left him thin and gaunt. His skin was gray, almost black in reaction to the chilly air, and showed early signs of the striations that mark old age.

But those who had fought under Poseen-Ka knew that the inner being was unchanged, except for the shame that accompanied defeat, and the passion it fed. A passion far more complex than simple revenge, because the war commander was too honest to blame the enemy for his failures, and too professional to let emotion govern his actions.

No, the passion had to do with correcting a momentary imbalance, a time when one of the countless threats that confronted his race had gained the upper hand, a situation that could and would be reversed. If not by him, then by someone else. In fact, viewed from the perspective of a race used to a chaotic environment, the situation was normal. As was his response, which was to analyze his mistakes and figure out how to avoid them in the future.

The fact that there *was* no future to speak of, beyond another twenty or thirty years of imprisonment, made no difference. The humans had a saying that went something like "Where there is heart there is hope." A noble sentiment worthy of a Hudathan.

Poseen-Ka stood, clasped his hands behind his back, and circled the table. It modeled a section of a planet called Algeron. This particular piece of terrain lay just north of the world-spanning mountain range known as the Towers of Algeron. They were represented by fingers of reinforced clay that pointed toward the smoke-stained ceiling and the surveillance cameras that crawled buglike from one side of the room to the other. The Hudathan hated the cameras, and the knowledge that Norwood could watch his every move, but was determined to hide such emotions. Especially in light of the fact that the human had been his prisoner once and comported herself with warriorlike dignity.

The map had been constructed from memory, and was inaccurate to some extent, but not enough to matter. No, the foothills that fell away from the mountains, the plains that stretched to the north, those were as they had been. Would be if he returned. But what of the fort called Camerone? And the damnable cyborgs that infested it? Had the fort been rebuilt? Were the man-machines waiting as they had been before? Such were the questions he would ask in the highly unlikely event that he received a second chance.

A poisonous rain spattered against the plastic-covered door. The room felt suddenly small and confining. The war commander swept the plastic aside and stepped out into a bitter drizzle. Mud squished beneath massive sandals as he walked down a flight of steps and out into the military cemetery.

Lighting strobed in the distance and served to illuminate thousands of crosses that had managed to stay vertical when all else fell. They marked the graves of soldiers killed in previous wars, when the humans had fought each other, arguing over who should lead. An understandable if somewhat self-defeating activity that plagued Hudathan society as well.

Thunder rumbled across the land and Poseen-Ka looked upward. His eyes struggled to pierce the cloud cover and failed. The stars. What about the stars? Would he travel among them yet again? Or die on this accursed planet, his flesh and bones turning to soup, and seeping down to join the military dead? Acid rain spattered across the Hudathan's face and made his eyes sting. Only time would tell.

The Hudathan scout ship was small, fast, and lightly armed. It hardly even paused as it dropped hyper on the edge of the solar system, launched the Special Operations package, and disappeared back into the strange continuum where objects can travel faster than the speed of light.

The package, no bigger than a soccer ball, had been fired in a manner that allowed it to join company with a meteor stream that, like Worber's World itself, orbited the system's sun. The stream, which consisted of debris strewn along the path of a well-known periodic comet, intersected the planet's orbit a few weeks later.

Technicians aboard the *Old Lady* detected the meteor shower long before it arrived, checked to make sure that it coincided with computer projections based on past activity, ran routine detector scans on ten percent of total mass, and cleared the shower for atmospheric entry.

The Special Operations package, along with the true meteorites that surrounded it, entered the atmosphere at a velocity of approximately ten miles per second. Friction caused them to slow slightly while their outer surfaces melted and were swept away in the form of tiny droplets. Most of the heat was dissipated, leaving the inside of the objects cold. During the last seconds of flight a layer of solidified melt called fusion crust formed on the surface of the real meteorites while the Ops package exploded and scattered millions of peanut-sized metal capsules far and wide. The capsules spattered across the tortured landscape like metallic hail. Some ceased to exist. Some survived.

In fact, a full 94.2 percent of the capsules remained operational after impact with the ground, a much higher percentage than required for mission success, and a number that would have pleased a war scientist named Rimar Noda-Sa very much.

It took less than five seconds for the capsules to open and release their micro-robotic passengers. Designed to look like a locally mutated version of *B.germanica*, or the Earth-derived German cockroach, the tiny machines waited exactly ten minutes, identified themselves with a millisecond burst of code, activated their on-board navigation systems, and scuttled toward the primary assembly point. No one knew it yet, but the Confederacy of Sentient Beings was under attack, and would soon be involved in a full-scale war.

2

The only thing *worse* than the study of war, is the *failure* to study war, and life as a slave.

Mylo Nurlon-Da
The Life of a Warrior
Standard year 1703

Planet Earth, the Confederacy of Sentient Beings

Danjou Hall, the traditional residence of senior cadets, boasted four gargoyles. Booly straddled the one located at the building's northwest corner, just above the room he shared with Tom Riley. He wore black fatigues, the kind favored by the 2d REP, the Legion's elite airborne regiment, a climbing harness, and a day pack. His feet were bare.

The carefully maintained grounds were seventy feet beneath him. The campus was dark except for the light from an almost full moon, some streetlights that had been placed with military precision, and a scattering of still-lit windows. Booly looked at his wrist term, touched a button, and saw the multifunctional dial appear. It was exactly 2359 hours. One minute to go.

He took a deep breath and released a long, steady plume of lung-warmed air. His heart beat like a trip-hammer. It reminded him of how stupid he was. So stupid he'd allowed the very creatures Uncle Movefast had warned him against to manipulate his actions, because even though Booly was half-human himself, and therefore tainted with the blood of those who had tormented him for six long years, he thought of them as aliens. Aliens who wouldn't mind if he plunged to his death, or was caught trying to reach the admin building, as long as it reinforced their rather shaky sense of superiority. This was an attitude Booly found hard to understand, since he'd been raised in an atmosphere where tribal needs came first, and what after all was the Legion, if not a military tribe?

So there was only one thing left to do, and that was to succeed. Because if he made it to the admin building without getting caught, and hoisted the senior-class pennant to the top of the flagpole, he would not only uphold one of the academy's most venerable traditions, he would disappoint the bigots and graduate at 1000 hours the next morning. But it wouldn't be easy, because while hundreds of classes had tried to hoist their pennants, and roughly twenty-five percent of them had succeeded, *all* of them had moved their flags across the ground.

The "aerial route," as Riley liked to call it, was both untried and undeniably dangerous. Something the academy's staff would officially disapprove of, even punish if they could, but secretly admire, because it was very much in line with the Legion's culture of perseverance in the face of impossible odds, personal bravery, and death in battle.

The bell tower was located on the far side of the huge quad on which he and his classmates had spent countless hours marching back and forth. And even though the chimes were muted during the night, the sound still surprised him. He jerked, swayed, and regained his balance. It was midnight. Time to get going.

Checking to make sure that the pennant was tied around

his waist, and the knapsack securely fastened to his back, Booly stood on the long, flat cornice. It received direct sunlight during most of the day and he could feel what remained of the warmth through the soles of his bare feet. That ability was a gift from his mother's people, which, when combined with their superior sense of smell and the cape of short, thick fur that covered the upper part of his torso, accounted for much of the prejudice that he'd endured.

The rest flowed from his stubborn "screw you" personality, something he'd inherited from his father, a onetime legionnaire, currently serving as Naa ambassador to the Confederacy.

Like his classmates, Booly had spent a great deal of time in the field, learning how to move without being seen. But *unlike* his classmates, Booly had grown up on the planet Algeron, where tribe fought tribe, and bandits roamed the land. So it was second nature to avoid the skyline, to remain in the shadows, to seek warmth with his feet. He could almost hear his uncle saying, "Good rocks are like beautiful females, son—warm, clean, and pleasant to touch. Bad rocks are cold, wet, and slippery. Step on them and they will betray you."

The cornice felt like "good rock" and carried Booly to the northeast corner of the building, where the first of many challenges awaited him. He knew the gap between Danjou Hall and the library was less than six feet wide, a distance he had jumped countless times on the ground. But this was different. This was scary. He looked down, saw a flash of white as a legionnaire walked by, and jerked his head back. What was a drill instructor doing out at this time of night? Looking for him? No, checking the plebes, that's all, and handing out gigs to the jerks on guard duty.

Booly paused, brought his breathing under control, backed up about fifteen feet, and ran full tilt toward the abyss. His feet made slapping sounds as they hit the cornice. The edge appeared and he threw himself toward the library roof. It was made of copper and slanted up toward a highly polished dome. He hit harder than planned, felt the metal buckle slightly, and swore as he slid downward. His fingertips squeaked over bare metal and his toes sought something solid. There was a ridge, he knew there was a ridge, but where the hell was it? Finally. His toes hit the ridge and brought him to a stop.

Had anyone heard? The last of the chimes were supposed to cover whatever noise he made. Had it worked? There was no way to tell. Booly remained perfectly still. His breath came in short gasps and fogged the copper in front of his face. He heard a voice. It was a long way off.

"Sir! Cadet Private Maria Martinez, sir!" as a drill instructor ordered some poor slob to identify herself. The DI's reply was barely audible. Booly waited. A dog barked, a door slammed, and a shuttle rumbled by thousands of feet above. Good.

Leaning in toward the slanted roof, Booly edged his way to the right. It was dark, very dark, and hard to see. His toes were pressed against the ridge and hurt where the metal cut into them. The zipper on his jacket made a scraping sound and left a wavy line to mark where he'd been.

He reached out, sank his hand into empty space, and damn near followed it. A pigeon burst into flight. Wings brushed his shoulder. Booly felt the bottom of his stomach fall toward the ground and pulled back from the void. The bird circled and flew away. This was it, the one gap that was too large to jump, where the plan called for him to descend and cross on the ground.

Scared, and angry with himself for damn near shitting his pants, the cadet gritted his teeth. "The goal, stay focused on the goal, and the path becomes clear." That's what his uncle had taught him and it almost always worked.

Booly visualized the admin building, saw himself raising the pennant, and felt his emotions steady.

Days of careful reconnaissance had revealed that the library's architect had provided present and future maintenance workers with a row of evenly spaced eyebolts to which they could secure safety lines.

Booly reached up, grabbed the rope end taped to his right pack strap, and pulled it free. The line, which consisted of a half inch black, gold, and lavender kern mantle, had been "borrowed" from one of Staff Sergeant Ho's supply rooms, and coiled into the pack lest it interfere with his running and jumping. The rope flowed smoothly as the cadet pulled it out.

Booly reached up over his head, felt for an eyebolt, and found one. It was a simple matter to thread the rope through the hole and pass the slack out and into the void. Then, when the white tape that marked the kern mantle's middle point appeared, the cadet reached into a pocket, felt for the figure-eight descender, brought it out, and pulled the rope through the larger hole and over the connecting ring. With that accomplished, it was a simple matter to secure the descender to the front of his harness with a locking D carabiner and test the rig with his weight. It held just as he knew it would. The fact that he had learned these skills while growing up, and again during his years at the academy, made them all the more familiar.

He placed one hand above the descender and one below it. Confident that he could control what happened next, he backed off the ledge, swung in against the building's side, and allowed himself to slide silently downward. The trick was to keep his upper hand loose while using his lower hand to control the rate of descent. Booly knew that moving his lower hand *away* from his body would increase his speed while bringing it closer would have the opposite effect. He kept it close.

Suddenly, perhaps thirty feet from the ground, Booly smelled something that shouldn't have been there. The strong odor of a rather expensive cologne. The kind worn by some of his wealthier classmates.

Careful to make no sound lest it give him away, Booly stopped his descent, and used his feet to steady himself against the wall. The brick felt cold. He looked over his right shoulder. The shadows were ink black and impossible to penetrate. But the odor persisted, so he waited, and waited, until he began to question his own senses, and was just about to release some line when the sound of voices froze him in place.

"Hey, Reggie, how's it hangin'?"

"Long and low. Now shut the hell up. The geek should come along any moment now."

Booly didn't know a Reggie, and didn't recognize either one of the voices, but it didn't take a genius to know they were underclassmen, tipped off as to the route he would take, and eager to make a name for themselves by turning him in. Which would put a black mark next to his name and cause him to miss graduation as well. A graduation his parents had traveled millions of light-years to witness.

Booly looked upward, saw that clouds covered the moon, and understood why they hadn't managed to spot him. He couldn't go up, not without attracting their attention, so the decision came easily. Booly used his left hand to reach up and pull the watch cap down over his face. It took a moment to adjust the eye holes. Praying that the line would continue to run as silently as it had before, the cadet lowered himself to the ground in one smooth motion, landing within three feet of a surprised underclassman.

The plebe wore fatigues and the black arm band that signified guard duty. He saw Booly, opened his mouth, and folded with a knee in the gut. He was bent over, making retching sounds, when a blow to the back of the head put him down.

"Reggie?" The voice was tentative and came from the right. Booly released the climbing rope and eased that way. The senior did his best to sound annoyed. "Yeah? What now?"

The clouds moved out of the way and moonlight hit the plebe's face. His eyes were like saucers. "You're not Reggie . . . you're—"

Booly never got to hear who the cadet thought he was, because his hand went over the boy's mouth, and a hip throw took him down. He wasn't more than fifteen years old and a knee was sufficient to hold him in place. The senior barely had time to gag and hog-tie the underclassman when Reggie called for help. He had reached his knees and was struggling to stand. "Somebody! Quick! Over here!"

If Booly had been from a more civilized planet he might have hesitated, might have searched for a less brutal approach, but he wasn't, so he kicked Reggie in the head. The cadet slumped to ground. Booly checked both his pulse and airway prior to tying him up. It took five precious minutes to drag both plebes further into the shadows and stash them behind the shrubbery.

There was no way to know if the younger cadets had abandoned their posts as part of the attempt to intercept him but he hoped they hadn't. Curfew violation was one thing, but leaving one's post without permission was something else again. A rule that might seem silly on Earth, but was of extreme importance out on the frontier worlds, where it might mean the difference between life and death, and not just for one individual, but for his or her entire unit as well.

Whether the cadets accused him or not depended on how smart they were, and how well they had assimilated the Legion's culture. Because accusing a senior without proof was tantamount to accusing a senior officer without proof, a nearly suicidal thing to do. Add that to the fact that the academy's staff *expected* the seniors to make a run at the admin building, and the fact that the plebes had not only broken general orders, but been *caught* doing so, meant their best hope lay in keeping their mouths shut and taking whatever punishment came their way.

But those considerations were for the future. Now Booly had even less time than before. Odds were that the under-classmen would be missed, found, or both during the next thirty minutes or so. He had to move and move fast.

Booly shrugged the knapsack off his back, pulled the kern mantle through the eyebolt, and dodged the falling rope. It took three precious minutes to stuff it back into the pack.

With the rope stashed, and the pack on his back, Booly tackled Morzycki Hall. Like all the buildings on campus it was named after one of the men who had fought under Captain Jean Danjou at the Battle of Camerone, in April 1863.

The wall was made of brick. Most were set flush but some had been allowed to protrude, creating a textured look. These were placed in a manner that made them con-venient to Booly's feet and hands, a fact that hadn't escaped his attention when he marched by every day. And, given that the end pieces were slightly warmer than the surfaces around them, he could actually "feel" where they were. So he was able to free-climb the wall in practically no time at all. There were windows, but all were dark, and it was easy to avoid them.

Even so, the cadet had barely reached the roof when he heard someone shout for the sergeant of the guard, and knew that the plebes had been found. The odds against making it to the admin building seemed nearly impossible now, but Booly decided to try anyway, preferring to be caught in the attempt rather than wandering around on a rooftop. He sprinted for the far side of the building. The roofing material was textured and relatively warm beneath his feet. Suddenly he felt happy, exhilarated, and completely without fear. Adrenaline? Stupidity? He really didn't care.

The edge appeared and Booly skidded to a halt. The admin building stood thirty feet away. Like Morzycki Hall, it had a flat, rectangular roof. His objective, one of three flag poles arrayed along the structure's east side, was no more than a hundred feet away. Booly heard the sound of distant voices and sensed movement on the quad. He fought to maintain his focus.

The key to spanning the distance between Morzycki Hall and the admin building, more officially known as Tonel Hall, was the scaffolding that maintenance workers had built along the south wall. All Booly had to do was cross the approximately twelve feet that separated Morzycki and the scaffolding, scramble up one of many ladders, and make his way to the flagpoles. That and effect his escape. The original plan called for throwing a grappling hook over one of the cross-pieces, pulling the rope tight, and securing it to one of the air vents that protruded from the roof around him. Having done that, it would have been relatively simple to wrap his legs around the line and slide downward. Things had changed, however, and time was running out. The moment demanded what his father sometimes referred to as a "gut check."

Standing on top of the foot-high wall that ran the circumference of Morzycki Hall, Booly did a deep knee bend and hurled himself outward. Air whipped by his face. He wondered if he was about to die. He hoped not, because the pennant seemed like a stupid thing to die for.

The scaffolding came up with incredible speed. His hands hit a cross-piece, slipped, and hit the next one down.

He missed with his left hand, connected with his right, and gave an involuntary grunt as the weight of his entire body threatened to tear his arm out of its socket. But the cadet's highly conditioned musculature managed to absorb the punishment and he held on.

It hurt, though, and Booly grit his teeth as he climbed the scaffolding and scrambled onto the roof. The flagpoles were lit from below. The one on the far left bore the emblem of the 1st Foreign Infantry Regiment, or 1st RE, most of which was stationed on Algeron, but had overall responsibility for administrative affairs.

The center pole flew the flag of the Confederacy, just the latest in the long line of governments the Legion had sworn to defend since its creation more than five hundred years before.

But it was the pole on the right, the one that flew the academy's own emblem, that claimed his attention. Ignoring the ever-increasing hubbub below, and walking stiff legged as if on parade, Booly crossed the intervening distance while untying the pennant tied around his waist.

It took only moments to free the halyards from their cleat, to lower the tricolor for which so many legionnaires had died, and attach the pennant of those who aspired to follow. Then, after a series of quick, jerky movements, the pennant was up and snapping in the breeze.

A shout went up from down below. Booly tossed a salute toward the flags, spun, and ran for the small shack-sized structure that provided access to the roof. The door sensed his approach and slid aside. Stairs led downward and Booly took them two at a time. It was clear that escape plan ''A,'' which called for retracing his path back over the rooftops, had never been realistic to begin with, which meant that his only hope lay in Tom Riley and escape plan ''B.''

Fire doors provided access to hallways on each floor and they were numbered. The first read ''10,'' and he needed

"B-1," or basement level one. Gravity helped, and Booly went faster and faster, until he was in the midst of what amounted to a controlled fall. Suddenly, a man in a jogging suit stepped through the door labeled 2. Booly hit him head-on.

Both men went down, and when Booly sat up, he found himself looking into the face of none other than General Ian St. James. Not just *a* general, but the commanding officer of the *entire* Legion, and the next thing to god. A god Booly had met on two previous occasions and even shaken hands with. And, as if that wasn't bad enough, Booly realized that the makeshift hood had disappeared and left his face uncovered.

An eternity seemed to pass. The general had hard eyes. The mind behind them assessed Booly's equipment and came to the proper conclusion. His voice was matter-of-fact.

"Over the roofs. Very ingenious. A first, if I'm not mistaken. Let me be the first to congratulate you on your courage. Were it not for the fact that my eyes have grown older, and therefore less sharp, I would swear that you look exactly like the son of one of the most unreliable sergeant-majors I ever had the misfortune to command. A thankless man who later rose to the highly unlikely ranks of major and ambassador to the Confederacy. But it would be inappropriate to attempt such an identification without my glasses. That being the case, I suggest you rejoin your classmates as quickly as possible."

Booly leaped to his feet. The salute came automatically and was inappropriate while out of uniform. "Sir! Yes, sir! Thank you, sir!"

St. James smiled and jerked his head toward the stairs. The cadet disappeared. The stairs were still vibrating when the general began the first of what would eventually be five trips from bottom to top. It was the only way he could unwind and get to sleep. A staff sergeant appeared from above.

"Sorry to interrupt your workout, sir. A senior managed to reach the roof. He raised their pennant."

St. James did his best to look surprised. "Really? No harm done, I suppose. Haven't seen anyone, though . . . must have made his way down before I entered the stairwell."

The sergeant nodded respectfully. "Yes, sir. The cadets are slippery little devils. I imagine he's gone by now."

St. James smiled and started up the stairs. "You're right about that. Of course I was one myself once. But that was a long time ago."

The sergeant moved to get out of the general's way. "Yes, sir. Did someone from your class make it all the way onto the roof?"

St. James smiled as he toiled his way upward. "Yes, Sergeant. Someone certainly did."

3

To negotiate is to dance, to move to the music of mutual need, creating harmony where none existed before.

Lin Po Lee
Philosopher Emeritus
The League of Planets
Standard year 2164

Clone World Alpha-001, the Clone Hegemony

Moolu Rasha Anguar had an ongoing love-hate relationship with the exoskeleton that his duties forced him to wear. He loved what it enabled him to do but hated having to depend on it. Plus, the contrivance was too shiny for his Dweller sensibilities, and smacked of technological superiority, a negative where the less-than-advanced members of the third Confederacy were concerned. Still, it allowed him to venture where his frail, sticklike body would otherwise be unable to go, and that was good.

Anguar checked to make sure that all the contact points were secure, ran a mental check on the neural interface that linked his nervous system with the machine's microcomputer, and walked toward the center of the *Friendship*'s master stateroom. The exoskeleton felt ponderous inside the artificially low-gravity cell maintained for his comfort.

Though originally built for the Imperial Navy, and still quite capable of defending herself, the onetime battleship *Reliable* had been rechristened after the emperor's death and turned into a sort of traveling capital, complete with its own largely automated bureaucracy, and chambers for the two-tiered senate, mercifully on hiatus at the moment.

More than that, the ship was a conscious attempt to avoid the impression that the government was centered on any one planet or beholden to any particular race. Just one of many smart decisions made by Anguar's predecessor, a human named Sergi Chien-Chu, who had led the revolution against the empire, fought the Hudathan hordes to a standstill and laid the groundwork for the third Confederacy, the first and second having fallen to tyrants long before the time of the empire. He had died an untimely death two years previously, and Anguar was his somewhat reluctant successor.

Anguar circled the compartment. The exoskeleton operated smoothly and multiplied his strength. He grabbed the edge of the massive desk and exerted upward pressure. It was bolted to the deck but metal creaked before he let go. Anguar gloried in the machine-made power, realized what he was doing, and berated himself for his weakness. Because to seek power, to enjoy power, was to court the very thing that would destroy all that he sought to build. A government that would represent *all* the known races fairly and preside over a thousand years of peace.

Suitably chastised, Anguar took a turn in front of the gigantic mirror. Like most of his race, the president was vain and considered vanity a virtue. He looked past the exoskeleton and took a moment to admire his well-shaped head, the large ovoid eyes that humans found so appealing, the pleasingly thin body, the long, sleek limbs, and the dangly sex organ that had provided him with so much pleasure over the years. Yes, it was a sensible body for the low-gravity world on which his race had evolved, but far too delicate for use on the planets favored by humans and other muscle-bound species.

Still, many observers agreed that it had been Anguar's frail physiology, combined with his people's extremely low birthrate, that was at least partially responsible for his victory in the last election. It seemed that other races, humans included, found it difficult to see the Dwellers as a physical or cultural threat, and preferred them to representatives of more brawny and therefore more threatening species.

Anguar thought it strange, almost perverted to think about the ways in which aliens perceived his body, but knew that physical differences were important, especially to physiological bigots like those on the planet below, human clones, who were not only subject to the many weaknesses typical of that particular race, but followers of a science-derived religion that threatened to further weaken the already-shaky Confederacy by refusing to join it.

Anguar sighed and used his implant to summon his attendants. They would dress the exoskeleton, a humiliating affair, but necessary in order to make him appear even vaguely human. The humans had pungent sayings for almost every situation, but his favorite applied to the universe as a whole: "Life sucks."

Alpha Clone Marcus-Six rounded a corner and started down the marble-lined corridor that led to the Chamber of Governmental Process. Guards, their weapons, uniforms, and faces completely identical, lined both sides of the hall and snapped to attention as Marcus approached.

Their rifle salutes were identical, as they should have been, given the fact that every single one of them had been cloned from the badly mutilated body of a soldier named Jonathan Alan Sebo, a hero of a mostly forgotten war who was said to have embodied all the virtues of the perfect foot soldier, and had therefore been chosen as the donor from which entire armies had been cloned.

Each soldier had different experiences of course, giving rise to different personalities, but they still had a great deal in common, including durable bodies, enough intelligence to operate high-tech weapons, and an almost fanatical determination to carry out whatever orders they were given.

The clone army had already proved its worth, because while it had been defeated by the Legion, it had won some battles as well, and never permitted more than what the Alpha clone thought of as a temporary occupation of Alpha-001, just one of the many things he and his peers were about to discuss.

The last of the soldiers popped to attention, a laser beam scanned the pigment-based bar code on the Alpha clone's forehead, and the doors swished out of his way. Never breaking step, Marcus entered the Chamber of Governmental Process.

It was a large room, circular in shape, with a highly polished white floor. Triangles of shiny black marble pointed in towards the center of the room, where a beautifully wrought double helix served as both a pillar and sculpture. The Alpha clone knew that it was modeled after a single molecule of a chemical substance called deoxyribonucleic acid, or DNA, the basic building block for all living organisms, and the only symbol his religion permitted.

The sculpture shimmered as bars of light representing the four chemical compounds called bases floated upward and disappeared into the ceiling. A circular table fronted the symbol. A pair of men rose to greet him. An outsider would have been at a loss to know who was who but Marcus had no such difficulty.

Pietro looked much as he did himself, with light brown

skin, flashing black eyes, and perfect teeth. But the stylized silver clasp worn on the left shoulder of his carefully draped toga, and the almost military way in which he held himself were unmistakably his.

Antonio used pomade on his hair, and arranged it in ringlets, a conceit Marcus found especially unattractive. Still, Antonio was the less rigid of the two, and therefore the more likable.

Taken together, they were "The Triad of One," the supreme leaders of the Clone Hegemony, and outside of the donor duplicates kept on permanent standby at various medical centers, the only representatives of their particular parent currently alive.

Given the fact that life span is determined in part by heredity, and the previous generation had died in quick succession, the current triad had been decanted within a few years of one another. Others would follow of course—but that would be many years in the future.

Marcus nodded politely. "Greetings, Pietro. Welcome, Antonio. Sorry I'm late. The president's security people changed the landing site again. A standard counter-assassination tactic but bothersome nonetheless."

Both men bowed, not out of deference, for all three were of equal rank, but because this was *his* planet rather than one of theirs. They spoke in unison and their voices had exactly the same timbre. "Greetings, Marcus. You look wonderful."

It was an old joke but Marcus laughed anyway. "Thanks. So do you. Shall we sit?"

The other Alpha clones nodded and took their traditional places around the table. The chairs had been custom designed for their third-generation predecessors and still fit perfectly.

"So," Antonio said, allowing his eyes to droop slightly, "what will the alien propose?"

Marcus shrugged. "You've seen the intelligence reports. He will offer to withdraw most of his troops from Alpha-One in return for our support of the Confederacy."

Pietro shuddered. "Align ourselves with alien free-breeders? Never!"

Marcus nodded dutifully but felt vaguely unhappy. While he shared his counterpart's distaste for the completely laissez-faire manner in which the Confederacy's member races managed their respective gene pools, Marcus knew they outnumbered the Hegemony ten to one, and were a force to be reckoned with. Of course it wouldn't be politic to admit that—not directly, anyway—so he took a more circuitous route. "That's easy for you to say, Pietro, but you don't have a battalion of cyborgs strutting around your capital. Please allow me to remind you that it is *we* who serve as hostages to the Hegemony's good behavior."

Antonio played with a ringlet of hair. "Come now, Marcus . . . how dangerous can they be? Our intelligence reports indicate that their commanding officer uses drugs and their morale is at an all-time low. The legionnaires are tough but your troops could defeat them."

"Yes," Marcus replied, careful to keep his voice level. "We could defeat them. But what about the wave that would follow? And the wave after that?"

"So what are you suggesting?" Pietro demanded scornfully. "An alliance with the free breeders? Surrender all that we hold dear? I think not."

"No," Marcus replied testily, "the inference insults us both. I would never agree to that."

"Then what *do* you have in mind, brother dearest?" Antonio asked mildly. "I know you too well to think that you would raise questions for which there are no answers."

Marcus shrugged. The awful truth was that he *did* believe in some sort of accommodation but was afraid to say so. He searched for a graceful way out. "We need time. Time to build our industrial base, time to strengthen our military forces, and time to sow discord in the Confederation. I suggest we stall.''

Marcus felt the tingling sensation that signaled an urgent page. He touched his implant and rose to his feet. ''My apologies, brethren. Another security matter, I suspect. Would you excuse me? I'll take care of whatever it is and return as quickly as possible.''

The other men nodded, stood politely, and watched Marcus leave the room. They sat once he was gone. Pietro was the first to speak. ''So, Antonio, what do you think of our brother's plan?''

Antonio smiled lazily and leaned back in his chair. ''I think it's one-hundred-percent grade-A bullshit.''

Pietro nodded agreeably. ''I concur. Stalling is a form of accommodation. I say we resist. More than that, I say we attack.''

Antonio lifted a well-plucked eyebrow. ''Yes, brother dearest, but what of Marcus?''

Pietro looked thoughtful. ''Our brother wants to placate the monster. So let him lull the creature to sleep. A long sleep from which it will never awake.''

''But how?'' Antonio asked dreamily. ''What will we do?''

Pietro looked grim. ''We will shoot the monster where it is most vulnerable. Right between the eyes.''

The president of the Confederacy of Sentient Beings, defender of the Galactic Peace, and doer of deals, watched Clone World Alpha-001 grow larger beneath him. The shuttle shuddered as it hit the atmosphere and continued its way downward. Sleek aerospace fighters hung off each wing, ready to destroy anything the clones might send up, supposing they were stupid enough to do so.

The Clone World was rather average by the standards of

Anguar's race, having what he considered to be an excessive amount of surface water, and any number of unusable mountain ranges. Still, he could see how the high degree of match between Alpha-One and Earth would seem attractive to humans, and understood that it had been chosen for that reason.

Anguar had done his homework and knew that the personage the clones referred to as "the Founder," an award-winning geneticist named Carolyn Anne Hosokawa, had chosen Alpha-One, Two, and Three personally, seeing each planet as a sort of creche for her clone-based society, and spreading them out to increase their chances of survival.

Then, having chosen their homes for them, and seeded them on multiple planets, Hosokawa had further assisted her creations by planning exactly how they would live, including a ban on reproductive sex, the establishment of highly efficient agro-industrial sectors, a carefully designed transportation system, and a gridwork of cities so similar that a person "grown" in one town would know the others equally well.

And while Anguar found the whole thing depressingly regimented, he couldn't help but be impressed by the efficiencies gained through the Hegemony's rigid top-down style. It would be comparatively easy to lead a society like that, Anguar thought enviously, rather than cope with the diverse mishmash of races and cultures he dealt with.

Of course it would be boring, too, especially if he had to cope with two versions of himself and listen to their speeches. The president smiled at the thought and felt the weight of an additional gravity settle on his narrow shoulders. He would have been crushed if it hadn't been for the exoskeleton.

A thin layer of fluffy white cloud rose to meet the shuttle and momentarily obscured the president's vision before vanishing from sight. A neat patchwork quilt of farmland appeared, each field exactly the same size as the ones that bordered it, all fed by ruler-straight irrigation ditches.

Farmland gave way to housing, but it was nothing like the fanciful resin-reinforced rammed-earth homes that his people preferred, or the wildly diverse structures he'd seen on other human-settled planets. No, these were concrete gray high-rise buildings, each as identical to all the rest as the people who lived in them.

The shuttle dropped even lower and started its final approach. Anguar saw carefully spaced parks, broad avenues, and man-made lakes. They were pretty, and he said as much to his military aide, a marine major named Stephanie Warwick-Olson. She sat opposite Anguar, with her back toward the cockpit, and turned to look out the window. She was pretty by human standards, though too fleshy for any self-respecting Dweller, and somewhat intimidating. Her voice was calm and matter of fact. ''They're pretty, all right, but I notice that the parks command the high ground, the streets are wide enough to accommodate heavy armor, and the traffic circles could be used as choke points. Very professional.''

Anguar looked out the window again and found that Warwick-Olson had somehow transformed the previously pleasant scenery into a potential battlefield. Repellors flared as the shuttle hovered and touched the ground five hundred feet from the terminal building.

The next fifteen minutes or so were filled with hurried comings and goings, confused multilingual babbling, and the genial anarchy that accompanied the president everywhere he went. His multiracial staff provided him with reminders of protocol (all three of the Alpha clones must be addressed as ''Mr. President''), a list of primary objectives (secure Hegemony support), and a review of secondary objectives (evaluate the Legion's commanding officer in light of allegations regarding his conduct).

And then, just when Anguar thought his head would explode, the hatch cycled open and he stepped out into bright sunlight. Cameras swooped in, hovered, and captured the carefully managed moment. He squinted, pulled his thin, almost nonexistent lips into a human-style grin, and made his way down the roll-up stairs. Flags snapped in the breeze, rows of identical soldiers stood at attention, and a pylon in the shape of a double helix twisted up towards the sky. The exoskeleton performed flawlessly and he was glad of its strength when the first of three identical humans applied what could have been a bone-crushing grip. He had cautious brown eyes and a bar code on his forehead.

"President Anguar, welcome to Alpha-One. My name is Marcus-Six. I hope your journey was a pleasant one. May I present my peers? This is Antonio-Six, president of Hegemony planet Alpha-Two, and Pietro-Six, president of Hegemony planet Alpha-Three."

Anguar said polite things to the clones, was introduced to Legion colonel John M. Sinkler, the officer who might or might not represent a problem, and was led past the assembled ranks of the Hegemony's Lightning Brigade, a unit comprised of identical soldiers, all of whom wore red berets with silver flashes pinned to them.

Of equal or even more interest to Anguar were the seven-and-a-half-foot-tall, one-and-a-half-ton Trooper IIs that stalked along behind the last rank of clones, keeping pace with the president while covering the crowd with their laser cannon, machine guns, and shoulder-launched missiles. And, as if all the armament weren't sufficient, each cyborg also carried a heavily armed legionnaire on his or her back.

The Legion was something of mystery to Anguar, consisting as it did almost entirely of humans, and having what he considered to be masochistic values and traditions. Like bravery in the face of impossible odds, death in battle, and a brooding pessimism.

Why did they continue to fight? Their motto was The Legion Is My Country, a phrase that seemed to put their needs above all others, yet they had almost single-handedly fought off the Hudathans, and were sworn to defend the Confederacy, the latest in a long line of governmental sponsors that reached all the way back to a principality on their planet of origin.

And what of the cyborgs themselves? Men and women plucked from the very precipice of death to live on as machines of war. They were in their own way even stranger than the clones they guarded him against.

Anguar felt mixed emotions. On the one hand he was grateful for the cyborgs' presence, knowing they could and would protect him, but he was concerned as well. The purpose of his visit was to gain the Hegemony's support for the Confederacy—and aiming guns at its citizens seemed like a poor way to go about it.

The president's thoughts were forced off in another direction as a band struck up the human version of "All Hail The Confederacy." It sounded horrible to Dweller ears but Anguar smiled gamely and placed a hand over his uppermost stomach, a location roughly analogous with the location of the human heart.

Then, with an honor guard provided by members of the Lightning Brigade and a bodyguard composed of heavily armed cyborgs, Anguar was escorted to a limo for the drive to the capitol building. He noticed that the clones had opted to ride in a separate vehicle and wondered if it was because of his race. Major Warwick-Olson, his personal secretary, and a communications android capable of relaying messages throughout the Confederacy joined him.

Doors thumped, radios crackled, and they whirred onto a side street. Leather-clad police officers on gyrostabilized unicycles rode to either side. Anguar noticed that all of them were female, had a fringe of red hair hanging below the edge of their white helmets, and possessed the same laser blue eyes.

Though popular with politicians, motorcades and parades are a security being's worst nightmare, and this one was no exception. As the limo started into motion Anguar saw that no less than three Trooper IIs led the way, six guarded each flank, and who knows how many brought up the rear. They ran with an easy ground-eating pace. The president frowned and turned toward Warwick-Olson.

"Major, I understand the need for security, but this seems excessive. I question whether there is a real legitimate threat."

Warwick-Olson never took her eyes off the window, and her right hand never strayed far from the weapon concealed under her left armpit. A small, almost invisible receiver fed a constant stream of information into her right ear. "You're welcome to your opinion, sir, and free to replace me anytime you wish, but I respectfully disagree. The people of Alpha One were subdued by force of arms, live under foreign occupation, and are led by xenophobic human clones. They have a well-trained, well-equipped army that still has all of its weapons. If *they* don't constitute a real and legitimate threat, then who the hell does?"

Anguar's immediate reaction was anger, but it quickly gave way to an appreciation of her honesty and the knowledge that she was correct. He cleared his throat. "Point taken. Comment withdrawn."

Warwick-Olson turned toward Anguar, smiled, and turned back again. "And that's the other thing, sir; you're what we humans call a 'keeper,' and they don't come along every day."

The compliment was so genuine, and so unexpected, that it caught the president by surprise. It took a moment to frame a suitable reply, and the by the time he had it ready, the opportunity had passed. Anguar remained silent instead.

A pair of police clones motioned the limo out onto a broad tree-lined boulevard. It stretched two miles toward a perfectly positioned dome. Ranks of citizens lined both sides of the street. They had been drawn from various specialties and assembled into homogeneous groups. Medical technicians here, agricultural workers there, and so on. The people who for one reason or another had managed to outlive their peers had a tendency to stand out. The rest became a white, brown, black, or yellow blur, depending on the racial identity of the man or woman from whom the group had been cloned, something made all the more interesting by the fact that the rest of the human race had become more and more homogeneous over the last three hundred or so years until most were light brown in color. Light brown was a tint Anguar approved of because it matched his own.

But what *really* claimed Anguar's attention was the almost total silence that accompanied the ride. Like most democratically elected politicians, the Dweller had at one time or another been on the receiving end of twenty-one-gun salutes, fireworks, holo displays, applause, boos, catcalls, insults, and flying vegetables. But never, not once, had he been greeted with a complete and abiding silence. A silence made more ominous by the fact that thousands and thousands of blank faces were staring at him.

The president looked at Warwick-Olson. She shrugged. He turned toward the window. A block of all-black faces flashed by. A sense of hopelessness settled over his narrow shoulders. Deep down he knew the rest of the visit would be a waste of time. The Hegemony had one mind and it was made up.

The Legion has always accepted foreign nationals, so the decision to recruit non-humans was both logical, and in the political sense, absolutely necessary.

Zenelian Astrapazi-Klein
A Confederacy of Stars
Standard year 2620

Planet Earth, the Confederacy of Sentient Beings

The sun shone brightly, the air was crisp, and the field was newly mowed. A band, their instruments gleaming, struck up a dirge. Like most of the music the Legion loved, it had a funereal quality, as if already mourning for the 643 men and women who slow-stepped out onto the field, wheeled right, and marched toward the far end. Each movement, each step, was clearly delineated and as somber as the music that accompanied it.

Booly was about to graduate thirty-third in his class, and therefore marched three ranks back, just behind the much-vaunted top twenty. Various parts of his body were sore from the previous night's adventures but he hardly noticed. It was a proud moment, and one that he tried to memorize by absorbing the way it looked, smelled, and felt.

A row of Trooper IIs stood along the left side of the
field, tall, angular shapes capable of killing everyone present in a few short seconds. They had a brooding quality,
like pallbearers at graveside. Their armor was newly
painted and rows of medals hung from their ceremonial
harnesses. The cyborgs were fronted by rank after rank of
enlisted personnel, instructors mostly, and the officers who
ran the academy.

The enlisted people wore the epaulets, green shoulder
strap, and red fringe that had been standard since 1930,
with the green ties adopted in 1945, the scarlet waist sashes
authorized in 2090, and the collar comets added after the
disastrous Battle of Four Moons in 2417. Some of the instructors were on loan from line outfits but most were assigned to the 1st Foreign Regiment, which supplied
administrative services to the entire Legion.

But the item of clothing that gave the legionnaires their
distinctive look, and was most reminiscent of the thousands
who had preceded them, were the gleaming white hats they
wore. Hats with short black bills known as the *képi blanc*.

The stands, bright with bunting, lined the right side of
the field and they were packed with civilian spectators.
Careful to face forward, Booly searched the crowd from
the corner of his eye, but was unable to spot his mother
and father. But he knew they were there and the knowledge
made him move with even greater precision.

There, just beyond the stage where General Ian St. James
and other officials waited, Booly saw the tops of the flagpoles he had visited during the night, and the pennant he
had raised. It would fly all day and be lowered that evening.
And although no one would officially acknowledge the
flag's presence, or who had put it there, everyone knew.
While some were disappointed at his success, most of his
classmates seemed genuinely proud, something that gave
Booly hope.

After colliding with General St. James and being allowed to escape, Booly had continued down the stairs and into the basement. Like a lot of basements, this one was the province of the building's heating and cooling systems, all of which were computer controlled and tended by various kinds of low-order robots. They didn't even turn a sensor in the cadet's direction as he raced down the long underground passageway that connected Tonel Hall with Conrad Hall, better known to his peers as the "Ptomain Palace" after the seemingly poisonous meals served there.

A pair of double doors blocked his path and he shouldered them aside. The thick odor of cooking filled his nostrils and made him gag. A plebe picked the wrong moment to step out of a storeroom. The senior hit her and sent an avalanche of crockery crashing to the floor. Her arms windmilled and she landed on her butt. Booly knew she was in for a long session on the quad. He felt sorry for her but knew that turning himself in wouldn't lighten her punishment one iota.

The air was thick with moisture. An intersection loomed. Booly turned left, hit a puddle of water, and skidded into the opposite wall. He pushed off and resumed his race down the hall. An autocart full of kitchen garbage blocked the right side of the corridor. He dodged left. Another approached and he lunged right. The objective was in sight. A pair of double doors that led out onto the loading dock. The word Exit glowed above them.

Would Riley be there? Or had he given up and left? Good old Riley, who, in spite of the academy's best efforts to trim fifteen pounds off his five-and-a-half-foot frame, had not only retained the weight, but managed to add some more, and just barely squeaked through physical training. Still, Riley had the second highest GPA in the senior class, a fact that made him popular with instructors and a target for the same bullies who harassed Booly. A commonality that brought the two cadets together and forged a lasting friendship.

Booly hit the swinging doors. They banged on the outer walls. A pair of floods threw light across the loading dock. Riley heard the noise, popped to attention, saw who it was, and let his shoulders slump. His fatigues were rumpled and creased, as was any uniform that he wore longer than ten minutes. "Damn it, Booly . . . where the hell have you been? And what did you do? All hell broke loose on the quad."

"I ran into a little trouble, that's all. Is that the truck? Let's go."

Riley frowned and stood his ground. "Not till you give me a sitrep. Did you raise the pennant?"

Booly glanced at the doors. The kitchen plebe would have reported the collision by now and a noncom could arrive at any moment. "Yes, sir, General, sir, I raised the pennant, sir. Man, I feel sorry for any poor sonovabitch that ends up reporting to you!"

Riley grinned and punched Booly on the shoulder. "So do I! Come on . . . what are you waiting for? Let's haul ass!"

The truck was a glorified garbage wagon with separate sections for organic waste, metal, plastic, and paper. Booly figured the paper bin would be the most comfortable and least disgusting place to hide. He climbed in, pulled armfuls of paper over his head, and heard the lid slam shut. The truck jerked into motion a few moments later.

Riley had used his charm, his position as an upperclassman, and a hefty bribe to "borrow" the truck from a plebe on garbage duty. The plebe was now waiting at the campus transfer station hoping nothing went wrong.

Booly felt his heart skip a beat as the truck slowed and came to a halt. It was way too soon for the residence hall so that meant a check of some sort. Seconds became minutes. The cadet heard muffled voices. Metal squealed as a bin was opened, then clanged as someone let go.

Then it was his turn. A voice said "Let's take a look in here." Hinges squeaked and a flashlight played across the trash over Booly's head. Light leaked through layers of paper and he was ready to surrender when the lid crashed down.

Another bin was checked, followed by a period of silence and a distinct jerk, as Riley applied too much power and the truck lunged into motion. Fifteen minutes later he was in Danjou Hall, in his room, snuggled under the covers. Riley got rid of the truck and returned twenty minutes later. Booly described his journey over the roofs, Riley marveled over the encounter with General St. James, and they wondered how graduation would go. Riley dropped off after a while but Booly lay awake until reveille sounded. There was a lot to think about, including the upcoming visit with his parents, and the question of orders. He had put in for the 2d REP, the elite airborne regiment, but so had half of his peers.

A distant part of Booly's mind, the part that had learned to march while half-asleep, heard the preparatory command and came to a halt with the others. The sun warmed the left side of his face, the sweet scent of newly cut grass filled his nostrils, and birds chirped in the surrounding trees. This was the moment he had looked forward to for six long years. He looked up at the speaker's platform. It was white and draped with regimental flags.

General Ian St. James gazed out over a sea of gleaming white kepis and felt his chest swell with pride. There had been a time hundreds of years ago when the Legion had been led by French officers, some of whom sought such an assignment as the means to promotion, while others served because they had to. A few were outstanding officers, but many were not, and the Legion had suffered at their hands.

Which was why the academy was so important. By training its own leaders, by instilling them with pride, the Legion insured its future. He smiled. His voice boomed through the public-address system.

"You arrived as children. You survived six years of hard work to emerge as men and women. You are the best, and we will need the best to meet the challenges ahead, for freedom is never entirely won. Never forget that there are those who want what we have, who would enslave us, or kill us because of what we *might* do. You have the will, the strength, and the training to stop them. Your presence on this field is proof of that. Therefore it is my honor, no, my *privilege*, to grant you commissions in Confederacy's Armed Forces. *Vive la Légion!*"

The answering shout was so loud that it scared birds from the trees. *"Vive la Légion!"*

There were more speeches after that, including one from Anguar's secretary of defense, but they were more the benefit of the spectators and news media than the cadets themselves. Like his peers, Booly felt a sense of relief and anticipation when General St. James returned to the podium.

St. James took one last look at the cadets, the field, and the campus beyond. A robotic news cam floated in for a better shot. No one else knew it yet, but this was his final year in the Legion and his last appearance before a graduating class. He had given the Legion thirty-nine years of his life and that was enough. His wife would be pleased. He smiled and hundreds of upturned faces smiled back. "Well, ladies and gentlemen, all good things must come to an end, and that includes congratulatory speeches."

The words echoed off distant buildings, laughter rippled through the ranks, and St. James nodded sympathetically. "Yes, the time has come to leave the Academy and apply the knowledge gained here." His face grew serious. The laughter died away. "Cadet battalion, atten-hut!"

Six hundred forty-three men and women crashed to attention. A hush settled over the field. St. James paused, took a deep breath, and released it with two words: "Battalion . . . dismissed!"

A cheer went up, along with a blizzard of snowy white hats. Booly caught one, clapped it on his head, and exchanged high-fives with Riley. "Congratulations, Tom!"

"You too, Bill!"

"See you tonight?"

"Wouldn't miss it. Twenty hundred hours at the *Képi Blanc*."

Booly nodded, waved, and allowed the crowd to carry him toward the stands. He saw his mother first, partly because she was beautiful, and partly because she the only full-blooded Naa among the spectators. Booly found himself checking to see if his classmates were staring at her, felt ashamed of himself, and kept his eyes straight ahead. He loved his mother, and if the other cadets had a problem with that, then tough shit. He waved and forced his way through the crowd.

Windsweet waved back and swallowed the lump that filled her throat. Memories flooded back. She remembered how her father had ambushed a Legion patrol, how she had nursed a legionnaire back to health, how she had slowly but surely fallen in love with him, how he had fought a duel for the right to court her, how he had deserted to be with her, and how they had fled into the snow-capped mountains. And it was there, in the ruins of a long-abandoned Naa settlement, that her son had been conceived. A conception that some claimed was scientifically impossible, unless humans and Naa were related somehow, or a miracle had occurred.

But Windsweet cared about none of that, for the young man with the big grin owned every bit of her heart not already given to his father, and nothing else mattered. She opened her arms and was swept away as Bill Booly, Jr., grabbed his mother and whirled her around. She laughed. "Stop that! Put me down!"

The cadet did as he was told. He held his mother at arm's length. Her short, downy fur might have darkened a little, but the delicately shaped face, charcoal gray eyes, and the full, sensitive lips were just as he remembered them. She smelled like her name. Windsweet. Her voice was gentle and the words were Naa. Although the language *seemed* simple, different pitches could be employed to embellish or change meanings, making it quite complex. "Greetings, my son. I see you are a warrior now."

Booly felt his heart swell with pride, for in the Naa culture the words "warrior" and "man" were synonymous. His father stepped forward. He spoke Naa like a native but his words were in Standard. "Your mother is correct, son, you look like a recruiting poster. Congratulations."

Bill Booly, Jr., accepted the hand-to-forearm grip common to adult males and looked at his father. He had aged during the three years since they had last met. The hair, close cropped as always, was thinner now and shot with gray. And the eyes, while no less blue, looked tired, and a bit distracted. He smiled. "Thanks, Dad. That means a lot coming from you."

The elder Booly shrugged and smiled wryly. "I hope *your* career in the Legion goes better than mine did. Here . . . your mother has something for you."

Windsweet smiled and offered her husband a box. He removed the lid. A second lieutenant's blue kepi and shoulder boards were nestled inside. The gift was expected, and identical to ones being received all around him, but it felt special nonetheless. As his mother buttoned the shoulder boards into place, and his father placed the hat on his head, Booly was transformed from cadet to officer.

The moment felt good, so good he couldn't stop grinning, and still had a grin on his face when they left the stands and headed for the long black limo that hovered at the curb. It was then that a corporal in the famed 1st REC crossed their path and snapped a salute in Booly's direction. The young officer returned it just as smartly, asked the NCO to wait for a moment, and gave him the fifty-credit note he had pocketed for that very purpose. It was an old tradition that had originated in another army and been adopted by the first senior class. The corporal smiled, rendered a second salute, and did a neat about-face.

There was no way of knowing whether the corporal had simply happened along, or timed his passage to coincide with the flood of new lieutenants, but Booly saw what seemed like an unusual number of enlisted people lurking in the area, all saluting like mad. He laughed, waved to a distant Tom Riley, waited while his parents entered the car, and slid into the rear-facing seat. It was dark and smelled of leather.

A window sealed them away from the driver's compartment. Booly had caught a glimpse of a Naa warrior called Knifecut Easykill at the controls and was reminded of his father's unusual position as chief of chiefs, and ambassador to the Confederacy.

Partly hereditary, and partly based on a sort of democratic consensus, the interrelated positions had been granted to the elder Booly when Wayfar Hardman, Windsweet's father, had been killed in battle—a battle in which the Naa had joined forces with the Legion to fight the alien Hudatha. The senior Booly had then used that alliance to leverage a number of agreements, including formal recognition of the Naa race and the right of Naa nationals to enlist in the Legion if they so desired.

But politics were no less rife than they had been during the emperor's reign, which meant an appalling number of political assassinations and the precautions necessary to prevent them. Which was why Easykill was a highly qualified bodyguard as well as a driver and a loyal member of Windsweet's tribe. The car tilted slightly and pulled away from the curb. The senior Booly smiled, "You're awfully quiet, son."

Booly shrugged. "Thinking, that's all. Where are we headed?"

"Lunch at the beach . . . followed by whatever you want."

His mother was wearing one of the high-collared oriental sheath dresses currently popular with human females. It was jet black and looked wonderful against her light gray fur. Her voice was hopeful. "There's a reception tonight . . . your father and I have been asked to go. . . . Would you like to come?"

Booly had been dreading the moment and was just about to launch into a carefully prepared speech when his father rode to the rescue. "We'd love to have you, son, but it's only fair to warn you that it'll be pretty boring, so you might want to consider other invitations."

The younger man smiled gratefully. "Thanks for the offer, but Riley invited me to dinner, and it could be a long time before I see him again. Who knows where they'll send us."

Windsweet knew what was happening and was powerless to stop it. Her son was a warrior now and beyond her reach. She allowed herself the smallest of frowns. "You'll be careful? Celebrations get out of hand sometimes."

Bill Booly, Jr., took her hand in his. "Don't worry, Mother. Tom and I are straight-arrow types. We'll have some dinner, drink a couple of beers, and go to bed early."

Windsweet nodded agreeably, but doubt tickled the back of her mind and refused to go away.

• • •

The Kepi Blanc was located in the seedy area south of San Diego's main spaceport. It had been in business for more than a hundred years and catered entirely to legionnaires. Made from what looked like tan adobe, and topped with a crenelated roof line, it had the look of a nineteenth-century Algerian fort. A grove of bottom-lit palm trees surrounded the structure and added to the desertlike ambience.

Booly was halfway up the walk when the front door opened and a trio of legionnaires stumbled out. They staggered, saw Booly, and managed some sloppy salutes. Booly grinned, returned their salutes, and entered the restaurant. Smoke swirled, music pounded, and a scuffle broke out. Bouncers converged on the offending parties and order was restored.

The Kepi Blanc was packed, and Booly was busy working his way through the crowd when a waiter decked out in the red hat, blue cutaway coat, red pantaloons, and soft boots worn by legionnaires back in 1835 intercepted him. "Welcome to the Kepi Blanc, sir. Please follow me."

Booly obeyed and was soon steered out of the great room down a hall and into a series of interconnected lounges and dining rooms. The noise level dropped considerably. He saw plenty of senior officers, many of whom regarded his half-human, half-Naa features with open curiosity, but no enlisted personnel. A new waiter took over, this one attired in the khaki duster and cartridge belts worn in 1954 Algeria. He had just steered Booly towards a long wooden bar when a voice yelled, "Hey, Bill! Over here!"

Booly turned to find Riley seated about ten feet away. Two of the more cerebral members of their class—numbers ten and fourteen, to be exact—shared his table. Number ten was a rapier-thin woman named Kathy Harris, and number fourteen was a rather genial young man named Tony Lopez. They waved him over. Booly thanked the waiter, circumnavigated a portly colonel, and claimed a still-vacant chair. Harris offered her hand and he took it. She smelled like soap. "Nice going on the pennant, Booly . . . the entire class is proud of you."

Booly raised an eyebrow. "The *entire* class?"

Harris shrugged. *"Most* of the class. The ones who count. Hey, waiter! Yeah, you in the pith helmet, meet the man who hoisted our pennant! He needs a drink."

A waiter, fully rigged for combat in Tonkin circa 1885, took Booly's order and disappeared. He returned two minutes later. Booly tried to pay but the waiter shook his head. "Not tonight, sir. Congratulations on your accomplishment."

Surprised, and somewhat embarrassed by the praise, Booly thanked the waiter, pointed out that Riley deserved a lot of the credit, and changed the subject. "So, Tom . . . how did the afternoon go?"

Riley winced. "Mom and Dad got into a fight, the food was lousy, and I left as soon as I could. How 'bout you?"

Booly sipped his gin and tonic. The truth was that he had enjoyed the time with his parents but it didn't seem polite to say so. "It was fine. Say, have you people ordered yet? I'm starving."

It turned out that they hadn't ordered, so the next hour and a half was spent ordering food, eating it, and downing rounds of free drinks, so that by the time the desert tray finally arrived, Booly was light-headed. It was then that a hand fell on his shoulder and a voice he both feared and hated filled his ears. "Well, if it isn't the brain trust of Booly, Riley, Harris, and Lopez. . . . Hey, Booly, good going on the pennant thing, *vive la légion,* and that sort of rubbish. May we join you?"

None of the foursome wanted to play host to Kadien and his toadies, also known as numbers 503, 608, and 621, but good manners dictated that they do so. Kadien had worked especially hard at making Booly's life miserable over the last six years, so alarm bells went off in a distant and still-sober portion of the officer's mind, but were muted by excessive amounts of alcohol and a naive desire for acceptance.

More drinks arrived and were consumed. In spite of the fact that they had less than twelve hours of seniority and, with the single exception of Booly, had never heard a shot fired in anger, the newly made lieutenants had opinions on everything from their superior officers' sexual proclivities to the use of robo artillery as a means of night harassment.

Though he was often less knowledgeable than those around him, Kadien made up for average intelligence with the same sort of tenacity that had allowed him to outlast other more capable cadets, and might or might not win a battle someday. He liked to keep score and declared himself the winner in no less than three hotly contested arguments.

An hour had passed by the time Kadien looked at his watch, turned to the toady on his right, and said, "Well, old weasel, the night is young, and other, more sophisticated pleasures await. Anyone care to join us?"

Booly was surprised to discover that the question was directed to him. He searched Kadien's face for the usual signs of contempt and came up empty. Was this a peace offering? An attempt to make up for the racial slurs, the badgering, and the harassment of the last six years? He smiled and had the uncomfortable feeling that it looked like a silly grin. "Sure . . . what did you have in mind?"

Riley signaled "no" with subtle shakes of his head, Harris looked doubtful, and Lopez kept his face intentionally blank.

Kadien made a production of looking around, as if checking to make sure no one could hear. "Ever heard of a nightclub called the Cess Pool? No? Well, friends tell me they have a floor show that will put hair on your chest. Ooops! Sorry, Booly, no pun intended."

Not entirely sure whether Kadien had made fun of him or uttered an unintentional faux pas, Booly smiled and waved the comment away. Kadien surveyed the table. "So how 'bout it? You want to see some real honest-to-God action? Or sit around the Blanc pounding your puds? Except for Harris, that is, who doesn't have a pud, but would if she could. Isn't that right, Harris?"

Harris and Lopez wasted little time begging off, but Riley was concerned for Booly's safety, and agreed to go. It seemed like little more than moments later when the five of them piled into an auto cab. Someone had barfed on the floor, and even though a robot had removed the mess two hours before, the smell remained. Kadien issued the instructions. "Take us to the Cess Pool . . . and step on it."

The on-board computer analyzed the words, acted on those that were consistent with its programming, and discarded the rest. Booly stared out a window as the vehicle jerked into motion, attained maximum economical speed, and headed south towards old Mexico, the very country in which Danjou and his men had fought their much-celebrated battle in the tiny village of Camerone.

Persistent seediness quickly gave way to full-fledged urban blight as the taxi carried them deep into the famed DMZ, which was officially off limits to *all* military personnel, including newly commissioned lieutenants. Windows gaped like blinded eyes, doors swung in the breeze, and vandalized streetlights stood guard duty on every corner.

Rectangles of light showed here and there. Were they clues to the location of hardy souls who lived there? Or bait set by one predator for another? Booly shivered and felt his head start to clear. Riley sat across from him. Their knees touched. Riley looked worried. A tendril of doubt touched the back of Booly's mind. Was the trip what it seemed? A peace offering by Kadien and his friends? Or something more sinister? Kadien seemed to sense Booly's doubts and smiled reassuringly. "We're almost there, old sport—hope you like naked women 'cause this place is supposed to be packed with them!"

Booly gave what he hoped was an enthusiastic nod, and was thrown against the door as the auto cab's nav system misjudged the driveway and turned a hair too late. The taxi bumped its way over a wicked set of rotating spikes and entered a half-full parking lot. It contained an intriguing mix of gleaming limos, middle-of-the-road sedans, and do-it-yourself armored cars.

The cab eased to a stop, Kadien paid the fare, and a man dressed in an executioner's hood and cape opened the door. The legionnaires slid out, milled around for a moment, and started towards a low-slung building. There were no lights and no signs announcing what it was. You either knew or you didn't.

A grim reaper, dressed in long black robes, holding a razor-sharp scythe, opened the door. Kadien led the way and the rest of the officers followed. The hallway was shaped like a tunnel, or more likely a throat, since the walls looked and felt like human tissue.

Booly had expected bright lights and pounding music. There was none. What little bit of light there was came from sconce-mounted candles. Their flames burned yellow and were bent sideways when struck by a wall of mechanically propelled air. It had been scented to smell like a woman's breath and was accompanied by a long, slow groan. The effect was unabashedly erotic and Kadien grinned. "Interesting, wouldn't you say? Shall we proceed a little further down the old gastrointestinal tract?" Kadien led and the others followed.

Riley touched Booly's arm. "If this is the *front* door, what does the back door look like?"

Booly laughed, and even though he had some very real

concerns about what they were doing, felt a little better. The trip into the DMZ was an adventure, that was for sure, and would make for a great story. Assuming he survived to tell it.

Another blast of heavily scented air made its way down the hall, hit them, and kept on going. A groan, deeply sensual and full of unarticulated yearning, followed the air and died in the distance. What appeared as a fleshy constriction irised open and a woman greeted them. She was naked beyond a leather harness and some thigh-high boots. Booly was no prude, and far from virginal, but had never seen anything like this before. He gulped and felt blood color his face. The woman had a deep, throaty voice. "Good evening, gentlemen, and welcome to the Cess Pool. Would you like to be shown to one of our private rooms? Or would seats on the main floor be more to your liking?"

Kadien reached out to fondle one of the woman's breasts. She made no move to stop him but her voice was hard as steel. "Everything has a price, Lieutenant, and mine is far higher than you can afford to pay."

Kadien made a show of snatching his hand away and mugged for his friends, but there was no doubt as to who had won. Booly was pleased but careful to hide it.

The woman turned and led them down a flight of curving stairs. It turned out that the "main floor" consisted of the circular area that surrounded a pool filled with some sort of dark, oily liquid. Bubbles rose to the surface, popped, and released a musky scent. The legionnaires were in the process of taking seats poolside when a loud, obnoxious voice came from the other side of the room. "Well, look what we have here, boys, some brand-new pimple-heads taking their pet cat for a stroll."

Booly knew instantly whom the cat part referred to and turned in the direction of the threat. There were six marines, all junior officers like them, all very, very drunk. One was standing, his face red from too much drink, pointing at Booly. "What the hell is that thing anyway? A legionnaire or a laboratory experiment?"

Anger surged and Booly had already taken two steps forward by the time Riley grabbed him and a bouncer sidled up to the marine. Words were exchanged, the marine shrugged, and fell into his seat. The lights began to dim and Booly allowed Riley to guide him into a chair. He looked at Kadien, caught the tail end of a smirk, and knew he'd been had. The other officer wasn't in cahoots with the marines, but had invited Booly to the nightclub knowing something similar could happen, and hoping that it would.

Booly had no more than settled into his chair, and the knowledge of what was going on, when the bubbles stopped and the oily stuff started to quiver. An ominous hum came over the speakers, soft at first, then grew in intensity until it became a growl. A round black something forced its way up and out of the inky black depths. Eight blobs stood on the platform and became people as hundreds of gallons of thick oily fluid drained away. There were two women and six men. They were naked except for a coating of whatever the stuff was, and in the case of the men, ready for sex.

The hum died to be replaced by the complex sound of drums, their individual beats echoing and overlaying each other to form a rich tapestry of interwoven sound, something the human part of Booly had learned to appreciate and enjoy. But not here, not tonight, not with people like Kadien. The people on the platform started a slow, sensual dance as Booly nudged Riley with an elbow. "Come on, Tom . . . let's get the hell out of here."

Riley's eyes were locked on the now-writhing forms that occupied the oil-wet stage. "Sure, Bill, lead the way."

Booly rose, considered some sort of excuse for Kadien, and decided to hell with it. Let the racist bastard think whatever he wanted. Pausing only for a much-needed stop in the men's room, the legionnaires made their way out of the club, and into the parking lot. The grim reaper was on the door but the executioner was nowhere to be seen. They were halfway to the cab stand when the marines stepped out of the shadows. The same marine did all the talking.

"Look, fellas, the wuss patrol, headed for home. Whacha gonna do, pussy? Tell the big bad CO that some jarheads called you a pussy? Cause if that's whach your gonna do I'd be happy to write it all over your furry ass and sign my name."

Booly knew the marine wanted to fight and knew there was no way around it. He removed his hat and jacket. Riley wasn't so sure and tried to dissuade him. "Come on, Bill, let's get out of here. We're right smack in the middle of the DMZ. What if someone calls the MPs? We're screwed, that's what."

Booly kept his eyes on the marine. "Can't be helped, Tom . . . Watch my back."

Booly had retained his dress shirt but the marine had stripped to waist. He had the chest, abs, and biceps of a body builder. That meant he was strong, but strength wasn't everything. How much did he know about hand-to-hand combat? Not just the crap the DIs had taught him at OCS, but the down-and-dirty stuff older cubs beat into your head, until it became part and parcel of who you were. The answer would soon become apparent.

The marine wore his hair high and tight. His forehead, nose, and cheeks were sunburned from a field exercise the day before. He grimaced and growled the way his high school football coach had trained him to do, brought his fists up, and danced from one foot to the other. A boxer, Booly decided, or a kick boxer, either one of which he could handle.

A cheer went up from the marines as their champion

moved in. Riley started the Legion's chant: "Camerone! Camerone! Camerone!" and Booly waited the way his uncle Movefast Shootstraight had instructed him to do. He could see the big warrior in his mind's eye, orange fur rippling in the mountain breeze, the huge .50-caliber recoiless in the cross-draw holster, hands on narrow hips.

Stop dancing, boy. Posturing means nothing and wastes energy. You want the other cub to know how tough you are? Wait and teach him with your hands and feet.

The marine closed in. "Here kitty, kitty. Come to daddy, you goddamned freak. Daddy has something for you." Booly saw the thought pass through greenish brown eyes and flicked his head to the right. A fist brushed his ear. Another came right behind it. Booly ducked, landed two blows to the man's rock-hard abdomen, and did a backwards flip. The use of gymnastics as part of hand-to-hand combat was something of a Naa specialty and more than a little disconcerting where the marine was concerned. His spin kick traveled through empty air and left him momentarily open. Booly stepped in, delivered three quick blows to the man's face, and danced out again. Blood trickled from the marine's left nostril and he bellowed with rage. "You goddamned freak! I'll kill you!"

Booly didn't know where the knife came from, only that it appeared in the other man's right hand, and gleamed with reflected light. It was double edged and shaped like a dagger. The other marines roared their approval and one of them yelled "Skin the damned thing . . . we'll use it for a throw rug!"

Booly wished for his uniform jacket but knew he wouldn't be able to grab and wrap it around his arm quickly enough to do any good. But his uncle was there and served to calm him.

Knives are dangerous, boy. In order to use them you have to get up close and personal. That's why most sen-

tients invented guns. So the first thing to remember is this: If your opponent has a knife, and you don't, accept the fact that you're going to take a cut. You have no choice. But choose the cut the way you would choose a best friend, taking the one that will damage you the least, and help you when times are hard.

Booly circled left, his eyes on the marine's face, rather than the knife in his hand. He could almost feel his uncle's large, callused hands close around his boyish arm. *Look, son,* the warrior had said, *look at the inner surface of your arm. The blood flows here and muscles run here. . . . Never, ever, take a cut on the inside of your arm.*

But here, his uncle said, rotating the boy's arm so that the outer surface was uppermost, *we have a thin layer of skin followed by good, hard bone. Take your cut there, block the knife, and blind your opponent. A knife means nothing when you cannot see.*

So Booly waited, heard Riley yell words he couldn't understand, and allowed the marine to move in. He heard something wail in the distance and was trying to figure out what it was when the attack came. The marine held the knife in an overhand cutting rather than stabbing grip. He pulled his arm back and slashed down towards Booly's throat. The Legionnaire threw his left arm up, felt the sudden jolt as the knife sliced to the bone, and stabbed the other man's eyes with two stiffened fingers. The results were spectacular. The other officer dropped the knife, grabbed his eyes, and started to scream.

Booly had less than two seconds to take the scene in before both he and Riley were buried under an avalanche of marine green. The attack was painful, but short lived, since the faint wail had transformed itself into the full-fledged scream of sirens.

The marines, who were well aware of the penalties for entering the DMZ, delivered a flurry of kicks and disappeared, leaving their buddy behind. Booly felt strangely light, but not light enough to stand, and remained where he was. His left arm hurt, and he was just about to cradle it against his chest, when a boot pinned it in place. A face appeared over him. It was fuzzy at first but blinked into focus. Kadien smiled. "Ooops! Did the freak fall down and go boom? Too bad, old weasel . . . but that's life. See you around."

Booly heard laughter and the face disappeared. He tried to move but found that he couldn't. "Riley?"

"Yeah?"

"You okay?"

"No."

"Well, hang on, the MPs will be here in a minute."

The sirens grew louder, died abruptly, and gave way to the sound of turbines. They howled loudly and then died as a pair of ground-effect vehicles settled onto their skirts. Booly heard doors slam, the sound of voices, and the thump, thump, thump of combat boots. Riley sounded tired. "Booly?"

"Yeah?"

"The MPs are marines."

"Oh, shit."

"Yeah."

And there was nothing else to say, because the MPs took one look at their fallen comrade, still rolling around clutching his eyes, and went to work with their batons. Booly saw the first couple of blows. The third took him under.

5

In war important events are produced by trivial causes.

Julius Caesar
Standard year circa 74 B.C.

Planet Earth, the Confederacy of Sentient Beings

The being once known as Sergi Chien-Chu, president of Chien-Chu Enterprises, liberator of enslaved sentients, and father of the Confederacy, awoke. Chemicals flowed and electrons stirred as the machine that cradled his brain moved to a higher state of readiness.

He thought the word *vision* and "saw" through the vid cams that replaced his long-dead eyes. It was nearly pitch black inside the bedroom so he switched to infrared. The com console, the warm air duct, and his wife's electric blanket glowed luminescent green. He thought the word *time* and a digital readout appeared in lower right quadrant of his vision: 0544. Sixteen minutes before he had to get up and go to work. Except that he was "up" and standing in a corner. Though not much larger than his original body, the cybernetic version was a good deal heavier and not much fun to snuggle with. Which was why he had taken to sleeping standing up.

Chien-Chu scanned Nola's still-sleeping form and thought how strange his existence was. When a massive heart attack had claimed his life, Madam Chien-Chu had used a small portion of their vast wealth to bring him back. The technology had been around for a long time and had originally been used to snatch criminals and terminally ill citizens from the brink of death so they could serve the former empire as cybernetic legionnaires. But nothing beyond the high cost of buying and maintaining a cybernetic body prevented others from prolonging their lives in similar fashion.

This fact made Chien-Chu distinctly uncomfortable and explained why the company that still bore his name had invested millions of credits in cybernetic research. The day was coming when anyone, not just the wealthy, would be able to extend his or her life by ten, twenty, or even thirty years, depending on the condition and viability of his or her brain tissue. Then all these people would learn what the industrialist already knew, that physical pleasures such as eating, drinking, and sex are nothing when compared to the simple but now unattainable comfort of snuggling with a loved one.

Not that life wasn't better in some respects, since Nola had raised him from the dead with a veil of carefully maintained secrecy, and freed him from the life that he had learned to hate. She knew that he detested politics and would never have gotten involved if it hadn't been for the death of their son at the hands of the Hudathans, and the possibility that millions if not billions more would die before the then-emperor finally took action.

So with a fine being like Anguar ready to take over, Nola had made the right decision. Besides, the industrialist had enjoyed watching his own incredibly overproduced funeral on the television, and been moved by the number of beings that actually seemed to care.

The readout snapped to 0600 and Chien-Chu initiated the

diagnostic programs that had taken the place of his morning shower. It took 1.5 seconds for his on-board computer to check his electro-mechanical systems and deliver five green lights to the lower left quadrant of his vision. Chien-Chu sent a mental acknowledgment and the lights disappeared.

Servos whined softly as he padded his way over to the bed, checked his wife's soft breathing, and headed for the door. Her voice stopped him. She sounded sleepy. "Sergi?"

"Yes, dear?"

"Be careful."

Chien-Chu had the feelings that went with a smile and felt plasti-flesh lips curve upwards in response. "Yes, dear. I'll be careful."

There was little to no point to stopping for a breakfast he didn't need to eat, and he had changed clothes the night before, so the industrialist headed for the front door. The condominium was generously proportioned, but far from pretentious, and located in a building favored by a hundred or so upper-middle-class professionals, all of whom believed that he was Madam Chien-Chu's driver and butler. A nice fiction and one that served to protect their hard-won privacy.

The door saw him coming, checked his identity, and slid out of the way. The hallway was rich with deep pile carpeting, gilded mirrors, and an ornate table that served no purpose at all. Having been summoned by the condominium's household computer, the elevator was waiting and opened to admit him. He stepped inside and discovered that another of the building's residents, a judge named Margaret Bretnor, was already aboard. She nodded in the manner reserved for servants and lesser beings. "Good morning, James."

Chien-Chu remembered how the same woman had fawned over the previous and more powerful him at a party two years before and nodded in return. "Good morning, Judge Bretnor. You look especially radiant this morning."

Bretnor's aging face brightened considerably. "Why, thank you, James, I'm using some new skin cream. Perhaps that would account for it."

The elevator came to a gentle stop. Chien-Chu smiled. "Of course, ma'am. Have a nice day." Judge Bretnor sailed off the elevator feeling better than she had for weeks, sped off to work, and handed out some of the most lenient sentences defense attorneys had ever seen.

Chien-Chu paused in the entrance hall and checked his appearance. His new self looked absurdly young, perhaps twenty-five or so, and was slim in a way that his previously portly body had never been. Close-cropped blond hair, blue eyes, and a woodenly handsome face completed the somewhat unlikely picture. Quite a change from the body that had failed him. His Chinese-Russian ancestors would have been shocked.

The industrialist shook his head in disgust. Not everyone wanted to look young again and Chien-Chu Enterprises was working on more mature and ethnically correct models. He would ask Nola to arrange for a prototype the moment one became available.

The ornate lobby was empty as usual and the door leaped out of his way. Once on the street, Chien-Chu joined the early-morning throng of people who were headed for work. Most accepted the industrialist for what he seemed to be but some recognized him as a cyborg and edged away.

Unlike humanoid androids, many of whom *looked* human but had telltale *A*'s embossed on their foreheads to avoid any possibility of a mistake, civilian cyborgs were classified as sentients and bore no special markings. And, given the fact that civilian cyborgs were something of a new phenomenon, some people spent a lot of time and energy picking them out of a crowd, and having done so, subjecting them to the same kind of hatred reserved for aliens. Especially since civilian cyborgs tended to be wealthy and were assumed to be greedy, grasping, and dishonest. Just one of the many challenges poor old Anguar had to deal with.

Chien-Chu allowed the crowd to carry him down into the maze of tubeways that crisscrossed the ancient city of Los Angeles. A quick check showed that he was right on time, as was his train. It arrived with a whoosh of displaced air, slid to a silent stop, and hovered over the rails. Chien-Chu made his way aboard, found a seat, and wound up surrendering it to a woman and two children. He could tell she knew what he was and didn't approve. She accepted the seat as if it were hers by right and did everything she could to avoid eye contact from that point onward.

The train made two additional stops prior to arriving at Platform 47-East. It had been placed there for the convenience of Orion, Inc., a successful aerospace firm, and just one of the many companies owned by Chien-Chu Enterprises.

The industrialist had worked at Orion for two months now, just as he had worked at other Chien-Chu-owned companies since his well-publicized death, gathering data, evaluating procedures, and feeding the resulting information through Nola to the small cadre of managers who ran his empire, and never ceased to be amazed at Madam Chien-Chu's unexpected business acumen. The whole thing was sneaky and, given his current duties, lots of fun.

Workers flooded off the train. Some knew him and shouted their hellos. "Hey, Jim! How's it goin'? See ya on the line . . ."

Chien-Chu shouted back, traded friendly insults with the ones he knew best, and was carried up the escalator and into the locker rooms. The flat screen on the front of locker 1157 had a message on it. "Jim James . . . please report to the production manager's office prior to starting your shift.''

Chien-Chu sighed, hit the accept button, and entered his code. The door popped open. The dreaded Mr. Conklin again. The two of them had butted heads three or four times in the past and would continue to butt heads as long as the production manager continued to treat sentient workers the same way he dealt with androids.

Chien-Chu stripped off the conservative butler-type suit that served as protective camouflage within the condominium, and donned a pair of gray-blue overalls, safety boots, and the blue bandanna he used to keep his blond hair under control. A wiry black man, his forearms covered with tiny scars where droplets of molten metal had burned their way through his gauntlets, punched Chien-Chu in the shoulder.

"Hey, Jimbo, what this shit about Conklin calling you in? Is that asshole bothering you again?''

Chien-Chu smiled. "You should never jump to conclusions, Kato. Perhaps Conklin admires the quality of my work and wants to thank me for my outstanding performance.''

Kato had lots of white teeth and they showed when he laughed. "Right, and pigs fly, too. You let the crew know if Conklin gets out of hand. The floor is a busy place and accidents happen.''

Chien-Chu smiled, nodded, and was secretly concerned. It was hard if not impossible to measure the negative impact that a person like Conklin had on productivity until you replaced them. And, given the fact that problems usually stem from processes rather than people, he was hesitant to fire someone without careful investigation. But when a manager was so disliked that workers fantasized about killing him you had to wonder.

Chien-Chu exchanged hellos with other workers, made his way out of the locker room, and headed for the lift that would carry him to the top floor. Doors whispered open, wood paneling embraced him, and mood music filled the air—none of which added one iota to the plant's efficiency or made life more pleasant for the majority of the company's workers. Chien-Chu felt annoyed and an array of feedback circuits told him that his face had registered that fact.

The doors slid open and the industrialist stepped out into a luxurious reception area. A class VII android rose from behind a wall of mahogany and smiled. She-it had a halo of blond hair, blue eyes, red lips, and a voluptuous body. Rumor had it she was programmed to provide Conklin with more than just secretarial services. If so, that too went against company policy, and came out of the company's bottom line. The android smiled, and if it hadn't been for the *A* on her forehead, Chien-Chu would have sworn she was human. "Yes? How may I help you?"

"Jim James, here to see Mr. Conklin."

The robot nodded politely. "Of course. Mr. Conklin is on an important call at the moment but I'll let him know that you arrived."

Chien-Chu chose a seat with a good view of Conklin's glass-enclosed office. He couldn't see through the electronically generated privacy haze, so he activated some of the on-board equipment that made his body so heavy, and watched the interference disappear. It came as no surprise that Conklin was sipping coffee and reading a news fax instead of taking part in a video call as his secretary claimed.

Fifteen minutes had passed by the time Conklin shoved the news fax into a recycling slot, said something to his secretary, and leaned back in his chair. He was still there, leaning back and looking superior, when Chien-Chu entered the room. Rather than greet Conklin as he was supposed to, sweat dripping and knees knocking, the industrialist took a moment to look out through the production manager's floor-to-ceiling foot-thick armaplast window.

It provided a wonderful view of the main floor, where Chien-Chu worked. The frame of a Viper Class Interceptor had started to take shape. Clumsy forms moved here and there while jets of blue-green flame stabbed the murk. Welding was part science and part art, which explained why Chien-Chu liked it. The process itself involved heating two pieces of metal to the point where both were ready to melt, inserting filler metal between them, and allowing all three to mingle. The resulting seam, or fusion zone, would be as strong as any other part of the surrounding metal.

But, to guarantee the strength of the weld, the heated metals had to be protected from hydrogen, nitrogen, and oxygen in the atmosphere. There were various ways to accomplish that, such as spraying argon, helium, or carbon dioxide gases onto the metals while welding, or applying nonmetallic flux prior to welding, but Orion had chosen a third approach. By removing all air from the production area and creating a near-perfect vacuum, they had eliminated all contaminants, a much more efficient process when multiplied by thousands of welds.

Of course those savings were somewhat eroded by the fact that the welders had to wear bulky space armor and were therefore less efficient. Unless the welders were cyborgs, that is, men and women who needed very little oxygen, and carried what they needed within armored bodies. Which was the primary reason why Chien-Chu had been hired, although his previous knowledge of welding helped, as did the fact that he had excellent references from other Chien-Chu owned companies.

Conklin cleared his throat. His voice dripped with sarcasm. "Assuming you are finished admiring the view . . . I could use a moment of your time."

Chien-Chu turned and looked down at the man in the chair. He had bio-sculpted features, a jeweled temple jack, and a weak, dissipated mouth. The cyborg waited for an invitation to sit.

Cultural norms suggested that the person who was seated had the advantage but the production manager felt intimidated. An absurd notion since the creature in front of him was little more than semi-skilled labor and a freak at that. He hoped his voice would sound appropriately stern. "Sit down. A complaint has been filed and must be reviewed."

Chien-Chu took a seat. It was then that he realized Conklin's desk had been placed on a platform that enabled him to look down on his visitors. "A complaint? About me?"

"Of course about you!" Conklin said irritably. "Why summon you to my office if it wasn't about you?"

Chien-Chu shrugged innocently. "To jerk me around?"

Conklin flushed. He pointed a finger at Chien-Chu's chest. "Listen, mister, you pulled the red switch, which cost this company thirty-five thousand credits! If there was any justice in this world I'd deduct every goddamned one of them from *your* pay!"

Red handles were located throughout the production area and were used to restore a breathable atmosphere in case of a suit puncture or similar emergency. Chien-Chu had pulled one of the handles two days before, when a red-hot chunk of metal had fallen from the scaffolding's upper deck and landed on a worker's upturned back. She felt the impact and screamed as the metal burned a hole through her armor. The cyborg had grabbed a handle and pulled. Chien-Chu eyed the other man with something akin to disgust. "Yeah, you could dock my pay, *or* you could thank me for saving Risa's life."

Conklin's eyes were slits. "If you had, I would. But an examination of the woman's suit showed that while the metal penetrated the *first* layer of armor, the second layer was intact, and completely adequate for a normal exit."

"And how," Chien-Chu demanded levelly, "would *I* or

any other member of the floor crew know that?''

"By damned well taking the time to look!" Conklin said shrilly, "and pulling the handle in a genuine emergency!"

"Which would leave no time to save her," Chien-Chu said in the same calm voice, "and violates accepted safety procedures. Procedures you are paid to enforce . . . which is why you're afraid to fire me."

Conklin jumped to his feet and pointed towards the door. "Get out of my office!"

Chien-Chu ordered his body to stand and it obeyed. "And a nice office it is. Tell me something, are the people at HQ aware of it?"

Conklin tried to answer but was so angry the words were incoherent. "Office! Out! Get now!"

Chien-Chu nodded and strolled out of the office. The beautiful android wished the cyborg a nice day, picked up a radio-borne summons, and wondered how badly Conklin would beat her. Like all of the more sophisticated robots, she had feedback circuits that delivered something akin to human pain and didn't relish what was coming. But her preferences meant nothing in the face of the programming that overrode what little bit of free will she had. The android hurried into Conklin's office, closed the door, and disrobed. For reasons she couldn't fathom Conklin liked to beat her while he had sex with her. She bent over the desk and waited for him to get it over with.

Chien-Chu left the elevator on the main floor, stepped over to a bank of public com sets, and keyed some numbers. Nola was up and cheerful as usual. Her face was wrinkled but still beautiful. Chien-Chu inquired after her health, listened to the usual minor complaints, and her plans for the rest of the day. Then, when that part of the conversation had run its enjoyable but predictable course, he told her about Conklin. She agreed with his recommendations and promised to implement them within the hour.

Cheerful, and more than a little pleased with himself, Chien-Chu reentered the locker room, grabbed a protective vest, a helmet with face shield, a tool belt with power supply, and a pair of gauntlets. He was still pulling the gloves on when he approached the lock. Everyone else had cycled through thirty minutes before, so, with the exception of a rather taciturn low-grade robo-cart, the industrialist had the airtight enclosure to himself.

He checked to make sure that his body was sealed, received confirmation that it was, and waited while the atmosphere was removed from the lock. A green light signaled vacuum, the hatch irised open, and the robo-cart trundled out. Chien-Chu followed. The vacuum meant nothing to his internally pressurized body and he gloried in the atmosphere of the place.

The ship's U-shaped frame curved upwards like the ribs of some prehistoric beast. Lasers flashed as fellow workers used crosspieces to tie the frame together, cut holes for the fiber-optic cables that would tie the vessel's electronics together, and attached the first of the hull plates.

The truth was that he loved this work more than building Chien-Chu Enterprises and more than the sculptures he had cut and welded together in the old days. The fact was that it felt good to work with his hands, to build something strong, to bend metal to his will. He grinned, started up a ladder, and was hard at work five minutes later.

Meanwhile, high above, Conklin had turned his secretary so he could slap various parts of her plasti-flesh anatomy, dominate her with violent thrusts of his penis, and look out the window at the same time. Something about having sex while watching lesser beings work added spice to the occasion. Yes, some railed against what they called ''enhanced masturbation'' as being somehow evil, but would have been even more outraged had he forced *real* women to submit to his desires, which proved what idiots they were.

Conklin had just established a comfortable rhythm, and was building towards the inevitable climax, when the comset buzzed. He wanted to ignore it, wanted to achieve orgasm first, but there was no denying the call. His boss didn't call very often, but woe be to the person who wasn't there, or didn't respond when she did.

Conklin paused, killed the video pickup, and stabbed the "on" button. "Good morning, Veronica, how are you?" The answer was short and far from pleasant. It seemed that both of them had been fired and were to be off prem by noon. Not only that, but the luxuries they had afforded themselves would be deducted from their severance pay, and their benefits would end thirty days later. She didn't say as much, but the production manager knew the *real* purpose of her call was to give him sufficient time to destroy certain files, ensuring their mutual safety.

Conklin hit the off button and felt his heretofore rock-hard member wilt. He barely had his pants on when the security team arrived, deactivated the android, canceled his access codes, froze his files, and inventoried his office.

No wonder, then, that neither Conklin nor Chien-Chu noticed the small eraser-sized spy-eye that inched its way off the production manager's armored-glass window, onto a support beam, and out towards the main scaffolding. It was the same support scaffolding on which the industrialist was busily welding a support bracket into place.

6

Unless dragged before a tyrant, or an enemy with a grudge, the average miscreant is better-off taking whatever punishment the Chief may hand out rather than face a sometimes inebriated jury of his or her peers.

Narmu Ooomadu Tutweiler
A Year with the Naa
Standard year 2542

Planet Earth, the Confederacy of Sentient Beings

William Booly, Jr., was in deep, deep trouble. Just how much trouble was underscored by the fact that half the people in the waiting area wore shock cuffs, leg chains, and in some cases both.

The room he and the other prisoners occupied was large, institutional, and intentionally intimidating. MPs in full combat rig stood next to the doors, surveillance cameras peeked out of corners, two-way mirrors punctuated glossy green paint, and a host of mass-produced heroes stared at Booly from behind layers of protective plastic.

The prisoners were called in what seemed like random order and marched, shoved, or dragged through a door marked Summary Court. They emerged fifteen to twenty minutes later. Some blustered, some whined, and some cried. Booly knew how they felt. The majority of the accused were enlisted personnel but a slack-jawed unshaven captain was led past as well. Not a good omen.

Having beaten the two legionnaires unconscious, the marine MPs had dumped them into the back of an armored personnel carrier and hauled them to the Academy's dispensary. Once there, Booly surfaced long enough to watch a doctor put eight sutures in his arm before the combination of alcohol, drugs, and fatigue had pulled him under.

Morning arrived along with a blinding headache, a breakfast he couldn't bear to look at, and a corporal who was so thin that he looked like a skeleton come to life. His name was Parker and he was a stern taskmaster. The first thing he did was to open the blinds and allow sunshine to flood the room. Booly didn't recognize the room or its sparse furnishings but assumed it was the BOQ or something similar. The corporal was insistent. Beady eyes stared from heavily shadowed sockets.

"Begging the lieutenant's pardon, sir, but Summary Court begins in an hour, and the lieutenant should be on time. Now lean on me, that's it, and I'll take you to the shower. Does the lieutenant need any help in the shower? No? Well, I'll be outside just in case."

In addition to the headache and the recently sutured arm, Booly had countless aches and pains. Some stemmed from his rooftop adventures but most were the result of the beating he had taken the night before. He made a side trip to the tiny sink, found the pain tabs the doctor had provided, and swallowed two.

Three additional steps took him to the shower enclosure. It was difficult to keep the bandage dry but he managed to wash without Parker's assistance. The shower was followed by a shave and running commentary from the hollow-cheeked Corporal.

"The lieutenant might be interested to know that I held the rank of sergeant on six different occasions during the last fifteen years."

Knowing an offer when he heard one, and eager to learn anything that might help him out of his present difficulties, Booly forced a smile. "Knowledge should be shared, Corporal . . . please enlighten me."

Parker nodded, removed a heavily starched shirt from its hangar, and held it up. A set of lieutenant's boards had been buttoned onto the shoulder straps and Booly wondered how much longer he'd be entitled to wear them. He stuck his left arm into the appropriate sleeve, fought to pry it open, and winced at the pain. Parker showed no signs of sympathy.

"The first thing to remember is that a Summary Court consists of a single officer, and the accused—that's you, sir—must represent themselves. And that being the case, sir, you must look the exact *opposite* of the sort of person who would do what you are accused of doing, which is violating a standing order, assault on a member of the Confederacy's Armed Forces, and conduct unbecoming an officer. Here . . . allow me to help with those buttons."

The charges, and the certain knowledge that he was guilty, filled Booly's stomach with lead. Unless he insisted on a court-martial, and the military equivalent of a jury trial, the officer in charge of the Summary Court could punish him in any way that he or she chose, up to and including a reduction in the rank he had worked so long and hard to achieve. What would his parents think? Not to mention the tribal elders. But everyone knows a court martial is a two-edged sword, ensuring fairness on the one hand, and by-the-book rigidity on the other.

"So," the corporal continued, helping Booly into a pair of stiffly starched pants, "the lieutenant might consider the following advice: Accept full responsibility for your actions, look the presiding officer in the eye, and apologize for everything except hitting the marine. There ain't an officer in the Legion that would punish a man for that.''

Booly laughed and fastened his belt. It glowed from a good polishing. "Thanks, Corporal . . . you give good advice. Can I ask a couple of questions?''

Parker nodded politely. "Lock and load, sir. Ready on the range.''

"What happened to Lieutenant Riley?''

"The powers that be decided to cut Lieutenant Riley some slack. He was verbally reprimanded, confined to quarters, and assigned to Legion Outpost NA-45-16/R. He lifts two and a half hours from now. Or so I hear.''

Booly damned himself for the idiot he was. Not only had he let himself down, and embarrassed his parents, he had betrayed his best friend as well. So much for Riley's application to Staff College. He swallowed hard. "Thanks, Corporal . . . I appreciate your honesty. Now for my second question . . . How does a know-nothing, wet-behind-the-ears junior lieutenant rate help from someone like you?''

A smile stole over Parker's tightly stretched face. "Some people are born lucky, sir, like a sergeant-major I once knew who ran through a hail of lead to save my ass and escaped without a scratch.''

Suddenly a whole lot of things made sense. "You served with my father?''

"Yes, sir, I had that honor,'' Parker replied soberly, "and if ever you need a sometimes sergeant, keep me in mind. I like an officer who will stand and fight. That's what they pay us to do. Now time's a-wasting, sir . . . Let's lace them boots, set that sling, and move out. It ain't smart to be late.''

Booly wondered whether Parker had chosen to help an old friend's son or been asked to do so by the ex-sergeant-major himself. There was no way to tell and he couldn't think of a graceful way to phrase the question.

Booly donned his hat, checked the full-length mirror, and was surprised at how good he looked. Thanks to Parker's preparations, and expert assistance, he could have passed a general inspection. Even with the khaki-colored arm sling.

They left the BOQ together, and it wasn't until they were outside and quick-marching their way across the quad that Booly noticed Parker's MP arm band and holstered side-arm. He was a prisoner! And only by the grace of the un-official noncom network had he escaped the indignity of a jail cell and everything that went with it.

Cadets saluted smartly, frightened by the unexpected ap-pearance of an honest-to-God officer, and the spectral MP. Booly returned their salutes, hoped he wouldn't encounter anyone he knew, tried to look officerlike, and was relieved when they approached the admin building. He looked up and saw the pennant had been lowered. An omen? He hoped not.

Booly took his place in the green room and waited his turn. Time passed with excruciating slowness. The other miscreants were fascinated by the lieutenant in their midst. Some stared in openmouthed amazement, while others whispered among themselves and asked the guards for in-formation. Parker used a series of narrow-eyed looks to intimidate some of the worst offenders but the sidelong glances continued.

Finally, after what seemed like an eternity but was ac-tually only forty-five minutes or so, the door opened and a private was dragged out of the inner office. She was livid with rage and it took two MPs to control her. ''Screw you, bitch! I hope you rot in hell!''

Booly had spent the last six years in a tough but pro-tected environment, an environment where this sort of dis-cipline problem was discussed during leadership classes but never witnessed. He watched the private's heels leave two black skid marks across the highly polished floor and heard his name called. "Lieutenant William Booly! This way, sir . . ."

Booly looked at Parker, got a thumbs-up, and nodded. "Thanks, Corporal . . . see you shortly."

So saying, Booly placed his hat in the crook of his left elbow, marched through the open door, and stopped in front of an ancient desk. It was made of wood and was bare outside of a stylus and computer console. The colonel who sat behind the desk had a blond-gray crew cut, an undisguised bionic eye, and a ramrod-straight back. The name tag above her left breast pocket read D. A. Axler. Her face was devoid of all expression. Booly snapped to attention, used his right hand to salute, and ripped off the correct protocol. "Second Lieutenant William B. Booly, reporting as ordered, ma'am." He kept his eyes focused on the plaque over her head. It read Legio Patria Nostra, or "The Legion Is Our Country."

The colonel returned the salute but took her own sweet time before saying anything. Booly heard a mosquitolike whine as the bionic eye zoomed in and tilted down along his uniform. Finally, when the view was obscured by the edge of her desk, the colonel spoke. "You look pretty good for someone who spent the night disobeying general orders, wallowing in booze, and getting into fights."

It was a trap. Agreement would amount to a confession of guilt and denial could be construed as defiance. Silence could mean trouble, too, but seemed like the best alternative. The colonel stood, walked around the end of the table, and stood with her face two inches from his. Booly detected the faintest whiff of mint. She had a hard face and her good eye glittered with emotion. "Now, you listen to me, Lieutenant, and listen good. *I* think you're a furry no-good freak conceived by a worthless NCO who went over the hill so he could screw the local wildlife."

Blood rushed to Booly's face, the fur she had referred to stood on end, and adrenaline flooded his bloodstream. It was only through a major act of will that he kept his hands at his side and his eyes focused on hers. She might be the world's worst bigot, or she might be jerking him around, but the results were the same. He hated her guts. To talk about his parents that way, to call his mother an animal, went beyond any possible justification. But an attack would give her an easy way to put him in prison.

The colonel paused, her eyes still locked with his, well aware of his hatred. She clasped her hands behind her back and circled him. "See how easy it is, Lieutenant? See how easily I pushed your buttons? What the hell are you going to do next time? And the time after that? Are you going to fight every man or woman who calls you names? 'Cause if you are, Lieutenant, then you aren't worth shit, and I should bounce your ass out of the Legion right now."

The colonel completed her circuit. Her eyes found his. "And guess what, piss ant, if it was up to me I *would* toss your butt out of here, because I don't think you'll make it. I think you'll allow some two-bit asshole to lure you into one fight too many, or coddle your troops because you want them to fall in love with your furry ass, or make some other equally stupid mistake. But *I* don't run the Legion, and for reasons *I* don't understand, General St. James thinks you have potential. I just pray to God that he's right, and this isn't a manifestation of the political crap that generals swim through, the kind that gets a whole lot of good people killed someday. *Do you read me, Lieutenant?*"

"Yes, ma'am!"

Axler nodded grimly. "Well, I sure hope you do, because you are one sorry sonovabitch. Drinking is *stupid,* violating orders is *stupid,* and fighting is *stupid.* Even when they're marines. Now, here's the skinny. . . . You get to keep your shoulder boards, but I'm taking three months' worth of your pay, and sending you to a planet where you will either lead or die. The second alternative being best for the Confederacy. Your shuttle lifts at twenty-three hundred hours tonight. Make damned sure you're on it. Questions?''

"No, ma'am!"

"Then why are you still here? Get the hell out of my office!"

"Yes, ma'am!" Booly snapped off a salute, did a perfect about-face, and marched to the door. It opened, then closed behind him.

Axler watched the young man leave, waited for the door to close, and smiled. "He's gone, sir."

A section of wood paneling swiveled out of the way and General St. James stepped into the office. He had watched the whole thing on closed-circuit video and carried two cups of steaming-hot coffee. One went to the colonel. "Nice job, DeeDee, you scared the crap out of him."

Axler took a sip of her coffee. It had too much sugar in it but she wasn't about to tell the general that. "I thought he was going to take a swing at me when I insulted his mother."

St. James nodded. "Yeah, but it had to be done. The Legion needs to look more like the Confederacy that it's fighting for. That means officers and legionnaires of every possible race. Or combinations of races, assuming the Naa aren't of human stock themselves, which scientists are beginning to doubt. But we can't afford hotheads. Lieutenant Riley swore that Booly walked away from a confrontation inside that nightclub but I had to know for sure."

Axler nodded. "Yes, sir. Well, now you know."

The general smiled. "I sure do. Now tell me about all the 'political crap that generals swim in.' I'd like to know more."

The colonel checked to make sure the general was joking and they laughed together.

The better part of the afternoon was spent out-processing for Clone World Alpha-001. Parker, *sans* arm band and weapon, accompanied Booly through the process. The young officer had thanked the NCO, and tried to release him, but the cadaverous corporal refused to go.

The first stop was a normally quiet area three floors above the Green Room. Normally used for routine administrative purposes, the offices were temporarily transformed into processing centers whenever a class graduated from the academy. A sizable number of Booly's classmates were already there, talking, arguing, and trading friendly insults. Booly looked for Kadien and didn't know whether to be happy or sorry that he wasn't there. Colonel Axler had been right about the way he'd been manipulated, and the last thing he needed to do was get in a fight with a classmate. But if Kadien said one word, just one word about his race, Booly knew he would wipe the sneer off the other officer's face.

Habits are hard to break, so the newly minted lieutenants automatically formed six lines and put an arm's worth of distance between themselves and the person in front of them. Each line terminated in front of a door, and each door had a number stenciled on it. Everyone had heard Riley's or Kadien's version of what had taken place the night before and Booly was greeted with hoots and whistles.

"Hey, Booly! Some marines are looking for you!"

"Look! He kept his boards!"

"Bill, good to see you, man, how's the arm?"

"Hey, shithead, where'd they send you?"

A hush fell over the crowd. Everyone knew he'd been to Summary Court and was curious about his punishment.

Booly forced a smile and shrugged. "Clone World Alpha-001."

There were groans, words of commiseration, and a round of the usual clone jokes. But Booly knew most if not all of the men and women around him were secretly pleased. Not because they were bigots but because humans beings like to feel lucky.

Fortunately for Booly, his classmates' attention spans were notoriously short and conversation soon veered toward the eternal verities of sports, sex, music, and warfare, not necessarily in that order. Booly's headache had returned, and his arm hurt, but it felt good to be reabsorbed into the wrap and weave of military society. The line moved quickly and Booly found himself standing in front of it fifteen minutes later.

Door number three opened, he stepped through, and found himself in a brightly lit but otherwise unremarkable room. There were no furnishings other than a platform with a frame around it. A vaguely humanoid robot with an olive drab paint job greeted Booly with relentless courtesy. "Welcome to out-processing station three. Please step onto the platform. The platform will rotate. Do not be alarmed. A series of questions will be asked. Please answer in a loud, clear voice."

Booly obeyed and the platform started to rotate. A gender-neutral voice came from nowhere and everywhere at once. "You have been wounded. With the exception of your wound, are you in pain?"

Booly lied. "No."

"Do you have bouts of nausea? Blurred vision? Unexplained dizziness?"

Booly had all three but knew why. "No."

"Do you have regular bowel movements? Have you seen blood in your stool?" And on and on until the questions and the sound of his own replies became a distant drone.

In the meantime a complex tracery of laser beams roamed his body, hundreds of precise measurements were taken, and the resulting information was sent across campus to a series of one-story buildings where an entire set of perfectly tailored class-A, class-B, and utility uniforms were produced, along with body armor, shoes, boots, and a customized side arm. Additional weaponry if any would be issued on-station.

Once that process was complete, and the platform had stopped, Booly was directed to pass through another door. The second room was very much like the first, except that there was no platform, and the resident android had no human qualities whatsoever. It consisted of some tubes, a shiny metal arm that extended from the ceiling, and a sensor-equipped air gun. Like his peers, Booly had been inoculated many times during the last six years and undid his shirt before being asked to do so.

"Welcome to out-processing station three. You will receive a full set of inoculations appropriate to Clone World Alpha-001. If this is *not* your destination, or you have entered the room by mistake, please say so now."

Booly remained silent and the computer-controlled equipment picked up where it had left off. "Please expose both your shoulders."

The sling was a hassle but Booly got the job done. The robotic arm whined as it moved into place and the air gun felt cold against his skin. "Please stand still. The air-injection system will lacerate your skin if you move."

Booly stood perfectly still, flinched when the gun went off, and braced himself as it was positioned on his wounded arm. The injector fired again, the arm whirred up and away, and the officer checked to see if he was bleeding. He wasn't. The machine intoned its final blessing. "Thank you, and have a nice day."

The officer was still struggling to get all of his buttons

buttoned as he stepped out of the cubicle and into a room staffed with a real person. The private was twenty-something, reasonably attractive, and immune to Lieutenants. She noticed his fur but did a good job of hiding her curiosity. A com set, computer console, and mysterious black box sat on top of her well-worn desk. "Lieutenant Booly?"

"Yes?"

"Please take a seat, insert your right hand into the box, and remain still." Booly could have demanded an explanation and would have received one but found it difficult to overcome six years of unquestioning obedience. He did as he was told.

The black box hummed, something warm wrapped itself around his wrist, and a tingle ran up his arm. The private looked at her computer, then at him. "Each unit is keyed to a single person. Did you feel a tingling sensation, sir? Good. That was the page function. You may remove your hand. Your orders have been downloaded into your wrist term, along with a copy of your service record, Legion regs, and a few other odds and ends. This booklet covers the operational stuff. Questions, sir?"

Booly withdrew his hand and found that a small flat black box had been attached to his right wrist. It was identical to the units worn by enlisted people except that it had a command channel and more memory. Data that would automatically self-destruct if his vital signs fell below certain limits. Booly touched the case, watched the full-color screen come to life, and saw a five-item menu.

- PERSONAL
- COMMUNICATIONS
- NAVIGATION
- COMMAND
- E-LOCATOR

He knew that four of the five listings would provide access to sub-menus but would figure them out later. "No, thank you. I'll read the booklet."

The private looked relieved. She hated explaining things to lieutenants. They were so damned stupid. She smiled politely. "Thank you, sir. Have a nice day."

Booly nodded, adjusted his sling, and walked out into a sparsely populated hallway. Parker was waiting and led him off to get his uniforms and other gear. His career, already tarnished and somewhat in doubt, had started.

7

Where troops have been quartered, brambles and thorns spring up. In the track of great armies there must follow lean years.

Lao-tse
Standard year circa 604 B.C.

Worber's World, the Confederacy of Sentient Beings

True to their programming, and eager to carry out their missions, millions of maggotlike microbots burrowed down into the planet's slowly dying flesh. Most, but not all of the tiny machines dug down through soft, moist earth, followed fissures into the ground, scuttled through subsurface conduits, probed the depths of long destroyed buildings, and communicated their finds via bursts of low-frequency code.

Other robots gathered in remote caves, in damp subbasements, and at the bottom of lakes, where they electronically mated with one another over and over again until thousands of the tiny machines were linked into what amounted to massively parallel computers, and certain master-programs were brought on line—master-programs that were quite capable of receiving the bursts of low-frequency code and responding with clear-cut orders.

Orders that sent the worker-bots into a frenzy of activity

as many were disassembled and reconfigured so they could more efficiently mine the required ore, build the refineries, and construct the factories necessary to manufacture finished products.

Days, weeks, and months passed while the robots worked, and because their labors were carried out beneath the planet's surface, and because they made no attempt to establish contact with the heavily monitored Hudathan prisoners of war, their efforts went undetected.

Grain by grain, ounce by ounce, and pound by pound the necessary ores were mined, transported, refined, shaped, and manipulated until storerooms began to fill up with a variety of parts. Parts that any Hudathan trooper would have immediately recognized as those belonging to assault rifles, energy weapons, machine guns, grenade launchers, mortars, and shoulder-launched missiles.

And then, hidden in the bottom of a bombed-out building, and supervised by a computer located in the ruins under Black Lake, a team of specially programmed robots went to work. Unlike the assemblies created by their peers, this particular machine would be the only one of its kind. Following designs devised by War Scientist Rimar Noda-Sa, and careful to adhere to the usual standards of quality, the micromachines fashioned what looked like a Hudathan trooper.

Great care was taken to ensure that the resulting robot appeared to be middle aged and undernourished. When the last section of black plasti-flesh had been applied and all systems had been tested, the robot was given a limp to simulate an old war wound, what appeared to be a well-worn battle harness, and sandals similar to those the prisoners made for themselves.

And so it was that in the Stygian blackness of a long-forgotten subbasement a brand-new creation was born, tested, and charged with one of the most important tasks of the upcoming war: to find War Commander Poseen-Ka, or if he was dead, the current commanding officer, and prepare him for a revolt and mass escape. Slowly but surely, with its highly sophisticated sensors probing the darkness ahead, the messenger began its journey.

Specialist Third Class Jessica Clemmons frowned, ran a hand through her kinky black hair, and stabbed a key. The computer screen winked, lines of numbers rolled by, and the same old message popped up: "Probability of natural causation .00001." It was the third time she had run the data and received the same answer.

Clemmons felt vindication mixed with apprehension. The Hudathans were up to something, there was no doubt about that, but would Lieutenant Rawley believe her? He'd been on her ass about one thing or another ever since he'd boarded the *Old Lady* two weeks before. "Clemmons, press that uniform. Clemmons, where's that report? Clemmons, I see gear adrift."

The loot was a major pain in the butt. And even worse than that, a *nontechnical* pain in the butt, who was rotating through the Electronic Warfare (EW) section on his way to bigger and better things, and wouldn't recognize a chip if he found one floating in his coffee. All of which made it damned hard to explain technical matters to the idiot. Still, her duty was clear, so Clemmons ordered a printout of her findings, checked her uniform for ketchup stains, and wished she was one of the smoothies who could talk birds down from the trees. They seemed to get along with Rawley just fine and received favors as a result.

Very few people said hello or acknowledged the serious young technician as she wound her way out of the EW Ops room and entered one of the *Old Lady*'s busiest corridors. The loot's closet-sized office was a hundred yards down-ship and shoulder-to-shoulder with other similar cubicles occupied by his peers. Clemmons walked eyes down, careful to salute each officer's highly shined shoes, but otherwise disconnected from those around her.

Unlike most of the other officers aboard ship, Lieutenant Rawley routinely kept his hatch closed, a habit that forced subordinates and superiors alike to knock and announce themselves. Clemmons stopped in front of the door marked Electronic Warfare Officer, checked her uniform one last time, and rapped on the airtight door three times. "Specialist Third Class Clemmons! Requesting permission to enter!"

Rawley's voice was nearly inaudible from behind the thick metal. "Enter."

Clemmons touched the hand plate and the hatch slid out of the way. A single step carried her to the center of the office. It was furnished with a fold-down desk-computer unit and two chairs. Rawley occupied one of the chairs and had no intention of offering the other to her. He was handsome in a pretty sort of way, with a straight nose, large dark eyes, and pouty lips. He arched a perfectly shaped brow. The move was carefully rehearsed and would come in handy throughout what Rawley assumed would be a long and distinguished career. "Yes?"

Clemmons felt beads of sweat pop out on her forehead. She fought to suppress the stammer that had plagued her since childhood. "I-I-I have an anomaly to report."

Rawley frowned impatiently. "So report it. That's what the daily summaries are for."

Which you don't bother to read, and wouldn't understand if you did, Clemmons thought to herself. "Yes, sir. B-b-but this could be urgent, sir—and I thought you should see it."

Rawley liked the idea of people bringing urgent and possibly important matters to his attention. He treated Clemmons to a number-three smile, which was professional, but contained a hint of sexuality. A surefire strategy when applied to heterosexual females. "All right . . . let's see what you've got."

Clemmons gave him the printout, he pretended to scan it, and uttered some "uh-huhs" before handing it back. "So, Specialist Clemmons, I have my opinion, but I'd like to hear yours. What does this data mean?"

Clemmons had expected the question and was ready for it. "W-w-well, sir, we have passive pickups scattered all over the planet's surface, just to make sure the prisoners don't come up with some sort of homegrown radios. Y-y-you know, the kind of short-range stuff we might not receive in orbit."

Rawley *didn't* know about the passive pickups but filed the tidbit for future reference. "Of course . . . go on."

Encouraged by the fact that the interview was going better than expected, the stutter disappeared and the words flowed. "Well, we sort through all sorts of static and junk, but none of it has ever amounted to anything until now. About two days ago I started to notice some low-frequency stuff—nothing sustained, mind you—but short bursts of a second or two."

Clemmons waited for signs of interest that never came. Rawley was getting bored and allowed the tiniest of frowns to wrinkle the skin between his eyes. "Yes . . . and?"

And pay attention, the inner Clemmons screamed, it's obvious! The bastards are up to something! The technician suppressed the insubordinate thoughts and chose her words with care. "I-I-I ran our records for the last three standard months. The transmissions started exactly fifty-three days ago, were transient for a while, then settled into semipermanent locations. One of which is centered on a body of water called 'Black Lake.' I think the geeks are up to something . . . and I recommend that the old lady send some grunts down for a look."

Rawley spent a full five seconds visualizing himself taking Clemmons's concerns up the chain of command, tried to think of how such an activity might benefit his career, and came up empty. "Thank you for your concern, Clemmons. Naval tradition aside, I doubt that General Norwood appreciates being referred to as 'the old lady.' Leave the printout on my desk. I'll push it up the ladder and see what the number three thinks. Dismissed."

Clemmons saluted, did a sloppy about-face, and stepped into the corridor. The hatch closed behind her. She took a deep breath, threw her shoulders back, and marched down the hall. The lieutenant had taken her seriously! He had promised to kick the matter upstairs! The number three would value her report and do something about it. Clemmons started to whistle, caught herself, and settled for an ear-to-ear grin. Life wasn't so bad after all.

Rawley checked to make sure the hatch was closed and fed the printout into the disposal slot next to his desk. It made a sucking sound and disappeared. Just like Clemmons, if he could find a department head stupid enough to take her.

The door to the Operations and Command Center swished open. General Natalie Norwood strode into the room and her staff stood. There was her executive officer, and the *Old Lady*'s skipper, Naval Captain Ernest "Ernie" Big Bear, the commander of the 16th Battalion, 3rd Marines, Colonel Maria Chow, and the officer in charge of the ship's aerospace fighters, Wing Commander Mark Sabo. They didn't even begin to fill the large compartment. Worber's World hung beyond the view port like a picture in a frame. Norwood smiled and headed for the refreshment table located against the inner bulkhead. "At ease . . . coffee anyone?"

There was general assent as Norwood had known there

would be. This particular team had been together for some time now. Of course none had been on-station as long as she had nor would the high command have allowed them to. That privilege, if privilege it was, had been reserved for the single woman who had won almost every medal of valor the empire and Confederacy had to offer. And that, just like her habit of pouring and serving coffee to her staff, was part of the legend. A legend she was barely aware of, since it meant very little to her. The fact was that there was only one thing that she *really* cared about, and that was punishing the Hudathans for what they'd done, and making damned sure they never did it again. Which was what the meeting was all about.

Once everyone had their coffee, and had exchanged the usual bits of gossip, Norwood opened the meeting. "Okay . . . you know the drill. With the quarterly snoop and poop inspection less than two weeks away I want to make sure we have our act together."

The other officers smiled and nodded agreeably but exchanged sideways looks. The geeks had been dirtside for more than twenty years now and that equated to something like eighty quarterly inspections. Every one of them had turned up minor violations of the rules but nothing major. No homemade rocket ships, no jury-rigged energy weapons, and no rebellions. But that didn't mean diddly to Norwood, who was just as fanatical as the day she had assumed command, and if the scuttlebutt could be believed, a lot more tiresome. Especially when she talked about how dangerous the aliens were, a perception that not only failed to match the facts, but served to reinforce rumors that she was more than a little wacko, and ready for a psychological tune-up.

But the boss is the boss is the boss, especially in the military, and none of them dared voice their concerns. So Big Bear reported on the ship's readiness to provide orbital fire support, Sabo outlined plans to put the grunts on the ground, and Chow made the usual extravagant claims about her marines. The meeting lasted two hours and three out of the four participants thought it was a complete waste of time.

It had taken the messenger the better part of a week to travel the twenty-five miles that separated its birthplace from the coordinates the roach-shaped scouts had given him. Like the insects they modeled, the microbots had full access to the areas where the Hudathan prisoners spent most of their time, and were systematically ignored by the human detection devices.

Based on data they had provided to the widely dispersed brains, and through them to him, the messenger knew there were a total of fifty-three prisoner camps each housing between two and three thousand troops. But one of those camps, the one the lead computers had designated as "alpha," was twice the size of the others, and geographically central to their locations. All of which suggested a rough-and-ready headquarters or something very similar.

Working his way up through the skeletal remains of what had been an evergreen forest, the robot hit the ground just short of the skyline and wriggled his way forward. Alpha base was cradled in a small valley and had been constructed on the ruins of a city once known as Waterville. The messenger saw that while paths had been cleared through the rubble and crude repairs had been made to some of the less damaged buildings, the location was far from what its Hudathan creators would consider habitable.

The robot switched to infrared. He saw light green squares of carefully conserved light; darker, more intense areas where fires warmed concrete; and the thin, almost spectral images left by troopers who shambled through the ruins.

Having detected no danger, the messenger stood and picked its way down the slope towards the graveyard below. The crosses and monuments had no meaning beyond their status as obstacles through which the machine was forced to pass. The markers were staggered, as if to rise up and block the invaders' way, but stood immobile while the robot passed among them.

The messenger walked under a stone arch and out into a partially cleared street. Having no power to work with, and no beasts of burden at their disposal, the troopers had removed just enough rubble so that two carts could pass each other. A pair of tired-looking Hudathans plodded by, their eyes glued to the ground, a wagon loaded with stones creaking along behind.

The robot fell in behind them and imitated the way they walked. A box-shaped heat source swooped down and a cacaphony of internal alarms went off within the messenger's central processing unit. A variety of alternatives presented themselves and were compared with the machine's prime directives. "Stealth is all-important." "Do nothing to attract attention." "Rely on your camouflage."

The robot ignored the vid cam and shuffled forward. The spy-eye paced him for a while, saw nothing out of the ordinary, and drifted into the murk.

Lightning flashed and left a jagged afterimage across the messenger's infrared vision. Thunder rumbled in the distance, acid rain fell, and the mud made squishy noises beneath his feet. Most of the buildings the robot passed were little more than empty shells, picked clean of anything useful years before, and cold as death. The machine ignored them and continued down the street until one particular structure caught and held his attention. It radiated more heat than any other building in the area and was largely intact. Guards had been posted to either side of the main entranceway. All good signs.

The messenger angled off into the shadows, stopped, and sent a millisecond worth of code. Three scout roaches were within a hundred feet of his location and hurried to his side. The first machine scrambled up his leg and plugged itself into a tiny neck socket. The larger robot sought confirmation of the building's function, received it, and removed the microbot from his shoulder. Carefully, almost reverently, he placed it on the ground. It made a clicking sound as it dived down a drain.

Confident that it had the correct location, the messenger stepped out onto the street, approached the guards, and announced who he was. "Nolar Isam-Ka to see War Commander Poseen-Ka."

The sentry was bored. He scanned the stranger for weapons, saw none, and gave the standard response. "The war commander is busy. Do you have an appointment?"

The robot took note of what he had learned. This was the correct location and Poseen-Ka was alive. "No," it replied, "but he'll see me."

The sentry looked doubtful, but ducked inside and returned a short time later. Four troopers accompanied him. They pretended to step out onto the street, turned, and grabbed the messenger from behind. In spite of the fact that the machine could have killed every single one of them, it made no attempt to do so. Its hands were bound and the machine was pushed, shoved, and prodded through the door.

The building's interior was lit with makeshift lamps, heat radiated from jury-rigged sheet-metal stoves, and rows of cavelike cubicles lined the main corridors. The offices had been established for use by Poseen-Ka's staff, not that they had much to do beyond documenting the latest deaths and fantasizing about some sort of rescue. They watched the robot with dull, uninterested eyes.

War Commander Poseen-Ka was looking out his window

at the graveyard when the messenger entered the room. The sound caused him to turn and instinctively place his back against the wall. He looked at the prisoner, felt ice water shoot through his veins, and looked again. He opened his mouth to speak, remembered the vid cam that oozed along the ceiling, and thought better of it. Something strange was taking place and he would have to be extremely careful. The officer kept his voice calm and matter-of-fact. "Tell me your name."

The messenger was matter-of-fact. "Nolar Isam-Ka."

Poseen-Ka took another look. He had assumed the guard was joking or had mispronounced the name, but there was no doubt about it. Except for the fact that the *real* Isam-Ka would look twenty years older than this one did, and normally wore an eye patch, the imposter was a perfect likeness. He tried a test. "Yes, of course. The last time I saw you was aboard the *Light of Hudatha.*"

The messenger didn't hesitate. "I am sorry, but you are mistaken. The *Light of Hudatha,* along with the rest of Spear Three, was destroyed in battle. The last time you saw me was in the company of Grand Marshal Pem-Da and War Commander Dal-Ba. The occasion was a court of inquiry. You were exonerated."

Poseen-Ka felt a quickly growing sense of excitement. He remembered the day well. How could he forget? Grand Marshal Pem-Da had tried to use the loss of Spear Three as an excuse to replace him, but thanks in large part to support from Isam-Ka, Poseen-Ka had emerged victorious. He blinked. "I stand corrected. Guards, release the prisoner. You may leave."

Surprised, but too well trained to show it, the guards removed the rope from the robot's wrists and left the room. They were huge and had to back out one at a time. The door closed behind them. Poseen-Ka eyed the vid cam and it eyed him back. He gestured towards the outer door.

"Come, old friend. Let's go for a walk."

It took hours for the messenger to relay the instructions it had been given and to answer Poseen-Ka's voluminous questions. During that time the unlikely pair circled the huge graveyard many times. Their feet left tracks in the alien mud and destroyed what little ground cover there was. Finally, when the officer had asked every question he could think of, and planned for every contingency that his highly intelligent brain could come up with, the time came for them to part. Poseen-Ka knew the messenger was a machine, but saw it as a savior, too, and thanked it accordingly.

Unable to feel emotions, or to gauge the manner in which its actions would impact the future, the machine acknowledged the comment and left. It took two hours for the messenger to find a suitable hollow in the ground, to pull a layer of debris over its chest, and deactivate its CPU. The resulting fire burned white hot, showed up on of the *Old Lady*'s detectors, and disappeared. A report was submitted, ignored, and systematically filed in memory. Life such as it was went on.

8

Death holds no fear for those who died before.

Master Sergeant Frank Kagan (ret.)
The Legion Is My Country
Standard year 2172

Clone World Alpha-001, the Clone Hegemony

Booly got lost in spite of the fact that he had taken the precaution of downloading a nonclassified schematic of the ship into his wrist term. The optimistically named *Warm Wind That Blows Happiness Throughout the Galaxy* was better known to her crew as the *Iron Bitch,* and was absolutely huge. So huge that a substantial number of her crew had never seen the entire vessel or each other, for that matter. All of which meant that Booly's self-assigned mission had a somewhat quixotic quality.

Still, the borgs were *his* responsibility, and a visit was the right thing to do. Assuming he found them, that is, which seemed less likely all the time. His wrist term contained the information he needed but insisted on presenting it via naval jargon and hard-to-read schematics.

Booly saw a weapons tech coming his way and flagged her down. She wore a buzz cut, a navy-issue temple jack, and bright red lipstick. He produced his most dazzling smile and was pleased to receive one in return. "I'm looking for Compartment D-4/G-3 . . . where the hell is it?"

The tech laughed. "Well, you're on the correct deck, sir, but you need to head in one corridor, turn to starboard, and watch for passageway G. G-3 will be the third compartment on the left."

Booly thanked the tech and did as she had instructed. Much to his surprise, it worked. After a short walk down zero-g-equipped luminescent hallways, the young officer found himself standing in front of a hatch marked Cybernetic Life Support. He palmed the access panel and waited for the door to slide out of the way. A chief petty officer looked up from the skin fax he was reading, saw the lieutenant, and swung his feet off the desk. He had a paunch and it strained the front of his shirt as he stood. His voice was slow and close to insolent. "Welcome to the CLS, sir, what can I do for you?"

Booly nodded. "My name is Booly. You have three of my people down here. I came to say hello."

The CPO's eyes narrowed and nearly disappeared into his doughlike face. "Yes, sir. Well, that was thoughtful, sir, and I'm sure your borgs will appreciate the effort. I'll tell them the minute they wake up."

Booly knew that cyborgs were normally transported in racks of fifty, their brain boxes connected to a computer-controlled life-support system, their minds subsumed by an ocean of drugs. But his troopers had been awakened in preparation for the planet fall, which was twelve hours away. Or should have been, since Alpha-001 was classified as a class-III combat station, requiring all members of the Confederacy's armed forces to land ready to fight.

But Booly had heard stories about naval cyber techs who minimized the amount of time they had to deal with the sometimes contentious borgs by waiting until the very last moment to bring them back, a practice that could severely impact a cyborg's readiness to fight when it hit dirt. The young officer fought to keep his face completely impassive. "Really? Well, that would be extremely unfortunate, Chief, because those borgs were supposed to be conscious six hours ago. Or didn't you read your orders?"

The chief pursed his lips and a pair of well-built ratings drifted into the compartment. Booly felt his heart start to pound. They wouldn't really attack him, would they? Striking an officer was a court-martial offense. But how would he prove that they were the ones? Especially if they lied, which they were certain to do? In an effort to make sure that no single arm of the military would grow strong enough to challenge his power, the now-dead emperor had fostered interservice rivalries, and that could still be seen, heard, and felt in the schisms between the Navy, the Marine Corps, and Legion.

Booly heard the hatch open behind him and felt a wave of cool air touch his neck. More ratings? He had just started to turn when a now-familiar voice put his fears to rest. "There you are, sir . . . Good thing you know your way around. We damned near got lost."

Booly completed his turn and there stood Corporal—no, a third stripe had mysteriously appeared on his sleeve— *Sergeant* Parker. He was expressionless as usual. Four tough-looking legionnaires were right behind him. They crowded through the hatch. The compartment got smaller. Booly turned to the CPO. "So, Chief . . . where were we? A difference of opinion, as I recall?"

The petty officer's tongue slid back and forth across suddenly dry lips. "No, sir. A mix-up, that's all. Come back in a couple of hours and your borgs will be ready to go."

Booly nodded. "Excellent . . . Sergeant Parker and I will see you then."

Parker barked, "Make a hole!" and the legionnaires stepped away from the hatch. Booly stepped out into the corridor and the others followed. As soon as they had put some distance between themselves and the CLS, Booly stopped and looked Parker up and down. The other legionnaires hung back. "It's good to see you, Parker. I like the additional stripe. Where the hell did you come from?"

Parker raised an eyebrow. "Earth, sir, same as you."

Booly frowned. "Cut the crap, Sergeant. You know what I mean. How did you wind up here at this particular moment?"

The noncom shrugged his narrow shoulders. "Yes, sir. I requested assignment to Alpha-001 and somehow wound up in your platoon. I called, learned where you were headed, and came down to say hello."

Booly knew bullshit when he heard it. He punched up the main menu on his wrist term, chose the command function, and selected TO or table of organization. The name General Marianne Mosby appeared at the top and he scrolled down past his company commander to his own name. And there, in charge of the bio bods in squad one, was Sergeant (provisional) Sean Parker. The officer knew damned well the NCO hadn't been on the list the day before, so where had he come from? The most likely place was the unassigned draft that had been sent to Alpha-001 to replace legionnaires who had been wounded in action, killed in action, or were due for rotation. Once aboard ship Parker had used his connections and almost magical understanding of how the Legion worked to get the assignment he wanted. Provisional rank included. Booly nodded towards the others. "And your friends?"

Parker peered out of deeply set sockets. "Begging the lieutenant's pardon, sir, but when a junior LT arrives straight from the academy, there's a distinct tendency for the riffraff to accumulate in his or her platoon. That will still happen to some extent no matter what we do . . . but I took the liberty of recruiting a few vets to even things up a bit.''

Booly shook his head in amazement. ''Sergeant, I don't deserve you, but I sure appreciate your help.''

Parker glanced down corridor and back again. ''Only one officer out of ten would come all the way down here to check on his borgs . . . and that's the kind of officer I respect. Now, unless something changed since this morning, it's time to prepare for dinner. I'll meet you down here when the shindig is over.''

Booly laughed at the noncom's command of his itinerary. ''What? No advice on how to behave at dinner?''

The cadaverlike face remained serious. ''Yes, sir. If you want some, sir. Lieutenants, especially new ones, should be seen and not heard.''

The dinner prior to planet-fall was a naval custom and one rigidly adhered to except in times of war. Every officer not required for duty was invited, and they filled the generously proportioned wardroom to capacity. Side tables stood heaped with the ship's best silver, appetizers, and bottles of wine. Marine sentries, their uniforms impeccably blue, guarded the doors, and naval ratings, all dressed in white, had replaced the usual service bots. The table looked as if it were a mile long. Precisely aligned settings gleamed against snowy linen, and candles flickered at two-foot intervals.

Booly, extremely self-conscious in his brand-new dress uniform, felt his stomach start to growl and wished he were somewhere else. His place was at the very foot of the table, safely removed from the dangers inherent in conversing with senior officers, and equally removed from the interesting things they might say.

Or so he assumed until a chime sounded and the multitude sought their chairs. Each stood behind his or her chair and awaited an entrance by the ship's commanding officer, Captain Moshe Dinara. It was only then that Booly learned that tradition called for either the ship's executive officer, or the highest-ranking officer of a sister service to be seated at the *other* end of the table, both as an honor, and a means of exercising whatever wit the junior officers could bring to bear. All of which meant that he and a nervous-looking ensign would be seated right next to General Marianne Mosby, one of the most famous and some said infamous officers the Legion had ever produced.

Booly felt his jaw drop as the general entered the compartment, walked up to her chair, and nodded left and right. Though he was not normally interested in middle-aged women—the young officer was awestruck by the combination of her beauty, poise, and the authority inherent in the stars that rode her shoulders. "Good evening, Ensign. Good evening, Lieutenant. I see the gods of war have seen fit to grant me two handsome dinner companions."

With those words, and the smile that accompanied them, Mosby enslaved both men. And not just because of her physicality, which was considerable, but also because of what she had accomplished. Everyone knew, or thought they knew, that she'd been one of the emperor's many lovers, that she had tried to convince his not altogether sane mind that the empire should fight the Hudathans from the very beginning, and had been sent to a military prison for her efforts. Historians also gave Mosby credit for a massive prison break, for fighting her way to capital, and for driving the emperor off planet. His first defeat and the one that ultimately led to his death.

The rest of the facts were a good deal less clear. Some said the general was a libertine, indulging in all sorts of sensual pleasures, not all of which were appropriate to an officer of her seniority. Others said she was ruthless, and more than a little willing to throw lives away, especially if doing so led to victory and enhanced her career. But Booly didn't know or care, not at the moment anyway, because Parker's words echoed in his head: "Lieutenants, especially new ones, should be seen and not heard." Good advice . . . but impossible to obey seated where he was.

Booly's thoughts were interrupted by a commotion at the other end of the wardroom and a stentorian announcement: "Ladies and gentlemen . . . Captain Moshe Dinara."

Dinara was a small man, so small that he looked like a teenager dressed up in his father's uniform. But whatever he lacked in size he made up for in stature by projecting his personality into every corner of the room. Though technically on a par with the Legion's legion of colonels, the captain outranked everyone aboard while under way, and there was no mistaking the aura of power that surrounded him. The naval officer had eyes the color of well-washed denim, and they missed nothing as he strode to the head of the table, stepped in front of his chair, and sat down. There was a massive rustling of fabric, the low murmur of conversation, and the clink of dinnerware as the other officers took their chairs.

What followed was as orchestrated as a classical dance, starting with wine, the obligatory round of formal toasts, and the arrival and clearing away of the first two courses. Booly was far too nervous to notice what kind of food he ate and wondered later on. But even military rituals run their course, and by the time the main dish arrived, the guests had engaged those around them in polite conversation. General Mosby had the right to guide the conversation any way she chose and lost little time in doing so. Where another officer might have been shy about bringing up Booly's ancestry she was refreshingly direct.

"So, Lieutenant Booly, you grew up on Algeron, I presume?"

Booly swallowed a bite of half-chewed food, started to

choke, and managed to control it. "Yes, ma'am."

"And your father was a legionnaire?"

"Yes, ma'am. A sergeant-major."

General Mosby had a heart-shaped face; full, sensuous lips; and a firm chin. High-quality perma-dye treatments effectively hid the gray that would have otherwise dominated her hair. She smiled and revealed a line of perfect white teeth. "Really? What's his name? Maybe we served together."

Booly gulped. Although his father's status as an ambassador forced most people to overlook the fact that he'd been a deserter, it was still embarrassing. Especially in the Legion. "Bill Booly, ma'am. Same as mine."

Mosby looked blank. "No, I can't remember anyone by that name . . . but it's a big Legion. Congratulations on your graduation from the Academy."

Booly mumbled something appropriate and took refuge in his meal as the general turned her attention to the now red-faced ensign. But the intermission didn't last long and she was soon back to him. "Well, Lieutenant. It looks like you and I will be working together. Have you looked at the interim TO?"

"Yes, ma'am."

"And?"

The question wasn't absolutely clear but seemed to call for some sort of strategic summary. Booly chose his words with care. The objective was to provide enough substance to prove that he *had* looked at the TO and given the matter some thought *without* seeming presumptuous. "The TO indicates that we are fifteen percent short of full strength, and while I'm not very experienced, that seems dangerous on a class-three planet."

Mosby nodded her agreement. "Well said. And that's not the worst of it. From the sitreps I've seen . . . our troops are poorly positioned, indifferently led, and subject to low morale. A situation you and I have been ordered to reverse—and damned fast, too.''

Booly knew the ''you and I'' bit was calculated to make him feel good and discovered that it worked anyway. A fact that he stored away for future use on the people he led.

The main course was removed and the dessert arrived. Dinara stood and a new round of toasts began. Saved from the need for further conversation, Booly and the now-sweat-drenched ensign regarded each other with expressions of mutual relief, and turned their attention to the light frothy green concoctions that had appeared in front of them.

The whole thing was relatively easy after that, but by the time Booly was allowed to stand and had waited for his seniors to leave the wardroom, he felt as though he had been in combat. And while he hadn't exactly won, he hadn't lost, either, which felt just as good.

Long, thin fingers of pain reached down into the darkness where Starke hid, found his soft, vulnerable brain tissue, and squeezed. Pain lanced the center of his being as the fingers pulled him up out of the warm, comfortable darkness and into the relentless light of consciousness. ''No!'' he screamed. ''Let me die! Please let me die!'' But the fingers were made of chemical compounds and had no choice but to interact with what remained of his body in ways dictated by what? God? Evolution? Or one of the countless regulations that governed the Legion? There was no way to tell.

Thus a cyborg named Starke and two of his companions were brought on line and readied for installation. They were awake during the first stage of chemical conditioning but unable to access the outer world without benefit of the vid cams and sensors built into their Trooper II bodies.

Starke hated the first stage for a variety of reasons, not the least of which were the feelings of vulnerability, claustrophobia, and guilt that it produced. With nothing to distract him, the past had a way of closing in around the legionnaire, confronting his mind with images he wanted to forget, forcing him to relive the same horrible episode over and over again.

He'd been an engineer on the grav train that ran from old New York to San Diego. A good job, hell, a *great* job, that required little more than staying awake, since computers handled the whole trip all by themselves. Yes, his one and only job had been to function as the ultimate fail-safe in case the triple-redundant systems managed to fail.

For the first two years Starke had performed flawlessly, staring out the control compartment windows as dark wilderness alternated with the blip, blip, blip of small-town lights, the long, drawn-out smear of the middle-sized cities, and the brightly lit splendor of huge metro-plexes. He had watched the control board that never lit up, the idiot lights that burned eternally green, and the com screen that scrolled endlessly redundant routine messages.

Then Linda had left him, and he had found what he thought at the time was temporary solace in the arms of street corner chemicals. The relationship had grown deeper and deeper until it consumed all of his pay, and all of his time, and left him dog tired. So tired that he took little naps in the control compartment, always careful to set his battery-powered alarm clock and to pick the least dangerous sections of the journey in which to sleep.

He had gotten by, until the night when whatever gods ran the universe decided to destroy him, and an electrical fire consumed the number one guidance system, and the number two system failed for reasons they never did figure out, and the number three system, which was located in Omaha, and capable of running the train from there, went down in a localized power outage, and the batteries he had meant to replace, but never got around to, finally ran out of juice. Yup, the dead batteries, and the ensuing head-on collision, had killed his alarm clock, him, and 152 men, women, and children.

Most of the passengers were injured beyond the possibility of repair, or had been dead too long to bring back, but thirty-three brains had been resuscitated. Starke had been one of them.

The trial had taken less than three hours. An artificial intelligence known as JMS 12.7 had found him guilty of negligent homicide, had sentenced him to death, and offered to take him through a course of appeals. He had declined. But then, just as they had prepared to run his brain through a computer-simulated version of what his passengers had experienced, to be concluded with his very real death, they had offered him the possibility of life as a cyborg. Out of weakness, and fear of the unknown, Starke had accepted. A decision he still regretted but didn't have the courage to correct.

"Hey, Starke . . . rise 'n shine, dickhead. You got company." The "voice" cut through the cyborg's thoughts like a knife. Though not received as sound per se, the syntax belonged to CPO Huber—butthole extraordinaire. Starke started to formulate a rude response and stopped when an unfamiliar "voice" entered his mind.

"Legionnaire Starke? This is Lieutenant Booly. How are you feeling?"

Starke felt a variety of emotions, including surprise, apprehension, annoyance, and pleasure. The response was automatic. "Yes, sir. Like hell, sir."

"I'll bet," Booly said sympathetically, speaking into a microphone and ultimately a computer that digitized his words and reassembled them in the form of "speech" the cyborg could understand. "I can't claim to know what it feels like, but if it's even half as bad as the descriptions I've heard, then you're feeling pretty damned bad. The good news is that we're hitting dirt pretty soon.''

"Alpha-001?"

"That's right, soldier. Since you've been assigned to my platoon I thought I'd drop by and see how you are doing."

"Thank you, sir."

"It might be a little early to thank me," Booly said dryly. "But here's hoping. I'll see you dirtside."

The officer moved on after that, and while there was nothing that could make Starke feel human again, the contact meant a lot. The lieutenant didn't know it yet, but when the shit hit the fan, at least one cyborg would be covering his ass.

9

The survival of the Hudathan race cannot be left to chance. Anything that could threaten our people must be destroyed. Such is the warrior's task.

Mylo Nurlon-Da
The Life of a Warrior
Standard year 1703

Planet Hudatha, the Hudathan Empire

The Valley of Harmonious Conflict had played an important role in Hudathan military affairs for thousands of years. It had been created by a meteor strike long before recorded history and was circular in shape. Gray cliffs, dotted here and there with equally gray foliage, circled the crater like a curtain of stone. Two passageways, one to the east and one to the south, provided access to the valley and had been sealed until the advent of gunpowder and projectile weapons had rendered rock walls ineffective as a means of defense. Now the larger stones, too big to be carried off for use in primitive huts, lay across the openings like the vertebrae of a long-dead beast, and hinted at the barbaric past.

During feudal times the mountain-rimmed depression had been the site of numerous battles, culminating in the great slaughter known as the Harvest of a Million Heads, which had killed so many members of the aristocracy that a new order had been forced into being and what remained of the clans had formed a single government.

A government which, like the Hudathans who had created it, was shaped by the cruel and unpredictable surface conditions of the planet itself. A distant part of Rebor Raksala-Ba's mind took note of the fact that thick gray clouds had rolled in to obscure a previously clear sky and that the temperature had dropped thirty degrees since the ceremony had begun. Only the latest in the billions of wild fluctuations caused by Ember and the planet's Trojan relationship with a Jovian binary. Snowflakes, just a few at first, whirled down to form a whitish crust across the upper surfaces of the Hudathan troops.

The parade ground was huge and could have accommodated ten times the roughly three thousand Hudathans assembled there. They stood in harmonious rows, their backs vulnerable to the ranks behind them, not because they *wanted* to but because military necessity demanded it. Thousands of years' worth of military experience had proved the absolute necessity of teamwork, even if it went against the typical Hudathan persona, and generated a certain amount of stress.

Most of the assembled multitude, like Raksala-Ba, were about to graduate from basic training. The rest, like Grand Marshal Hisep Rula-Ka, were there to officiate. Rula-Ka appeared as little more than a distant dot from where Raksala-Ba stood, but he had a powerful voice, and it boomed through a multitude of speakers.

"Each and every one of you is to be congratulated. You have completed basic training and are now ready for Advanced Combat School or technical training. Your strength, your courage, and your intelligence are critical to the future of our race. The galaxy, and indeed the universe, teems with intelligent life, all of which represents a threat to our people. Nowhere does the old adage 'If a variable *can be* controlled it *must be* controlled' apply more than in the area of military policy. Only a fool waits for his neighbor to mine the ore, build the forge, and temper the steel that will be used to kill him. I submit that the so-called Confederacy of Sentient Beings is such a neighbor, and that steel must be met with steel, and blood must be answered with blood.''

Raksala-Ba watched for the subtle hand movement from his recruit-dagger commander, saw it, and joined the ancient cry. ''*Blood!*''

The word was like thunder and echoed off the crater walls. The cry was as ancient as the warrior code that had spawned it. Raksala-Ba reacted to the shout as his father had, and as his grandfather had, with a surge of patriotism. Not for the family that had pushed him out into a blizzard at the age of sixteen, or the clan that had done little more than endorse his enlistment chip, but for his eternally threatened race.

Rula-Ka continued. ''It is my pleasure to announce that some of you, a tiny fraction of the whole, have been selected for special recognition. Even now monitor drones are passing among you, identifying the chosen few, and touching them with the glow of honor. Those so identified are ordered forward that all might see and know them.''

Careful not to move his head from the mandatory eyes-forward position, Raksala-Ba checked his peripheral vision. The snow was falling more thickly now but the monitors had little difficulty bobbing through it. They were shaped like globes and held aloft by small antigrav generators. There were fifty or sixty of the machines and the air hummed as they passed. Suddenly intense beams of white light flashed down to touch individual troopers. Raksala-Ba felt fear followed by pride as a beam found and held him in its actinic glare. The recruit was careful to walk with his head up and his back straight as he marched all the way to the front, did an about-face, and joined the others who had been chosen. They stood at parade rest and he did likewise.

Rula-Ka was getting old now and the crest that ran from the front of his head to the back was even more prominent than it had been when childhood playmates had called him "shovel head." His eyes were like lasers as they swept the ranks before him. "Meet the chosen ones, first of a new breed, best of the best. It is *they* who will meet the human-machine warriors in combat, *they* who will reign victorious, and *they* who will prevent defeat."

Raksala-Ba heard the words but had difficulty under-standing them. "Chosen ones?" "Machine warriors?" But the machine warriors were cyborgs, brains that controlled electro-mechanical bodies, freaks that . . . He wanted to run, wanted to hide, but knew it was unthinkable. Fear, pride, and discipline held him in place.

"And that," Rula-Ka continued, "is why they will sac-rifice their bodies and join the ranks of a new spear. A spear so honored that it will have a name instead of a number . . . and has already been added to the scroll of racial he-roes. For these troopers, and those yet to come, will be known as the 'Regiment of the Living Dead.' "

The name sent a tingle through Raksala-Ba's entire body as did the cry of "*Blood!*" that followed and the certain knowledge that he was about to die.

A huge drill instructor named Drak-Sa, "the Beast," had been chosen to perform the executions. He took ten paces forward, stopped before the recruit to Raksala-Ba's far left, and drew his side arm. It was a projectile weapon loaded with ultra-low-velocity ammunition. He looked up at Rula-Ka and waited for the war commander's signal.

In the meantime, a small army of medics, festooned with the equipment necessary to prevent clinical brain death, had appeared off to one side, and stood like ghosts in waiting.

Rula-Ka allowed the moment to stretch tight, taking pleasure in the discipline of his troops, and the wind that nipped at his skin. The snow fell thickly now hiding the furthest ranks of troopers behind a curtain of white. He looked at the noncom and inclined his head.

Drak-Sa leveled his pistol at the recruit's chest. The trooper had developed a never-before-seen twitch in the muscles of his right cheek but still came to attention. The weapon made a dull thumping noise as the slug penetrated his chest, mushroomed, and broke his spine. The body crumpled to the ground and medics rushed to the warrior's side.

Raksala-Ba found himself praying for death as his knees grew weaker and threatened to betray him. For to fall, and lie crumpled on the ground, *that* was a fate even worse than death. The recruit felt his sphincter loosen and something warm trickle down the back of his leg.

The weapon thumped again, and again, and again, until the drill instructor looked Raksala-Ba in the eye and aimed the pistol at his chest. Snow fell like a shroud and the barrel gaped like the entrance to a clan tunnel. Raksala-Ba wondered if he would see the bullet or hear the sound it made. He didn't.

The technicians used chemicals to pull Raksala-Ba out of his cave. He screamed soundlessly as they rolled his consciousness out over an endless red plain, secured it in place, and forced him to listen.

"YOU ARE NOT DEAD. THE FUTURE IS UP TO YOU. YOU ARE NOT DEAD. THE FUTURE IS UP TO YOU. YOU ARE NOT DEAD. THE FUTURE IS UP TO YOU."

The words went on forever.

• • •

Like a dreamer who has experienced a dream before, and knows how it will end, Raksala-Ba felt himself pulled out and up. He wasted no energy fighting the sensation because he knew it would do no good. The red plain was as before, except that a variety of strange shapes and icons had been added to its surface. The voice returned.

"LOOK AROUND YOU."

Raksala-Ba did as instructed.

"IDENTIFY THE ICON THAT LOOKS LIKE A CYL-INDER."

Raksala-Ba turned and saw a pink cylinder that stood on end.

"GO TO THE CYLINDER."

"Go to the cylinder?" What in the four devils were they talking about? He was dead and couldn't "go" anywhere.

Excruciating pain lanced through Raksala-Ba's mind-body. He screamed soundless obscenities at the voice and sent the same signal that had moved his body. Something happened. Did he move? Or did the cylinder move to him? Raksala-Ba wasn't sure but the result was the same. He mind-touched the icon and felt something akin to a mild sexual orgasm. The voice boomed in his head. "THINK ABOUT WHAT YOU LEARNED." Darkness closed around him.

Raksala-Ba found himself on the red plain once more. The icons were as they had been. But others were present this time. Dark amorphous bodies stalked the land, their shadows crossing his, their thoughts like static in his mind. They were threatening, dangerous somehow, and he growled in a nonexistent throat.

"YOU ARE PART OF A TEAM," the voice said. "TAKE ALL OF THE ICONS AND PLACE THEM ON THE EAST SIDE OF THE PLAIN."

Somehow, without quite knowing how, Raksala-Ba knew

east from west. Eager to complete the exercise and get away from creatures around him, the recruit thought his way to a pyramid-shaped icon. It was bright green. He tried to "think" the object across the plain but it refused to budge. A mild electric shock buzzed through his brain. The voice was calm and unemotional: "YOU ARE PART OF A TEAM."

Raksala-Ba looked around. Some of his fellow beings stood alone but three had gathered around a blue cube. He thought himself in that direction. The closer he got the better he could see. Although the "creatures" had heads, torsos, arms, and legs, all of which added to their somewhat Hudathoid appearance, they were different, too, and had a robotlike aspect. Suddenly the recruit thought to look down at his own body and discovered that he looked as they did. What had been static became language.

"Welcome, comrade. We have been unable to move the cube by ourselves. Let's find out whether the addition of your strength will prove sufficient. Please join in 'thinking' the cube towards the east."

Raksala-Ba did as instructed but the cube remained where it was. An idea occurred to him. "The voice said to 'place' the icons on the east side of the plain. We have bodies now. Let's lift the cube and carry it across."

There was a moment of silence as the others considered the proposal, followed by general agreement. They bent at the waist, slid their hands under the cube, and lifted. The icon proved to be light as a feather and the foursome had little difficulty moving it to the "east."

Having seen their example, others gathered together, lifted their respective icons, and moved them to where the cube now stood. All were intelligent and understood the lesson: A team can accomplish that which an individual cannot.

• • •

Raksala-Ba stood on the surface of a computer-generated planet. The grass, trees, rocks, and other objects were recognizable but lacked detail and definition. The voice was unemotional as always. "YOUR CYBERNETIC BODY HAS BEEN EQUIPPED WITH A VARIETY OF WEAPONS. YOUR RIGHT ARM CONSISTS OF AN ELECTRONICALLY DRIVEN, SIX-BARRELED, FULLY AUTOMATIC PROJECTILE WEAPON. AIM AT ROCK NUMBER THREE AND FIRE."

The numeral 3 appeared over a distant rock. Raksala-Ba raised his arm and saw a set of cross hairs slide across his mental view screen and pause over the boulder in question. In the meantime, information regarding windage, target density, and a dozen other factors scrolled down the right side of his electronic vision. He thought the word *fire* and felt his arm shudder as simulated feedback reached his brain. Rock chips flew in every direction and the target seemed to go out of focus as a haze filled the air. Raksala-Ba thought the word *stop* and the weapon obeyed. A programmed wind blew the dust away and the recruit saw that the rock had been shattered and reduced to four or five large chunks. The voice returned:

"YOUR LEFT ARM HAS BEEN EQUIPPED WITH A THREE-PINCER TOOL HAND AND AN EXTERNAL MISSILE RACK. PROVISION HAS BEEN MADE FOR SIX PROJECTILES. EACH WEAPON CAN BE INDIVIDUALLY CONFIGURED FOR ANTIPERSONNEL, ANTIARMOR, OR ANTIAIRCRAFT MISSIONS. ALL OF THESE MUNITIONS CAN BE GUIDED TO THE TARGET IN THE HEAT-SEEKING, ELECTRONIC-ACTIVITY, OR OPTICAL MODES. AIM AT TREE SIX AND FIRE."

Raksala-Ba brought his arm up, allowed the cross hairs to settle in over the designated tree, and ordered the launcher to fire. The force of the recoil caught him by surprise and pushed him backwards. The missile hit the tree. Bark flew and a chunk of wood disappeared, followed by a series of individual explosions. Raksala-Ba jerked as an electric shock stabbed at the tender flesh of his brain.

"YOU FIRED WITHOUT SELECTING WEAPON MODE OR TRACKING PROGRAM. TRY AGAIN."

Raksala-Ba raised his arm and selected the antiarmor mode with optical targeting. When the missile fired he was braced for the recoil. It flew straight and true. The recruit heard the electronic analog of a sharp cracking noise as the war-head detonated and the tree toppled. He shuddered slightly as a mild orgasm rippled through organs he no longer had. He remembered his body and wondered where it was buried.

Like those around him, Raksala-Ba felt nervous. Computer simulations were one thing but real combat was something else. Yes, the hostiles were an inferior race called the Muldag, and no match for Hudathan regulars, much less cyborgs, but the voice had gone to great lengths to explain that the aliens had been equipped with high-quality human weapons, and promised that their eggs would be allowed to hatch if they won the upcoming battle. Raksala-Ba had his doubts about that, but really didn't care, since a Hudathan defeat would most likely mean death. And, though he had doubted it at first, he *did* want to live. Even if that meant life in a metal brain box.

Others felt differently of course, which accounted for the fact that more than a third of the recruits chosen on graduation day had been killed by the psychological trauma involved, or "excused" from further service by the seldom-seen observers.

The shuttle shuddered as it dropped down through the planet's atmosphere. Like the other cyborgs who sat knee to knee in the cargo bay, Raksala-Ba was linked with the ship's sensors and could see the richly green continent rising to meet them, studded here and there with mirror-bright lakes, and bound together with lazily flowing rivers.

The Muldag were a relatively obscure race. They had colonized only two planets in their home system, and had no particular need to find more. That hadn't saved them from the attentions of a Hudathan expeditionary force however, a force that had taken less than three planetary rotations to defeat what little military the Muldag had and turn their home planet into a combat range.

The target, such as it was, consisted of an already bombed-out city. Having been armed with human weapons, Muldag prisoners of war had been dropped into the area with orders to fight for their lives *and* their unhatched offspring. Which was more than sufficient motivation in the minds of those who had designed and would observe the exercise.

Freed from the unpleasant necessity of dodging antiaircraft fire, the Hudathan shuttles made long approaches and zigzagged in towards landing zones located along the city's western perimeter.

The plan called for each dagger to move inwards, secure designated objectives, and rendezvous on the main plaza, where the shuttles would pick them up. Still linked with the ship's external sensors, Raksala-Ba felt his heart beat a little bit faster as the trees reached up for the shuttle's landing skids, and gunfire winked at him from below. Something rattled against the heavily armored hull and he knew it was ground fire.

The shuttle landed with a heavy thump, Commander Naga-Ka gave the appropriate command, and led his fellow cyborgs into a full-fledged ambush. Realizing the Hudathans would have to land somewhere, and knowing the jungle would force them to put down in one of a limited number of clearings, the Muldag had laid thirty or forty ambushes in hopes of killing the Hudathans as they de-assed their transports. And, if Raksala-Ba and his companions had been run-of-the-mill troopers, the plan might have worked.

But Raksala-Ba and his comrades *weren't* run-of-the-mill troopers, they were cyborgs, and that made all the difference. Most of Dagger Two's borgs were hit within seconds of their arrival. Some of what the Muldag threw at the Hudathans was of questionable quality but the rest consisted of human-manufactured armor-piercing rounds and should have cut the landing force to shreds. But it took the cyborgs only seconds to realize that what they'd been taught was true—their armor *was* proof against anything short of an antitank weapon, or one of the Legion's quads. That reduced fear to little more than pleasant tension. The cyborg Hudathans went to work.

Thanks to their sophisticated sensors, the cyborgs had little difficulty finding pockets of heat and electro-mechanical activity in the surrounding forest. Raksala-Ba established a rhythm: Target, aim, select, fire . . . Target, aim, select, fire . . . Target, aim, select, fire.

The ground heaved as salvos of grenades searched for and found Muldag automatic-weapon pits. Leaves rippled and disappeared as bullets tore through them and found Muldag snipers. A tree swayed, then toppled as a flight of missiles locked onto a makeshift antenna and exploded on impact.

But the battle was not entirely one-sided, as Raksala-Ba learned when the cyborg to his right took a shoulder-launched heat-seeking missile directly in the center of his chest and disappeared in a ball of flame.

Raksala-Ba moved more carefully after that, and took better advantage of available cover, but there would be no more than four such deaths during the exercise, which was well within the number of missile-inflicted casualties the observers were willing to sustain. They wanted the newly blooded cyborgs to know they were powerful, but mortal as well, so they would protect the bodies they had been given.

But Raksala-Ba was oblivious to that, and much more interested in the fact that each time a furry brown body fell in front of his weapons, he was rewarded with a mild orgasm. Killing the Muldag became a game, an effort to string the kills together in a long, uninterrupted sequence, so the pleasure never stopped. Others did likewise and it was hard to find enough indigs to make everyone happy.

It took the Hudathans little more than six hours to reach the ancient limestone city and sweep through the already devastated streets. The observers noted that by the time the shuttles landed and the cyborgs climbed aboard, only a handful of Muldag had survived.

And so it was that congratulations were exchanged, toasts were drunk, and the Regiment of the Living Dead won its first battle.

10

An intelligent enemy is better than a stupid friend.

African proverb
Author and date unknown

Clone World Alpha-001, the Clone Hegemony

The light from the holo table lit Parker's face from below and made him appear even more cadaverous than usual. Booly had summoned the noncom to one of the ship's many conference rooms to review the plan by which their personnel would be moved from the spaceport to the fortified control point that was their particular responsibility.

The map occupied the entire eight-by-four-foot holo surface. Everything from hills to fire hydrants appeared to be three dimensional and threw shadows that were synchronized with the time of day. There was a great deal of surface detail since all of the necessary vid scans had been conducted from low orbit. Sewer lines and fiber-optic cables were represented by nearly invisible pastel lines or were missing altogether.

Parker ran a slender, almost delicate finger along a major arterial, paused at one of the many traffic circles, and speared the next intersection. ''There it is, sir. Checkpoint X Ray.''

Booly nodded his agreement. ''So, Sergeant, given that company HQ will send hover trucks to carry the troops, how long will it take our personnel to join the rest of the platoon?''

Parker frowned. ''Assuming the transport is on time, assuming the drivers know their way around the city, and assuming our borgs are fully operational, about thirty minutes or so. A question, sir?''

''Shoot.''

''Does the lieutenant mean to say that the troops will travel without us?''

Booly grinned. ''Yup, that's what the lieutenant means to say. You and I have special authorization to travel with General Mosby's party. It departs approximately four hours *before* our people are scheduled to go and will pass within three city blocks of Checkpoint X Ray.''

Parker looked thoughtful. ''That would allow the lieutenant to arrive unannounced.''

Booly's grin grew wider. ''The sergeant has an excellent grasp of tactics.''

Parker nodded slowly. ''It occurs to me that the lieutenant has the makings of one grade-A sonovabitch. No offense intended.''

''And none taken,'' Booly said cheerfully. ''Grab your kit, Sergeant. The captain's gig departs forty from now.''

Legion general Marianne Mosby settled into one of the gig's large leather-covered acceleration couches, assumed the ''don't bother me'' frown that functioned to keep staffers at arm's length, and concentrated on the palm top's color screen. Shuttle trips had long ceased to fascinate her, and think time was hard to find. The trip from Earth had given her plenty of opportunity to study the strategic situation vis-à-vis the Clone Hegemony, but she hadn't gotten around to the key personalities involved, and they were fascinating. Especially the men, who were identically handsome, and if the intelligence summaries could be believed, as different as flakes of snow.

Mosby scrolled downwards, came to a 3-D color image of the Alpha clone Marcus-Six, and paused. Like his brothers, Marcus-Six was *very, very* good looking, even *with* a bar code printed across the middle of his forehead. Unlike his siblings, however, Marcus-Six had some ineffable quality that she found appealing. Sensitivity? Concern? Whatever it was triggered her rather active libido. Which was a waste of time, since like his subjects, Marcus-Six was not allowed to engage in sexual activity. Or, according to some of the rumors she'd heard, not *able* to.

Which reminded Mosby of her own situation, and the fact that she'd be fifty soon, an age when the prospect of babies becomes less and less likely. Oh sure, there were plenty of options, including sperm donors, in vitro fertilization, surrogate mothers, auto wombs, and other less savory possibilities. But she wanted the *real* thing, including hot, steamy sex, a full-term pregnancy, and a traditional delivery. Never mind the fact that she was a general, or that she had turned down numerous offers of marriage, or that she was too blasted old. She wanted a baby, damn it . . . and was in the habit of getting her way.

"General?"

Mosby found the intrusion annoying and switched to her "you'd better have one helluva good reason for bothering me" expression. "Yes? What is it?"

The petty officer quailed. "Thirty to touch-down, ma-'am. The pilot said you'd want to know."

Mosby *did* want to know and felt guilty about what she'd done. She mustered a smile and thanked the NCO for passing the message. He blushed and hurried away. Mosby sighed. Men were such simple creatures. Boring and predictable. Then why were they such a problem?

Alpha Clone Marcus-Six stood before a huge window and stared out over the city. It was a study in symmetry. Carefully spaced streets intersected each other at precise right angles; apartment buildings, office towers, and dispersal centers stood shoulder to shoulder like well-disciplined troops; and traffic moved with computer-controlled efficiency.

But like his life, the city only *appeared* to be orderly. Because just beneath the neat, seemingly orderly surface, a witch's brew of ideas, thoughts, beliefs, truths, perceptions, lies, theories, ambitions, fears, and hopes churned and bubbled like a cauldron on the boil.

Less than two months had passed since President Anguar's visit, and the only thing that had changed was the level of danger that Alpha-001 faced. While pretending to stall the confederacy, and seeming to humor their brother, Pietro and Antonio were secretly preparing for war. They had, among other things, seeded agents on Alpha-001, funded a low-key but effective anti-Confederacy propaganda campaign, and sponsored isolated "guerrilla" attacks on Legion outposts. All in the twin names of "freedom" and "autonomy."

But how much "freedom" and "autonomy" would the Clone Hegemony find under the heel of a Hudathan combat boot? Not very much. Yes, the free breeders were disgusting, but at least they were human, and might eventually see the error of their ways. Which was why Marcus continued to favor an accommodation with the Confederacy. His sibling's delusions of grandeur aside, the Hegemony was too small to stand against the Hudathan Empire alone, and unlikely to survive once the Confederacy was defeated, an outcome that an alliance might forestall.

But it would be difficult if not impossible to come out in favor of an alliance with the very government that viewed genetic planning as a violation of individual rights and had garrisoned troops on his planet. Especially when a large segment of the population approved of and supported the so-called freedom fighters.

Now, with the departure of the wonderfully incompetent General Sinkler, and the arrival of equally competent General Mosby, a bad situation had suddenly turned worse. Or had it? Assuming that the new officer was as capable as the intelligence reports claimed she was, and assuming that he provided some carefully disguised assistance, it *might* be possible to slow or even stop the rot his siblings had started. Discrediting his brothers' freedom fighters would be a good place to start. Yes, a promising thought indeed, which in conjunction with other plans, might turn things around.

Marcus turned his back on the window, checked his watch, and saw that General Mosby was scheduled to pay him a courtesy call in an hour or so. There was a spring in the Alpha clone's step as he passed the double helix that dominated the center of his office and headed for the door. Opportunity, as the old saying goes, waits for no man.

In order to maintain an appropriately low profile, and to facilitate the dropoff, Booly had talked his way aboard the last unit in the convoy. Like all of its kind, the quad stood twenty-five feet tall, weighed about fifty tons, and was heavily armed. Each of the four-legged cyborgs mounted multiple energy cannons, an extendable gatling gun, missile racks, grenade launchers, and a variety of light machine guns. All of which would make it damned hard for someone to attack the convoy from the rear. The quad had no difficulty matching the lead vehicle's forty-mile-per-hour pace and ran with surprising grace. Booly, Parker, and a squad of legionnaires rode in the cyborg's belly compartment. The up-and-down motion took some getting used to but was no worse than riding an armored personnel carrier cross-country. The noncom tapped his wrist term. "We're just about there, sir."

Booly nodded and slapped the ready button next to his helmet. "Hey, Grady, thanks for the ride. The next corner would be fine."

The cyborg "heard" the officer electronically and swept the area for any sign of an ambush. His sensors detected lots of everything but nothing unusual. "That's a roger, Lieutenant . . . welcome to the neighborhood."

The enormous cyborg paused, lowered its belly to a point only six feet off the street, and opened the starboard-side personnel hatch. Knowing the quad would catch hell if he fell too far behind, the legionnaires hurried to bail out. A host of strange odors filled Booly's supersensitive nostrils and the concrete felt good as it smacked the bottom of his boots.

Servos whined as the hatch closed above them and the cyborg took off. A pair of identical unicycle cops followed along behind. All three accelerated smoothly, closed the gap between themselves and the convoy, and slowed accordingly. Traffic, which had been delayed so the convoy could pass, flooded the intersection.

Booly looked around. Apartment buildings rose on all sides, windows staring down onto the street, walls hemming him in. Everything was spotlessly clean, boringly consistent, and broodingly hostile. The legionnaire sensed a presence behind him, and turned to find six identical children standing there, watching him with open curiosity. They were of African descent and had kinky black hair, dark brown skin, and large, expressive eyes. They all appeared to be seven or eight.

Booly smiled and saw that their expressions remained

unchanged. The children were afraid of him. Why? Because he was a stranger? A soldier? No, they had seen legionnaires before, so it was something else. Then it came to him.

Moving slowly, so he wouldn't scare them away, Booly lowered himself to one knee. The children looked at each other questioningly but stood their ground. The officer smiled reassuringly, reached for the nearest child's hand, and pulled it towards his face. Large eyes grew even larger as Booly took the little boy's hand and rubbed it against a furry cheek.

Suddenly there was a giggle, followed by laughter, and a wholesale rush to run grubby hands through short, soft fur. Suddenly Booly was transported back to his childhood when he and the other cubs had followed groups of legionnaires as they made their way between the earthen domes collectively known as "Naa town." The odor of incense had hung heavy on the air while smoke drifted upwards from dooth-dung fires and barely heard commands issued from inside the fort. The fort that had been constructed to keep the Naa out—until the Hudathans attacked, that is—and the tribes sided with the Legion. The right decision . . . but not one born of mutual respect.

Though never hesitant to make use of Naa labor, or to avail themselves of Naa prostitutes, the troopers had treated the inhabitants of Naa town with undisguised contempt, as did most of their "wild" and therefore "pure" brethren, his mother's tribe included.

But Windsweet had been more understanding, and explained that the Naa who lived in Naa town did so for a reason, and could not be judged except by those with similar experiences. Which might or might not account for the fact that she occasionally left him with a cousin while she and his father took part in meetings within the fort.

His cousin had been a beautiful little female, all laughter

and smiles, who had not only been partner to his first kiss, but had subsequently led him through the rubble that lay heaped at one end of the high walls, and into an old storm drain, which led back through the original structure's foundation and into the fort, where bars prevented access.

The memory gave Booly an idea. He stood with exaggerated slowness. Parker watched, half-bored, half-annoyed. His assault rifle was slung across his chest and ready for use. The pre-drop briefings had been very specific regarding the danger of lingering too long in one place or of socializing with the locals. "We'd better get a move on, sir."

Booly nodded and held out his hand. "Give me a fragmentation grenade."

Parker had several. He released one from its pouch and handed it over. "Yes, sir. May I ask the lieutenant what he plans to do with the grenade?"

"Yes," Booly replied thoughtfully, "you may. Children should have toys. A grenade will do nicely."

The office was large and almost spartan in its white-walled simplicity. A painting, one of thousands produced by the same group of artistically gifted clones, hung over a glass-topped credenza. The Alpha clone sat in a high-backed executive-style chair. His touch-sensitive desk had been tilted upwards to take the glare off the built-in screen and keyboard. A pair of intentionally uncomfortable chairs completed the decor.

Marcus-Six timed his motions so that General Mosby would see that he'd been working rather than waiting for her, yet feel honored by the speed with which he abandoned that activity, and came to meet her. The Alpha clone could be quite charming when he wanted to be.

"General Sinkler! How nice to see you again. And this must be General Mosby. Your courage in the face of the emperor's tyranny is legendary. It's an honor to meet you.''

Mosby had dealt with more than the emperor's tyranny, including a rather erotic interlude involving the emperor, his clone, and a huge bed. But she saw no reason to mention that. Especially since Marcus-Six had been brainwashed to think that sex, any kind of sex, was a crime against science. Mosby accepted the Alpha clone's outstretched hand and felt something pass between them. He sensed it too and a look of surprise registered on his face. "The honor is mine, Mr. President. I look forward to working with you."

"And I with you," Marcus-Six replied smoothly. "Come . . . I took the liberty of arranging for an early dinner. I hope both of you will join me."

Checkpoint X Ray occupied what had been a small park, a park the Hegemony's city planners had funded with an eye to recreational *and* military needs since it served a densely populated neighborhood and commanded an important intersection. Which was why the Legion had placed a platoon-sized reaction force there and why the locals resented it.

In addition, the off-worlders had cut down fifty identical oak trees to create a free-fire zone, dug a network of interconnected underground bunkers, and built a five-foot-high berm around the park's perimeter. Not to mention the eight-foot-tall electrified fence that topped the berm, the reinforced-concrete pillbox–control center that crouched behind the only gate, the floodlights that blazed around the clock, the ominous-looking cyborgs that patrolled the grounds, and the grotesque fly forms that dropped from the sky like dragonflies onto a steel-reinforced lily pad.

None of which mattered to Corporal Sanford, who yawned and wished her semipermanent hangover would go away. Of course that was unlikely, what with the loot spending most of his time at HQ, the top kick dogging it as much as she could, and Sergeant Yang running his jury-rigged still around the clock. Nope, Sanford decided, there was very little chance of sobriety in *her* future. She grinned and scanned the monitors racked in front of her.

Two people were supposed to be on duty inside the control center, but *supposed to* didn't mean much at Checkpoint X Ray, so Sanford was alone. That being the case, she was glad that all seventy-three of the checkpoint's surveillance cameras were up and running. The shots they provided clicked on and off with monotonous regularity and painted an ever-changing mosaic across the monitors in front of her.

Sanford looked up E Street towards the north . . . down West Twenty-fifth at the never-ending traffic . . . up at a section of uniform roof line . . . and out at a row of sterile facades. Her eyelids grew heavy and started to fall. Sleep tugged, trying to pull her down into its warm embrace, but a proximity alarm jerked her back. Within seconds other alarms had joined the first and the legionnaire was blasted with an annoying chorus of beeps, squeals, and tones. Eager to silence them, she scanned the screens. The children were familiar figures that hopped, skipped, and jumped through the outermost threat zone, and tripped her sensors as they had many times before.

Sanford was just about to activate the PA system, and order the little beggars to leave, when one of them threw something into the air, and another caught it. The object in question *looked* like a grenade but that was impossible. Wasn't it?

A sudden rush of adrenaline cleared Sanford's head and served to heighten her senses. She selected the appropriate camera, ordered it to zoom in, and found that her worst fears had been realized. Some idiot had allowed the children to get their hands on a Legion-issue grenade!

To her credit, Sanford thought of the children's welfare first, but rather than call for backup as she should have, she left the control center without her TO weapon and rushed to intervene. Which was a violation of general orders and a serious breach of security procedures.

It was a relatively simple matter for Booly and Parker to cross the street, identify themselves, take Sanford "prisoner," retrieve the disarmed grenade, and pay the children with some local currency. Booly laughed when all six of them flashed identical smiles, giggled, and skipped away.

Sanford, white faced, and clearly shaken up, was marched through the unlocked gate and into the pillbox–control center where she was secured to a chair. It took Booly only seconds to locate the controls for the perimeter security system and turn them off. He knew that doing so would trigger alarm units worn by the platoon commander and by his or her first sergeant. They would be pissed, *real* pissed, but helpless to do anything about it. Or so he hoped.

Seconds passed, followed by minutes, and no reaction at all. Had the two men been enemy commandos the entire platoon would have been dead by now. Booly shook his head in disgust. He turned to Sanford. There were sweat-stained half-moons under her armpits. "So, where *is* your CO?"

Sanford devoted the better part of a second to deciding whether to cover for the loot or let his ass swing in the breeze. The second alternative seemed a lot more appealing. "He's not here, sir."

Booly frowned. "Where the hell is he? On patrol?"

Sanford had never seen a half-human officer before and found the sight fascinating. "No, sir. Lieutenant Fedderman prefers to sleep at HQ. We see him once or twice a week."

"And the borgs? There should be at least one Trooper II on duty at all times."

"The borgs are with the lieutenant."

Booly and Parker looked at each other. The legionnaire's replies spoke volumes. Rather than bunk with his troops Fedderman preferred to kiss REMF (rear echelon mother-fucker) ass and have steak for dinner. And, as if that wasn't bad enough, he had taken the platoon's borgs along to func-tion as his personal bodyguard. Parker lifted an eyebrow. "And the first sergeant?"

Sanford didn't care anymore. Her ass was grass and every-one could damned well fend for themselves. She shrugged. "He's passed out somewhere."

Booly nodded. There was no doubt about it. Discipline was seriously screwed up. He motioned to Parker. "Turn the corporal loose." He squinted at the name tag sewn over the legionnaire's left pocket. "Sanford, is it? All right, San-ford, I want you to call company HQ. Tell 'em were gonna run a drill out here, and not to worry if they hear about some sort of disturbance. Got it?"

Sanford had decided that the new loot was a lot more attractive than the old loot and wished she looked better. "Yes, sir."

Booly smiled. "Good. Restore the security system and hold the fort while Sergeant Parker and I play reveille."

It took them less than five minutes to weave their way through a series of sandbagged walkways and down into a labyrinth of underground bunkers. Mud squished beneath their combat boots as they walked the length of a hand-dug tunnel and entered a large chamber.

At least twenty-five legionnaires occupied what looked like twenty bunks. Some wore clothes, some didn't. Layers of thick gray smoke hung in the air along with the almost nauseating odor of sweat, booze, and vomit. A wild as-sortment of scavenged beams held the spray-plas reinforced ceiling in place. Jury-rigged lamps threw light down onto a floor strewn with dirty uniforms, poorly maintained field gear, mud-caked boots. A beeper beeped and Parker picked up a pair of olive drab pants. The beeper was attached and he turned off. "Don't know which one is the first sergeant, sir, but here's his pants."

"He won't be first sergeant for long," Booly said grimly. "Lock and load."

Both men released their safeties, put a round in the chamber, and aimed their weapons at floor. Booly grinned. "Time to wake the troops, Sergeant . . . let 'em have it."

The assault rifles made more noise than usual within such an enclosed space. Every single one of the legionnaires was awake within the first two seconds. Some tried to get up, to leave their racks, but retreated as a hail of bullets tore through the jumble of uniforms, gear, and boots that littered the floor. Eventually, after both men had fired full thirty-round magazines, the noise died away. Dust motes drifted through the light and fell towards the floor.

Booly looked around. Some of the faces were black, some were white, but most were brown. Some of the legionnaires met his eyes, daring him to think whatever he chose, but most slid away. He had them by the short hairs and they knew it. The future looked dark. Booly nodded as if in agreement. "That's right, assholes. Life sucks. Now roll out of those racks. We have work to do."

Marcus-Six heaved a sigh of relief as the door slid shut on General Sinkler's rather corpulent posterior. Both he and General Mosby had spent the last two hours maneuvering towards some time alone. He, because he wanted to build a working alliance as quickly as possible, and she, because the Alpha clone was the most fascinating man she had encountered in some time, made all the more interesting by the fact that he was supposed to be celibate.

In fact, the degree of polarity between them had been *so* strong that the average person would have detected and responded to it in a matter of minutes instead of hours.

But Sinkler loved to talk, and worse than that loved to sing, having a pleasant though not spectacular baritone. This gift he generously shared with all and sundry, especially those who reported to him, and had heard his rendition of "Sky Legion" more times than they cared to remember.

So, by the time Sinkler had finished the first part of his repertoire, and the dinner dishes had been cleared, the other two had built the beginnings of a relationship via sidelong glances and repressed laughter.

Having seen Sinkler off, Marcus-Six returned to find that Mosby had left the table and made herself at home in the sitting area of his private quarters. Although the occasion had forced Mosby to wear her dress uniform, it did feature a skirt, which Mosby wore slightly shorter than regulations allowed. It had ridden up to reveal a few inches of thigh. Marcus found the combination of the uniform and creamy-colored flesh to be more than a little intriguing and accepted the general's invitation to sit next to her. He moved even closer when she pouted and patted the leather at her side. "Don't be shy, Marcus . . . I won't bite."

Though not experienced at the social-sex rituals practiced by free breeders, Marcus did his best to come up with a lighthearted response. "Really? Remind me to fire the head of our intelligence service. She claims you are one of the toughest officers the confederacy has."

Mosby looked pleased. "How nice of her. But that's on the battlefield. This is closer to the boudoir."

Marcus-Six felt beads of sweat break out across his forehead. He had heard the rumors but assumed they were exaggerated. The fact that free-breeder women really *were* aggressive came as a shock. "Yes, well not *too* close, since our society made a conscious decision to *control* evolution rather than simply experience it."

"Yes," Mosby said agreeably, her perfume lapping

around his head, "I'm so glad we can discuss that. It seems that sexual reproduction is central to the differences between our governments. Tell me, have you ever had physical sex?"

Marcus-Six had lost control of the situation and knew it. He felt flushed, and found it difficult to breathe. "Why, no . . . I . . ."

"You *can* have sex, can't you?" Mosby interrupted. "I mean, they didn't cut anything off, did they?"

The question, followed by the warmth of the hand that she placed on his thigh, gave Marcus-Six an erection. Not a new sensation but one he had tried to minimize. He babbled nervously. "Approximately two percent of the population is left intact to protect against the possibility that some unforeseen catastrophe might destroy the sperm and egg repositories."

"And the rest?"

"Are sterilized to prevent unplanned births and given chemicals to inhibit their sex drives."

Mosby nodded thoughtfully and allowed her hand to drift upwards along the Alpha clone's leg. His erection was a long, hard bulge under the tight cloth of the pants he wore. She smiled. "Don't tell me . . . let me guess. Two percent?"

Marcus-Six nodded wordlessly, removed the general's hand from where it had come to rest, and prayed for strength. He needed this woman to help find and put a stop to the world-destroying insanity his brothers had launched. But at what cost? He looked into her eyes and realized that an already difficult life had just become more complex.

11

. . . The way of the warrior is resolute acceptance of death.

Miyamoto Musashi
A Book of Five Rings
Standard year 1643

Worber's World, the Confederacy of Sentient Beings

General Natalie Norwood felt the usual sense of anticipation as she strode into her quarters, discarded her clothes, and settled into the big black chair. Only this session was different, because knowing she would be down among the Hudathans *made* it different, though she wasn't sure why. The quarterly inspections were a source of joy and despair. Joy, at seeing the extent to which the Hudathans suffered, and despair at walking through the charred ruins of cities she had loved.

Still, it had to be done, just as so many other things had to be done, most of them unpleasant. She scanned through a variety of shots, found one that looked promising, and locked on. Twelve Hudathans, part of a work party, were building a rock wall. They looked woefully thin and ragged. Just one of many such efforts she had noticed of late. But why?

Although some of the work was focused on strengthening their dwellings, a substantial part of it appeared to be random in nature. An effort to keep the troops busy? Norwood could understand the need to do that since she did the same thing herself. Troops have a tendency to get into trouble when they have too much free time.

But the temptation to ascribe human motivations to the aliens was a dangerous one and Norwood struggled to resist it. After all, that's what the landings were for, to perform on-site assessments of prisoner conditions and activities. Once she was there, once on the ground, the purpose of the walls would become apparent.

The shots changed, Norwood found some images that gave her pleasure, and slowly but surely pushed each of the psychological-physical buttons that normally led to release, and from there to oblivion. Nothing. She tried again. Still nothing. Something, she wasn't sure what, was getting in the way. Finally, feeling tired, worried, and frustrated, she went to sleep. Her dreams were dark and troubled.

War Commander Poseen-Ka had never been more frightened. Not of death, which would come as a welcome relief after years of imprisonment, but of failure. Failure to take advantage of the opportunity he had been given, failure to revenge himself on the humans, and failure to escape from his planetary prison.

There had never been a question as to *if* they would come, only *when* they would come, and his intelligence officers had predicted that with almost perfect accuracy. And why not? The humans adhered to consistent schedules and always inserted additional surveillance cameras just prior to an inspection. Cameras that could be tallied and tracked. Yes, Norwood had grown careless over the years, and would soon pay the price.

Poseen-Ka, his factory-new weapons bundled at his feet,

stood on the hill above the graveyard and gazed skywards. Human troop carriers had left white claw marks across the unusually blue sky as if proclaiming their ownership of it and all that lay below.

But not anymore. Not after they landed and he took possession of both their ships *and* their battle station. Then, depending on what the high command had ordained for him, he would be rescued or killed during a human counterattack. But that was then and this was now. There was work to do. Soldier's work, the kind he'd done his entire adult life, and would continue to do until the day he died.

The war commander gathered his weapons and started down the slope. His skin started to turn black in the sun, his sandals slid on a scattering of pebbles, and a half-buried skull stared up at him from a rain-eroded grave.

Something was amiss but Norwood couldn't decide what it was. And because generals are supposed to base their decisions on more than just gut instinct, there wasn't a damned thing she could do about it. Besides, the landing force consisted of more than a thousand heavily armed marines and legionnaires. More than a match for the bows and arrows the Hudathans could theoretically come up with. The thought should have alleviated the hollow feeling in the pit of her stomach but didn't.

Master Sergeant Max Meyers more than occupied the jump seat across from her. The light machine gun, often served by a two-person crew, looked like a toy in his massive hands. Linked ammo crisscrossed his chest, the butt of a handgun protruded from his left armpit, and a commando knife hung hilt-down from his harness. He smiled and Norwood responded in kind. It was impossible not to. "Nothin' like a little stroll to keep a soldier in shape, General."

Norwood eyed the small paunch that pressed against his

shirt. "Really? Well, maybe we oughtta come dirtside a little more often, then."

Meyers laughed, as did those seated around them, and the shuttle leveled out. There weren't any windows, so Norwood couldn't see the surface, but she had little difficulty imagining the ocean of rubble that passed beneath the shuttle's stubby wings.

Cities, towns, homes, businesses, schools, churches, and millions of people all murdered by the Hudathans. Yes, the aliens had their virtues, but what good is bravery without compassion? Intelligence without empathy? Strength without kindness? And so it fell to her, and the men and women under her command, to keep chaos at bay, at least on Worber's World. She couldn't do much about the Confederacy as a whole.

Due to the fact that the snoop-and-poop inspections had taken place for about twenty years now, and that the Hudathans were unarmed, airstrips had been cleared near their centers of population and were reused as needed. That's why marine recon dropped first, checked the runways for booby traps, and reestablished a defensive perimeter *prior* to each landing.

So when Norwood's shuttle thumped down, dumped forward momentum, and taxied towards a berm-protected parking area, she knew the immediate area was secure. Ramps were lowered, dust spurted upwards, and metal clanked as she made her way down and onto the surface of her home planet.

Colonel Maria Chow, the highly capable commander of the 16th Battalion, 3rd Marines, was waiting, as was the irrepressible Major Ricardo Hussein, commanding officer of the Legion contingent, which had been temporarily detached from the 5th Foreign Infantry Regiment to reinforce the marines.

Both popped to attention and held their salutes. Norwood

returned them in kind and shook their hands. "Maria . . . Ricky . . . it's good to see you. Is everything secure?"

Hussein had brown skin and a lot of extremely white teeth. His uniform was heavily starched and he looked like a recruiting holo. "The grunts needed lots of help, General, but we showed 'em what to do."

It was a running joke and Chow played along. She was short and squat, like the mortars she had commanded as a lieutenant. "Shit. If it wasn't for us, Ricky and the rest of his cyber-weenies would be up in orbit drinking hot chocolate and reading each other bedtime stories."

Norwood shook her head in mock disgust. "I have a whole planet to run and this is what they send me. So how 'bout it? Did either one of you slackers get a sitrep on zones one and three?"

Both officers nodded their heads but it was Chow who answered. "Yes, ma'am. Both teams have landed and report their perimeters are secure. Ricky will lead the One Team . . . and I have Three."

Norwood nodded. The fact that she had divided her team into three roughly equal parts might have been a mistake had they been landing on an enemy-held planet, but the Hudathans were unarmed, so a reinforced company should be adequate for each major location. "Good. Let's saddle up."

It took the better part of an hour to reinforce the marine perimeter with four of the Legion's Trooper IIs, load the APCs and head for the Hudathan-occupied ruins. A flight of aerospace fighters, fighting to keep their speed down, roared overhead. They were gone a few seconds later. Both Chow and Hussein had joined their respective teams and were closing on their objectives.

Norwood rode in the lead vehicle with her head and shoulders sticking up through a hatch. Master Sergeant Meyers didn't approve . . . but Norwood wanted to see the terrain with her own eyes. The APC lurched as the right-hand track rode up and over a concrete block. Norwood braced herself against the motion. The metal felt warm beneath her fingers.

A knowledgeable eye could still tell the difference between the rubble created by a bombed-out apartment complex and a high-rise business office. Signs advertised services no longer available, arrows guided nonexistent traffic, and lampposts, heated by the same energy beams that had burned huge swathes across the city, drooped like dying flowers. Protruding from a sidewalk that had flowed like lava, Norwood saw the head and shoulders of a man, arms raised in supplication, forever entombed in a suit of glassified concrete.

Norwood felt her anger return and used it to feed the moment, to immunize herself against the feelings of pity that threatened to dilute her hatred. Strength, that was the answer, and Norwood took pleasure in the fact that there was nothing subtle about the robo scouts that swept the area ahead, the quads who guarded the convoy's flanks, or the main battle tank that brought up the rear. The message was clear: "Do what we say or die."

Hard eyes watched the convoy pass and waited for the prearranged signal. The Hudathans emerged from their hiding places. They knew every square inch of the surrounding terrain, were heavily armed, and willing to die. A dozen or so started to work on ambush number two. The rest, some two hundred in all, headed for Landing Zone Two.

Elsewhere, hundreds of miles away, similar activities took place in the vicinity of Landing Zones One and Three. A surveillance camera drifted in from the surrounding badlands, spotted unexpected movement around Zone One, and was destroyed with a shoulder-launched missile. The battle had begun.

Specialist Third Class Jessica Clemmons heard the buzzer, touched a series of keys, and watched the last thirty seconds of video from SURCAM 1147. The images she saw were so jarring, so unexpected, that she ran it again. The camera drifted around the corner of a tumbledown building and out over a street. About fifteen Hudathans were digging some sort of trench. Four of them saw the surveillance device, one gave an order, and the other three aimed weapons towards the camera. The video went to black.

Clemmons gulped, stabbed the button that would download her screen to Lieutenant Rawley, and hit the intercom. The connection was voice only. He sounded ragged, and slightly out of breath. "Lieutenant Rawley here."

"I-i-it's Clemmons, sir. Th-th-the Hudathans destroyed SURCAM 1147. R-r-request permission to notify Ops."

The voice was annoyed. "What did they do? Beat the damn thing with a stick?"

"N-n-no, sir. Th-th-they hit it with a shoulder-launched missile."

Rawley gave an exasperated sigh. "I'm surprised at you, Clemmons . . . drinking on duty is a court-martial offense. Log off, inform the duty NCO, and report to quarters. I'll deal with you later."

Clemmons started to reply, started to object, but knew it was hopeless. She broke the connection, stood, and had started to log off when it hit her. There were a thousand people on the surface, and if the Hudathans had weapons, *all* of them were in danger. She sat, downloaded her screen to the Ops Center, and activated the intercom. The response was immediate. "Ops Center."

Clemmons spoke and discovered her stutter had disappeared. "EW Section here, sir. The enemy attacked and destroyed SURCAM 1147. Video confirmation is available on channel one-three-six.''

There was a momentary pause as the Ops officer checked the video, followed by the words ''Holy shit! Good work, EW. Stay on it.''

General quarters sounded just as Lieutenant Rawley was about to come between Ensign Ngundo's rather shapely legs. He didn't appreciate the way Ngundo pushed him to one side and reached for her pants. Goddamn the navy anyway! Would the bullshit never end?

Norwood got the word on SURCAM 1147 only seconds after War Commander Poseen-Ka received the same news via the low-powered radio relay system that tied his forces together. The lag time made little or no difference. Though not completely within his trap, the convoy was two-thirds of the way into Hudathan kill zone. Not perfect, but good enough.

Norwood was still in the process of deciding what to do when the Hudathans opened fire. Not at the bio bods, who were vastly outnumbered, but at the quads and the single tank.

Poseen-Ka always made it a point to avoid making the same mistake twice in a row. So, having underestimated the effectiveness of human cyborgs during the Battle for Algeron, and having paid for his error, the Hudathan had no intention of doing so again. And, given the fact that the micro-bots had not been equipped to manufacture the heavy artillery, rocket launchers, or other weapons that would normally be used on armored targets, he'd been forced to improvise.

Which explained why both quads had been targeted by three suicide teams, each consisting of two troopers, carrying twenty-five pounds' worth of explosives apiece.

All of the teams had prepositioned themselves along the

quad's line of march in hopes that one of them would be relatively close when the moment came. But the radio transmission ruined that and the Hudathans were forced to sprint towards their respective targets.

Drulo Baka-Sa, leader of team three, had been a world-class athlete twenty years before. He was older now, but still powerful, and put everything he had into the effort. Bullets started to fly, and his target quad, the one guarding the convoy's western flank, was in the process of lowering its body to the ground. Once there, the cyborg would become impregnable to anything the Hudathans could presently bring to bear. Everything, literally everything, depended on Baka-Sa's ability to close the gap and get beneath the behemoth *before* it settled in. The Hudathan looked back over his shoulder, saw that Nola-Da was only steps behind, and redoubled his efforts.

The quad known as Abdul had been a legionnaire for thirteen years, ever since a mining accident had claimed his body, and thought he'd seen it all. Not the *big* war of course, the one that put the Hudathans on Worber's World to begin with, but two or three smaller conflicts and a police action or two.

But prisoners who suddenly had weapons, that was a new and not especially pleasant surprise. Still, there was no real cause for alarm, since there was no sign of enemy artillery, which along with heavy armor, was the only thing that quads fear. No one needed to order him down, which they did anyway, or to open fire, which they also did anyway. There were damned few targets, though, excepting the two greenish blobs who had appeared in the middle of his electronic vision and were headed his way.

Abdul zoomed in and saw no sign of the assault rifles he might have expected, and was not especially concerned in any case, since they could do little more than chip his carefully applied paint job. Then he saw the packs they wore, received a warning from his brain-linked on-board computer, and knew what they were. A demo team! Hell bent on placing explosives under his belly!

Already moving downwards as fast as his hydraulics would permit, Abdul directed most of his fire to the oncoming blobs, and the rest to the backup teams coming along behind them.

Baka-Sa felt his abdominal muscles tighten as dirt geysered to his right and an energy beam pulsed overhead. The cyborg had seen the danger and was focusing its considerable weaponry on the threat. The Hudathan leaped over a huge chunk of concrete, shouted his clan's ancestral war cry, and pounded towards the alien quad. He heard a grunt through his ear plug and knew Nola-Da had been hit. A series of bright blue energy beams stuttered by his shoulder and caused his radio to crackle. He tripped, caught himself, and staggered ahead. The rubble made it difficult to run and also made it hard for the quad's computer to predict where he would go next. Grenades popped out of the quad's launchers, tumbled end over end, and exploded in midair. Shrapnel whined past the Hudathan's head and peppered his three-hundred-pound body. He kept on going.

The quad was lower now, no more than six feet off the ground, and steadily falling. Something thumped into Baka-Sa's shoulder and hurt. But there were only feet to go before he crossed the finish line, before he showed the others who was fastest, before the race was won.

Antipersonnel mines exploded, triggered by Abdul's last-ditch attempt to save himself, but it was too late. Suddenly Baka-Sa was there, rolling into the cyborg's enormous shadow, looking up at camouflaged metal. He wanted to detonate the pack himself, to control his last few moments of existence, but that was denied him.

Seeing Baka-Sa's success via his high-powered spotting scope, and not inclined to take any chances, Dagger Commander Enora-Ka activated the remote triggering device. Baka-Sa, and the legionnaire known to his friends as Abdul, died in the same flash of light.

The second quad, the one covering the convoy's eastern flank, survived the initial assault, but lost both legs on one side, and was effectively immobilized. And, as if that wasn't bad enough, a full fifty percent of the APCs in the first half of the convoy, or the part fully enmeshed in the Hudathan kill zone, had been destroyed by prepositioned command-detonated mines. So, badly outnumbered, and stripped of a good deal of her mobility, Norwood had little choice but to retreat.

Three legionnaires died while trying to pull the second quad's brain box, and more would have made the attempt, if the cyborg in question hadn't threatened to fire on them, and promised to cover their retreat. And cover them she did, hurling a sleet of lead in every direction as the APCs pulled back, hunting the Hudathans like rats in a gravel pit.

Twice the APC Norwood was riding was blown out from under her, twice she was helped to safety, and twice she stopped to pull dead and dying soldiers out of the wreckage. And always with the same thoughts burning through her mind. Where had the weapons come from? How had they done it? And what could they possible hope to gain?

Because no matter how many humans they killed in the coming hours, and given the reports coming from Landing Zones One and Three, the butcher's bill would be high indeed, she could *still* call for reinforcements, or retreat to her fortress in the sky and sterilize the entire planet from there. And the aerospace fighters were still up, too, ready to inflict damage.

A sniper opened fire from the cover of a recently repaired stone wall. Lead spanged off metal and Norwood ducked. A huge bandage-wrapped hand touched her shoulder. It was

Meyers, wounded, grimy, but still smiling. "It's the Bear, ma'am. He says it's urgent."

Norwood grimaced and accepted the hand-held com set. If her XO wanted something it would be important. A shoulder-launched missile hit an APC and detonated with a sharp, cracking sound. Her latest vehicle lurched and someone started to scream. "Yeah, Ernie . . . what's up?"

The *Old Lady*'s skipper was a big man, made seemingly bigger by the personality he projected, and the entire Ops Center hung on his every word. Quite a few of the SUR-CAMs were still operational and provided live coverage of the battle. "We've got trouble, General, *big* trouble."

"Gee, Ernie, thanks for the insight."

The naval officer ignored Norwood's sarcasm. "No, boss, I mean *real* trouble, fleet-sized trouble. There are approximately fifty ships. Each and every damned one of them is a ninety-six-point-eight percent match with known Hudathan designs. They dropped hyper ten minutes ago and are headed this way."

Norwood felt her heart sink. Suddenly it all made sense. The purpose of the ground action had been to weaken the battle station. The destruction of the battle station would be but the first highly symbolic blow in an all-out war to destroy the Confederacy. And it was her fault. Every decision she'd made had been predicated on the same faulty assumption: that the Hudathans were unarmed. How they obtained the arms no longer mattered. The damage was done. She chose her words with care.

"I'll attempt to regroup in the LZ, Ernie . . . but things don't look very good. Program a full flight of message torps. I want five-hundred-percent redundancy on all priority-one destinations. Give 'em what we have so far . . . and tell them to get ready . . . this is only the beginning."

Big Bear nodded. "Yes, ma'am."

"And, Ernie?"

"Yes, General?"

"Pull our air support . . . use them to attack the Hudathan fleet . . . and make the bastards pay."

Captain Ernie Big Bear looked up at the screen. He knew he'd never see Norwood again, not in the physical world anyway, and wanted to cry. But warriors don't cry, not with the entire Ops Center looking on, so he didn't. "Roger that, General . . . Good luck . . . Ops out."

Norwood handed the com set to Meyers. "All right, Sergeant . . . let's fall back on the airstrip. Warn the perimeter guards and order the Trooper IIs to dig in."

Meyer's reply was lost in the sound of a tremendous explosion. The Hudathans had detonated an enormous mine under the up-till-now undamaged battle tank. It was built to survive such explosions and did. But one of the machine's massive fans had been damaged, forcing the tank to remain where it was. Explosions rippled across its surface as the Hudathans unleashed a storm of shoulder-launched missiles. The marines answered by traversing their still-potent weapons across the surrounding ruins, tracking and eventually finding many of their attackers.

Norwood wanted to come to the tank's assistance, wanted to rescue the crew, but knew it was hopeless. A hundred yards separated the slowly retreating convoy from the now-isolated tank and every inch of it was swept by enemy fire.

A hand grabbed her arm, pulled her towards the rear of the vehicle, and down the ramp. Norwood looked back to see that smoke had started to boil up from the badly damaged engine. The next piece of bad news came with mind-numbing speed.

A grimy face appeared next to hers. She had seen it before but couldn't put a name to it. "We got through to the landing zone, ma'am. They're cut off and taking heavy fire. Two of the drop ships were destroyed by command-detonated mines, a Trooper II is down, another is damaged, and the entire west side of the perimeter is under heavy pressure. Lieutenant Alvarez requests permission to abandon sixty percent of the LZ and consolidate her position.''

Random thoughts chased important thoughts through Norwood's mind. Alvarez? What about Captain Horowitz? Dead or wounded. All was not lost, though. Yes, two of the landing craft had been destroyed, and so had at least fifty percent of her force. The remaining ships would be sufficient if they could reach them. "Permission granted. Tell Alvarez to defend the remaining ships.''

The face nodded. "Yes, ma'am.''

The next fifteen minutes passed with agonizing slowness as the convoy tried to disengage and the Hudathans refused to cooperate. Then, just when Norwood could see the smoke pouring up from the vicinity of the landing strip, Poseen-Ka triggered the second ambush. It was as he had intended to be, the blow that broke the convoy's spine.

The hand-dug trench ran the width of the road along which the convoy had traveled and was packed with explosives. When detonated, the resulting explosion threw soldiers fifty feet in the air, cut an APC loaded with wounded marines in half, and disabled two more.

Norwood, walking backwards and firing from the hip, had her feet knocked out from under her. The ground hit hard. She tried to rise, saw a stump where her left foot had been, and started to scream. Meyers appeared, applied a tourniquet, and injected something into her thigh. Then, ignoring her orders to the contrary, the master sergeant tossed the general over a massive shoulder, and jogged towards the drop zone. A mere handful of survivors, twenty at best, followed along behind.

The battle for *Battle Station Alpha XIV,* better known to the humans as *The Old Lady,* went entirely according to plan. The *Hudathan plan*, as visualized and carried out by none other than Grand Marshal Hisep Rula-Ka, onetime protégé to War Commander Niman Poseen-Ka, father of the Hudathan Cyber Corps, and intellectual architect of the coming war.

Upon emerging from hyperspace, it had come as no surprise to him that the weapons he had so carefully placed in his former leader's hands had not only been used, but used in a strategically thoughtful manner, weakening the human battle station, and opening it to the very real possibility of an attack from below.

Now, as his attack ships slashed their way in through the human fighters, victory seemed certain. The only items left unresolved were the number of ships destroyed, the number of lives lost, and the fate of his old comrade. Would Poseen-Ka emerge alive? It wouldn't make much difference to the overall war effort, but he'd look good on the propaganda holos, and the old fart would make a good ally in the days to come.

Rula-Ka sat in his oval-shaped command center, his back comfortably protected by two inches of solid steel, and watched the three-dimensional holo that dominated the center of the room. The other fourteen niches were empty due to the fact that his immediate subordinates were spread out over the fleet.

Another officer might have been busy issuing commands, giving orders that no one needed, or generally getting in the way. But not Rula-Ka. No, he had learned the art of war from Niman Poseen-Ka, and knew that less was more. Yes, he thought contentedly, a well-thought-out plan, executed by well-trained troops, needs only the occasional nudge or adjustment in order to succeed.

Such seemed to be the case as the lights that represented individual human fighters winked out one by one, and the battle station's main batteries were engaged. Not without loss of course, because the assault cost Rula-Ka a carrier, a cruiser, and two light destroyers, some twenty-five hundred lives in all. But well worth the price. The Hudathan forced himself to relax and savor the moment. The old saying was correct. "A dish delayed tastes all the sweeter for the waiting."

Poseen-Ka wound his way through a maze of crumbled walls, rusted vehicles, and twisted steel. The human bodies, interspersed here and there with their Hudathan counterparts, were like a bloody trail that led towards the airstrip. There were a great number of them and it seemed unlikely that anything more than a handful had escaped the second ambush.

As the Hudathan war commander reached what had been the outermost line of human defenses, the scene changed. Here the Hudathan bodies lay like waves lapping on a beach, each having conquered just a little more sand, until the last line of bodies was intermixed with those belonging to the defenders.

Poseen-Ka passed what remained of a burned-out Trooper II, its massive body dwarfing the three- and four-hundred-pound Hudathans who lay dead around it, a giant among Liliputians.

Then came the weapons pits, which would also serve as ready-made graves for the men and women who had died in them, and a series of serpentine skid marks. Poseen-Ka could imagine the humans, many of them wounded, dragging their heaviest weapons back towards hastily prepared backup positions, and firing till attrition wore them down. Now they lay alongside their enemies, an interspecies jumble of arms and legs, their blood commingled in the dirt beneath them.

Poseen-Ka paused, looked out over the battlefield, and waited for the sense of jubilation that should surely come.

It didn't. He felt only sadness at the use to which his intelligence and creativity had been put.

The war commander continued his walk. A berm stood in the way and he climbed to the top of it. Two ships had been destroyed and were still on fire. The rest stood untouched and were the subjects of intensive scrutiny by teams of pilots and technicians who hadn't flown Hudathan ships in twenty years, much less human models, all of which were reasonably new.

But it had to be done. Horrible though the slaughter was, even more would be necessary. The battle station was a threat, and threats must be destroyed.

A trooper approached. His body was filthy, and blood stained his rags, but his weapon was clean. His salute was crisp with reborn pride. "Three of the humans continue to live. Do you wish to interrogate them?"

Poseen-Ka had little interest in whatever the humans might have to say but wanted to see them. He followed the trooper to a place where three humans sat propped up against some sandbags. Guards stood all around. There were two males and a female. All had been wounded. It took him a moment to recognize Norwood. She had aged since the last time he had seen her and was white from loss of blood. Her eyes were as he remembered them, though, filled with intelligence and carefully focused animosity. She spoke his language with a heavy accent. "You survived."

"As did you."

"But not for long."

"No," Poseen-Ka agreed soberly, "not for long. It was a mistake to let you live. I won't make it twice."

Norwood nodded. "I didn't think you would."

The Hudathan drew his never-before-fired side arm, released the safety, and aimed it at her head. Norwood spent the last microsecond of her life wondering why she had been destined to survive the first battle for Worber's World only to die in the second. She took the first bullet, followed by a semiconscious Meyers, and a tight-lipped com tech. It took three additional hours to load the human ships, lift, and close with the battle station.

Clemmons lived long enough to see the end. There wasn't much need for electronic warfare specialists after the main batteries were destroyed and the aliens forced their way in through Lock Number 4, so the technician donned her space armor and joined the marines. Energy weapon in hand, she followed a ragtag squad of volunteers down a smoke-filled corridor, and wished she were somewhere else. Anywhere else.

Everyone knew the Hudathans didn't take prisoners, not because they were cruel, but there was no logical reason to do so. After all, the Hudathans reasoned, why risk your life to kill the enemy, then allow them to live? It didn't make alien sense.

Besides, live prisoners were a continual threat, and anyone who didn't believe that could take a look at the gaunt scarecrow-like figures who had made their way up from the planet's surface and forced their way in through Lock Number 12. Not that it got them very far, since they lacked space armor, and were temporarily trapped in a single airtight compartment.

The formerly clean, almost sterile corridors were gone, now filled with portable fire-fighting equipment, makeshift com centers, aide stations, emergency rations, ammo boxes, and recently dead bodies. There had been wounded hours? Or was it days ago? But most had been killed when the sick bay took a direct hit from a Hudathan torpedo. Now, with sixty percent of the Station's airtight compartments holed, even a wound meant almost certain death.

Clemmons felt a tremendous almost overwhelming sense of sorrow. Sorrow for herself and the others as well. Tears ran down her face but she didn't care. She would do her best, and kill some Hudathans if she could, but there was no point in hiding what she felt. There wouldn't be anyone left to criticize her before long.

The squad stopped in front of a black-and-yellow-striped hatch. Clemmons recognized it as providing access to the flight deck, where the aerospace fighters, shuttles, and hundreds of lesser craft were normally kept. A pair of tough-looking legionnaires guarded it. Her squad leader, a lance corporal up until an hour ago, gave a password and ordered the legionnaires to open it. They obeyed.

The lock contained six dead bodies, or what remained of six bodies, since there wouldn't be much more than mush inside the decompressed suits.

Clemmons didn't look, didn't want to know what would happen to her, and bit her lip. The outer hatch opened and the squad stepped out onto the flight deck. With the exception of a pristine shuttle known as "the hangar queen," and some skeletal maintenance sleds, the normally crowded space was completely empty. Everything that could fly, armed or unarmed, had gone out against the Hudathans and never come back. The corporal's voice was artificially gruff and made the technician jump.

"All right, people . . . form a single rank. That's right . . . your other left, dip shit . . . that's better. At ease."

Clemmons had always known that the grunts were crazy and this proved it. A drill for God's sake!

But it wasn't a drill as the men and women soon found out. A marine lieutenant and an MP appeared. They dragged a space-suited figure between them. Judging from the noises coming over the suit-to-suit tac frequency, the prisoner was male. The words were punctuated with sobs.

"Please! Don't shoot me! What's the point? We'll die if we stay. Why not escape? That's our duty, isn't it? To escape and fight another day?"

"You make me sick."

Clemmons assumed that the second male voice belonged to the marine lieutenant, and the impression was confirmed as the officer continued to speak. He scanned the helmets before him. "You've been summoned here to act as a firing squad. The thing in front of you is named Alan Rawley and used to be a lieutenant. He left his duty station, tried to activate a life pod, and was found guilty of desertion in the face of the enemy. The sentence is death."

Clemmons could hardly believe it. Lieutenant Rawley of all people! Sentenced to death, just like the rest of them. The technician's name had been printed in block letters across the front of her suit. Rawley saw it. "Clemmons! It's you, isn't it? Tell them I'm innocent. Tell them what a good officer I am!"

The corporal's voice was hard like the sergeant he'd copied it from. "Atten-hut!"

Clemmons snapped to attention. The deck shuddered under her boots and tilted to port. She leaned the other way to compensate.

"Prepare to fire on my command!"

Clemmons brought her weapon up and tried to hold it steady. The sight drifted back and forth across Rawley's chest.

"Ready!"

Clemmons fumbled with the safety and managed to release it.

"Aim!"

Clemmons wondered if she should sight on Rawley's head instead of his chest. She moved the sights and was surprised by the fear that appeared in the officer's eyes. "No! Please! I beg you!"

"Fire!"

Clemmons allowed the barrel to drift off target and pressed the firing stud. The energy bolt passed Rawley's helmet and scorched the paint on the bulkhead beyond. Not everyone was so kind. Clemmons closed her eyes as Rawley's chest exploded inwards and his suit decompressed. The body was left where it fell.

A Hudathan shuttle landed on the flight deck twenty minutes later. The officer in charge timed his troopers and noted that they were able to kill the human defenders in record time. Still another example of Hudathan superiority. He hardly even noticed Clemmons as he stepped over the technician's decompressed body and headed for the blast-damaged hatch. The battle was over.

12

The principal study and care and the especial profession of a prince should be warfare and its attendant rules and discipline.

Niccolò Machiavelli
The Prince
Standard year 1513

Planet Earth, the Confederacy of Sentient Beings

The police came for Sergi Chien-Chu while he was welding
a strut. They didn't wear uniforms or wave badges, but
there was no mistaking what they were. The short hair, hard
eyes, and plastic good looks were dead giveaways, as was
the fact that they were cyborgs and entered the vacuum
chamber without suits.

The Viper was nearing completion now and would be
removed within the next day or so. Men, women, cyborgs,
and robots walked, climbed, scurried, rolled, and oozed
over the hull as they hurried to complete their last-minute
tasks. Chien-Chu stood at the point where a short, stubby
wing intersected the ship's hull. A mask covered his face
and metal glowed blue as he worked a seam. The industrialist became aware of the police when a voice came over
his seldom-used transceiver. "Sorry to interrupt your work,

citizen James, but we would like a word with you."

Chien-Chu turned, saw what appeared to be two impossibly clean people, and knew who they were. Police. Not the "chase a purse snatcher down the street" type, but the high-level "I wear suits, too" variety that had guarded him when he was president, and spent a lot of time looking under beds. But why him? He killed the torch and was amused when they moved closer. The agents received his thoughts as electronically transmitted words. "Me? What on Earth for?"

The male looked around as if checking to see who might be equipped to listen in. "Can we discuss this privately?"

The industrialist shrugged and ordered his face to smile. "Sure . . . if such a thing exists."

But the police had little interest in debating questions of personal freedom, not with their supervisor spot-checking their electronic conversations, and a tiny pinhead-sized microbug roaming around the top of Chien-Chu's helmet. They waited patiently while the industrialist gathered his tools, made his way across the equipment-strewn floor, and entered the lock. The three-way silence was more than a little uncomfortable by the time they had cycled through.

Co-workers stared sideways as Chien-Chu opened his locker, replaced his tools, and removed his overalls. The industrialist could practically hear their thoughts: I wonder what the poor schmuck did? I hope they don't search my locker. . . . Damn, that cop looks good . . . I wonder if?

But their questions went unanswered as Chien-Chu led the agents out into the hall and looked around. It was temporarily empty. "Okay, whoever you are, this is as far as I go without some I.D. and a *lot* more information."

The cops held up their hands palm out. Badges had been woven into the plastiskin that covered their wires, cables, and servos. The oval areas contained a back-lit confederate seal, a number, and a bar code. They *looked* authentic. But looks could be deceiving. Still, one of the agents activated a high-end portable scrambler, and Chien-Chu had the feeling they were for real.

The man spoke without moving his lips. He had police-issue black hair, non-confrontational brown skin, and hazel eyes. "My name is Lopez. Her name is Johnson. The president wants to see you."

Chien-Chu was surprised and allowed it to show. "The president? As in President Anguar? You've got to be kidding. What would the president want with a welder?"

Johnson was pretty in a predictable sort of blond way. Her voice was firm but respectful. "Please, citizen Chien-Chu, we know who you are, as does President Anguar. He sent a note."

Chien-Chu felt mixed emotions as Johnson unsnapped her belt purse and removed an envelope. Anger at the violation of his privacy, fear of what it might portend, and curiosity regarding the note she handed him.

The industrialist saw that his real name had been handwritten on the outside of the envelope and recognized Anguar's semi-incomprehensible scrawl. He tore the envelope and removed a heavily embossed card. The words sent synthetic adrenaline coursing through what was left of his circulatory system.

Dear Sergi,

Sorry to bother you, but the Hudathans
attacked Worber's World, and I could use some advice.

Respectfully Yours,
Moolu Rasha Anguar

One aspect of his personality experienced a mixture of emotions, including anger, sorrow, and fear. The rest, the part that had run a large company, and been head of an interstellar government, focused on the intellectual side of things. Who won the battle? How many casualties had been suffered? When would the Confederacy respond?

Of more importance, however, was the question he *didn't* ask because the answer was so apparent. The Hudathans had attacked because they had no choice. They believed that *any* sentient represented a threat, so a Confederacy of sentients represented multiple threats, and must be destroyed. Not just the government, but the member races as well, until all were eradicated.

Chien-Chu felt his knees grow weak under the weight of the guilt that rode his shoulders. Many of his advisers, General Norwood among them, had urged him to attack the Hudathan homeworlds immediately after the victory on Algeron.

But in spite of his son's death at Hudathan hands, and the deaths of billions more, Chien-Chu had resisted their counsel, and pursued what he believed was the wiser, more humane course. By imprisoning the Hudathan POWs on Worber's World and dismantling their war fleet, he sought to bring their leaders to the negotiating table. Yes, the Hudathans might choose continued isolation over membership in the Confederacy, but surely they would see the error of their ways and forsake conquest as the means to physical and psychological security.

But negotiations had dragged on, years had passed, and it now seemed that the Hudathans had used the time to build another fleet. A fleet with only one purpose, murder on a scale never seen before. So, like it or not, the responsibility was his, and Anguar would have his help. He looked from Lopez to Johnson. "The president wants to see me. Let's get going."

Even with a high-priority clearance it still took the better part of four hours to reach the spaceport, make their way through security, board a six-place shuttle, and blast up through the atmosphere. The government was in session aboard the *Friendship* and there was a constant flow of ships in and out of the ex-battleship's overcrowded flight deck. Finally, after sitting in a holding orbit for more than thirty minutes, the pilot received permission to "come aboard."

Computer-controlled co-orbiting robo-beacons lit the way and outlined a path so clear, so obvious, that even the most besotted fly-it-yourself senator should have been able to land without crashing into the larger ship's hull. A few still managed to do so, of course, which explained why the spacegoing capital boasted twice the number of repeller-beam projectors a ship of her size would normally carry, plus six search-and-rescue craft all ready for immediate launch.

But their pilot was sharp and ran the beacon-lit gauntlet with the surety of the ex–fighter pilot that she was, slowing her craft just so, and dropping the shuttle into the exact center of their designated parking space.

It took the three cyborgs only minutes to cycle through the ship's tiny lock and step down onto the repulsor-blackened flight deck. There was motion all around them as space-suited bio bods hurried to service newly arrived ships, robotic hoses snaked their way towards waiting fuel tanks, and small two-person maintenance sleds zipped over their heads. But outside of a wealth of radio traffic that Chien-Chu could access if he chose, the motion produced no sound.

A path that consisted of two equidistant yellow lines led them through a maze of spacecraft and equipment towards an official-looking hatch. Chien-Chu watched as a methane-breathing senator, safely ensconced in its own portable environment, was welcomed and ushered into the lock.

Then it was their turn. Coded radio transmissions zipped

back and forth between the agents and the officer of the guard. Four Trooper IIs, their armor buffed to a dull sheen, snapped to attention. Machine guns were extremely dangerous aboard any sort of habitat, so the borgs had been equipped with two arm-mounted energy cannons instead of just one. Their elbows came forward and their forearms went vertical.

Chien-Chu realized that he'd been honored with the Trooper II version of a rifle salute and nodded in response. *Everyone* seemed to know who he was. So much for his carefully constructed cover.

Like the Confederacy itself, the *Friendship* had been the subject of many compromises. Signs of that were immediately visible in the large, immaculately clean lock. Rather than the animated holo-art humans might have chosen for the bulkheads, or the multicolored gas swirls favored by the Dwellers, a numerically small but still influential race called the Turr had thrown their support behind an increase in the heavy metals export tax in return for the infrared diorama that occupied all four walls. Never mind the fact that only the Turr, specially equipped cyborgs like Chien-Chu, and certain classes of robots could see the ever-changing panorama of blue-green blotches, Turr honor had been served. That, and countless episodes like it, were a major reason why Chien-Chu had exited politics as quickly as he could.

The hatch opened to reveal a Ramanthian tri-person. Their space suits, luggage, and food grubs were racked on a heavily overloaded robo-floater. All three aliens wore identical black cowls that served to hide most of their insectoid-looking faces. They touched pincers to proboscis and bowed in unison. Chien-Chu did likewise. The formalities thus observed, both parties went their separate ways.

The industrialist hadn't taken more than three steps when

one of Anguar's many aides came rushing up. He was human, balding, and somewhat chubby. Beads of perspiration dotted a heavily furrowed brow. His hand felt damp and weak. "Citizen Chien-Chu! My name is Burton. Halworthy Burton, assistant to the president. I'm sorry I wasn't here to greet you at the lock. Please allow me to extend my heartfelt apologies. . . . The reception for the new senator from Drath ran five minutes over, Governor Bork had a heart attack in chambers, and the Haldar Amendment is coming up for a vote. Not that any of those matters excuse the way you've been treated. No, no, certainly not. The president left strict instructions. Come . . . I'll take you to his office."

Much to his combined relief and amusement Chien-Chu was never called upon to say a single word during the journey from the lock to Anguar's heavily guarded office. Burton had nothing to say and was happy to say it.

But the trip through *Friendship*'s maze of corridors and halls was fascinating nonetheless. Chien-Chu never ceased to be amazed by the diversity of intelligent life that flourished in one little corner of the galaxy. Amazed, and awed, for like the many races of man, each species brought its own science, art, music, literature, and traditions to an interstellar civilization that was unparalleled in its complexity, richness, and depth.

Yes, the necessary accommodations were almost always difficult, and very often messy, but well worth the effort. How horrible it would be if the Hudathans managed to destroy this rich tapestry of life, only to hang a single monochromatic shroud in its place.

"And this," Burton said grandly, "is the president's office."

Chien-Chu looked around and was amazed by the extent to which a decorator-being had managed to take artifacts, paintings, sculptures, and fabrics from dozens of worlds and integrate them into a wonderfully subtle and eclectic whole.

But as positive as the coming together of disparate races might be, there were plenty of problems, and Anguar had security to match. Lopez and Johnson disappeared, Burton excused himself, and a new set of agents, six in all, supervised as Chien-Chu passed through the latest in scanning frames, and was ushered into a spacious suite.

Anguar had increased the gravity within his quarters and worn the dreaded exoskeleton with an eye to his visitor's comfort and the requirements of the day ahead. He hurried forward. Both men embraced.

"Sergi! The new you looks wonderful! How clever you were . . . staging your own death. I was most upset. And it worked for quite a while. Our intelligence people stumbled onto your true identity while investigating a man named Harold Conklin. Sorry about that . . . but I wouldn't want you to think we did it on purpose."

Chien-Chu was relieved to hear it, assuming Anguar was telling the truth, which he probably was. His answer did credit to the politician he'd been in the past. "And you look even younger than the last time I saw you. How do you manage it?"

Though fully aware that the human was playing to his well-known vanity, Anguar was honored by the fact that the industrialist would go to the trouble, and generated a human-style smile. "By having sex every chance I get. Which is damned seldom anymore. Too much work. How 'bout you? Is that rig fully functional?"

Chien-Chu laughed at Anguar's directness and brushed the question aside. "Why Conklin? How did he come to your attention?"

Anguar had side-articulated eyelids. They opened and closed. The smile disappeared. "Simple. When not stealing money from your company, or abusing his position as an executive, Citizen Conklin passed his time selling secrets to the Clone Hegemony. The design specs for the Viper are an excellent example.''

Chien-Chu was shocked. "The Viper? It's the best we have.''

"Exactly,'' Anguar agreed. "Come, you'll be more comfortable in the sitting area.''

Once both beings were seated and the industrialist had refused the refreshments that his body no longer needed, the conversation turned even more serious. Anguar's huge light-gathering eyes had a slightly luminous quality. They were locked on the cyborg's twin-vid cams. "Never mind the Viper technology Sergi, it's a minor problem compared to the one we need to discuss. The Hudathans are the *real* threat.''

Chien-Chu nodded soberly. "Tell me what happened.''

"Better yet I'll *show* you,'' Anguar replied. "The first part anyway . . . before General Norwood was killed and the battle station fell to the Hudathans.''

The industrialist's heart sank as a wall holo popped on. What followed was a monotone-voiced narration of some of the most horrific battle footage he'd ever seen, complete with multiple SURCAM-generated angles, and background sound. The last shots, those of General Norwood's brutal execution by War Commander Poseen-Ka, and Hudathan troopers fighting their way through the battle station's corridors, confirmed his worst fears. The prisoners had escaped, a brand-new Hudathan fleet was on the loose, and every single human being on or around Worber's World had been murdered. All hope that war might still be avoided faded to black in concert with the video.

Both beings were silent for a moment, shaken by the images they'd seen, and depressed by the enormity of the task ahead. Chien-Chu remembered the seemingly normal, almost cheerful corridors. "Do the senators know?''

Anguar replied with a human-style shake of the head.

"No, not yet. I will tell them in my address to the general assembly, scheduled two hours from now. I wanted to speak with you first."

The industrialist spread his hands. "I'm honored . . . but don't know what to say beyond the obvious. We must learn from past mistakes. The emperor waited too long. We must respond quickly, respond with everything we have, and show no mercy. I was weak and the men and women of *Battle Station Alpha XIV* paid for my mistakes."

Anguar looked concerned. "Do not blame yourself, Sergi. My people have a saying: 'Strength can be found in common rock, compassion lives in the heart.' You did the right thing. And I agree with your analysis. As do my generals and admirals. Assuming that the Senate grants us the authority, the Confederacy will respond with all the force at its command, but certain problems will remain."

Chien-Chu knew a cue when he heard one. "Problems? What sort of problems?"

Anguar was silent for a moment, as if considering his answer. "Please don't be offended by what I'm about to say."

Chien-Chu shrugged. "Be direct, old friend, I can take it."

"Yes," the Dweller said thoughtfully, "I think you can. The problem is that the human race is the most warlike species the Confederacy has, and due to your remarkable fecundity, one of the most populous."

"Excuse me," Chien-Chu interjected angrily, "but the Confederacy has been attacked, and it seems to me that you *need* a warlike species or two."

"Of course we do," Anguar replied evenly, "the outcome of the war will depend on our largely human military forces. And that means that a disproportionate number of humans will be wounded or killed. Thousands, perhaps millions of human lives will be lost, all under the direction of a government they don't fully control. How long will your species put up with that before the calls for secession begin?''

Chien-Chu considered what Anguar had said. He was right of course. There had always been people who thought mankind should go it alone. And a disproportionate number of human casualties, coming so soon after the disastrous first war, would play right into their hands. "So spread the responsibility, arm *all* of the member races, and insist that they fight."

"Ahh," the president said, "if only it were that simple. The Dra'Nath are in hibernation and will remain there for another two years. The Arballazanies are shaped like gigantic worms. It would take a ship the size of this one to accommodate two of them. The Poooonara are even more fragile than my race and have no word for 'weapon.' The Say'lynt occupy thousands of square miles of ocean. I could go on and on. The point is that while all the member races evolved to deal with the conditions found on their particular home worlds, only a few, like the Ramanthians, the Naa, and the humans, evolved to deal with a threat like the Hudathans."

"So, what are you saying?" Chien-Chu asked impatiently. "That a defense is doomed to failure?"

"Of course not," Anguar said dismissively. "I'm saying that some species will be critical to the war effort, others will be useful, and some will play no role at all. What I need, no, what the *Confederacy* needs, is someone to study that middle category, to find ways to utilize their various abilities, and publicize whatever success they have."

"So that we humans will feel better about the massive casualties we're about to take."

"Exactly," Anguar agreed cheerfully. "And that's where you come in."

Chien-Chu stared into the other being's huge eyes. He

had underestimated his successor. The Dweller didn't want advice . . . he wanted cannon fodder. Happy cannon fodder.

For one brief moment the industrialist wondered if the separatists were right, if the human race should go its own way, but the knowledge of what would happen to the undefended races drove the thought from his mind. "All right, I understand the necessity, but why me?"

The politician mustered a human smile. "Who better to convince the human race than another human? And not just *any* human, but a past president? And not just *any* past president, but one returned from the dead?"

The counterattack had begun.

13

Accurate information cuts deeper than the finest blade.

Grand Marshal Nimu Wurla-Ka (ret.)
Instructor, Hudathan War College
Standard year 1956

Clone World Alpha-001, the Clone Hegemony

Booly thought Marine Major Stephanie Warwick-Olson was the smartest, sexiest, most fascinating woman he'd ever met. When he tried to figure out why, he couldn't quite decide. Was it the way she paced back and forth like an animal in a cage? The long, angular body? So skinny it shouldn't be sexy but was? The big eyes? High cheekbones? Lips? Or was it her mind? Laser fast and hard as steel . . . Yes, there was an age difference, but so what? Her voice jerked him back to reality. "Wouldn't you agree, Lieutenant Booly?"

The briefing room was large enough to accommodate the platoon's Trooper IIs plus the quad that had been assigned to him for this particular mission. Every one of Booly's eighty-plus legionnaires were staring at him and he didn't have the foggiest idea of what to say. He felt sweat surface through his fur, knew his mouth was hanging open, and wanted to die. In fact he was just about to admit that he didn't know what she'd said when a now-familiar voice came over his ear plug. "Yes, ma'am . . . surprise *is* the key."

Booly echoed Parker's words, saw Warwick-Olson nod thoughtfully, and knew that she knew. He wasn't sure *how* she knew, since the noncom had transmitted the message via the platoon's command frequency, but she knew nonetheless. Did she know *why* as well? He hoped not, and forced himself to concentrate on the briefing.

"So," Warwick-Olson continued evenly, "that's the high-level view. By eliminating the cell, we silence a source of anti-Confederacy propaganda *and* make the planet more secure for President Anguar's upcoming visit. Which is why I have temporary command of your platoon. Questions? No? Good. Now that we have the high-altitude stuff out of the way, let's take a stroll through the rocks and trees."

The next hour was packed with a detailed assessment of how the underground cell operated, its well-documented ties to Clone World Beta-002, and a wealth of other information, including each member's genetic makeup, their relationships to each other, the weapons they preferred, favorite foods, and other personal minutia. So much information. Booly started to wonder: How had the major or the spooks she worked with obtained this stuff anyway? The academy's instructors had taught him that even good intelligence summaries were about half fact and half guess work . . . so where did all the hard facts come from? He waited for a pause and raised his hand. Warwick-Olson nodded in response. "Yes, Lieutenant?"

"We seem to have an unusual amount of information at our disposal. Could the major comment on how it was gathered? And how reliable it is?"

Warwick-Olson was already looking his way. Her words

leaped the gap like electricity arcing between opposite poles. Or so it seemed to Booly, although the older officer showed no signs of similar feelings. "A fair question, Lieutenant. But one I can't answer without compromising classified information. Suffice it to say that I have a high level of confidence in this intelligence. . . . So high that I'd be happy to take the point. Good enough?" There were chuckles from around the room. The legionnaires weren't all that fond of marines but the major was okay.

Booly swallowed the lump that had formed in his throat. "Yes, ma'am. That's more than good enough."

"Excellent. Now, let's take a look at the neighborhood. Routes in, routes out, and our control points."

An aerial map filled the wall behind her and Warwick-Olson produced a light pointer. It circled the blocks in question, stabbed major arterials, and hovered over one particular building. It grew larger, filled the screen, and rotated.

Booly tried to concentrate, tried to hear what she said, but discovered that the major's olive green utilities had an unfortunate tendency to disappear without warning.

Whenever that occurred, the legionnaire found Warwick-Olson's pert breasts, narrow waist, slim hips, and long, lean legs to be very distracting. So much so that it would have been quite embarrassing had he been forced to stand up. No such disaster took place, however, so that he was able to get the major properly clothed by the time the briefing was over, and the troops were dismissed. There was a lot of good-natured talking and laughing as the platoon cleared the hall. Booly lingered for a moment and was rewarded with a private audience. It didn't go well. "Lieutenant."

"Yes, ma'am?"

"You seemed distracted during the briefing. Is there a problem? A gap in my presentation skills, perhaps?"

"No, ma'am! You have excellent presentation skills."

Warwick-Olson nodded slowly. Her lips made a hard, thin line. "I agree. I *do* have good presentation skills ... which means that the problem lies elsewhere. I could have chosen any platoon in this damned city but I chose yours. Why? Because *you* made an instant reputation for yourself by restoring discipline to a neglected command. Your CO was impressed, General Mosby was impressed, and *I* was impressed. All by a piss-ant wet-behind-the-ears lieutenant who can't pay attention to a briefing."

The major's eyes narrowed down to little more than slits. "Well, listen, Lieutenant, and listen good. Because if I catch a bullet tomorrow morning, that will leave *you* in command, and the way things stand right now, half the platoon might die because you were daydreaming. Now take this disk, study my plan, and have it memorized by morning. Fail, and I will drag your ass in front of the company CO. Get it?"

The disk was no larger than an antique quarter and hit the center of his palm with enough force to depress his hand. Booly hadn't been so thoroughly chewed out since his first year at the academy. A bullet would have been preferable to the shame and embarrassment he felt at that moment. His voice was a croak. "Ma'am! Yes, ma'am!"

"Good. Now get your ass out of here."

Booly snapped to attention, did a textbook-perfect about-face, and marched towards the door. It was the longest walk of his life.

It had been scheduled to be a sunny day, but the morning brought fog and a thin, steady drizzle. The platoon, formed up into heavily armed squads, stood waiting by their vehicles. Booly, exhausted from a sleepless night spent studying the major's plan, noticed that she was the only one who had equipped herself with rain gear. Did that mean what he thought it meant? That she had some clout with the

Clone Weather Control people? No, the clones wouldn't even give the Confederacy the time of day, much less the kind of weather they wanted. The woman was maddening.

Booly ran his eye over his troops one last time, checked what he saw against the carefully memorized plan, and found everything to his liking. He gathered his courage, closed on the spot where Warwick-Olson stood consulting an olive drab porta-comp, and offered a snappy salute.

The major paused and looked down her nose at him. "Good morning, Lieutenant. Thanks for pointing me out to any snipers that might be lurking around."

Booly felt stupid and let his hand fall like a wing-shot bird. "Sorry, ma'am. It won't happen again."

Warwick-Olson nodded. "Good. I'd like to live long enough to see my thirtieth birthday. Now, describe plan Alpha."

Booly fought the desire to think about the years that separated them and forced himself to focus on the plan of attack. "We move into the designated area from four different directions, seal the main arterials with Trooper IIs, and close on building 4321. The quad will deal with enemy armor should any appear. A pair of Marine assault boats will close off any possibility of an airborne escape.

"You will effect entry with Squad One, I will cover the back with Squad Two, Sergeant Parker will seal the secondary streets with Squad Three, and Sergeant Hafney will position Squad Four as a ready reserve. We will fire if fired upon but every effort should be made to capture the subjects alive."

Warwick-Olson nodded approvingly. "Excellent. It would seem I picked the right officer after all. Load 'em up."

The compliment felt good in spite of the fact that it didn't mean much after screwing up the day before. Which meant that Warwick-Olson was a good leader, he was one helluva pathetic s.o.b., or both.

The troops piled into their vehicles, the security gate slid clear, and the APCs growled out onto empty streets. Consistent with standard security procedures, and true to her word, Warwick-Olson took the point while Booly rode drag. If either were killed, or the convoy was cut in half, one officer would probably survive.

Trooper IIs, backed by the massive quad, loped along behind. The time of day, combined with the bad weather, reminded Booly of his childhood on Algeron.

He would always remember the sound of his uncle's voice as it woke him from a deep sleep; the soup's creamy texture as he spooned it into his mouth; the hard, almost unbearable pressure on his bladder; the trip to the freezing cold underground privy; wonderfully warm clothes snatched from beside the eternally burning fire; the ascent to the world above, where snowflakes flew, wooly dooths awaited their owners, and mountain trails led towards adventure.

Yes, his father had come along occasionally, but his duties as chief and ambassador left little time for hunting. It was one of the few things Booly regretted about his early childhood—that his father was missing from so many of his favorite memories. A radio transmission interrupted his thoughts. The voice belonged to Warwick-Olson. "Green One to green Two."

"Green Two. Go."

"Checkpoint One coming up. Execute. Over."

"Roger that. Out."

The plan called for the APCs and cyborgs to part company at the intersection designated as Checkpoint One and follow different routes to the objective. It was common knowledge that the clones kept a close eye on the Legion's movements so it was important to make the whole thing look as innocuous as possible.

Seated next to the APC's driver, Booly watched the appropriate intersection appear on the control screen, gave the necessary order, and felt the vehicle swivel to the right. A quick check of a smaller screen confirmed that a Trooper II named Omanski had peeled off and was following behind.

True to the regimented way in which the clones chose to live, the streets were empty, and would remain so until 0700 when everyone would pour out of their nearly identical apartment buildings and head for whatever work their genetic inheritance dictated. It made life in the Legion seem free by comparison.

Terrified of missing one of the turns necessary to reach their objective, Booly monitored street signs with extra care, *and* tracked the APC's position via a Confederacy-controlled global positioning satellite. This backup procedure took into account the possibility that the clone underground might have changed the street signs in an effort to confuse Legion forces. Just one of the many variables Warwick-Olson had planned for and he hadn't thought of. Her voice sounded in his ears. "Green One to Green Two."

"Green Two. Go."

"Position check, over."

"Position confirmed, over."

"Roger that, Green Two. Green One out."

Booly felt his stomach muscles tighten as the APC turned the last corner and headed for their final destination. A robo-cleaner, its lights flashing yellow, scurried to get out of the way. Booly ignored the warnings that bleated over the public com channel and sent a message to his squad. "All right, folks . . . we're almost there. Prepare to de-ass the vehicle. Don't fire unless fired upon. Lock and load."

Warwick-Olson's voice was crisp. "Green One to Green units . . . objective in sight. Two?"

Booly checked the picture supplied by the rearwards-facing vid cam. The Trooper II named Omanski had taken up his position at the last intersection and was quickly dwindling in size. "Check, over."

"Three?"

"Check, over."

"Four?"

"Check, over."

"All units are in position. Execute Option A, I repeat, execute Option A. Over."

The APC swung into an alley and stopped so as to block the ramp that led up and out of the apartment building's underground parking facility. The rear hatch made a clanging sound as it hit the concrete and the squad de-assed the vehicle. Booly opened the side door, looked to make sure he wasn't jumping into a hole of some sort, and bailed out. He checked, saw his legionnaires were headed for their pre-assigned positions, and turned towards the elephant gray building. In spite of all the preparation, all the prior thought, what happened next came as a surprise.

There was a barely heard thump as Warwick-Olson and the first squad blew the security door, effected entry, and raced up towards the sixth-floor apartment where the cell was headquartered. Glass shattered over Booly's head and a gun barrel poked out. Armor-piercing rounds had already started to punch divots into the APC's armor by the time he found cover behind a rusty red dumpster. The building housed hundreds of innocent people and a hail of bullets would almost certainly kill some of them. Booly gave his first combat order. "Hold your fire! Donk . . . be careful . . . but nail 'em if you can."

Legionnaire LeRoy Donk, a graduate of the famed "one

for one,'' or ''one round for each kill'' sniper school on Algeron, was still taking aim when Warwick-Olson screamed into Booly's ear. ''We've got a runner, Green Two! He's on a unicycle and coming your way!''

Booly had barely enough time to remember the gyro-stabilized units used by the local police, and to visualize how one could be ridden inside the building, when the back door exploded, and a man on a unicycle surged out through an avalanche of safety glass. He had a mini-launcher in one hand and a machine pistol in the other. The one-wheeled vehicle was controlled by a combination of foot pedals and pressure-sensitive knee pads. It bumped its way down the short flight of stairs without the slightest hint of difficulty.

Time slowed as the launcher fired and a series of mini-ature explosions marched across the area and flashed around the APC. Booly was in motion by that time, sprint-ing towards the point where his path would intersect with the unicycle's, firing low in hopes of disabling the machine. Rain spattered against his face and the smell of garbage filled his nostrils as the machine pistol winked red and brass casing arced through the air. He saw the man's face, read the hatred written there, and fell as a bullet slammed into the center of his chest. He tried to scream, tried to call for help, but couldn't get his lungs to work. Pain squeezed and darkness pulled him down.

The room was large, open, and tastefully decorated. A gas fire burned in the large tile-framed fireplace and care-fully arranged lights added to the overall sense of warmth. It was midmorning and General Marianne Mosby was talk-ing via a scrambled satellite link. She listened carefully, asked some questions, and nodded approvingly.

''Thanks, Major . . . I'm sorry the runner escaped, but outside of three casualties, that was the only flaw in an otherwise perfect operation. Congratulations. I'll see you at oh six hundred tomorrow.''

Marcus-Six, his day robes swirling around his legs, entered with a tray. Steam rose from a pair of ceramic mugs and filled the air with the rich scent of chocolate. He put them down on a low-slung table as Mosby folded her communicator in half and dropped it into a civilian-style handbag. ''The chocolate smells delicious, Marcus, thank you.''

Marcus smiled, reveled in the scent of her perfume, and sat down beside her. He knew he shouldn't, knew she would test his resolve, but did so anyway. The truth was that he found her aggressive free-breeder ways strangely attractive and couldn't help himself. ''I'm glad you like it. How did the raid go?''

Mosby lifted a cup, tested the liquid against her lips, and decided to let it cool. ''Very well indeed. Thanks to the information you provided. One person got away. The rest were captured and will be interrogated.''

Marcus shrugged noncommittally. ''The interrogators won't learn much. All of the cell members trace their lineage back to five or six sets of political fanatics who were quite willing to die rather than to compromise their cause. Our founder thought such individuals might come in handy and my brothers have taken full advantage of their existence. They will be furious when they learn what the Legion has accomplished.''

''Which is one more reason why you should consider an alliance with us,'' Mosby said smoothly, ''before your brothers destroy all that the founder sought to build.''

It was the perfect argument, directed at his brothers rather than the system the three of them represented, and the Alpha-Clone knew that. *Knew* she was manipulating him. Then why did it work? How could he know what she was doing and be so powerless to stop it? And what did she want? An alliance with him, or with the Hegemony he represented?

Then he looked into her eyes, felt himself drawn slowly but surely to the eager softness of her lips, and knew the truth. General Marianne Mosby wanted both.

14

There is no better remedy against an enemy than another enemy.

Fredrich Nietzsche
Standard year circa 1875

With the Hudathan Fleet off Worber's World

Poseen-Ka strode into the *Death Dealer*'s enormous wardroom and saw that the necessary preparations had been made. The court, comprised of his old protégé Grand Marshal Hisep Rula-Ka, a relatively young war commander named Mimbu Zender-Ka, and a grizzled old sector marshal named Hulu Hasa-Na were already seated.

In keeping with the nature of the occasion, their chairs were backed by solid steel. His seat had an open back that symbolized his complete vulnerability and was located in front of them. He strode towards the chair and sat down. This was the second occasion on which he had faced a court of inquiry during his career and would almost certainly be the last. Not only had he lost an entire fleet to the humans, but the war as well, and the penalty was obvious. Death. It was an ignominious but altogether appropriate end to a failed career.

Rula-Ka wasted no time in calling the court to order. He

was splendid in his crossed battle harness and ruby red command stone. His voice filled the room. "By the authority of the ruling Triad, Section 3458 of military regulations, and the authority vested in me, this court of inquiry is now in session. War Commander Zender-Ka will read the charges."

Zender-Ka's skin was gray and tight across the plane of his face. He cleared his throat, glanced towards Poseen-Ka, and read from the printout in his hand. "Given that the fleet under War Commander Poseen-Ka's command was committed to action more than twenty annual units ago, and was subsequently destroyed, with collateral loss of lives and material, the court calls on said officer to answer such questions as seem pertinent, and to justify his actions. Failure to answer these questions, or to cooperate with this court, is punishable by imprisonment or death. Are there questions?"

There were none so Zender-Ka continued. "When the court is satisfied that the relevant facts have been heard, evaluated, and understood, a decision shall be rendered. The decision will be binding, final, and implemented within a single cycle." Zender-Ka's eyes darted around the room. "Questions?"

There were no questions so Zender-Ka gestured assent. "The relevant regulations having been read, and there being no questions, the court may proceed."

"Good," Rula-Ka said cheerfully. "It's my hope to have this nonsense completed in time for mid-meal. War Commander Poseen-Ka, you heard the charges, how do you respond?"

No one rises to the rank of war commander without developing political as well as military skills, so Poseen-Ka had taken note of the routine, almost lighthearted tone in Rula-Ka's voice and knew it meant something. But what? That the officers in front of him were simply going through

motions? That he'd be exonerated? Or that they didn't care
and were eager to rid themselves of a minor irritant. He
had witnessed and heard stories about both situations. He
worked to keep his voice level and calm.

"The charges are factually correct. I *was* in command of
a fleet . . . and it *was* destroyed. The enemy proved a good
deal stronger and more resourceful than previous encounters had led us to expect."

"Previous encounters that led to the destruction of seven
human-occupied systems, hundreds of ships, 1,237 research
stations, fuel depots, habitats, as well as isolated colonies,"
Rula-Ka put in sternly, "and were praised by the Triad."

Poseen-Ka kept his face impassive but felt a keen sense
of gratitude towards this onetime subordinate. What had
started as little more than a flicker of hope burned more
brightly now and warmed his body. The other officers nodded dutifully and did their best to look interested. All of
which suggested that the outcome was a foregone conclusion. Not to be acknowledged as such, but understood by
the same mysterious process by which so many things were
understood, and occasionally *misunderstood,* so that otherwise promising careers were sometimes terminated while
less deserving records won praise and promotion.

It was what Poseen-Ka privately thought of as the dark
side of a culture in which the deep-seated need for individual survival was so strong that larger social structures were
tolerated only because they provided the means by which
to dominate other sentient and therefore threatening races.
But his desire to survive was equally strong so he listened
for his cues. They weren't long in coming.

"The court thanks Grand Marshal Rula-Ka for setting
the record straight," Zender-Ka said soberly. "Please continue."

Poseen-Ka chose his words with care. "After the battle,
my troops and I were confined on the surface of a planet

the humans call Worber's World. We remained there until freed by a fleet commanded by Grand Marshal Rula-Ka.''

"Who is well aware of the valiant assistance rendered by War Commander Poseen-Ka and his troops," Rula-Ka intoned, "saving thousands of Hudathan lives. Video of that battle has been forwarded to the Triad and will be seen by millions of Hudathan citizens.''

Poseen-Ka looked at his onetime subordinate and realized that his previous assumptions were wrong. This was *more* than a well-orchestrated attempt to save what was left of a mentor's career, this was part of a carefully designed public relations campaign calculated to build civilian support for another war and the sacrifice it would entail. The microbots, the secret weapons factories, and the ensuing ambush were all part of an elaborate script. A script written by Grand Marshal Rula-Ka.

Rula-Ka inclined his head as if reading Poseen-Ka's thoughts and confirming his conclusions. It was Zender-Ka who spoke. "The court is once again indebted to Grand Marshal Rula-Ka for his timely observation. Would War Commander Poseen-Ka care to add anything to the account?''

"No," Poseen-Ka replied, "that covers it.''

"Thank you," Zender-Ka said politely. "Are there any questions for the war commander? No? That being the case, I see no impediment to a vote. Grand Marshal Rula-Ka? How do you vote?''

"War Commander Poseen-Ka executed his duties to the best of his ability. Not guilty.''

"Sector Marshal Hasa-Na?''

Hasa-Na, only barely awake by now, motioned with his right hand. "Not guilty.''

Zender-Ka inclined his head to the subordinate open-neck position. "Thank you. I vote 'not guilty' as well. Let the record show that War Commander Poseen-Ka is found innocent of all charges real or potential and declared fit for command. The court is adjourned.''

Stunned by both the outcome and the unexpected speed with which it had been achieved, Poseen-Ka stood to accept the congratulations of the officers who had judged him. Moments later he was ushered out of the wardroom and into Rula-Ka's private quarters, where a table had been set and a feast awaited.

Although the Hudathan had already enjoyed some excellent meals since his release, he still felt the urge to gorge himself on all the foods he'd been denied for the last twenty years. But the military surgeons had warned him against the dangers of excess so he limited himself to small, carefully chosen portions.

Knowing Poseen-Ka would want to devote most of his attention to the food, Rula-Ka used the opportunity to brief the recently freed officer on the strategic situation. ''Here . . . have some marinated tripe. A favorite, as I recall. At least that remains the same. Many things have changed. Take the Triad, for example . . . Ibaba-Sa finally died. Some say of natural causes. Others aren't so sure. Kora-Ka had the good sense to retire and Taga-Ba grew so senile the clan had him institutionalized. Poor old fart. Here . . . try some sour bread. All of which means increased opportunity for those who were not closely aligned with the previous Triad and are on friendly terms with the new one.''

''And Grand Marshal Rula-Ka?'' Poseen-Ka asked politely. ''Would it be fair to say that he falls into the latter category?''

''Yes, it would,'' Rula-Ka said smugly, helping himself to a second portion of his favorite pudding. ''So much so that I will need some capable officers if I am to accomplish all that the new Triad expects of me.''

Well aware that the conversation was proceeding exactly as Rula-Ka wanted it to, Poseen-Ka had no choice but to go along. "I'm pleased to hear it. Is there any way in which I could be of assistance?"

The pudding rattled as it was drawn up through a large straw and into Rula-Ka's slit-shaped mouth. He talked with his mouth full. "Yes, old comrade, there is. It isn't fair, what with your imprisonment and all, but the race requires your skills. I want you to accept a jump to sector marshal and command the new fleet."

Suddenly, Rula-Ka's eyes burned with internal fire, and eating utensils jumped as his fist hit the table. "More than that, I want you to *destroy* the Confederacy with the same ruthless efficiency a doctor reserves for disease-bearing bacteria! Not a single life, race, or ecology will be spared. Your job is revenge. Give it to us . . . and the entire race will be grateful."

A lifetime of obedience urged Poseen-Ka to say yes, to grab the chance at redemption and never look back. But experience had taught him that humans were extremely hard to kill. He gestured his respect. "Your offer does me great honor. I hesitate to speak lest I shame myself and therefore you."

Rula-Ka wiped his mouth with the back of a gigantic fist. "Never. You had a saying when I was young. 'Silence teaches nothing.' Teach me that I might learn."

Poseen-Ka spoke carefully. "I know nothing of the fleet that you spoke of . . . but I know this: The last fleet under my command was equal, if not superior to what the humans eventually brought to bear, and it was destroyed. We lost because I was too cautious, because the human cyborgs defeated us on the ground, and because the humans came together at the critical moment. I promise to learn from *my* mistake . . . but what of the rest?"

Rula-Ka hissed his approval. "An excellent analysis! Correct in every detail. Which is why we spent years developing cyborgs of our own, and are taking steps to divide

the enemy into at least two warring factions. Are you finished? Excellent. Come. We have a meeting to attend.''

The Alpha clone known as Antonio knew the Hudathans
would have little or no interest in what he looked like, but
couldn't resist the temptation to check his reflection in the
mirror anyway. He was well aware of the fact that his
brothers were contemptuous of the carefully arranged ringlets of hair and that was a large part of the reason why he
liked them. They made him different and therefore more
significant. But what of the horizontal worry lines that ran
the width of his forehead? Were they deeper now? More
prominent? He knew they were.

What had started as cheerful acquiescence to Pietro's latest plan had turned into a source of unremitting worry.
What if Marcus was correct? What if the Confederacy really *was* the lesser of the two evils? What if the Hudathans
had lured them into a carefully laid trap? A somewhat unlikely possibility given the number of Hegemony ships on
hand . . . but what if?

Still, it wouldn't do to reveal his doubts to Pietro, not
with the aliens already aboard. He shook his head, saw his
reflection do likewise, and turned away. Ten steps carried
him through the hatch and out into a busy corridor. Crew
people, all copies of ten basic tech types, saluted respectfully. Antonio nodded politely, turned down the appropriate
passageway, and found his brother waiting by the main
lock. He wore the usual toga, clasp, and frown. He started
to say something but a light flashed green and a tone cut
him off. The hatch cycled open.

Antonio had seen holovids of course, but was psycho-
logically unprepared for how large the Hudathans were.
Large and menacing. It took an act of will to remember
that the aliens were on *his* turf rather than the other way
around. Pietro did the talking. ''Welcome aboard! Please

accept our apologies if we inadvertently omitted courtesies of rank or title.''

The lead Hudathan, an imposing specimen who wore shoulder belts with a ruby red stone set where they crossed each other, spoke via the translator that rode his waist strap and fed his implant. His voice had a hissing quality. ''Thank you for your concern, and please accept our apologies for failing to observe whatever protocols apply to guests. While we have killed millions of your kind we have never had a reason to learn about your culture.''

Antonio felt his blood turn ice cold. Were the words intended as a threat? Or a simple statement of fact? Pietro opted for the second and less ominous interpretation. ''Of course. I am known as Pietro and this is Antonio. Together with our brother Marcus we rule the Clone Hegemony and are known as 'The Triad of One.' ''

''I am Grand Marshal Hisep Rula-Ka,'' the first Hudathan said tightly. ''This is Sector Marshal Poseen-Ka, his adjutant Arrow Commander Nagwa Isaba-Ra, and my adjutant, Spear Commander Pasem Dwaneka-Ba. We have a tripartite leadership council as well, which gives us something in common, and bodes well for an agreement.''

Antonio noticed that the second Hudathan was visibly older than the first, and somewhat shrunken, as if he were recovering from an extended illness. The other two were as healthy as the first and just as intimidating.

Happy to let Pietro take the lead, Antonio found himself paired with the alien known as Poseen-Ka and was interested to note that he wore no translator and spoke standard with a minimal accent. ''I haven't seen any human ships since the war. Is this one typical?''

Antonio knew that an honest answer could have military value but figured the Hudathan spy drones had already furnished them with the information anyway. ''Yes, it's typical of Hegemony invader-class cruisers, but not of

Confederacy ships, which tend to be larger and more heavily armed. We prefer to have smaller vessels but more of them.''

Poseen-Ka nodded the way humans do and committed everything he saw to memory. Based on what he'd learned in the past from the renegade named Baldwin, he knew that the humans saw Rula-Ka's willingness to board one of their ships as a sign of weakness, which served to emphasize their stupidity. Who in their right mind invites a member of another clan into the ancestral fortress? No one, that's who.

So it was with considerable interest that Poseen-Ka observed the way in which the ship was laid out, the mostly identical crew, and the body language of those around him. A rather useful gift, courtesy of two dead humans. Baldwin and the female named Norwood.

The briefing room was quite large but had been made smaller through the addition of movable partitions. Chairs, each specially constructed, were positioned so that each Hudathan would have a section of wall protecting his back. Poseen-Ka was impressed by his hosts' attention to detail and raised his estimates of their intelligence. Once seated, and supplied with refreshments he had absolutely no intention of consuming, Rula-Ka got to the point.

''Our forces attacked and destroyed the Confederacy habitat known as *Battle Station Alpha XIV*. This is but the first step of what will be an all-out effort to impose Hudathan control over this sector of the galaxy. The Clone Hegemony has two choices: you can stand with the Confederacy and die, or stand against them and live. Which will it be?''

Pietro found the blunt, almost insulting language hard to bear, but managed a smile. ''You get right to the point, Grand Marshal Rula-Ka . . . and I admire that. Please allow me to be equally frank. . . . While there is little doubt as to the strength of the forces under your command, the ultimate outcome of the war is still very much in question, as your presence aboard this ship proves. That means our choices are a good deal more complex than you indicated. We can side with the Confederacy, which could lead to your defeat, we could side with you, increasing the likelihood of victory, or we could sit on the sidelines and see what happens.''

Poseen-Ka saw Rula-Ka's eyes flash as they had a few hours earlier. ''Neutrality means nothing! Your are either for or against us! There is no middle ground.''

Antonio saw tiny beads of sweat pop out on his brother's forehead and knew his looked the same. His stomach churned and his hands began to shake. He lowered them to his lap.

Pietro struggled to sound casual and to fight the rising panic. ''Yes, of course. But under what terms? Suppose we side with you, and emerge victorious, what then?''

It was a key question and Poseen-Ka was curious to see how his new superior would answer. Rula-Ka leaned back and seemed to relax. ''The Hegemony would be free to live life as it does now but would not be allowed to expand.''

It was a rather obvious lie, since the entire point of the Hudathan offensive was to exterminate *all* sentient races, with an emphasis on humans. The female called Norwood would have laughed at such words and Poseen-Ka expected Pietro to do the same. He didn't. Much to the Hudathan's amazement, and subsequent contempt, the clone nodded, smiled, and accepted Rula-Ka's offer at face value. Documents were signed within the hour. A single lie, convincingly told, had reduced the enemy by 25 percent. Victory was possible.

15

How laudable it is for a prince to keep his word and govern his actions by integrity rather than trickery. . . . Nonetheless we have in our times seen great things accomplished by many princes who thought little of keeping their promises and have known the art of mystifying the minds of men.

Niccolò Machiavelli
The Prince
Standard year 1513

Clone World Alpha-001, the Clone Hegemony

Booly awoke to the smell of a perfume so delicate it reminded him of the scent his mother wore. But there was nothing motherly about the hand that slid down across the flat plane of his stomach to touch the quickly growing member between his legs. He opened his eyes, tried to sit, and winced at the pain, which was not just in his chest where the bullet had slammed the body armor against his sternum, but in his head as well, which had bounced off the concrete. Marine Major Stephanie Warwick-Olson nuzzled his shoulder and made soothing noises. "Shame on you, Lieutenant . . . the doctor ordered bed rest."

"But what . . ."

"Am I doing here?" Warwick-Olson finished for him.

"Visiting a sick comrade. That's what visiting hours are for, aren't they? And you were so sound asleep it seemed cruel to wake you . . . although that's what I decided to do. Oh my, something's standing at attention, and a nice one it is, too. I like your fur . . . it's soft and kind of bristly at the same time."

Booly felt blood rush to his face and wondered if it was all part of some erotic dream. The major began to move her hand up and down and he knew it wasn't. "But you and I . . ."

"Shouldn't be in bed together?" Warwick-Olson asked softly. "Oh, but we should, especially since we want each other, and are no longer part of the same chain of command. You *do* want me . . . don't you, Lieutenant?"

"Yes, ma'am, I mean yes, Major."

"Stephanie . . . please. Now, fortunately for you I am about to dispense a remedy that will improve your circulation, enhance your respiration, and ease the pain. Conventional practitioners might suggest that I wait until you are more fully recovered . . . but I subscribe to a more aggressive approach. Are you ready?"

"No, I mean yes, I think so," Booly said, glancing around the room. "What if someone comes in?"

"With Sergeant Parker standing guard? Not likely."

Booly started to wonder what Parker would think of the closed door but all such thoughts were washed away as Stephanie sat up and allowed the covers to drop away from her body. She was extremely slender, with breasts just as he had imagined, and delicately defined ribs. She watched his reaction, smiled at the response, and moved to her hands and knees. No sooner had the sheet-and-blanket combination been pulled away from his body than she swung a leg over Booly and straddled his torso. The glimpse of the dark triangle between her legs combined with her firm yet gentle touch sent even more blood to his already engorged penis and threatened a premature ejaculation. Booly bit the inside of his lip as Stephanie bent forward and electricity jumped between their lips.

What followed felt better than anything he had ever experienced before, including the experimental sex with his cousin and a subsequent encounter with another plebe. And if the sounds Stephanie made were any indication, she was enjoying it, too. The whole thing left him both figuratively and literally drained. They collapsed and lay in a tangle of arms and legs. "So," Stephanie asked, "how was I?"

Booly let his hand glide across the velvety smooth skin of her back and down along the bumps made by her vertebrae. "You were fantastic! The best senior officer I ever had sex with."

Stephanie laughed. "What? There were others?"

Booly kissed her lips. "A colonel and two generals. No majors."

"Good," Stephanie replied contentedly. "I'd hate to think there were any majors."

"Never," Booly said, his hand sliding down between her silky-smooth legs. What happened next took longer, and involved a more detailed exploration of each other's bodies, but was equally satisfying. When it was over Stephanie kissed him, made a trip to the bathroom, and started to get dressed. Her voice was businesslike. "Thanks, Lieutenant . . . do us both a favor and keep it to yourself. Hard though that may be."

"Of course," Booly said, wincing as his headache returned. "When can I see you again?"

Stephanie pulled uniform trousers up over long, slim legs and turned in his direction. "Whenever duty brings us together."

"So this is it? Slam, bang, thank you, Lieutenant?"

"Yup, that's about the size of it."

Booly felt hurt. "But why?"

Stephanie paused, sat down on the bed, and took his hand. Her eyes were serious. "Because there's a war on, Lieutenant. The news arrived this morning. The Hudathans attacked Worber's World, freed their POWs, and destroyed the orbital battle station. The president is headed this way, but once he's gone, I'll get orders and so will you. One or both of us is likely to get killed. Besides, I'm too old for you."

Booly searched her face. The war was news but secondary to the thought of losing what he'd just managed to find. "There's no way I can change your mind?"

Stephanie released his hand. "None."

Booly felt helpless. He remembered the way she had treated him. "I thought you didn't like me."

Stephanie smiled and tugged at her bra. "I *always* liked you. That was the problem."

Booly didn't know what to say so he remained silent as she finished dressing and headed for the door. She stopped just short of it and turned around. What followed was the first and only time she ever used his first name. "Good luck, Bill. You did a helluva job the other morning. You'll make a fine officer. Take care of yourself."

Booly mustered some words but the door opened and closed before he could say them. Life had given him something good and taken it away just as quickly. He swore at his luck, activated the holo set, and found some news. There was no mention of a war. The clones were sitting on it. Gritting his teeth against the pain, Booly looked for and found a uniform. It was clean and crackled as he pulled it on.

Fifteen minutes later, with his side arm riding his hip, Booly opened the door. Sergeant Parker, the latest in the nonstop round of volunteer guards supplied by his platoon, snapped to attention. If the noncom suspected that something had taken place between Booly and Major Warwick-

Olson, there was no sign of it on his cadaverous face. "Good morning, sir. It's good to see you up and around."

Booly nodded. "Likewise, Sergeant. I hear there's a war on. Let's see if the rumors are true."

Marcus saw Mosby long before she reached his office. She knew about the war, her uniform attested to that, and strode down the hall like the warrior she was. The security cameras tracked her one after the other while a computer spliced the shots together.

The clone watched the Confederacy officer approach with the usual mix of anticipation and alarm. General Marianne Mosby managed to be dangerous and alluring at the same time, qualities reminiscent of the founder, or the stories he'd heard about her, and wanted to believe. He stood as Mosby approached the door to his office. Her pace was just slow enough that the automated security system had time to scan her retinas and open the door before she ran into it. He was halfway there when she entered. "Marianne! You heard the news?"

Mosby nodded and accepted a brotherly embrace. "Yes, I'm sorry to say that I did. There was more than enough slaughter last time." She backed away to scan his face. "Why the news blackout? You can't keep an interstellar war secret for very long."

"Nor will I try," Marcus replied, glancing at a wall clock. "We are more disciplined in the way we distribute information, that's all. The four o'clock news will carry a full account."

"And which side will the Hegemony take?" Mosby demanded, passing through his office area and into the private quarters beyond. "The Confederacy's? Or the Hudathans'?"

"Who's to say?" Marcus replied evasively. "And why take sides at all?"

"Because there will be no room for neutrality," Mosby said sternly. "The Hudathans don't operate that way and neither do we."

They sat down at opposite ends of a white couch. Marcus knew the Confederacy was a good deal less unified than Mosby's statement suggested but made no attempt to counter her argument. Especially in light of the fact that Hudathan part was true and accounted for the considerable misgivings he had about the secret alliance that his siblings had established with the aliens.

Well, not exactly *secret,* since one of his spies had been present at their meeting. Which left Marcus in a terrible dilemma. Should he remain loyal to his brothers in spite of what they had done? Or side with the Confederacy, thereby splitting the Hegemony's forces and reducing the impact of the secret alliance? Mosby interrupted his thoughts. "I have some news for you."

"Yes?"

"The president's ship will drop hyper tomorrow morning. He will shorten his stay because of the war but still plans to come."

Marcus spoke automatically. "Most of the arrangements have been made. We will welcome President Anguar as we have in the past."

Mosby scanned the clone's face in an effort to discern what lay beneath the surface. She saw concern but couldn't see further. "We both know why he's coming. He'll ask where you stand."

Marcus forced a smile. "And I'll tell him, or at least I hope I will."

Mosby nodded deliberately. "Good . . . but there's more."

"More?"

"Yes, more. I want to know where you stand as far as *I'm* concerned."

Marcus felt his palms grow sweaty and his heart beat faster. "I don't understand."

Mosby got up and sat down beside him. She wore the slightest hint of perfume. The uniform wasn't sexy, or shouldn't have been, but seemed strangely attractive. Marcus fought the desire to reach for the big metal buttons, to undo the high-collared jacket, to hold the soft warmth of her breasts.

"Oh, yes you do," Mosby replied confidently. "It has to do with the way free breeders reproduce. No labs, no test tubes, and no syringes. We just say what we feel, strip off our clothes, and have honest-to-goodness sex. Sometimes we do it for fun and sometimes we do it to make babies. *Surprise* babies that don't necessarily have a gift for any one thing. And that's the fun of it, Marcus, *not* knowing and waiting to see. So what do you think? What would our baby be like? Would she be a politician like you? A soldier like me? Or something else altogether?"

Marcus knew that free-breeder sex led to chaos, knew that what Marianne suggested was wrong, but couldn't help himself. He reached for the topmost metal button, pushed it through the buttonhole, and started down a path from which he could never return.

Fisk-Eight turned the corner, stopped to look into a shop-front window, and used the reflection to check his back trail. He'd always been careful but never more so since the narrow escape from the apartment building. The off-worlders had come very close to neutralizing his entire cell and his escape aboard the unicycle had been more a matter of luck than skill. There was no doubt of the fact that they had been betrayed, and betrayed at the highest levels, since the location of the safe house had been a closely guarded secret, known only to those who lived there, and a tiny handful of high-level cadre.

Fisk checked the reflection one more time, assured himself that it was clear, and headed down the street. He was an average-looking man who had gone to great lengths to look even more so, a task made easier by his even features, light brown skin, and nondescript clothes.

But in a society made up of millions of look-alike soldiers, technicians, laborers, teachers, and cops, and less than a hundred anarchists, Fisk stood out as much as any free breeder would have, and had to fight for his anonymity. A check? Put in place by the Founder to make sure that her homegrown revolutionaries never got out of hand? There was no way to be sure.

The clone turned into an alley, walked twenty feet or so, and slipped into a doorway. He waited five minutes for a tail to appear but none did. Satisfied that it was safe, he touched a carefully concealed button, stepped out into the alley, and continued on his way. Cameras hidden under the eaves of nearby buildings swiveled, captured his image, and fed it to a nearby control room. Fisk-Three saw it, confirmed his brother's identity, and was waiting when Eight took a sharp right-hand turn and descended a short flight of stairs.

Fisk-Eight waited for the steel fire door to slide open, stepped into a small metal-walled room, and heard it close behind him. A full minute passed while he was X-rayed, weighed, and retina-scanned. Eight felt no resentment, no impatience, because security was of the utmost importance. The final door slid open and Three stood waiting to greet him. They embraced. "Greetings, brother."

"Greetings . . . I rejoiced at the news of your escape."

Eight held his sibling at arm's length. "Thank you. Fisk-Twenty was not so lucky. A sniper shot him through the head."

Three nodded grimly. "The free breeders will pay. As will the sympathizers who coddle them. Come, I will show you the progress we have made.''

Eight followed Three down a hall, through a door, and out into a carefully sealed warehouse. The windows were located high above the concrete floor and painted black. Smoke drifted through the light provided by six ceiling-mounted fixtures. There, supported by a maze of scaffolding, and served by a crew of androids, was an eight-foot-tall Trooper II. Or what *looked* like a Trooper II, since the fabrication of a *real* cyborg was way beyond the amount of technological-biological expertise that the Fisk brothers could bring to bear, or *needed* to bring to bear, considering the fact the machine had never been intended as anything more than an elaborate disguise. Three had been working on the project for the better part of a month and hurried to explain.

''This baby is a lot slower than a *real* Trooper II, which can reach speeds of fifty mph over relatively flat terrain . . . but that won't matter where our application is concerned. The electronics *are* important, though, especially the radios and the transponder.

''As with the real thing, this machine has a fast-recovery laser cannon in place of its right arm and an articulated fifty-caliber machine gun where its left arm should be. I had hoped to obtain *real* surface-to-surface missiles for the shoulder launchers but haven't been able to steal any. The replicas will pass any but the most detailed inspection.''

''Don't worry about it,'' Eight said reassuringly, ''you've done a remarkable job. Given the fact that the machine will be part of the presidential guard, the laser cannon and machine gun will be more than adequate. I look forward to using both on the free-breeder president and his Hegemony sympathizers.''

Three frowned. ''I mean no disrespect, brother Eight, but *I* built the machine, so *I* should have the honor of taking it into battle.''

Eight pretended to take the matter under consideration. The truth was that he had never for a moment intended to operate the machine himself. Yes, it was true that the person who killed Anguar, and thereby destroyed any chance of a Confederacy-Hegemony alliance would be venerated for hundreds if not thousands of years to come, but it was also true that he would be dead, a condition that Eight wanted to postpone as long as possible.

Eight thought it was particularly interesting that while physically identical, his brother and he were so different where certain key attitudes were concerned, and theorized that it was due to the different environmental stimuli they had experienced while growing up. He had grown up largely on his own, while Three had been reared in a state-run school, where he had been heavily indoctrinated. He did his best to look peeved.

"Well, if you insist, but it hardly seems fair. I've been working towards the same goal, after all . . . and that should count for something."

"And it does," Three said soothingly. "I'll make explicit mention of your contribution in my report."

Your *last* report, Eight thought cynically, soon to be filed. Externally he nodded his head agreeably, followed Three to the place where an android was testing a leg servo, and listened politely as Three went on. His sibling was an idiot but he couldn't help but feel cheerful. In a relatively short period of time, days at most, President Moolu Rasha Anguar would be dead.

16

And bow begat bow, and cannon begat cannon, and missile begat missile. Such is the lineage of war that each generation of weaponry is copied by the enemy and added to the inheritance of death.

Hoda Ibin Ragnatha
Turr Truth Sayer
Standard year 2201

Planet Drang, the Confederacy of Sentient Beings

O'Neal stepped out into the main channel and leaned into the oncoming current. The water pushed hard, but her Trooper II body weighed half a ton, and pushed even harder. A quick check of her sensors confirmed that the squad had followed her lead. They were blips on her heads-up targeting system and spread out to lessen the effect of an ambush. First came Yang, followed by Tyler, Hata, and Verbeek, with Khyla on drag. She had the unenviable job of walking backwards most of the time, guarding against an attack from the rear.

O'Neal listened to her servos whine as she forced her way through the oncoming water. Her readouts informed her that the river was flowing at a steady five mph, that the visibility index was seven on a scale of ten, and that the ambient temperature was 52°F.

The cyborg knew that an attack if any would almost certainly come from upstream, which would allow the frogs to ride the swift-flowing current and rake the patrol as they swept by. There were alternatives of course, like wading through the maze of stagnant channels that paralleled the river, but that meant forcing their way through knee-deep mud. A fate worse than a frog harpoon.

With that in mind, the squad leader kept to the right side of the river, where the current was weaker, and took full advantage of the relatively firm footing offered by the gravelly bottom. Depth varied as the cyborg moved upstream. Her headlike brain box broke the surface occasionally, providing glimpses of the river up ahead and the triple-canopy jungle that obscured the sky. Not that it mattered much, since it was pouring down rain, and almost as wet as being in the river. It was a crappy way to make a living, and only slightly better than being dead, which was where she'd been when the medics had jerked her back.

They said the odds against a meteor holing a habitat and doing significant damage were millions to one, but that hadn't stopped one of the little buggers from hitting the *High Stakes IV* at about thirty miles a second, punching a hole through the triple-thick hull, shooting the width of a large gaming room, and burying itself in the far bulkhead.

O'Neal, who had been hired to deal black jack, and show a bit of leg, remembered klaxons, a strong wind that snatched the cards off her table, along with anything else that was loose, and sucked the whole mess through a hole that had appeared on the far side of the room.

People screamed and ran for the door. Like the rest of the casino's staff, O'Neal had been through intensive safety instruction and knew exactly what to do. She stepped in front of the hatch, held up her hands, and shouted for calm. A dozen panic-stricken customers charged her. A ham-sized fist hit her chin and she went over backwards. The crowd stampeded over her body, crashed into the automatically locked doors, and screamed as more people collided them from behind.

The safety systems worked of course, just as the ship's architect had promised that they would, and sealed the puncture within the legally mandated five minutes, which was why most of compartment's occupants survived. But three people, O'Neal included, were killed. Killed, and brought back to life, *if* they would accept life as a cyborg, *if* they would serve the Legion, and *if* they made it through basic training.

Life over death had seemed like an easy choice at the time, a real no-brainer, but O'Neal wasn't so sure anymore. Not after eight long years on pus balls like Drang, fighting every kind of weirdo geek the Confederacy got into an argument with, while living in an artificial body. No, it wasn't much fun, and given the chance to make the decision all over again, O'Neal knew she might go the other way.

The attack came from the one direction the frogs had never used before . . . above. In spite of the fact that everyone had *seen* the beehive-shaped mud huts that lined certain riverbanks, and *knew* that the indigs were amphibious, they had assumed things wouldn't change. And they were wrong.

Bubbles exploded as mottled green-black bodies splashed into the river and allowed the current to carry them downstream. O'Neal barely had time to transmit a warning before she was locked in combat. "Frogs! Dropping from above! Backs to the riverbank and don't shoot each other!"

Outside of the fact that they had webbed feet, the indigs didn't look like frogs at all. They were skinnier, for one thing, with snakelike heads and long, willowy limbs. Their arms terminated in three-fingered hands that lacked the opposable thumb common to many bipedal tool-users but had skin-covered bone spurs that served the same purpose.

O'Neal saw that the first one was armed with the usual gun runner–supplied harpoon launcher and a wicked-looking belt knife. The frog brought the weapon up, grinned a toothy grin, and fired. A stream of bubbles trailed the spear as compressed air was forced through its tiny propulsion unit.

O'Neal's on-board computer identified the threat, acquired the target, and requested permission to fire. The cyborg provided mental authorization and felt the recoil as a pair of mini-torps left her shoulder launchers and sped away. The left one found the incoming harpoon, exploded, and neutralized the threat. The second weapon homed on the frog, followed the creature through a series of evasive maneuvers, and ran up its ass. The explosion was muffled and felt like a mild nudge. A curtain of pulverized frog drifted downstream, wrapped O'Neal in a bloody embrace, and was pulled away.

O'Neal felt an unexpected weight land on her shoulders. An indig had dropped from above and was busy sawing on her neck seal. A primitive but potentially lethal strategy. First, because of the fact that no one was supposed to get that close to a Trooper II, second, because her weapons-heavy arms weren't capable of reaching behind her head, and third, because joint seals were the softest and most vulnerable spot in her duraplast anatomy. Given a sharp knife, and a sufficient amount of time, there was a very real possibility that the warrior would cut its way through.

O'Neal turned, backed her way into the riverbank, and tried to rub the indig off. It didn't work. The frog's long, slender legs made good anchors and it was tough. The cyborg needed help and needed it fast. She triggered the radio. "Red leader to red team . . . I have a rider . . . and can't peel it off. Coming your way."

Cybernetic bodies were expensive, so the men, women, and computers that had put the Trooper II design together had been careful to establish bionic linkages between the legionnaires' brains and their electro-mechanical bodies. That's why O'Neal felt pain as the frog managed to cut through the first layer of the neck seal. The flashing red light that appeared in the upper left-hand corner of her vision was both redundant and unnecessary.

The cyborg swore as her right foot hit a rock and threw her head over heels downriver. Perfectly content to be underwater and upside down, the indig continued to saw.

Yang had killed a frog by breaking its neck and was waiting as the noncom tumbled in his direction. Unlike O'Neal and some of the others in the company, he *liked* killing geeks. His psych profile described it as ''. . . a typical displacement phenomena, common to military cyborgs, in which the subject hopes to reclaim some of their lost humanity by killing as many non-humans as possible.''

Yang felt what would have manifested as a grin on his original body and launched himself out into the current. It took a moment to sort out the intertwined bodies but Yang managed to wrap an enormous arm around the frog's neck and started to squeeze. The warrior, obviously still hoping to kill one of the monsters, continued to saw. Yang squeezed harder. The threesome hit a large water-smoothed boulder and bounced off. ''Don't worry, Sarge . . . I've got it.''

O'Neal was surprised and somewhat alarmed to find that she *wasn't* worried, and, if it hadn't been for the pain, would have been almost disinterested in the outcome. So she died . . . so what? What difference would that make? To her or anyone else? Maybe death would end the loneliness and the terrible sense of isolation.

But it was the frog who died, choked to death by Yang's relentless arm, and released into the current.

By the time O'Neal was freed the attack was over. Most of the frogs had been killed but a few had managed to escape downstream.

Khyla had taken a harpoon in a major subprocessor and had lost control of her right arm and all of its weaponry but everyone else was okay.

O'Neal moved her to the middle of line, ordered Verbeek to take the drag position, and cautioned the squad to keep their sensors peeled. The noncom didn't think the frogs had the command and control structures necessary to lay sequential ambushes, each attack driving the squad into the next, but she hadn't figured them for a vertical attack either, and had been lucky to escape with only light casualties.

It was a long, hard slog back to Firebase Victor and relative safety. "Relative" because the Confederacy base had been built on a platform that stood over a lake teeming with frog warriors. At night anyway, when they liked to serenade the legionnaires with eerie hoots, and long nerve-wracking screams.

The patrol was still two miles from base when O'Neal called in. "Red Leader to Victor Six. We're coming in."

The voice belonged to a bio bod nicknamed "Zits," after the condition of his skin. "Roger that, Red Leader. Camerone is . . ."

"The place where Danjou fought and died," O'Neal replied automatically. The pass phrase had always seemed a bit silly, especially in light of the fact that no one had ever heard the frogs speak a single word of standard without benefit of an electronic translator, but the major was a stickler for procedure, and based on experiences earlier in the day, rightly so.

The patrol climbed up and out of the river, swept the surrounding jungle for signs of an ambush, and trudged around the boulder-strewn outflow. The lake was large and calm. The never-ending rain made thousands of overlapping circles for as far as the eye could see. Firebase Victor was a dimly seen gray smudge a mile and a half out. Beacons flashed on and off, signaling its location to the shuttles that came and went. Some of the legionnaires were critical of the location, sitting as it did over a large body of frog-occupied water, but O'Neal disagreed. The lake provided and maintained a natural free-fire zone that would have been impossible deep in the jungle. They waded in and soon disappeared.

The lake bottom was muddy, which was why the Legion had laid down miles of elevated matting that radiated out from the platform like the arms of a starfish. The indigs destroyed pieces of the walkways every now and then, but the maintenance bots had always managed to repair them, so the game went on.

O'Neal fought the temptation to focus her underwater floodlights straight ahead and swept them left and right. The water was thick with silt, free-floating plant life, and other, less identifiable debris. The spots reached twenty feet out where they were lost in the surrounding gloom.

The problem with the walkways was that the indigs could lay ambushes to either side of them with the almost certain knowledge that a patrol would come along eventually. Of course that advantage was lessened to some extent by the fact that the Legion's tireless aqua drones identified 96.2 percent of such ambushes before they could be sprung.

Still, O'Neal had no desire to fall into one of the 3.8 percent of the ambushes that *weren't* detected, and kept her sensors cranked to the max, a policy that resulted in any number of scares as dimly seen fish glided by, but was necessary nonetheless. Nothing happened and the march was uneventful.

The cyborg sent a burst of code to the automatic defenses designed to protect the firebases's enormous support columns, received a tone, and led her patrol into the floodlit area directly beneath the platform.

The lock located in the base of Support Column Six opened, allowed the squad to enter, and closed behind them. The water level dropped as air was pumped in. O'Neal felt the elevator move upwards and was ready when the chemical spray came on. It was green and had been formulated to kill all of the spores and bacteria that clung to their armor.

The only problem was that it couldn't reach all of the nooks and crannies of a Trooper II's anatomy without some help. Which was why the squad raised their arms above their heads and shuffled in a circle like primitives worshiping the sun. Khyla needed help with her wounded arm, which would have made the whole thing look even stranger had there been someone there to witness the event.

Dripping, and as clean as technology could make them, the squad left the elevator and entered Firebase Victor. Gratings clanged underfoot, a maintenance bot slid along the ceiling, and a holo-projected likeness of the 3rd REI's flaming grenade insignia, with the words: Legio Patria Nostra (The Legion Is Our Country) filled the opposite wall.

The next two hours were spent being debriefed by a fuzzy-cheeked second lieutenant. He asked every question on his list, and freaked when the ambush came up, since it didn't fit any of the patterns he'd been told to expect. The result was a long series of tedious questions. The cyborgs had answered every one of them three times before the lieutenant called it quits.

Finally free, and looking forward to some well-deserved down-time, O'Neal was stopped in the hall. Clubacek was short and skinny but a whole lot tougher than he looked. "Hey, Sarge, the major wants to see you, on the double."

O'Neal nodded her massive head. "Thanks, Corp . . . I'm on the way."

Major Harlan's office was located one level up, and like

everything else on Firebase Victor, was intentionally large to accommodate Trooper IIs. O'Neal rapped on the door three times, and announced her name, rank, and serial number. The single word "Come" was sufficient to bring her inside. She snapped to attention. Armored shutters had been opened to let in the soft gray light. The furnishings were as plain and austere as the man they served. He had a receding hairline, a hooked nose, and a pencil-thin moustache. "At ease, Sergeant . . . welcome home."

O'Neal knew, as did all the other legionnaires stationed on Firebase Victor, that rather than allow his company to be overrun during the Battle of Algeron, Harlan had called on orbiting battleships to attack his own position, decimating both the Hudathans and what was left of his command. No one could say with certainty *why* the major had volunteered for a long series of commands such as the one on Drang, but some said it was a self-imposed penance for what he had done, while others swore he was crazy. Whatever the reason, he was a good officer and they were lucky to have him. He smiled. "I'd invite you to take a seat but there are regulations concerning the destruction of government property."

O'Neal had heard the joke before but laughed anyway. "Thank you, sir, but I prefer to stand."

Harlan nodded. "I hear you ran into some trouble out there." The fact that the CO knew about the ambush didn't surprise O'Neal in the least. He knew *everything,* or that was the impression she had, as did everyone else.

"Yes, sir. The frogs dropped from overhanging trees into the river. I was asleep at the switch and Khyla took a harpoon."

Harlan noted the factual response, the acceptance of responsibility, and the resulting consequence. He also knew that part of the blame was his, for failing to anticipate such an attack, and taking steps to prevent it. But that was for later. The noncom's response confirmed a decision made earlier. He sat on the edge of his desk. "These things happen. We learned something today. Everybody's alive. That's what counts."

"Yes, sir."

Harlan looked at her, as if trying to penetrate the armor, to get at the person within. "I have news for you, Sergeant."

O'Neal felt the bottom drop out of her nonexistent stomach. Mom? Dad? Were they okay? "Sir?"

"You have orders for a new unit being formed on a planet called Adobe. A very special unit that could play an important role in the war."

In spite of the fact that O'Neal wasn't especially happy about life as a cyborg, she hated what the Hudathans had done, and was ready to do her part. "Thank you, sir. May I ask what sort of unit? And what makes it special?"

Harlan smiled. "Beats the heck out of me, Sergeant. Drop me a line when you find out."

"Yes, sir."

"Good luck, Sergeant. You did a fine job here on Drang. We'll miss you."

"Thank you, sir." O'Neal clanked to attention, delivered a crisp salute, waited for the acknowledgement, and turned towards the door. Sixteen short hours later her brain-box had been pulled, lifted into orbit along with five others, and plugged into a special life-support system that allowed them to remain conscious. The cyborgs could sleep, play games, listen to music, live alternate lives, or sharpen their military skills via the ship's virtual-reality matrix.

O'Neal tried to enjoy herself, tried to see the journey as a much-needed vacation, but couldn't escape the feeling that something nasty waited at the other end of the trip.

17

The general who advances without coveting fame and retreats without fearing disgrace, whose only thought is to protect his country and do good service for his sovereign, is the jewel of the kingdom.

Sun Tzu
The Art of War
Standard year circa 500 B.C.

Clone World Alpha-001, the Clone Hegemony

President Moolu Rasha Anguar lay suspended in the gossamer-light silk-thread hammock and stared at the ceiling over his head. Some idiot or collection of idiots had painted a Confederacy seal up there so he could never forget who or what he was. The last thing the Dweller wanted to do was to strap himself into the exoskeleton and spend the day on the surface of Alpha-001. But that's what he had to do. Now that the Hudathans had declared war, the Hegemony was even more important than before.

The fact that he had fifty thousand troops plus the infrastructure needed to support them tied up on the Clone Worlds was bad enough, but the possibility that the Hegemony would actually side with the Hudathans was truly terrifying. Not because the Clones were a serious military threat, but because they could open a second front, and thereby siphon off resources that would otherwise have been directed towards the Hudathans.

That was why Anguar had agreed to visit Alpha-001 and take one last crack at diplomacy. The planet's ranking officer, one Marianne Mosby, thought it was worth a try, and had made some progress on her own. Of course she was sleeping with an Alpha clone, or so his intelligence network claimed, but that could be an advantage, depending on whether the general used the leverage to help the Confederacy or herself.

The Dweller made the purring sound that signaled amusement. Did the Confederacy have a decoration for heroic screwing? If so, he would make sure that Mosby received one. Unless she supported the other side, that is, which would make him angry, and result in her almost certain death.

A tone signaled the start of a long miserable day. Anguar swung his feet out of the hammock, found the floor, and shuffled towards the bathroom. He might be president but he still had to pee.

It could have been any time of day or night, thanks to the blacked-out windows and the artificial light. Previously busy androids stood here and there, frozen in place, their work complete.

Fisk-Eight felt a sense of anticipation as he watched Fisk-Three climb into the Trooper II's cramped control space and strap himself in. Unlike a lot of the things his cell had attempted, this plan could actually work, and assuming it did, the Alpha Clones known as Antonio and Pietro would be grateful. Yes, the morning would be an interesting one, and he looked forward to it.

"You look happy," Three said as he connected the last of the sensor pads to his legs.

Eight gave himself a mental kick in the pants for allowing his semipermanent scowl to slip. "I'm pleased with the quality of our work, that's all," he replied gravely. "And for the cell. *Your* victory will be *our* victory."

Servos whined as Three tested his controls. "I'm glad you feel that way, my brother. I was afraid that you envied my role in the assassination."

Eight shrugged. "I know it isn't seemly, but the truth is that I *do* envy your role, although I'm doing my best to fight it."

Three looked sympathetic. "And you're doing a wonderful job. I said so in the report I submitted last night. Is the truck ready?"

Eight nodded. "Ready and waiting."

Three attempted to look at his wristwatch and a huge arm moved in response. He laughed. "Good. Close the hatch and secure the seals. It's time to go."

Starke was tired, which was the way he usually felt after he dreamed about the crash that had destroyed his body along with those belonging to 152 other men, women, and children. He hadn't seen it, of course, or even been awake at the moment of impact, but he'd watched the computer-generated court-holos hundreds of times.

But reveille is reveille, and when Parker said "Jump," it was time to move. Starke released his joint locks, ran a systems check, and followed the other cyborgs out of the maintenance bay. The platoon had been stationed at Checkpoint X Ray for so long that the small parking lot seemed like home.

The unit formed by squads and came to attention as Booly appeared. Like the bio bods and cyborgs that fronted him, the young officer had paid special attention to his uniform. His fatigues crackled, light winked off his highly polished belt buckle, and his kepi sat just so. He stopped in front of Parker, returned the noncom's salute, and the inspection began.

The platoon had been chosen to be part of the presidential guard, a high honor indeed, and one that General Mosby took seriously. Which meant that the colonel, the major, and the captain took it seriously, too, as did Booly, who had no choice in the matter. He made a show of pausing in front of each cyborg, of flipping one of their multiple inspection plates open, and peering at the readouts within. But given the fact the platoon's maintenance techs had fussed over the Trooper IIs well into the night, there was very little chance he'd find something to complain about.

The same was true of the bio bods, all of whom had been preinspected by Parker and the other noncoms. That left Booly with little more to do than nod and mumble a litany of compliments. "Nice turnout, Paxton . . . good job, Starke . . . keep it up, Minh . . ." and so on, until the entire platoon had been inspected and found fit for duty.

Then it was time to form up and move out. The president and his entourage were supposed to arrive in front of the hat-box-shaped governmental complex at 1100 hours sharp. That meant the honor guard must arrive at 0800 so they could secure the area and still have time to complain about the rotten duty they had pulled. There were the usual orders, last-minute screw-ups, and unforeseen changes. Starke "heard" his name come over the radio and gave the mental equivalent of a groan. "Hey, Starke! Shake a leg. D'Costa has a warning light and the techs need time to scope it out. She pulled drag and I want you to replace her."

Drag sucked, but it wouldn't pay to say so, which left Starke with no choice. "Got it, Sarge . . . I'm on the way."

Finally, Booly led his platoon out of the compound and into early-morning traffic. It was morning rush hour and the noncoms struggled to keep the column "right and tight." But the Legion had been dirtside for a couple of years now and familiarity breeds contempt. Rather than avoid the off-worlders as they had during the early days of occupation, the clones used their three-wheeled cars to weave in and out of the convoy, pulled in front of the APCs, and peppered the legionnaires with rude gestures. The air turned blue with Parker's invective. It made absolutely no difference. Within five minutes of hitting the street the column was stretched out over twelve city blocks.

Starke tried to walk backwards, mindful of his responsibility to watch the platoon's rear, but it was hard to do, especially as vehicles swerved in front of him, pedestrians jay-walked every which way, and children hurled the usual insults. "Hey, freak! Hey half-man! Death to free breeders!"

Starke ignored the insults and the occasional rocks that bounced off his armor. It was tough, but the job was to keep a sensor out for *real* threats, the kind posed by people with shoulder-launched missiles, remotely piloted attack drones, and explosive-packed suicide droids. His surroundings were transformed into a blur of threat readings, trajectories, vectors, ranges, and heat sources, all flooding his senses, lighting up his displays, and vying for the cyborg's attention. Which was why he missed the significance of a little boy named Fisk Twenty-seven trotting alongside him on the sidewalk, why he ignored the truck that cut him off from the rest of the platoon, and why he died.

Fisk-Eight monitored the rear-facing camera. His truck was a large, boxy affair that smelled of freshly baked bread. By placing it where he had, the lead elements of the column would be unable to see what happened next. He spoke the word "now" into the voice-activated microphone and knew the right person would hear it.

Trotski-Eleven was twelve blocks away in a beat-up sedan. It hadn't been easy to stay in front of the military convoy but he had managed. The word *now* was all the stimulus he needed to side-swipe a triple-decker bus. The larger vehicle screeched to a halt, followed by Trotski and the entire column of legionnaires. The anarchist tilted his chin down towards his lapel mike, said "Done," and triggered the timer on the thermite bomb that rode in the passenger's seat. The car was completely engulfed in flames by the time he reached the sidewalk and vanished into the quickly growing crowd.

Fisk-Eight smiled happily as thick black smoke poured upwards to stain the sky. Traffic ground to a halt and he glanced at the ceiling-mounted monitor just in time to see the boy named Fisk Twenty-seven dart out from between a pair of stalled vehicles and slap a disk against the lower part of the Trooper II's back. Only the most careful observer would have noticed the manner in which the cyborg jerked as a half million volts of electricity were discharged into the legionnaire's electro-mechanical body. The electricity fried Starke's circuits, burned his subprocessors, and cooked his brain. A wisp of gray smoke drifted away from a heat vent on his port side.

It took less than three minutes for Fisk-Eight to lower the truck's ramp so that Fisk-Three, still encased in the Trooper II-like exoskeleton, could clank down and onto the finely grained pavement. Which was almost exactly the amount of time it took Booly's APC to push the still-burning car out of the way, put a call in to the local fire department, and move forward again.

Fisk-Three had walked around in front of the truck by that time, and was easy to spot when Booly checked the number of transponders in his heads-up helmet display, and found the correct number. The van, still manned by Fisk-Eight, stayed where it was just long enough for Twenty-seven to hook a cable around one of the Trooper II's enormous ankles, activate the winch that had been bolted to the truck bed, and jerk the now-dead cyborg off its feet. There was a loud crash as it hit the street. With that accomplished, it was a relatively simple matter to winch the carcass into the truck and close the door. The sight of this activity elicited cheers from the clone-packed crowd, who, while unsure of what had taken place, sensed that the Legion had received the short end of the stick, and heartily approved.

Eight smiled, nodded to the crowd, and pulled away from the place where Starke had died. Fifteen minutes later the truck was full of bread, Starke's body was being stripped of its armament, and the anarchist was having breakfast in his favorite café. There would be plenty of time to read the morning newsfax, trade insults with the regulars, and watch the assassination live. Life was good.

Marcus wore a formal toga secured with a double-helix-shaped silver pin. Mosby wore her full dress uniform with medals. They had spent the night together in the Alpha Clone's quarters and were waiting for Anguar to arrive from the spaceport. Marcus had suggested sex, and while Mosby would have agreed under normal circumstances, to-day was different. Duty came first, which was why she took the opportunity to slip a small disk into the Alpha clone's holo player, and waited for the video to appear.

Marcus frowned. "What's this?"

"Some propaganda," Mosby said honestly. "Ignore the narration and watch the pictures. They were taken on the surface of Worber's World, but it could have been Alpha-001, or 002, or 003, and *will be* if we lose the war."

Marcus watched Norwood and her troops walk into the Hudathan ambush, watched them fight, and watched them die. The narration had been created with the Confederacy's citizens in mind, and was therefore open to question, but the video was undeniably real, not because it *couldn't* be faked, but because he knew it *hadn't* been faked, and the knowledge made him sick. He watched a Hudathan execute a female general and knew it could have been Marianne. Could *still* be Marianne. He thought about what she had come to mean to him, about the life that could be growing inside her belly, and knew he could never allow it.

The Alpha clone touched the coffee table's control corner and the holo tank snapped to black. "Marianne, there are some things that you and President Anguar need to know. My brothers entered a pact with the Hudathans. They agreed to open a second front that will split your forces between the aliens and the Hegemony."

Mosby nodded calmly. She was disappointed but not especially surprised. "They told you this?"

Marcus shook his head. "No. I have a spy that they don't know about. A clone taken from an officer named Arrow Commander Nagwa Isaba-Ra. The real Isaba-Ra was tracked and killed while taking long-range sensor scans of Alpha-001. Knowing the Hudathans would continue to be a threat, I gave my scientists permission to replicate the scout's body, scrub the resulting brain, and download one of our most experienced agents into the newly vacated tissue. He returned home to the Hudathan fleet, received a hero's welcome, and was assigned to War Commander Poseen-Ka. He was present when my brothers cut their treacherous deal."

Mosby's eyebrows shot upwards. She was surprised. Not so much by the technology involved, since that had been around for a long time, and been outlawed by the rest of the human race, but by her lover's foresight, and ruthless attention to what he believed to be his duty. It was a quality they shared and she had thought about. To what extent does the means justify the end? The question was as old as her profession and nearly impossible to answer. She focused on other more immediate concerns. "Your spy is an aide to

Poseen-Ka? *War Commander Poseen-Ka?* The same one we just watched?''

Marcus had been unaware that the Hudathan he'd seen put a bullet between General Norwood's eyes, and the officer to whom his spy had been assigned were one and the same. The knowledge came as a shock and served to reinforce the appropriateness of his decision.

Mosby started to pace back and forth between the coffee table and the gas fireplace. ''So Poseen-Ka is still in a position of power . . . and we have a spy on his staff. This changes everything.''

Marcus noted the ''we,'' started to correct her, and thought better of it. Right or wrong, the decision was made.

Convinced that ornamental office buildings did little but instill distrust in the general population, the Founder had specified that all such buildings would be plain and drab, and there was little doubt that her architects had taken the good doctor at her word. Booly could not remember seeing a less interesting building in his entire life. It was large, gray, and with the exception of its cylindrical shape and unblinking windows, completely without ornamentation of any kind. A park, which fronted the building, and was of the same diameter, served to complete one of the figure eights that Hosokawa seemed to favor, and could be seen on any aerial map of the city.

Color, such as it was, came from the bunting that had been draped over the reviewing stand, the dress uniforms that swarmed over the area, and the standards that snapped atop the long, slender flagpoles.

The gaiety, or appearance of it, was a nearly meaningless gesture, since the citizens who had been commanded to line the U-shaped drive were a somber bunch, and clearly wanted to be somewhere else. Still, matters of protocol had to observed, so Marcus had ordered a sufficient number of bystanders to give the occasion some weight.

Although the president's civilian bodyguards retained responsibility for overall security, Booly had been given secondary control of the area immediately surrounding the review stand, and took the assignment seriously. During the hours since he and his platoon had arrived, they had swept the area for bombs, set up lanes of fire that could be used to repulse a full-scale military attack, and stepped through a variety of maneuvers that had been devised and rehearsed via interactive virtual-reality training scenarios. As a result, Booly's troops could handle anything from an unexpected plane crash to an outbreak of food poisoning.

Still, there's no such thing as being *too* ready, and the president was due to arrive in fifteen minutes, so Booly took one last tour of his platoon and their positions. While the bio bods could be useful in a single assassin scenario, the president's bodyguards were the primary line of defense, and the legionnaires were there to handle crowd control, or in the unlikely event of a massed assault, to add their firepower to that of the security detail.

The cyborgs were more critical, however, since they were the president's *only* defense against an armored attack, or aircraft that somehow managed to elude the fighters that prowled the sky overhead.

With that in mind, Booly paid close attention to the way the Trooper IIs were situated and wished he'd been allowed to bring some quads. Their heavy weaponry would have been welcome at either end of the drive, but they were bulky, and thought to be too imposing, especially on the evening news, where it might appear as if the already-subdued crowd were there at gunpoint. So the Trooper IIs would have to do, and Booly approached each one looking for weak points.

Fisk-Three watched the legionnaire's slow, methodical approach with butterflies in his stomach. Each and every moment since joining the column had been fraught with danger. Would someone notice a difference between the way his exoskeleton looked and the real thing? Would they ask a question he didn't know the answer to? Would he unintentionally draw attention to himself? These questions and more had haunted him ever since the charade had begun. Now an officer was approaching, speaking with each borg in turn, and making small adjustments to the way they were positioned. Beads of sweat broke out on Three's forehead. He wanted to wipe them away but couldn't.

"This is Big Dog Four. We are mean, green, and clean. Five from the door."

The voice boomed through Booly's ear plug and belonged to the huge black man who headed Anguar's mostly human security detail. His name was Slozo, Jack Slozo, and Booly feared him more than potential assassins. The message meant that the trip from the spaceport had gone smoothly, there were no signs of opposition, and the motorcade would arrive in less than five minutes.

Booly debated whether to inspect Starke at all, decided to give the cyborg a quick once-over, and beat feet back to his command position. He analyzed the cyborg's field of fire as he approached.

Fisk-Three had excellent optics at his disposal and used them to switch back and forth between the quickly approaching officer and the review stand. It was thick with minor functionaries. They swirled suddenly as two additional figures appeared, one of whom was clad in a toga, the other in full military uniform. This was the part that Fisk Eight didn't know about, the fact that he had been given orders to waste the traitorous Marcus, *and* his free-breeding military whore, before she corrupted the entire planet with her perverted ways. Because when Marcus died, killed by a berserk Trooper II, any chance of an alliance with the Confederacy would die with him. Anguar amounted to a desirable but almost secondary target.

"Starke?"

Three jerked his attention back to the officer who stood in front of him. There was something about the legionnaire's tone of voice, and the expression on his face, that signaled danger. The anarchist felt a tremendous need to go to the bathroom and fought to keep it in. "Sir?"

"Your voice synthesizer sounds different."

"Yes, sir. I'm having some trouble with my radio. That could account for it."

Booly nodded thoughtfully. "Yes, I suppose it could. But what happened to the unit decal on your right shoulder? The dent over your right knee joint? And the death's head that Private Leiber painted on your left forearm? Where are they?"

Fisk-Three began to fire before his arm was pointed at the review stand. Dirt geysered next to Booly's left boot as the armor-piercing bullets hit the ground, dug a trench to the curb, and sparked their way towards the bunting-draped platform. Booly reacted without thinking and was hanging from the Trooper II's gun arm by the time the words came out of his mouth.

"Green Two to Big Dog Four . . . condition red! I repeat, condition red!"

Slozo was far too professional to question or ignore the report. The machine-gun bullets were still ricocheting off the cement and screaming through the park when the presidential motorcade pulled a U-turn and headed for the airport. Assault craft, each loaded with a platoon of legionnaires, took off from checkpoints located throughout the city, and converged over the convoy. A thousand fingers rested on a thousand triggers. One threat, one hostile move, and everything within a half-mile of the main boulevard would be destroyed.

Mosby's combat-trained reflexes were quicker and more appropriate than the Alpha clone's. She pushed him down and crouched over his body with side arm drawn. The functionaries, all members of three basic administrative genotypes, acted in concert. Two groups dived for cover, many screaming in fear, while the third stood as a bulwark between their leader and the crazed Trooper II.

Servos whined in protest as Booly pulled down on the exoskeleton's gun arm. But the exoskeleton's laser arm was unencumbered and there was no way to stop it. He yelled into his helmet-mounted boom mike. "Platoon! I am your target! Fire!"

Fisk-Three felt something warm flood down his right leg as he shook the officer free and aligned both weapons on the review stand. Splinters flew, bunting sagged, and bodies were tossed into the air under the impact of his bullets. Had he hit the targets? The anarchist was trying to see when two shoulder-launched missiles, hundreds of rounds of armor-piercing ammunition, and six laser beams all converged on his position. The resulting explosion left nothing larger than an I.D. card for the investigators to find and piece together. Booly, momentarily deafened, but otherwise unhurt, lay on his back and watched contrails stretch themselves across the sky. It felt good to be alive.

Many miles away, in a café full of stunned and amazed people, all watching the ceiling-mounted monitors, a man named Fisk-Eight shook his head sadly, wiped his mouth with a cloth napkin, and got to his feet. It had been a good plan, a fine plan, but Three had fired too early. What could he have been thinking of anyway? Ah well, such is the lot of the revolutionary. Here today and gone tomorrow. Eight smiled, left a tip, and walked out the door. Sirens screamed in the distance.

• • •

Explosions are funny things, and unless carefully planned, produce unpredictable results. So, in spite of the fact that Booly was spared when the exoskeleton blew up, a woman standing a hundred yards away had been killed by a piece of flying shrapnel. He had been very, very lucky, as had Alpha Clone Marcus, General Mosby, and President Anguar, all of whom had emerged from the assassination attempt not only alive, but in some ways better off, unlikely though that might have seemed.

Which explained why Booly was dressed in his number one uniform, and waiting nervously in one of *Friendship*'s well-appointed corridors, while his superiors finished a meeting in Anguar's office. The waiting was even worse than combat, and the young officer had sweated through the inner layers of his uniform by the time one of the president's many assistants, a chubby young man named Halworthy Burton, appeared and led him inside.

The artifacts, paintings, and sculptures were little more than a blur as the legionnaire followed Burton through a scanning frame, past some heavily armed bodyguards, and into the president's inner sanctum. Anguar, Marcus, Mosby, and some other sentients that Booly had never seen before stood as he entered, and looked at him with open curiosity. But it was the president himself who stepped forward to greet Booly. The smile had a forced quality but was reassuring nonetheless. "Lieutenant Booly . . . welcome aboard. My staff treated you well, I trust?"

What Booly had hoped would emerge as a confident baritone came out as a broken croak. "Yes, sir. Everyone has been most kind."

"Excellent," Anguar replied jovially. "Please allow me to introduce Alpha Clone Marcus, General Mosby, who tells me that in addition to being both resourceful and brave, you are an excellent dinner companion. Ambassador

Undula represents the Sovereign Worlds of Tull . . ."

The names and titles started to blend together after a while, and Booly found himself nodding and mumbling "glad to meet you, gentle being," over and over again. Finally, when the introductions were over, the young officer was invited to sit, which he did, with his back ramrod straight and his hands folded in his lap. The compartment was warm and he felt a little light-headed.

"So," Anguar began, "I imagine that you're impatient to get this over and return to your unit. That being the case, we will be as efficient as possible. We brought you here to let you know how much we appreciate your attention to duty, quick thinking, and personal bravery. Thanks to you and your platoon, we are not only alive, but better off than before. In spite of the fact that the people of Alpha-001 have no great love for the Confederacy, they *do* have feelings for our friend Marcus, and were quite disturbed about the attempt to assassinate him. And while we have reason to believe that his brothers may still open a second front, their efforts will be substantially weakened. On behalf of the entire Confederacy I would like to thank you. General Mosby?"

Mosby nodded, stood, and walked over to where Booly sat. He stood without being asked. The general smiled and undid his shoulder boards. "Lieutenant to captain in less than a year . . . Not bad for someone who got drunk, lost a knife fight, and received one last chance."

Booly was still blushing from the general's blunt, rather negative appraisal of his career, when he was ushered out and into the hall. Still, he should have been happy, the legionnaire knew that, but Starke's death, combined with those of twelve bystanders, made that impossible.

He fingered the hard copy Burton had handed him on

the way out, removed the protective tab, and pressed his right index finger against the print-sensitive dot. Words appeared out of nowhere. Algeron! He had orders for Algeron! Booly was going home.

18

Just as we are one with the ocean, and the ocean is one with the planet, the planet is one with the cosmos. In unity lies perfection.

The Say'lynt Group Mind known as "Raft One"
As dictated to Dr. Valerie Reeman
Standard year 2836

Planet Earth, the Confederacy of Sentient Beings

Dr. Cynthia Harmon was angry, an emotion that showed in the way she slammed the auto cab's door, and stepped into traffic. She was a small woman, with a pinched face, and the body of a natural gymnast. Her clothes were casual and nearly identical to the ones back at the hotel. She squinted at a building on the far side of the street. It looked more like the warehouse it had been than headquarters for the Department of Interspecies Cooperation. Whatever that might be.

Ground cars screeched to a halt and drivers swore as Harmon stepped out into the middle of the street, pulled a much-folded piece of official-looking stationery out of her purse, and checked the address in the upper right-hand corner. This was the place, all right, the place to which she had been ordered to come, or risk losing her grant, which was the only thing that kept the undersea research facility going. All because of some bureaucratic whim. How dare they interfere with her work! Someone would pay.

Oblivious to the horns and insults that sounded all around her, Harmon crossed the street, took the stairs two at a time, and was surprised when a uniformed guard smiled, opened the armor-plated door, and said, "Good morning, Dr. Harmon. The director is expecting you."

Harmon nodded brusquely, resolved to keep her attitude firmly in place, and realized that she didn't have the foggiest idea of where to go next. The hallway was large enough to accommodate an auto-loader. Sun streamed down through highly placed windows and threw rectangles of light across the concrete floor. A hand touched her elbow. "Dr. Harmon? This way, please. The director is expecting you."

The director's assistant, if that's what the machine was, had been painted olive drab and had a military-style bar code stenciled on its chest. Did that imply a connection with the military? The whole thing seemed stranger all the time.

Harmon followed the android down the hall and was struck by the feeling of quiet efficiency that permeated the building. It reminded her of an ancient library, or a monastery, except there were no books, and damned few humans. In fact, judging from those she saw in the hall, and in the offices to either side, most of the staff consisted of androids, cyborgs, and aliens. Some of whom wore elaborate life-support systems or sat, hung, or wallowed in specially designed environments. Just another way to waste taxpayer money, Harmon thought bitterly, while the suits strangled her research and jerked her around. Her black high-tops, standard wear on Marianna Three, squeaked against the highly polished floor.

The hall ended in front of massive double doors. They

opened on their own and Harmon followed the android into a spacious waiting area. The machine indicated some mismatched but comfortable-looking chairs. "Please take a seat—"

Harmon held up a hand in protest. "I know . . . the director is expecting me." The android nodded expressionlessly and withdrew.

The doctor considered her alternatives, chose the chair with the least padding, and planned her strategy. She would husband her anger at first, allowing it to build while the no-doubt-idiotic director prattled on, and then, just when he or she was least expecting it, Harmon would jump in, rip the worthless bureaucrat to shreds, reduce the shreds to a quivering mass of jelly, and return to her habitat, grant intact. It had worked before and would work again. "Dr. Harmon? The director will see you now."

Harmon stood and followed the robot into a small antechamber, and from there into a large, rather spartan office, dominated by the same wooden desk that had served the warehouse manager eons before. Her host was younger than she had expected, good looking if you liked that sort of thing, and somewhat wooden. He rose to greet her. "Dr. Harmon! How good of you to come! You had a pleasant journey, I trust?"

Harmon shook the man's hand. It was firm and dry. "The plane didn't crash, if that's what you mean."

The man laughed. "You're everything they said you'd be. Please have a seat."

Harmon eyed the director suspiciously. "And you are?"

The man shook his head as if disappointed in himself.

"I'm sorry . . . where are my manners? My name is Sergi Chien-Chu. I'm the director of the Department of Interspecies Cooperation."

Harmon felt her mouth drop open. "*The* Sergi Chien-Chu? The one everyone thought was dead?"

"One and the same," Chien-Chu agreed cheerfully. "And I'd still be dead if wasn't for the blasted Hudathans." His plastiskin face turned grim. "We must stop them. And soon."

Harmon searched for the anger that she had brought into the room and couldn't find it. Chien-Chu! Industrialist, patriot, savior, the list went on and on. She didn't watch a lot of news, but even *she* had been aware of the enormous media hoopla that had surrounded his return from the dead, and his promise to help President Anguar against the Hudathans. Public confidence had soared after that in spite of the defeat off Worber's World. Harmon was impressed in spite of herself. But why was Chien-Chu in charge of some low-rent government agency? And what did he want with her?

Chien-Chu smiled as if able to read her thoughts. He perched on the corner of the desk. "Which brings us to you. The Confederacy needs your help."

Harmon frowned. "*My* help? What could I do?"

Chien-Chu looked her straight in the eye. "We want you to travel to a planet designated IH-4762-ASX41, contact the sentients known as the Say'lynt, and recruit them into our armed forces."

Harmon looked at the industrialist as if he were certifiably insane. "Have you lost your mind? I'm a scientist, not a recruiter. Surely you have other, more qualified candidates."

"No," Chien-Chu answered evenly, "we don't. Did you know a woman named Dr. Valerie Reeman?"

Harmon felt cold liquid run through her veins. There wasn't a day that went by that she didn't think about Valerie. Dead these many years, killed when the Hudathans overran her research station, and buried in alien soil. They had gone to college together, majored in marine biology together, and formed the only relationship that Harmon had ever cared about. Yes, she had known Valerie Reeman, and dreamed of her every night. "Yes, I knew Valerie. What about her?"

"She was working with the Say'lynt at the time of her death. They thought very highly of her."

Harmon *knew* she was being manipulated, *knew* she was being used, but couldn't help herself. "The Say'lynt . . . what are they like?"

"Their bodies are similar to Terran phytoplankton," Chien-Chu replied, "linked together via hundreds of miles' worth of translucent fiber, into what amounts to a group consciousness. Each mind, and there are only three or four, incorporates billions of individual plankton, and occupies up to a thousand square miles of ocean."

"Then what good are they?" Harmon demanded skeptically. "How could they hold a weapon? Program a computer? Or do anything else worthwhile?"

"They have unusual powers," Chien-Chu said gently. "Based on firsthand observations by General Natalie Norwood, we know the Say'lynt can control sentient minds from hundreds, even thousands of miles away. They did it to the Hudathans. An ability like that could come in handy."

"But how?" Harmon asked desperately, fearful of what she was being asked to do, but curious just the same. "You said each individual entity takes up a thousand square miles of ocean. Why bother to recruit them if they can't be moved?"

"Ah, but they *can* be moved," Chien-Chu replied smoothly. "Or at least two of them can. And a colony-class freighter has been converted to that very purpose. It's in orbit waiting for you to board."

Harmon was silent for a moment. "And if I refuse? If I return to Marianna Three?"

Chien-Chu shrugged. "You won't refuse, but if you did,

I'd have you court-martialed, for disobeying a direct order.''

The scientist stood. Her eyes flashed. "Except that you *can't* have me court-martialed . . . because I'm a civilian!''

Chien-Chu smiled. "You *were* a civilian. Your commission as a captain in the Naval Reserve was approved five days ago. Congratulations.''

Harmon clenched and unclenched her fists. She would have hit him but knew he wouldn't feel much. "You are a one-hundred-percent dyed-in-the-wool sonofabitch.''

Chien-Chu seemed to give it some thought. He nodded slowly. "Yup, it goes with the job.''

The *D'Nooni Dai* looked more like a moon than a spaceship. That's because she was big, round, and covered with what might have been craters, but were actually recessed solar panels, heat exchangers, and beam projectors. And the *Nooni*, as the crew called her, was old—not as old as Earth's moon, perhaps, but old enough to have carried two colonies into space. No small feat, given the time and distance involved.

Which helped explain why she was considered to be a good-luck ship, and would no doubt survive her current assignment, or so the ensign believed. His name was Hajin, he was fresh out of the academy, and liked to talk, something he might have done less of had he known that the plain-looking woman who sat next to him was a captain, equivalent in rank to a Marine or Legion colonel, and his commanding officer. He gestured towards the shuttle's viewscreen. "Would you like the guided tour?''

A full week had passed since Harmon's conversation with Chien-Chu. During that time she had learned what there was to know about IH-4762-ASX41, read all of the research that Valerie had sent home prior to her death, and been imbued with her friend's passion for the Say'lynt.

But of even more importance to Harmon was the fact that the sentients had *known* Valerie, had liked her, and could describe the circumstances of her death. Perhaps learning more about the way her friend had died would provide a sense of closure and free Harmon from the memories that haunted her. In any case, the biologist had used what little leverage she had to obtain five years' worth of government funding for Marianna Three, and the staff she'd left behind.

That left her free to take on a new commitment, and as with every commitment made during her life, Harmon intended to give it all of her time, energy, and intelligence. She nodded. "Yes, give the guided tour. Tell me about the big things that stick out from the side of the ship."

Hajin nodded eagerly, advised the larger ship of his passenger's desire for a "fly-by," and banked for a better view. "Like all colony-class ships, the *Nooni* was built in space. That's because she's too big to lift under Earth-normal conditions. The structures you referred to are 'bolt-on' propulsion engines designed to provide the old girl with a whole lot of extra power. I don't know what the brass have up their sleeves, but it must be heavy, because they reinforced the hull, and more than doubled her power."

Harmon nodded. Water was heavy, all right, as were the Say'lynt themselves, and the alterations made sense. Chien-Chu might be a scum-sucking sonofabitch, but he was a smart sonofabitch, and a good planner.

The ensign brought the tiny shuttle into the *Nooni*'s landing bay with a little more of a flourish than the occasion demanded, put his ship down with a gentle thump, and helped the scientist collect her belongings. He noticed that Harmon had twenty-five pounds' worth of personal gear and two hundred pounds of disks, cubes, books, and other paraphernalia.

Air had been pumped into the bay by the time they were

finished, allowing them to exit through the claustrophobic lock. Both were surprised by the shrill sound of the bosun's pipe, the sight of the ship's marines standing at present arms, and the officer who came forward to greet them. He wore a dress uniform, a chest full of medals won during the first Hudathan war, and a neatly trimmed beard. Blue eyes twinkled from deeply set sockets. He considered a salute but held out his hand instead. "Commander Tom Duncan, ma'am, welcome aboard."

Though nominally in command of the ship *and* the mission, Harmon didn't take the first part of the job very seriously, nor had she taken the time to read up on naval traditions. She shook Duncan's hand, nodded dutifully as he introduced the rest of the ship's officers, and wondered why Chien-Chu had seen fit to assign her a public relations specialist, not to mention his four-person holo crew.

Then, when the introductions were complete, Harmon read the one-size-fits-all "I'm taking command" speech handed to her by Duncan, faked her way through a cursory inspection, and heaved a gigantic sigh of relief when shown to her private quarters. They were spacious and well appointed. A tad too much brass for Harmon's taste but appropriately spartan. Her baggage had preceded her into the cabin and was stacked in the middle of the well-carpeted deck. She saw a bar and waved Duncan in that direction. "So, Commander, how about a drink? Assuming the bar is stocked."

Duncan smiled and moved towards the bar. He'd been worried about Harmon, and still had some concerns, but felt encouraged. "Thanks . . . I'm on duty at the moment, but a soft drink would be nice. What can I get for you?"

Harmon dropped into a chair and found that it was too soft. "Am I on duty?"

Duncan popped the lid on a soda and poured the contents over some ice. "The captain of a naval vessel is *always* on duty . . . but allowed to have a drink anyway.''

Harmon laughed. "A gin and tonic, then . . . to celebrate the fact that I didn't toss my cookies on the way up through the atmosphere.''

Duncan frowned. "Ensign Hajin thinks he's a hot pilot. Did he get carried away?''

Harmon shook her head. "No, he was fine. I tend to get air sick, that's all.''

Duncan brought her the gin and tonic. "Well, don't worry about it. You're in space now . . . and we won't have to worry about atmospheric conditions until we orbit ASX41.''

Harmon sipped her drink. It tasted good. "How about the crew . . . do they know about our mission?''

Duncan shook his head. "No. My orders were to keep the lid on until you came aboard. That's why Hajin was so surprised to learn that his passenger was our commanding officer. They have theories, of course . . . and who wouldn't, given the way the ship has been configured.''

Harmon pressed the coolness of the glass against the side of her face, realized what she was doing, and pulled it away. "Let's talk about that if we can. How do you feel about working for what amounts to a civilian?''

Duncan looked at Harmon, trying to gauge her personality. How direct could he afford to be? And did it really matter? Unlike most officers his age, he had come up through the ranks during the last war. He had made lieutenant as a reward for bringing his heavily damaged destroyer into port after every single line officer had been killed. More promotions had followed until the war ended and he had been pushed into early retirement so younger officers could have a chance. All of which meant that he didn't give a shit about politics, promotion, or a career that never should have been. He shrugged. "I was worried.''

Harmon nodded approvingly. "*Was?* Or are?''

Duncan chuckled. "Both."

Harmon smiled. "Me too. I know about marine biology, and I know about leading people, but I don't know anything about spaceships. Let's say you run the ship, and I handle the Say'lynt?"

Duncan beamed his approval. "Sounds good to me, assuming that you're willing to observe the forms, and that includes a uniform. The crew expects it."

Harmon indicated her khaki shirt and pants. "I don't spend much time thinking about clothes. I'll wear anything you want."

Duncan nodded. "Excellent. I'll have a full set of uniforms delivered to your cabin. The everyday one looks pretty much like what you have on."

"So," Harmon said, "now that we have the 'how we're gonna work together' stuff out of the way, how about showing me around?"

"It's called an 'inspection,' " Duncan said patiently, "and I'd love to show you around."

Harmon smiled. "Right. Got it. And there's one more thing . . . Some people say I have a temper. They're wrong, of course, but it keeps cropping up. Let me know if someone starts a rumor like that."

Duncan raised his glass in acknowledgment. "No offense, ma'am, but commanding officers tend to be temperamental anyway, and nobody would be especially surprised."

Harmon's eyebrows shot up. She got to her feet. "Really? I'm starting to like the military. Civilians get all pissy the minute you blow off some steam. So, time to inspect the troops."

"Sailors, ratings, or the ship's company," Duncan corrected her, "unless referring to the marines when dirtside, where the term 'troops' would apply."

"Whatever," Harmon said impatiently. "Let's go."

If the *Nooni* could be said to have a "bow" it was the topmost part of the ship. The control, living, and environmental spaces were located below that, and weren't especially interesting, not to Harmon's eye anyway, especially when compared to the vast emptiness that filled the center portion of the ship. This was where hundreds of compartments had once been, filled with thousands of "sleepers," each sealed in his or her high-tech coffin, slumbering away the years as the ship made the long sublight journey to a distant star.

But that had been towards the end of the Second Confederacy, before a reliable hyperdrive had been discovered, and the need for such journeys ended. All of which meant that the ship was what? Three, four hundred years old? Or even more than that? It hardly made a difference. The point was that she had survived, been hollowed out, and reinforced to handle her next set of passengers.

As Harmon followed Duncan out onto the catwalk following the circumference of the hull she felt a momentary dizziness as the deck disappeared and it seemed as if she might fall. But the grating was firm beneath her sneakers and the solidity of the handrail served to restore her sense of equilibrium. The space was absolutely huge, like the inside of the sports dome in Sydney, except with the field scooped away to match the openess above. A large column ran down through the center of the space. Duncan pointed to it.

"That's the ship's keel, or spine, and plays a major role in holding her together. Lift tubes run to either side of it so that the crew can move back and forth between their quarters and the engineering spaces without climbing up and over the tank.

"When the tank is filled, an artificial current will be set in motion by the nozzles located around the sides of the habitat, the water will be filtered through the units down there, and real sunlight will be brought in via external collectors and fiber-optic pathways.''

Large though the tank was, Harmon wondered how the Say'lynt would feel, assuming they agreed to come aboard. Would the tank seem claustrophobic after a thousand square miles of ocean? Would their health be affected? There were all sorts of questions, and with the exception of the relatively small amount of data sent in by Valerie prior to her death, damned few answers.

Which brought her back to a fundamental question: The Say'lynt's special talent not withstanding, why go to all this trouble and expense, when the same amount of money spent on conventional weapons might produce considerably higher returns? Unless there was another, deeper reason, a political reason, which would explain why someone like Chien-Chu was involved.

Harmon stopped abruptly. She'd come to the moment of truth that sometimes follows the right question: the Confederacy of Sentient Beings was just that, a collection of self-aware beings, many of whom were completely unequipped for war with a race like the Hudathans. Humans and similar races would have to do most of the actual fighting and suffer most of the casualties; a fact that could weaken if not destroy the Confederacy. Which not only explained the need to recruit the Say'lynt, but the need to *publicize* the recruitment. Now Harmon knew why the holo crew was aboard.

The biologist looked at Duncan, then out over the manmade abyss. What had seemed eccentric and wasteful suddenly seemed important. The Hudathans had killed Valerie. Now they would pay. And Harmon would do her part.

19

The effects of gunpowder, that great agent in our military activity, were learnt by experience, and up to this hour experiments are continually in progress to investigate them more fully.

Carl von Clausewitz
On War
Standard year 1832

Planet Jericho, the Confederacy of Sentient Beings

In spite of the fact that he had killed hundreds of sentient beings since becoming a machine-thing, and taken part in three planetary assaults, Rebor Raksala-Ba was scared. As were most of his comrades, because even though the Regiment of the Living Dead had acquired an awesome reputation in the minds of the Hudathan people, they had never gone head to head with the Legion's much-vaunted cyborgs. They were about to do so.

What if their armor couldn't handle the Trooper IIs' offensive weaponry? What if there were more quads than they'd been led to expect? What if the humans had new weapons against which they had no defense? Those questions and more haunted the Hudathan as his shuttle bucked its way down through Jericho's Earth-normal atmosphere.

So, even though the pep talk was all too predictable, Rak-sala-Ba listened anyway, preferring it to the voices in his head. As usual, there was no way to know whether the Observer was on-board or had been recorded earlier.

"Like a disease that spreads via the blood, the humans make their way from system to system, leaving corruption behind them. Our job is to find such pustules, lance them, and cauterize the resulting wound."

The ship rocked violently from side to side as a volley of surface-to-air missiles exploded nearby and transformed one of the assault boats into a cloud of metallic confetti.

Unable to see beyond the bulkhead opposite him, and terrified of his own fear, Raksala-Ba concentrated on the Observer's voice. It continued unchanged. "Once on the ground, you will disembark, move in a northerly direction, and engage the human Legion. Yes, they will place their Trooper IIs in your way, but the alien cyborgs will fall by the scores as your superior weaponry cuts them down. The quads will be more difficult, but there will be relatively few of them to contend with, and you will emerge victorious.

"Once that task has been accomplished, you must seek out and kill the regular troops, remembering that the humans breed like Radu, and even a handful could reinfect the stars."

The cyborgs knew a cue when they heard one, and the word "*Blood!*" reverberated through the troop bay. Up forward, in a jump-seat behind the copilot's position, the Observer ran one last check on their vital signs, found everything to his liking, and closed his eyes against the explosions outside. The arrow had been released and would fly straight and true.

There had been silence within the temple of the Lords. A deep abiding silence that had lasted for a hundred thousand years and never been broken. Until the humans arrived, that is. They worked softly at first, walking, talking, and prying, deciding how to proceed. Then came the growl of heavy equipment, the rattle of drills, and the whine of laser cutters.

But the ruins had survived a great deal over the millennia, and were so huge that their very size was a more than adequate defense against the not-always-gentle probings of the archaeologists, xeno-biologists, and fortune hunters who sought to understand their secrets. Until now, that is, and the advent of a war that the long-dead builders would have considered to be barbaric, and more than sufficient reason to go wherever they had gone.

The temple of the Lords was so huge, so vast, that the twelve aerospace fighters occupied no more than a small portion of the tightly set stone floor. Huge figures, each different from all the rest, stared down at the machines much as they had looked down at what? Members of a long-vanished religion? Representatives from different star-faring races? The scientists were still arguing over the statues and their possible significance.

So the scientists objected when Lieutenant Commander Angela Ritter removed her fighters from the spaceport and installed them in the great hall. As a matter of fact, they were *still* talking about the reports they would file and the penalties they would levy when the orbital barrage began. Some died in their burning prefabs, some vanished in the explosion that took the spaceport, and some survived to learn the intricacies of the Mark IV power rifle.

Suddenly the scientists knew what the military had known all along: the Hudathans would give no quarter, show no mercy, and accept nothing less than total victory. The simple fact was that they didn't care about human suffering, they didn't care about preserving the ruins, and they didn't care about the planet's ecology. All the humans could do was even the odds a little, take some of the bastards with them, and avenge their own deaths.

A voice sounded in Ritter's helmet. "Delta Base to Delta Leader . . . condition green . . . repeat . . . condition green."

Ritter eyed her heads-up displays, confirmed the ready lights, and spoke into the voice-activated mike. "Roger that, Delta Base . . . wish us luck."

"What for?" the voice inquired. "You never needed it before."

But the comment was pure bravado, and both parties knew it. Ritter switched frequencies. "Delta Leader to Delta Wing . . . condition green . . . let's crank 'em up. Remember . . . stick with your wingman, conserve your offensive load, and stay in atmosphere. Even the smallest ship in orbit would eat you alive."

A whole chorus of "rogers" came back and Ritter struggled to ignore the fact that all the voices she heard would be stilled by sundown.

Compressors whined, engines fired, and thunder echoed between ancient walls. Hundreds of green flockers, their nests tucked here and there throughout the ruins, shot outwards to escape the noise, and headed east towards what had been a bowl-shaped reservoir and currently served as a gigantic birdbath. Other creatures, reacting to the unexpected disturbance, ran, jumped, and wiggled towards safety.

But there was no safety as death rained down from the sky, and Ritter lifted her aircraft away from ancient stones. She hovered for a moment, dust billowing up to either side, and checked to confirm that the rest of her tiny command had done likewise. Then, ready as she'd ever be, Ritter took a moment to cross herself, and sent the appropriate command to the plane's fly-by-wire control system. Heavy gee's forced the pilot back into the seat as the fighter passed between vine-covered columns and climbed towards the enemy-held sky.

The flat-roofed structure might have been a dwelling, set into the side of the hill, where it would catch the evening breeze, and cool the rooms within. But a profusion of plants had grown up around ancient walls, blurring the angles and softening the lines so they were indistinguishable from the jungle around them. With strong stone walls, a good line of retreat, and the ridge that stretched left and right, the villa, if that's what it could properly be called, made an excellent weapons emplacement and company HQ.

By all rights First Lieutenant Connie Chrobuck should have led a platoon, and taken orders from a more experienced officer, but infantry expertise was in short supply on Jericho, which meant that she was in charge of a full company, half of which consisted of legionnaires, while the rest had been patched together with biologists, archaeologists, geologists, technicians, and various port trash who would rather fight than sit on their cans.

Interestingly enough, it was this last category that had turned out to be the most useful, having as they did a more than passing familiarity with weapons, some of which had been garnered while serving with the Legion. Though unsure of the exact number of deserters under her command, Chrobuck judged there were quite a few, and took full advantage of the fact.

She was lying on the roof, scanning the jungle in front of her with a computer-enhanced scope, when a curly-haired cargo jockey named Louie flopped down beside her. He wore a utility vest loaded with gear, fatigue pants, jungle boots, and was armed with a power pistol and an assault weapon. His breezy informality was typical of the civilians in her company. "Hey, Loot . . . I did like you said. Any geek that decides to come up along the stream is going to get one nasty-assed surprise."

Chrobuck nodded. She wore a green beret over short hair

and looked at him with large gray eyes. Her single gold earring gave her a piratical air. "Good work, Louie. Now, remember, let the Trooper II handle the heavy lifting, while you and your squad watch his flanks and add to the suppressive fire."

Louie grinned. "Yeah, yeah, yeah. Don't worry, honey, we'll cover the tin man's ass. And when this thing's over you and me can have a beer. Whaddya say?"

Chrobuck thought about shoving the words down the man's throat, or telling him that she didn't date idiots, but what was the point? Louie would be dead soon. "Sure, Louie, you hold the line, and the beer's on me."

Louie grinned, gave her a confident thumbs-up, and rolled away. The manner in which he stayed below the skyline and handled his weapon testified to military training. An ex-marine? Legionnaire? She'd never know. Chrobuck looked upwards, saw no sign of the bad weather the Met officer had promised, and swore as contrails raced each other across the sky.

Raksala-Ba gave thanks that he no longer had a flesh-and-blood face to signal the fear he felt. He braced himself against the boat's infernal rocking motion and tried to look relaxed. The others did likewise. The pilot came over the command frequency. "Hold on . . . we're going in."

The assault craft had lost sixty percent of its control surfaces, and one of its two engines, so what happened next was more like a controlled crash than a normal landing. The ship hit the middle of a clearing, went airborne like a stone skipping over the surface of a lake, and smashed into the jungle. Half the cyborgs were crushed when the ship hit the side of a vine-covered building but the rest survived.

Raksala-Ba was among the lucky ones. He released the harness that had held him in place, made his way out through an opening that hadn't been there before, and looked around. The wreckage was at his back, an ancient vine-covered building stood to the right, a ridge rose up ahead, and a stream gurgled to the left. Bullets rattled against his armor.

There was no time to think or strategize. Months of training took over. The Hudathan tracked the incoming fire to its source, selected a high-explosive warhead, and fired. An explosion blossomed on the ridgeline above. He felt a mild orgasm and was still enjoying the afterglow when the pleasure disappeared.

The Trooper II named Quanto had fought under the famous Colonel Pierre Legaux on Algeron, had kicked some serious Hudathan butt during the first war, and forgotten more tricks than the newbies were ever likely to learn. Not the least of which involved concealing his heat under the surface of a lake, stream, or in one case, four feet of dirt, only to pop up and surprise the enemy. And surprise them he did, emerging from the swift-flowing stream like an avenging spirit, missiles leaping away from each shoulder as water cascaded down off his jungle green camouflage. One surface-to-surface missile found the still-warm wreckage and exploded. The other hit the borg off to Raksala-Ba's right and blew him to bits. Although impervious to .50-caliber bullets, the Hudathan armor could not withstand high-explosive missile hits.

Raksala-Ba felt a piece of shrapnel clang off his shoulder, swiveled to the right, and fired. The mini-missile blew Quanto in half. A Trooper II was dead. Raksala-Ba felt a powerful orgasm ripple through his nonexistent genitals and started up the slope in front of him. The fear that had plagued him earlier was momentarily gone.

Ritter and the wing under her command arrived at 15,000 feet in time to slice through the second wave of Hudathan assault boats. It was easy at first, maneuvering until a ship filled her sights, then blowing it out of the air. At least fifteen of the incoming ships were destroyed within the three short minutes that it took the Hudathan fighters to react. They came out of the sun and destroyed two defenders on their first pass. Ritter bit her lower lip as the eternally cheerful Roo vanished in a ball of flame and "Nags" Naglie hit the side of a jungle-clad mountain.

The fighting grew fast and furious. Ritter flamed a fighter, caught a glimpse of empty sky, and ordered the fighter to climb. Radio discipline had gone to hell in a handcart but it was too late to do anything about it.

"Watch your tail, Logan . . . damn, that was close."

"May day, May day, I'm going in . . ."

"Come to Momma, geek face . . . Come to Momma."

"Hey, Bones, did you see that? I . . ."

"They're on my ass! Get 'em off! Get 'em off!"

"Break left, Snakeyes . . . I've got 'em."

A tone sounded and a target appeared on Ritter's display. The parameters didn't match anything in memory so she ran them again. Nothing changed. Whatever the Hudathans had sent down was *big,* real *big,* and coming her way. A strategic target, then, something worth dying for. The flight leader glanced at the place where her wingman should be and saw that he was there. His name was Kisley, but was better known as "Kisser," since he had a tendency to kiss anything with lips, especially when drunk. "Hey, Kisser, do you see what I see?"

"That's a roger, Delta Leader. It's big, it's fat, and it's ours."

"Exactamundo . . . let's engage."

Arrow Commander Indu Korma-Sa stared into the holo tank with a sublime sense of detachment. The fact that two fighters had appeared, and were getting ready to attack his large, rather awkward surface support ship, bothered him not at all. For unlike all but a few of his peers, Korma-Sa had taken the time and trouble to read many of the data cubes captured during the first war, and had discovered something called *A Book of Five Rings* by a human named Miyamoto Musashi. Not just *any* human, but a warrior who had killed more than sixty samurai in personal combat, before retiring to a cave and writing his book. A book that Korma-Sa knew by heart. The situation gave rise to the appropriate quote.

"To attain the Way of strategy as a warrior you must study fully other martial arts and not deviate even a little from the Way of the warrior. With your spirit settled, accumulate practice day by day, and hour by hour. Polish the twofold spirit heart and mind, and sharpen the twofold gaze perception and sight. When your spirit is not in the least clouded, when the clouds of bewilderment clear away, there is the true void."

Korma-Sa looked into the true void, saw that which should be done, and gave the necessary orders. "Allow the enemy to close and use the short sword to destroy them."

Long accustomed to his commanding officer's almost allegorical orders, the hard-faced weapons officer signaled willing assent, waited as the fighters closed with the ship, and readied the short-range weapons.

Ritter and Kisley expected to die at any moment and fired all their long-range weapons in hopes of a lucky hit. They exploded harmlessly against the supply ship's protective shields. Both pilots waited for the inevitable response and were surprised when it failed to materialize. Thus encouraged, they readied their short-range armament, and arrowed in for the kill. They were only twenty miles away when the alien ship opened fire. Kisley died immediately. Ritter was hit but kept on going. Hudathan computers tracked her, but the flight leader was good, and managed to stay alive for another 10.7 seconds. She didn't see the torpedo that hit her aircraft or feel the explosion that took her life. Korma-Sa honored her bravery, cleared the episode from his mind, and reentered the void.

Chrobuck watched Quanto die through her scope, bounced a signal of a low-flying drone, and sent the video to Brigade HQ. "Zulu Four to Bravo One."

The first voice she heard belonged to Colonel Wesley Worthington himself, C in C, Jericho ground forces. "This is Bravo One . . . Go."

"Sending video on freq four. We are in contact with what appear to be military androids or enemy cyborgs. They eat fifty-caliber ammo for lunch but don't like missiles. I am one T-Two, sorry, make that deuce T-Two's down, and fading fast. Over."

There was a moment of silence while Chrobuck watched her four remaining Trooper IIs fire their laser cannons to no visible effect. Whatever the things were shrugged the energy off, unleashed a flight of mini-missiles, and halved what was left of her cybernetic armor. She didn't have to tell Worthington because he'd seen the firefight firsthand. For him it would be just one more piece of bad news in a day filled with nothing else. Worthington had deployed what troops he had around what the archaeologists had named the "Valley of Temples," which featured a Class III spaceport, some fairly well fortified SAM launchers, and the colonel's underground command post.

"Bravo One to Zulu Four. Assume cyborgs for now. Pull back but make 'em pay. Help is on the way. Bravo One out."

Chrobuck grimaced. "Make 'em pay?" With what? But orders are orders, and she knew Worthington didn't have a whole lot of choice. She ordered the surviving cyborgs to fall back to a point where hastily trained civilian support teams could rearm their missile racks, called in an artillery mission on the area between them and the enemy LZ, and called for the company supply sergeant. Her name was Horowitz and she was built like a truck. She didn't have a lot of respect for lieutenants and let it show as she low-crawled onto the roof. "So, Lieutenant . . . what's up?" Horowitz had to yell to make herself heard over the shriek of outgoing arty, the thump, thump, thump of HE a half-mile in front of her position, and the cloth-ripping sound of machine-gun fire.

Chrobuck ignored the lack of respect and cut straight to the point. "How many shoulder-launched missiles have we got?"

Horowitz knew exactly how many SLM's she had, but pretended to consult her wrist term. Never one to give *all* of anything, the supply sergeant took ten percent off the top. "I issued twelve SLMs day before yesterday with forty-three stashed to the rear. We didn't think we'd need that many of them."

Chrobuck nodded. "Well, conditions have changed. Order some professors to bring the slims forward. They will be issued to uniformed personnel only. We can't afford to waste them on trees."

Horowitz remained impassive. "Yes, ma'am."

"And, Horowitz?"

"Ma'am?"

"Have the eggheads bring the rest of the SLMs, too. There's no point in saving them."

Horowitz was embarrassed but tried not to show it. She looked into the young officer's face, saw the determination in her eyes, and nodded slowly. "Yes, ma'am. Camerone."

Chrobuck nodded. "That's right, Sergeant . . . Camerone."

The sergeant back-wiggled into the jungle while Chrobuck continued to observe. The artillery mission came to an end, and with the exception of some intermittent machine-gun fire in the jungle below, a temporary silence settled over the ruins. The arty had carved an arc-shaped swath through the jungle and Chrobuck saw a number of Hudathan casualties. The only problem was that for every enemy casualty she saw two of her own.

She pulled back from the scope just in time to see something pass through her peripheral vision. It was a spy-eye, one of thousands released by the Hudathans, and was held aloft by a tiny antigrav generator. A legionnaire saw the device, nailed it with his energy rifle, and returned to the mines he was placing.

The momentary respite ended as a flight of Hudathan ground-support craft appeared out of the south and swept in at treetop level. Missiles leaped away from their wings and homed on the artillery pods located to the rear. They responded with motor-driven gatling guns, antimissile missiles, and a full-spectrum electronic-counter-measure defense. Most of the incoming weapons were destroyed or misdirected but a few got through. They destroyed three large-caliber tubes, an ammo dump, and the quad that had been ordered to move up in support of Chrobuck's company. Twenty-three bio bods were killed. The explosions shook Chrobuck's command post and sent flames soaring into the sky.

But the enemy aircraft were still coming, ejecting chaff, and jinking back and forth to evade surface-to-air missiles. Chrobuck saw bombs drop from their wing racks and watched a line of explosions march her way. Entire trees, blocks of stone, and the occasional body were tossed into the air. It was only when she saw lights winking along the leading edge of their wings, and felt rock chips hit the side of her face, that Chrobuck realized how exposed she was. She scrambled to her feet and was halfway to the jungle when the line of planes roared overhead. They flew so low that she could feel the air that they displaced and see the alien unit designators.

A storm of small-arms fire, along with the hail of slugs produced by the two remaining gatling guns, formed a curtain of lead. A pair of SAMs reached up, didn't have time to arm themselves, and zigzagged towards the sun. One of the planes staggered as it hit the line of fire, performed an unintentional wing-over, and crashed into an ancient temple. Chrobuck heard a series of secondary explosions as she slipped into the coolness of the jungle and tried to reestablish contact with her platoon leaders.

The resulting reports weren't very positive. Staff Sergeant Nibo, who had the first platoon, and a hodgepodge of legionnaires, desk jockeys, and port trash, had linked up with Master Sergeant Fhad, who led the third platoon, comprised of the remaining Trooper IIs, some archaeologists, and two squads from the 2nd REP. Together, both platoons were falling back. Louie's booby trap had accounted for one of the Hudathan cyborgs, and some well-placed slims had destroyed two more, but the rest kept on coming.

Chrobuck did what she could to encourage Nibo and Fhad, checked to make sure that the second and fourth platoons were in position along the ridgeline, and laid down covering fire. The moment that the first and third passed through the defensive line, Chrobuck planned to put mortar fire on the slope in front of her, stiffen her defenses with whatever remained of the third and fourth, and hold the ridge for as long as she could. She knew it wouldn't make much difference in the long run, but Worthington was counting on her to hold his right flank, and every Hudathan killed was one less for the Confederacy to deal with.

Raksala-Ba proceeded more cautiously now that Tornu-Ka had been killed by means of a booby trap. Like all such devices, its real value lay not in the number of casualties actually inflicted, but in the amount of fear generated, and the degree to which that fear inhibited the enemy's activities. And while Raksala-Ba couldn't speak for the other cyborgs, he knew that the explosion had inhibited *his* activities, and caused him to pay greater attention to his surroundings. They spy-eyes helped a lot, floating ahead and broadcasting videos of everything they saw, so the cyborgs knew what they were facing.

The humans had been falling back for some time now, or "up" as the case might be, since they had the rather unenviable task of fighting a rear-guard action while climbing a steep slope. The combination of the jungle and tumbledown ruins provided the enemy with excellent cover, which allowed them to pause every now and then, and fire on the steadily advancing cyborgs.

Regular troops would have been decimated long before, but the humans' SLMs were of only limited value at close range, and almost impossible to use with thick foliage blocking the way. So the cyborgs kept coming, their automatic weapons pumping death up towards the ridge, while their energy cannon probed the jungle and started innumerable smoky fires.

In the meantime Raksala-Ba prayed for an air strike. Anything that would prevent another devastating artillery attack. But the planes were busy elsewhere, and the moment that the last of the humans made it to the ridgeline, and were pulled into hastily dug fox holes, mortar shells began to fall.

The earth shook as 120-mike-mike mortar shells detonated on the forward incline while 105-mike-mike artillery rounds pounded the lower slope. Geysers of earth and vegetation shot skywards, a cyborg screamed on channel three, and the attack stalled.

Crouched in whatever shelter they could find, Raksala-Ba and his comrades had a limited number of choices: they could stay put, and wait for the assault to end, an almost unbearable alternative given the ferocity of the attack, they could retreat, and face the possibility of execution at the hands of the Observers, or they could attack, overrun the human positions, and silence the mortars and artillery. They chose to attack. Dagger Commander Wala Prolla-Ka uttered the cry *"Blood!"* and was answered by every cyborg that could transmit. *"Blood! Blood! Blood!"* Raksala-Ba stood, gritted nonexistent teeth, and started uphill.

"Here they come!" The words originated from one of the civilians and were heard on freq four. Chrobuck ignored the break in radio discipline and used the command override. "Save your ammo! Prepare your grenades. Don't throw until I give the word."

Some of the humans had grenades, and some had home-made bombs, thanks to Louie and a demolitions expert from the 2nd REP. Given the effectiveness of the Hudathan armor, Chrobuck figured they were the only close-in weapons likely to make much of a dent on the advancing cyborgs. The problem was to determine the exact moment to use them.

The officer stood, forced herself to ignore the death that whistled all around her, and looked down into the shell-tossed jungle. Shadows moved here and there as the Hudathans fought their way upwards. They were getting close and so was the appropriate moment. "Okay . . . wait . . . wait . . . wait . . . arm your weapons . . . hold . . . hold . . . hold . . . throw!"

At least one of the homemade bombs went off in a dock walloper's hand, killing her along with two legionnaires. But the rest sailed out and down, hitting, then bouncing into the air, where most of them exploded. The force of the explosions, plus the shrapnel they produced, killed a number of the Hudathans, but the rest, Raksala-Ba included, kept on climbing.

His mind had gone somewhere safe, and was only partially aware of the command-detonated mines that went off just before he reached the top, or the fact that whoever was in command of the humans had called for an artillery attack on the ridge itself, slaughtering even more of his comrades, along with an equal number of defenders. All he knew was that he had survived the slope, had reached the top, and was wading through the enemy bio bods as if they weren't even there. Orgasm after orgasm racked his nervous system as he killed and killed and killed. *Blood! Blood! Blood!* It was all that mattered.

Chrobuck fought her way up through a heavy, almost smothering darkness. Her eyelids seemed to weigh a ton each and opened with great difficulty. A dull, throbbing pain probed the side of her head. She tried to sit. A hand pushed her down. A face interposed itself between her and the ceiling-mounted light. It belonged to none other than Colonel Wesley Worthington. "So, you aren't dead after all. Lord knows you tried."

Chrobuck frowned. She remembered the Hudathan charge, the exploding bombs, and the exploding mines. Things became confused after that, but she remembered a cyborg climbing up over the ridge, firing her handgun in a futile attempt to hit its vid cams, and the way that its wedge-shaped brain case had looked her way. The rest was darkness. "Yes, sir, I mean no, sir. Sorry I lost the ridge."

Worthington shook his head grimly. "You did all you could, Lieutenant. And then some. Like calling for an artillery mission on your own position."

Chrobuck thought about all the people who had died and felt a tear trickle down her cheek. She didn't want the colonel to see and wiped it away. He nodded understandingly. "I'd cry too if I had the time. Now listen, Lieutenant, because I need your help, and I need it badly. I asked the Navy to keep a scout ship in reserve. It's fueled, armed, and ready to lift. I need an officer to board that ship along with all that we've learned, cyborgs included, and get the information to General St. James on Algeron. You're the one I picked.''

Chrobuck realized what Worthington had said, what it would mean, and managed a sit-up. It made her head pound. ''No disrespect intended, sir, but screw that. Give me a company, a platoon, or a squad. I'm going to work.''

Worthington smiled sadly. ''No, child. You aren't. Give St. James my regards, and tell him I'll be waiting in hell. Lord knows he ordered me to go there often enough.''

Chrobuck frowned, opened her mouth to say something, and never got it out. The colonel nodded to a medic, a needle bit her arm, and darkness pulled her down.

Like most long-range recon ships, about 75 percent of the LRS-236's mass was devoted to a pair of powerful engines, plus a hyperdrive that would have done justice to a destroyer. The rest of her payload was devoted to an enormous array of high-powered sensors and automated weaponry, with only a minimal amount of space being left over for environmental-support equipment and a two-person crew.

Lieutenant Bruce Jensen paced back and forth in front of his ship, sucked on the unlit cigar that protruded from the corner of his mouth, and cursed the double-dipped ground-pounding sonofabitch that had kept him dirtside while the Hudathans took control of the sky. It was stupid, that's what it was, especially if they wanted their dispatches to get through.

Jensen wore a red baseball cap, olive drab flight suit, and a shoulder holster. He had brown eyes, a straight nose, and three days' worth of black beard. A pair of medics emerged from the ship's airlock. The larger of the two gestured back over his shoulder. ''She's all strapped in, sir. Should come around in a couple of hours. Change her dressing twice a day.''

Jensen nodded, couldn't think of anyone he wanted to say good-bye to, and entered the lock. It took fifteen minutes to run a systems check, fire up the engines, and signal his readiness.

A hundred miles away a flight of six carefully husbanded surface-to-orbit missiles took off, locked onto their various targets, and zigzagged towards space. Short of massive incompetence the STOs presented no real danger to the Hudathan ships but the attack did serve to distract them. That's when the bomb-proof lid slid back, and the *LRS-236* lifted off and screamed away. It took Jensen less than one sweat-soaked hour to fight his way clear of Jericho, make the hyperspace jump, and escape his pursuers. That was when he lit the cigar, noticed that his passenger was kind of pretty, and decided that life could be worse.

It took the Hudathans twenty-three days to crush all resistance, to hunt down the last of the humans, and kill them. In all, 12,643 humans had been killed, but so had 4,281 Hudathans. It was one week later when Sector Marshal Poseen-Ka read the battle summaries, looked up at his adjutant, and gestured distress. ''If this is the price of victory . . . then defeat is beyond our ability to pay.''

20

If the second war proved anything, it proved that warriors come in all shapes and sizes, their only commonality being a willingness to risk all for the greater good.

Keenmind Wordwriter
Words on War
Standard year 2859

Planet IH-4762-ASX41, the Confederacy of Sentient Beings

There was no doubt about it, ASX41 was a beautiful planet. The seemingly endless cobalt blue sky arched down to meet an equally blue ocean. Light sparkled off the waves as they ran before the wind, chasing each other across the world-spanning ocean. The planet was so beautiful, so benign, that the air seemed to welcome the shuttle, lowering it through the atmosphere with nary a bump, and setting it free to roam.

A wild assortment of emotions clamored for Dr. Harmon's attention as the ocean passed beneath her. She felt relief at escaping the *Nooni* for a while, apprehension regarding the Say'lynt, and sadness about Valerie's death. Ensign Hajin, voluble as always, was at the shuttle's controls, and bore no such burdens. The transformation from lowest-ranking officer aboard the *Nooni* to commanding officer of the shuttle always made him happy, and today was no exception. "Captain! Look! There's the wreckage of the Hudathan destroyer!"

Harmon looked, and sure enough, there, sticking up out of the steadily shallowing sea was the unmistakable shape of a Hudathan spaceship, waves washing the length of its rusty hull.

She had seen the wreck before, of course, but that had been on video, and the real thing was a lot more impressive. It and a few lonely graves on a nearby island were the only signs of a war that had left many planets completely devastated.

It had been in the closing days of the long, bloody conflict that the then-Imperial Navy had dropped into the system, found three Hudathan warships standing guard, and given chase. None had been willing to surrender, and this one, the wreck that had already slipped beneath the shuttle and disappeared to the rear, had made the mistake of passing through the upper reaches of the planet's atmosphere, where the Say'lynt group minds known as Rafts One, Two, and Three had seized control of the crew's higher-thought processes, and forced them to crash.

Harmon had studied the Say'lynt, or what there was to know about them, so she knew how important the planet's ecology was to them, and understood the bravery of what they had done. The act of pulling the alien ship down out of the sky had been analogous to taking a poison-laden dagger and plunging it into one's own chest. There was no doubt that all sorts of toxins were leaking out of the Hudathan warship and would be for hundreds of years to come. Toxins that could harm the Say'lynt. So if it was courage that Chien-Chu was looking for, or the willingness to sacrifice oneself for the greater good, then the Say'lynt were on a par with the most decorated soldiers in the Legion.

Something tickled the back of Harmon's mind, or she thought it did, but a glance at Hajin was enough to establish that he felt nothing of the kind. "There's the island, Captain . . . shall I put her down?"

Harmon considered carrying out a brief aerial survey first, but decided it could wait, and nodded her head. "Sure, put her down. I'd like to take a look at the site where the research station was located. Maybe I can learn something." The order *sounded* official but Harmon knew that her real motivation was personal. A chance to see Valerie's grave and make peace with the past.

The island looked like something from a travel feelie. Harmon saw white sand, a curving beach, and a crystal-clear lagoon. The ship slowed, flattened the water beneath it, and flared in for one of Hajin's picture-perfect landings. The sand gave slightly as the aircraft settled on its skids. The purpose of the mission was to make contact with the Say'lynt and determine their willingness to serve in the Confederacy's armed services. So with the exception of Hajin, and over the objections of the public-relations specialist sent to make sure that everyone knew about an agreement that hadn't been negotiated yet, Harmon arrived alone.

The pilot was still at the controls, still in his shut-down sequence, when the scientist cycled through the lock and jumped to the ground. The sand was smooth and outside of the wavy lines left by the wind, completely untouched. It gave under her sneakers as she made her way between clumps of lush vegetation and into a clearing.

Energy weapons had reduced the closely clustered prefabs to a pool of brittle brown glass. Temperature fluctuations had shattered the material into a thousand pieces. Harmon made her way around it and towards the dozen or so stainless steel grave markers that signaled where Valerie and her companions had been buried by the Hudathans, dug up, and reburied by the Imperial Navy. Similar monuments had sprouted by the millions all over what had been the empire, and given the way things were going, more would be needed.

It took little more than a moment to locate the stake that had Valerie's name on it, to kneel in the sand, and rest her forehead against the sun-hot metal. The tears came in a flood, along with deep, racking sobs, and the combination left her trembling.

But a tremendous weariness settled over her shoulders, the sobbing slowed, and a wonderful sense of peace flooded her body. Harmon felt light, so light that she could float away. Which was exactly what she did. She found that she was everywhere yet nowhere at all. It felt particularly odd because she was used to having her thoughts centered in one place rather than scattered across the surface of a planet.

But she liked it, or thought she did, and was still trying to come to terms with the feeling when a voice entered her mind. "Welcome, Dr. Harmon. We share your feelings of sorrow. Valerie was our friend. She is dead now but lives on in our memories."

Then, as if the word *memories* were some kind of cue, Harmon was transported back in time, and found herself watching Valerie. But from where? From the surface of the sea, it seemed, because she had a plankton-eye view of the beach, which bobbed up and down with each passing wave. Valerie wore a two-piece bathing suit, her hair was pulled back into a ponytail, and a patch of white sunscreen protected her nose. There were other humans, too, milling around behind her friend, and joking with each other, but Harmon ignored them. Valerie filled her eyes, her mind, and her heart. Long white legs flashed in the tropical sunshine as her friend ran down the beach, splashed out into the bathtub-warm water, and dived through an oncoming wave. Harmon was all around her, viewing Valerie from a multiplicity of angles, recording what she looked like while sending the image elsewhere.

Valerie paused, put her feet on the sandy bottom, and touched one of the long white filaments that floated next to her. She frowned and called to the others. "Look! An organism of some kind . . . I wonder what the rest of it looks like."

"Be careful," someone cautioned, their thoughts echoing through Harmon's mind, "we haven't even started to catalog the life-forms in that ocean. Who knows what sort of defense mechanisms it might have."

"It seems harmless to me," Valerie replied, but released the filament nonetheless, and moved to an open section of water. The memory faded and was gone.

Suddenly Harmon was back, her forehead pressed against warm metal, tears dried on her face. She stood and looked around. "Can you hear me?"

"Of course we can hear you," a voice said from inside her head. "We heard you from the moment that you entered orbit. Come, wade into the sea, that we might feel you."

Harmon felt a mixture of fear and wonder as she walked down onto the beach, kicked off her sneakers, and waded out into the water. Other than the gentle passing of the waves and the distant call of a seabird, nothing happened at first. Then, with a gentleness that seemed almost accidental, fifteen or twenty long white tendrils drifted in with the waves, caressed her calves, and stopped just short of the beach. "You are as beautiful as Valerie's memories said you would be."

A feeling of incredible joy filled Harmon's heart. She *wasn't* beautiful, and was well aware of it, but the fact that Valerie had thought of her that way meant everything. "Thank you. Thank you for everything! I read the reports that Valerie wrote about you. She was right. You *are* gentle beings.''

''*Too* gentle to be soldiers?'' a voice asked mockingly. Harmon wasn't sure how she knew, but it was different from the first one, and more distant. She scanned the horizon. ''You know about that? About why I came?''

''Of course,'' the voices said in perfect unison. ''We knew from the moment you arrived. You think of little else.''

Harmon smiled at the rather accurate assessment of her mental processes. She was somewhat obsessive at times and the Say'lynt had said as much. ''Then you understand my concerns.''

''Yes,'' the voices agreed, ''we do. You question the motivation behind your orders, the practicality of transporting bodies such as ours, and the risk involved.''

''Yes,'' Harmon replied soberly, ''I do.''

''Then consider this,'' the second voice said. ''Millions of your kind have perished at the hands of the Hudathans. Even now your soldiers fight distant battles in behalf of the organization that you call the Confederacy. Why should we be exempt? We have visited their minds, we know the Hudathans would have killed us during the first war, if it hadn't been for their desire to study us first. So we have every reason to fight, and as the one you call Chien-Chu pointed out, the ability to do so. You saw the wreckage?''

Harmon nodded, realized how stupid it was, and thought her reply. ''Yes, I saw the wreckage.''

''Then you know what we are capable of,'' the first voice said sternly.

''But there are only three of you,'' Harmon objected, ''or were as of twenty years ago.''

''Four,'' an additional voice corrected her. ''There are four of us. Three of what you would consider to be adults, plus Raft Four, who hasn't matured yet. I will take care of

Four. One and Two will fight the Hudathans.''

The statement was made with such authority and with such certainty that Harmon knew the decision had been made. She cleared her throat, realized there was no reason to speak, and projected her thoughts. ''All right . . . if that's your decision . . . then so be it. By the authority vested in me, I hereby name Rafts One and Two as privates in the Confederacy's Marine Corps, and order them to active duty. Orientation and basic training will take place during trans-shipment.''

''Thank you, ma'am,'' Raft One said respectfully,'' but we took the liberty of absorbing all of Captain Ward's military training, and will act accordingly. *Semper Fi.*''

Harmon thought about what the ramrod-straight Marine Corps officer would say when he learned that his memories had been stolen for use by aliens, and grinned. ''Well done, Private. Carry on.''

The *Nooni* was little more than a dot at first, a fly speck against an otherwise unmarred sky, nearly lost in the vastness of the planet's atmosphere. Bit by bit the ship grew larger, until it looked like what it was, and Harmon could hear the high-pitched whine of its main drive, along with the deeper rumble of the bolt-on propulsion units. They weren't working very hard now, but soon would be, as both the Say'lynt and the water necessary to sustain them were brought aboard.

Down, down, down the spaceship came until the huge globe hovered only fifty feet above the now-flattened water. The public relations specialist and his assistants had launched an airborne robo cam, which when combined with four different surface cameras, plus two remote-controlled subsurface units, would provide them with every possible angle on what promised to be the most exciting footage the mission had to provide. Harmon did her best to ignore them.

The inflatable jet-powered work boat, one of four brought down via shuttle, moved up and down on the waves generated by the *Nooni*'s overpressure. Harmon, who had spent thousands of hours at the helm of small boats, barely noticed the motion. She turned the bow into the waves and kept her attention on the ship. She wore a mask pushed up onto her forehead and full scuba gear.

High above, strapped into his command chair, and surrounded by the bridge crew, Naval Commander Tom Duncan fought to retain his composure. The *Nooni* had never been designed to hover for five minutes, much less the hour or so required to load the Say'lynt, and hundreds of things could go wrong. A sudden storm could develop, his primary control system could go belly up, or one of the bolt-on propulsion units could fail. And, with only fifty feet between the ship and the ocean, any one of those possibilities would result in almost certain disaster. Some or all of the crew might survive, but the ship would go down, leaving the mission in shambles. A thin sheen of sweat glistened on his forehead and he wiped it away. "Stand by to deploy the siphon."

A technician, her eyes glued to the screen in front of her, answered without looking his way. "The siphon is ready, sir. All systems green."

Duncan took one last look at the control boards. Once the siphon had been deployed, and a Say'lynt had entered it, there would be no turning back. They would succeed or crash . . . simple as that. His throat felt dry and he swallowed some saliva. "Deploy the siphon."

Harmon heard the words at the same moment the technician did and watched with a growing sense of suspense as a circular hatch irised open and a large, nearly transparent tube appeared. It was at least six feet in diameter and pleated like an accordion. She had sat next to Duncan during countless virtual-reality simulations but nothing could have prepared her for the real thing. The way the *Nooni* hung there, suspended between sky and water, the nearly deafening noises as engines fought to keep the ship aloft, and the size of the tube that splashed into the water below. The technician's voice accompanied the spray. She sounded relieved. "Siphon deployed, sir."

"Excellent. Captain Harmon, the siphon has been deployed. Please ask the marines to board as quickly as they can."

Harmon grinned at the reference to "marines," knew that the Say'lynt had "heard" the order, but passed it along as a matter of form. She did her best to imitate Ward's gruff-voiced style. "All right, you know the drill, let's do it by the numbers."

A considerable amount of thought had gone into what was to happen next. Although Say'lynt intelligence was broadly distributed across thousands of brain nodes, some were more critical than others, and tended to be grouped within the same hundred square miles of ocean. These would be boarded first, since they were analogous to the human brain, and therefore critical to survival. Maneuvering them into the proper position had taken six days of hard work.

Due to the fact that the Rafts had only limited means of self-propulsion, and normally relied on the wind and currents to take them from one place to another, Harmon and her makeshift staff had used the work boats to tow the alien brain nodes to the pickup zone, which was no small task, since in spite of the fact that each Raft weighed hundreds of tons, they were still rather fragile, and it was difficult to pull on them without doing damage.

But, after a series of near disasters, much maneuvering, and a good deal of profanity, the task was accomplished.

The most critical parts of Raft One were in the pickup zone and ready to embark. The Say'lynt was cheerful as always and a lot more composed than Harmon was.

"Raft One, ready to embark, ma'am."

Harmon spoke into the small boom mike. "The marines are ready to board. Start the pumps."

High above, on the *Nooni*'s bridge, a technician touched a button. A pair of powerful pumps started to work, salt water was sucked up through the massive siphon, and Raft One went with it. Harmon held her breath at first, fearful that something would go terribly wrong, but all of the careful preparation paid off, as mile after mile of the Say'lynt disappeared up and into the ship's bio tank. It even became boring after a while, as seconds stretched into minutes, and minutes accumulated towards an hour.

Things went well until all of Raft One was in the tank, and Raft Two was in the process of coming aboard. Duncan knew a problem had developed when the sound of the main drive rose an octave and the entire ship started to vibrate. "What the hell was that?"

"*That* was bolt-on number three, sir," a tech replied calmly. "It just went down. The NAVCOM compensated by demanding more power from the main drive, but it's beginning to overheat, and the loss of number three threw everything out of balance. The vibration is stressing the hull, and what with the extra weight, we could have some stress fractures."

Duncan looked at the elapsed time, saw that it would take another fifteen minutes to load the rest of Raft Two, and knew what had to be done. But the decision belonged to his CO, and for better or for worse, that was Captain Cynthia Harmon. The vibration had increased. A thousand unseen pieces of metal started to rattle. A coffee cup crashed to the deck. The XO fought to keep his voice level. "Captain . . . this is Duncan. I recommend that we abort . . .

repeat . . . abort the embarkation procedure.''

Harmon felt something heavy fall into her stomach. They had a contingency plan for this kind of situation, but it was far from pleasant, and could imperil the mission. More than a mile out from the pickup zone the Say'lynt had been pushed, pulled, and prodded between a pair of bottom-mounted pylons. The purpose of this evolution was to concentrate their long white filaments and loosely strung nodes into a tightly packed mass that would enter into the siphon as easily as possible. One of the side effects of this strategy, however, was to concentrate the alien flesh in a manner that would allow a second party to cut it in half, thereby saving the sentient's control nodules, but sacrificing its extremities, including parts of its mind.

Valerie had reported that the Say'lynt had at least some ability to regenerate their more distal body parts, but the extent of this ability wasn't clear or the effect it would have on the sentient itself. What about shock? Loss of cognitive function? There was no way to know. But to hesitate, to push the ship too far, could mean death for everyone aboard. This was not the sort of decision that a marine biologist normally had to face, and Harmon wondered if she was qualified.

All those thoughts flashed through Harmon's mind in a fraction of a second and were followed by a voice inside her head. ''You *are* qualified. Do what has to be done.''

Harmon was surprised at the strength of her voice. ''That's affirmative, Commander . . . hang in there as long as you can. Let's go, Delta Team . . . you know what to do.''

Harmon pulled her mask down over her face, bit down on her mouthpiece, and tested the regulator. The air was there and she hit the water feetfirst. It took two minutes to swim the distance between the still-anchored work boat and the fibrous mass that was Raft Two's highly compacted body. It was moving right to left as the siphon sucked it up. The scientist turned to the right and kicked. The international orange pylons came steadily closer. The other three members of the special function team did likewise. A self-propelled underwater camera tracked their movements. The plan was to amputate as far back as they could, using the pylons as a marker.

The scientist felt for and found the power baton holstered along her right thigh. It came on at the touch of a button and projected a three-foot cutting beam. Water boiled all around the bar of blue-white energy. Harmon felt the resulting warmth sweep back along the length of her arm. Safety was an important concern so they had agreed that only two members of the team would cut while the other two acted as backups and kept an eye on the big picture.

Harmon had designated herself as one of the two cutters. She swam into position, checked to make sure that she could see cutter number two on the far side of the undulating biomass, and gave the necessary order. "Okay, Neely, remember to move with the cut . . . and keep an eye on me. One amputation is more than enough for today."

Neely, a hard-eyed medical tech, said, "Aye, aye, ma'am," and brought his baton down in a two-handed grip. Stretched as they were between the siphon and the weight of the Say'lynt's body the filaments seemed to leap away from each other. Harmon duplicated the rating's move and saw the same thing happen on her side. A milky-looking substance shot out of the severed ends, a horrible scream filled Harmon's mind, and she saw Neely grab his ears. The more distal brain nodes were dying and broadcasting their pain.

Harmon wanted to tell the med tech that the sound hadn't come through his ears, and that it was imperative that he retrieve the slowly falling baton and finish the job, but there was no time. Propelling herself forward, and moving sideways with the incision, Harmon cut again and again. More and more of the milky white fluid entered the sea until the scientist couldn't see what she was doing and all semblance of method was gone.

Harmon was hacking now, using the baton like a primitive ax, bringing it down time after time, as long, drawn-out screams filled her mind and radio babble assaulted her ears. But there was no time to tell Delta team what to do, only to act, and hope for the best.

Duncan held on to the command chair with both hands. Out of balance, underpowered, and with an ever-growing amount of weight to cope with, the *Nooni* was in the process of shaking herself apart. The main drive, stressed to the very limits of its emergency limiters, was severly overheated. Klaxons, buzzers, and beepers sounded all around. He had never felt so helpless, so powerless, as he did right now. All he could do was wait, hope that the inexperienced scientist could save his ship, and pray. "Yea, though we walk through the valley of the shadow of death, we fear no evil . . ."

The last strands broke before Harmon could cut them. The ends whipped around, wrapped her in a network of fibers, and pulled her towards the siphon. The scientist realized the danger, flailed about her, and became even more entangled. The baton! She could cut her way out! But the baton was gone, lost during the initial whiplash, and as distant as Earth itself. Harmon felt for her diving knife, found it, and had just started to cut her way out when she heard a rumbling noise. Water swirled, something pulled at her, and the knife fell away. The siphon!

Harmon had no more than had the thought when she was inside the tube and being lifted up and into the *Nooni*'s bio tank. She tumbled head over heels, bounced off the sides of the tube, and was sucked into the ship.

Duncan read the sensors, got confirmation from what was

left of Delta team, and ordered full power. The *Nooni* shuddered as the weight of the siphon fell away, lurched sideways as the NAVCOM did its best to compensate for the malfunctioning bolt-on, and groaned as the now-screaming thrusters fought to push it upwards. Inch by inch, foot by foot, the *Nooni* and her crew fought their way up through the resisting air, rejoicing as it grew thinner, and heaving a final sigh of relief as she broke out into the emptiness of space. They had made it.

Meanwhile, down in the bio tank, a much-battered Captain Cynthia Harmon floated on her back, and gazed upwards into a steel gray bulkhead. Raft One was humming what it called the "Healing Song," while Two lay quiescent towards the bottom of the tank. Both had assured her that Two would live and regain full functionality. The scientist thought about that which might lie ahead and wondered if it was worth it. For better or worse, two additional marines had been recruited to the cause, and would soon join the battle.

No, Harmon decided, make that *three* more beings, since she would add her 130 pounds to the fray. She thought of Valerie and found sadness, but none of the anguish that had been there before, or the anger that had so often accompanied it. At least one battle had been won.

21

He who will win must know the enemy better than he knows himself.

Naa proverb
Author and date unknown

With the Hudathan Fleet, off the Planet Prospect II, the Confederacy of Sentient Beings

War Commander Niman Poseen-Ka sat in the semidarkened command center. It was oval in shape and could accommodate up to fifteen officers in the alcoves around the central holo tank. But they were where they should be, out leading their troopers to victory. Or so the Hudathan hoped. Although his fleet had racked up some impressive victories, the action on Jericho being an excellent example, there had been reverses as well, like the disaster at Rork's Drift, where an entire task force had been destroyed. The Confederacy was fighting, and in many cases, fighting well. He looked up at the view screen. It was empty save for the distant image of a brown-blue planet and a scattering of stars.

Poseen-Ka shifted his considerable weight into a more comfortable position and stared out into the void. The In-

thulu System lay helpless before him. It had taken less than
five standard days to destroy its once-powerful fleet along
with the weapons platforms that orbited the two populated
planets. Not because of any lack of skill on the part of the
defenders, or a paucity of courage, but because they had
been outnumbered three to one. Still some danger remained. There was little doubt that the humans had sent
message torps to their high command. That meant the odds
were excellent that a Confederacy battle group was on its
way. However, intelligence had assured him that it would
be more than a week before any such force arrived. At this
point his flagship, the *Hand of Hudatha*, could sterilize
Prospect I and II by itself should he give the orders to do
so, but he hadn't. Why?

Perhaps the five fates were angry with him. Perhaps he'd
been *too* successful, *too* proud, and this was their way of
punishing him. Or maybe they were upset with Grand Marshal Hisep Rula-Ka, who had ridden a long streak of good
luck. Until a strange fate that had befallen him.

It still wasn't clear what had happened, how Rula-Ka's
personal gig had been taken by a human destroyer, but it
had, and his onetime protégé turned commanding officer
was in enemy hands. Fortunately the humans didn't realize
who they had captured, or they would have demanded a lot
more than the Inthulu System's two inhabitable planets as
ransom.

Not that such efforts would avail them much, since the
Triad would expect Poseen-Ka to abandon his senior officer, assume his duties, and lay waste to the entire system
by last meal the same day. And he should have done so by
now.

So why hadn't he? His excuses were feeble. Yes, Rula-
Ka had been his onetime protégé, but so had many others,
and the war commander knew he would sacrifice any of
them in an instant. True, Rula-Ka had freed him from Wor-

ber's World, but that had been incidental to a larger plan that met racial needs. Even the restoration of his rank and reputation had served a larger purpose, not the least of which was to create a figure on whom failure could be blamed should that become necessary. So why the hesitancy to act?

The answer was obvious. Somewhere, hidden where only he could see it, Poseen-Ka was weak. A weakness that could be seen in the fact that he had allowed himself to form a sentimental attachment to Rula-Ka. An attachment so strong that he had actually considered a trade. The out-and-out folly of it astounded him. The solution was obvious. He must ignore his emotions, order an attack, and emerge victorious. Over the humans *and* himself. Still . . . what if there was another way?

Poseen-Ka touched one of a dozen buttons recessed into the armrest of his chair. The response was nearly instantaneous. His aide, a highly decorated recon pilot named Nagwa Isaba-Ra, appeared as if by magic. He was the most efficient assistant the war commander had ever been lucky enough to have. A recessed spot threw a slash of light down across the younger officer's face. It reflected strength and determination. "Sir? You called?"

"Yes," Poseen-Ka replied. "I did. To what extent was the Inthulu System damaged during the last war?"

There was absolutely no reason why Isaba-Ra should have that particular piece of information at his fingertips but he did. "The Inthulu System was barely touched during the first war, sir. It was bypassed during the leap to the inner planets."

Poseen-Ka signaled understanding, as well he could, for he had commanded the fleet his subordinate referred to. "So while the indigenous population will have *heard* about our methods, they don't *know* about them."

The thought was rather abstract and Poseen-Ka took

pleasure in the fact that Isaba-Ra understood what he meant. "No, sir. Most of the humans in this system have had little or no personal experience with our culture."

"So, they would believe an offer of terms?"

The Hudathan known as Isaba-Ra felt his heart hammer against his lab-grown chest. They had warned him that this might happen, that in order to maintain his cover as a spy, the *only* spy the Hegemony had within the alien ranks, he might have to say or do something that would cost human lives. The fact that they would be *non-Hegemony* lives helped to some extent, but didn't entirely eliminate the nausea in his stomach. "Yes, sir. Based on what I've read about human psychology, they would *want* to believe such an offer."

"Exactly," Poseen-Ka said thoughtfully. "All the humans I knew placed great store in discussion. Let's give it a try. Contact intelligence. Tell them to dangle the possibility of a trade in front of the humans. A planet in return for our crew. Make sure they do nothing to make Rula-Ka seem special."

Isaba-Ra signaled his understanding. "It shall be as you say, War Commander. Where should this meeting take place?"

Poseen-Ka thought for a moment. "Somewhere they will see as neutral ground. An asteroid, perhaps?"

Isaba-Ra gestured assent. "I will examine the possibilities."

Poseen-Ka watched the youngster leave the compartment and turned to the view screen. The planet was still there, as were the stars.

Deep inside a blast-proof command bunker on the planet Prospect II, wall monitors flickered and radio traffic murmured in the background. The air was filter-fresh and cold enough to raise goose bumps on unprotected arms.

Admiral Maria Salgado had short black hair touched with gray, a blaster scar down the right side of her face, and a two-pack-a-day stim-stick habit. She exhaled a thin stream of smoke and touched a remote. The wall screen faded to black. She had seen the video twenty-seven times. "So, Phillip, do you believe them?"

"Hell, no," Captain Phillip Hastings replied matter-of-factly. "The geeks don't negotiate. Never have, never will. Everyone knows that." He was a thin man who liked to run. He felt closed in and did his best to hide it.

"Well, Governor Kogan doesn't," Salgado replied dryly. "She believes in the tooth fairy, pots of gold, and Lord knows what else. She's been all over me ever since the message came in."

Hastings shrugged. "You can't really blame her, Admiral. Barring some sort of miracle, the geeks can finish us anytime they want. It'll be a week or a week and a half before reinforcements arrive. She figures that even the *possibility* of a deal is better than certain death."

Salgado sighed. "I suppose you're right. What have we got to lose? Send for the prisoners and request my shuttle. This mission belongs to me."

Isaba-Ra was cold, tired, and increasingly pissed off. He, along with a dagger of specially trained naval commandos, had been waiting in the wreckage for sixteen hours. During that time he had gone through four sets of oxygen tanks, filled his liquid waste container to capacity, taken three uneasy naps, and consumed six of the foul-tasting food wafers.

Human scouts had come, inspected the wreckage for any signs of an ambush, missed the twelve Hudathan troopers hidden deep among the twisted steel girders, and left some spy eyes to watch for them. Their failure was understandable, since the wreck was huge, and the commandos were equipped with heat cloaks and ECM gear.

Still, if the humans didn't hurry up and get there, the spy would go crazy. Not that he was exactly sane, especially given the fact that he felt more and more Hudathan with each passing day, and had an increasing amount of difficulty remembering his past identity.

Maybe it would have been easier if he'd been a less successful Hudathan. But Isaba-Ra was a hero, universally judged to be good at what he did, and rewarded accordingly. A helluva lot different from the man he'd been, a know-nothing intelligence tech, genetically destined for a boring life. Not so for Isaba-Ra, who might rise as high as his talent and luck would take him. Spear commander? War commander? Grand marshal? Nothing was beyond the realm of possibility. It was tempting, very tempting, and increasingly on his mind.

Isaba-Ra heard three clicks over the speakers inside his helmet. The humans were coming! He answered with two clicks, the signal to feed looped video to the spy eyes, and prepare for action. Quickly, and with a minimum of fuss, the commandos took their assigned positions. There was no gravity to speak of so it was important to move with great care. Then, with everyone in place, the second, more important wait began.

Admiral Salgado hadn't worn battle armor in a long time. She had nearly forgotten how confining it could be, how certain odors built up over time, and how vulnerable she felt, knowing that the only thing between her and hard vacuum was what amounted to six layers of bonded fabric. Sure it was tough, sure it was strong, but there were plenty of weapons capable of punching holes through it. The officer pushed the thought away, wished she could light a stim stick, and checked to see how the rest of her party was doing. They were in the final stages of boarding the shuttle.

The *Victory*'s launch bay was a cavernous space that dated back to the bad old days when the emperor and his advisers had favored size over nearly everything else. The *Victory,* which normally served as a training vessel, along with a handful of smaller ships, were all that remained of the small but potent planetary defense force she had commanded. A combination of sorrow, bitterness, and guilt nearly overwhelmed Salgado as she boarded the shuttle, signaled for the deck crew to remove the roll-around stairs, and took a seat on the starboard bulkhead.

The Hudathans sat across from her. They were huge hulking figures who gazed impassively through their face plates and seemed anything but cowed. Salgado wondered what they were thinking, especially the oldest of the four, who claimed to be a noncom, but received a lot more deference than the rank called for. Was he an officer, perhaps? Claiming a lower rank in an effort to mislead his captors? That might account for the rather unusual willingness to negotiate, something she had made clear to Governor Kogan, who had acknowledged the possibility, and made it equally clear she didn't give a damn what rank the prisoners were, as long as the negotiations were successful.

Salgado sighed. As presently constituted, the deal wasn't much of a deal. They had a promise and nothing more. There were no precedents to follow, no bilateral guarantees, and no one to act as a witness if the Hudathans broke their word. The only comfort the officer had was the knowledge that her advance team had planted an extremely powerful command-triggered mine aboard the wreck, which she could detonate at the first sign of treachery. She wanted to live, but had already lost nearly everyone she cared about, and was quite willing to trade her life for the enemy's.

It took less than an hour to make the trip to the slowly

drifting wreck. Salgado fought the temptation to think about how many valiant men and women had died aboard the one-time cruiser, and how many *would* die during the days, weeks, and months ahead. The pilot interrupted her thoughts. "I have visual contact with the wreck, Admiral. Visual, electronic, and IR scans confirm six, repeat six, suits of armor, all radiating within normal parameters."

Salgado, a damned good rocket jockey in her younger days, wished she were in the cockpit, seeing the wreck with her own eyes, but knew that would undermine the pilot's confidence. "And the spy eyes?"

"Nothing out of the ordinary, ma'am. The negotiating team and that's all."

"Very well, then, close on the wreck, but keep your finger on the trigger. The numbers match . . . but the possibility of an ambush continues to exist."

"Aye, aye, ma'am. Closing now."

By prior agreement the shuttle fired its retros while still a long ways off, slowed, matched the wreck's rate of drift, and assumed a position one mile out. A Hudathan vessel of similar size and capability could be seen in the corresponding slot two miles away. The pilot announced their arrival. "We are in position, Admiral. All sensor readings normal."

Admiral Salgado looked around the already depressurized cargo compartment and grinned through her face plate. "All right, ladies and gentlemen, time to de-ass the shuttle, and see what the geeks have to say."

The cargo door slid open and the Hudathan prisoners were ushered out into the void. They were closely followed by the guards and negotiating team. All of them fired their suit jets and moved away in a sloppy sort of formation. It took them less than five minutes to cross the intervening space and land on the wreck.

Salgado was interested to note that although three of the

aliens had no difficulty landing on the wreck, the oldest, and the one she suspected of being an officer, misjudged the situation, and would have overshot the target entirely if his guards had failed to intervene. A problem the human understood, since she didn't get much suit time, either, and could easily make a fool of herself. It might be meaningful, or it might not, but one thing was for sure: if she bought the farm, the geek sonofabitch was going with her.

Isaba-Ra waited until the grand marshal was aboard and the humans had committed themselves before making his move. Though not an actual Hudathan, the spy executed the plan in much the same manner as a *real* Hudathan would have, straight ahead, and balls to the wall. He didn't like what he was about to do, but felt that it had to be done, and was determined to be successful. He gave the only order his troops needed to hear. "Kill the humans."

The Hudathan shuttle launched a pair of torpedos at the very same moment as Isaba-Ra's commandos opened fire from their carefully concealed positions. Their fire, plus that of the heavily armed Hudathan negotiating team, was nearly irresistible. Suits were already imploding all around her when Salgado felt a weight drop into the pit of her stomach, said, "Aw shit," and detonated the well-hidden mine. The ensuing explosion ripped 25 percent of the wreck apart, killed most of those present, and propelled the rest into space.

Isaba-Ra was among the fortunate few who managed to survive. His first reaction was one of surprise, followed in quick succession by suspicion and fear. Who had planted the bomb? The humans or Hudathans? And if the Hudathans were responsible, had they been *trying* to kill him? Or was he simply viewed as expendable? Lord knew Po-seen-Ka was capable of a move like that, and due to the fact that the human had been raised in a culture where societal needs came first, he could understand the underlying mind set.

But why? There would have been no need had the original plan been given enough time to succeed. That left the humans, and the strong possibility that their advance team had planted a command-detonated mine, and done so right under his nose. How would Poseen-Ka react to that? Would the war commander see it as a regrettable but understandable artifact of war? Or as an act of massive incompetence punishable by death? Both were within the realm of possibility.

Isaba-Ra fired his jets in quick succession, stabilized his suit, and scanned the heavens. He found the still-battling shuttles, zoomed in, and watched the human vessel explode. Part of him felt a terrible sense of sadness while another reacted with almost clinical detachment. The decision was made. For better or for worse, for life or for death, he would contact the only ship likely to pick him up. Isaba-Ra activated his emergency beacon, announced his situation via radio, and waited to see what the five fates had in store for him.

Poseen-Ka stared into the holo tank. The analog was twenty feet across, and looked exactly like Prospect II, all the way down to the scientifically precise pattern of fires that crisscrossed its surface, the clouds of thick black smoke, the still-glowing lakes of molten slag, and the strange lightning storms that played across the once-fertile farmland. The globe rotated before him and the Hudathan knew that this part of his job was nearly done.

The war commander looked up and found eleven sets of eyes waiting to meet his. All the members of his staff who were still alive and able to attend in person. Two more, their images projected onto a long curvilinear screen, hung in what seemed like midair. Their eyes met his as well. All wore cross-straps and a single red gem. They waited for him to speak. He allowed the silence to stretch long and thin before he broke it.

"The humans have paid for their treachery, for the cowardly way in which they murdered Grand Marshal Rula-Ka, and our unsuspecting negotiating team. Should any of you wish to hear the details of what happened, Arrow Commander Nagwa Isaba-Ra was there, and will be glad to describe what took place."

Isaba-Ra, who stood at parade rest off to one side of Poseen-Ka, felt their stone-cold eyes turn his way. He had been exonerated of all responsibility, praised for his valor in the face of the enemy, and submitted for another medal. What should he feel? Relief at being alive? Pride in having murdered a party of unsuspecting humans? And what was he anyway? A clone? A human? A Hudathan? He wasn't sure anymore. Poseen-Ka spoke and the spy gave a sigh of relief as the eyes shifted away.

"The war has entered a new phase. In spite of our many victories, and the success of our valiant cyborgs, the humans fight on. Their strategy has been to slow the force of our attack while they ready themselves for the climactic battle. This stems from their essential weakness, from the fact that the Confederacy consists of many races, all of whom put their interests first. Discussion, negotiation, and compromise. Those are the flaws that will bring them down. For while our enemies dither, we shall strike, and strike hard, aiming our blow for the very place where defeat claimed our honor, and so many of us died. The planet called Algeron."

A human audience might have applauded or given some other external sign of approval. The Hudathans did no such thing, but Isaba-Ra could tell that they were impressed nonetheless, and ready to follow Poseen-Ka's lead. It showed in barely seen hand gestures, in the way they looked at each other, and the hardening of their expressions. If Poseen-Ka wanted to attack Algeron they were ready.

It was, Isaba-Ra knew, the kind of information he had been sent to get, and worth thousands, maybe millions of human lives, because a warning, given in time, could enable the Confederacy to prepare. Assuming he gave the information to the Hegemony, and assuming they saw fit to pass it along to the Confederacy. So what would he do? Confirm his external identity and remain silent? Or act in concert with the inner voice that was so distinctly human? The choice was his and his alone. The voices droned on while the man called Isaba-Ra searched for his soul.

22

One should know one's enemies, their alliances,
their resources and nature of their country, in order
to plan a campaign. . . .

Frederick the Great
Instructions to his generals
Standard year 1747

Planet Algeron, the Confederacy of Sentient Beings

Easytalk Nightkiller elbowed his way out onto the sun-
warmed rock, brought a pair of Confederacy-issue bino-
finders up to his eyes and scanned the flatlands below. He
saw piles of rain-rounded boulders, lots of low-lying scrub,
and water-cut ravines. Due to the fact that the planet had
an extremely short rotation, he could actually *see* the long,
dark shadows crawl towards the east. Dust spiraled up and
away from whatever had disturbed it. The Naa moved the
binoculars to the right, racked focus, and found what he'd
been looking for. Nightkiller felt honored. The Legion had
seen fit to send a full platoon after him. Scouts forward,
bio bods behind, Trooper IIs on the flanks, and a quad to
bring up the rear. Just like they had taught him at NCO
school, never for a moment suspecting that he'd take the
knowledge over the hill and use it against them.

The Naa thumbed the zoom control, watched a Trooper II leap towards him, and focused on the half-visored face visible just beyond an armor-clad shoulder. Nightkiller didn't like officers *or* half-breeds, so greasing the captain wouldn't bother him in the least. The fact that he'd get paid for it was icing on the cake.

It seemed that the breed's father, an ex-officer, had gained more influence than certain chieftains thought a human should have, and was marked for death. But his followers, the tribe once led by the famous Wayfar Hardman, were skilled warriors and continued to protect him. Until now, that is, since his efforts to unite the tribes against the alien Hudatha had forced the human to travel more than usual, and left him vulnerable to attack. But that was an opportunity for someone else. His job was to limit the human's effectiveness by terminating his son.

The deserter understood why that was important, because should the off-worlder manage to unite the tribes against the Hudathans, he might also convince them to remain together when the war was over, which would have the effect of reducing the chieftains' autonomy and power. A definite no-no.

A relatively harmless raid had been sufficient to pull the unsuspecting breed away from his company HQ and into the foothills. The bandit grinned and back-wiggled into the safety of some randomly piled rocks. Muscle rippled under his gray-striped fur as he stood. He wore a weapons harness, pistol belt, leather pants, and Legion-issue combat boots. His dooth smelled him, grunted in recognition, and pawed the ground. The Naa scrambled down out of the rocks, put a foot into a stirrup, grabbed onto the side-mounted saddle handle, and pulled himself up and onto the beast's shaggy back. The raiding party consisted of six Naa and two humans. All of them were deserters who hated the

Legion. He gave a hand signal, gestured towards the trail, and led them upwards.

The flat scrub-covered plain had given way to steeply slanted slopes and a jumble of rocks. Booly scanned the area, saw what he recognized as the mouth of an arroyo, and used hand signals to send his scouts in that direction. Both were full-blooded Naa, *and* members of the 13e Démi-Brigade de la Légion Étrangère, better known as the 13th DBLE.

As presently constituted, the brigade consisted of a command and services company, a works company, a reconnaissance squadron, and a combat company, presently commanded by none other than Captain William Booly, Jr. An officer who had not only been raised on Algeron but was personally familiar with large sections of it.

The scouts signaled their understanding, and moved out up the ravine with the easygoing confidence of the veterans they were, for in keeping with Naa tradition, and the nature of the world on which they'd been raised, both had been blooded long before they joined the Legion.

The ravine made for relatively easy going but could also lead them into an ambush. To counter that threat Booly gave his scouts a good head start, pulled his four Trooper IIs down off the flanks, and replaced them with the more agile bio bods.

The young officer's knees hurt from riding a Trooper II for the last six hours. He could have dismounted, but was reluctant to do so since it would cost him the additional range obtained by jacking into the cyborg's com system. And communications were essential. Still, he felt guilty about riding while some of his troops walked, and took the point position by way of penance. A decision that his ride, a legionnaire named Helmo, reacted to with disgust.

It wasn't fair! Not only did she have to haul the company

commander's butt all over hell's half acre, *she* had to take the point as well, along with all the additional risks attendant on that position. Like taking an SLM between the vid cams, stepping on a mine, or triggering a full-scale ambush.

But orders were orders, so the cyborg brought her weapons systems up to condition-five readiness, and boosted her sensors to high gain. The light had started to fade and the darkness would bring added danger. Mom had been right. War sucks.

Thanks to the fact that she was the only ground pounder to make it off Jericho alive, and had dispatches for LE-GCOM Algeron, Chrobuck was hustled down out of orbit, given high-priority ground transportation, escorted through what seemed like a hundred miles of Fort Cameronc's busiest underground corridors, and left to rot in the anteroom outside General Ian St. James's office.

She was far from alone. The room held approximately twenty chairs and most were occupied. Chrobuck was the most junior officer present. She saw colonels, lieutenant colonels, a host of majors, and a civilian with a briefcase chained to her wrist. Some spoke to each other in low, confidential tones as others whispered instructions into their hand comps or scanned the month-old multimedia mags that lay scattered about.

The doors that provided access to the general's office would open every fifteen minutes or so, an officer would emerge, and a name would be called. When this occurred, the fortunate man or woman would look up, receive a confirming nod, drop what he or she was doing, glance at a conveniently placed mirror, and disappear into the inner sanctum.

There was no discernible pattern to this activity, since a number of people who had arrived *after* Chrobuck had already been called, so she gave up trying to make sense of it. An hour had passed, and a snack had been served, when the young officer allowed her mind to drift.

The trip from Jericho had been relatively fast, only twelve days, but intensely miserable. Once Chrobuck came to, and realized where she was, a profound depression set in. The knowledge that her friends and comrades were dead, and that she had survived, triggered successive waves of guilt, sorrow, and anger.

Making a bad situation even worse was the lack of privacy, and the fact that her sole companion, Flight Lieutenant Bruce Jensen, didn't care what happened on Jericho, as long as it didn't happen to him, and spent all of his spare time trying to get into her pants. By the time the *LRS-236* dropped into orbit they were barely speaking and Jensen had a black eye.

"Lieutenant Chrobuck?"

The voice jolted the officer out of her reverie. The other officers looked up, ran appraising eyes over her badly creased uniform, noted the not-very-clean bandage that decorated the side of her head, frowned, gave thanks that the ratty-looking lieutenant was someone else's problem, and returned to whatever they'd been doing.

Chrobuck stood, glanced in the mirror, and wrote her uniform off as hopeless. She had never seen St. James, much less met him, but he had a reputation as a fighting general, more concerned with deeds than declarations, and she hoped it was true.

A heavily decorated sergeant major held the door open. A quarter of his face had been blown away during the first battle of Algeron and the resulting scar tissue transformed a smile into a grimace. "Right this way, Lieutenant . . . the general is waiting for you."

Chrobuck entered a spacious but somewhat spartan office and saw that St. James was taking a com call. He was a handsome man, quickly going gray, with the quick, lean body of a mountain climber. He smiled, continued to speak into a wireless handset, and gestured towards one of two chairs that faced his desk. Chrobuck sat, took note of the carefully framed regimental photos that hung on the walls, the climbing mementos that filled a plexiglass case, and the brass plaque that had been mounted on the desk in front of her. It read, "Be bright, be brief, and be gone." A picture of a beautiful Eurasian woman and two teenage boys occupied a side table and softened the overall effect.

Still, there was an almost palpable feeling of authority in the room, and Chrobuck felt tiny beads of sweat pop out on her forehead, and was about to wipe them away when St. James replaced the handset. He smiled. "Sorry about that, Lieutenant. I don't know who frightens me the most, the homicidal Hudathans, or our own supply people. Lord knows both are out to get us."

Chrobuck laughed in spite of herself. She knew St. James was putting her at ease and appreciated the effort. "Yes, sir. I know what you mean."

St. James perched on a corner of his desk. His face grew serious. "I'm sorry about what happened on Jericho. We sent a relief force as soon as we could. It should have arrived by now. I hope it catches the bastards red-handed and erases them from the face of the cosmos. You'll be interested to know that two of Worthington's message torps made it through. The last one made mention of Hudathan cyborgs and the fact that you would be coming our way. Have you got something for me?"

Chrobuck nodded miserably and pulled a tiny data disk out of her belt pouch. It was just like her commanding officer to let St. James know that she was coming and thereby prevent any possibility that she would be treated as a deserter. She handed him the disk. "Yes, sir. The colonel sent you this."

St. James took the disk, walked over to a wall-mounted

holo player, and slipped it in. The room lights dimmed, colors chased each other through the air, and an image appeared. It was Colonel Wesley Worthington. He was on the edge of exhaustion but still managed a crooked smile. "Hello, Ian, you old bastard. If you're watching this then Lieutenant Chrobuck made it through. Take care of her . . . she's one helluva fine officer."

It was then that Worthington consulted some handwritten notes and launched into his report. He narrated some video of the Hudathan cyborgs, provided an analysis of their strengths and weaknesses, and sketched in what he knew about the enemy task force.

It was a masterful briefing and during the last part of the report Chrobuck had the rather unsettling experience of watching herself retreat to the ridge, get hit, and fall. She was grateful when the holo collapsed and the lights came up. St. James looked grim.

"*Hearing* about the Hudathan cyborgs and *seeing* them in action are two different things. No wonder the geeks have done so well. You did the Confederacy a great service, Lieutenant. This holo is just what we need to obtain more resources and kick certain programs into high gear. I'm just sorry that we paid such a high price to get it."

Chrobuck nodded and stood. She fought to control the flood of tears that threatened to come. "Thank you, sir. Will there be anything else?"

St. James looked thoughtful. "I'm no shrink, but I'd say you need some time off, but not too much. Report to the BOQ. I'll find you a slot. Lord knows it won't be difficult. We need every officer we can get. Any requests?"

Chrobuck came to attention. Her salute was as crisp as she could make it. "Sir, yes, sir. I would prefer an infantry assignment if that's possible."

St. James nodded and returned her salute. "I'll see what I can do."

Chrobuck did an about-face and was halfway to the door when the general spoke again. "One more thing, Lieutenant . . ."

The younger officer turned. "Sir?"

"I'm putting you in for the Legion of Valor. It's the least I can do after what you did on Jericho. The joint chiefs will have to pass on it but my recommendations are generally approved."

Chrobuck swallowed the lump that had formed in her throat. She knew the *real* heros lay dead on Jericho. And she knew that it would always be like this. The dead are dead; the living go on living. She forced a smile. "Thank you, sir."

The horribly wounded sergeant major appeared out of nowhere, escorted her to the anteroom door, and called another name. A major stood, checked his uniform in the mirror, and entered behind her. The officers' club was due for a party . . . and there were questions about the guest list.

They had climbed steadily upwards through another two-hour-and-forty-two-minute day. The ravine had played out long ago and given way to an ancient trail. It switchbacked endlessly upwards and vanished between two peaks. The sun had risen in the east and threw pink light across the mountains known as the Towers of Algeron. Some of the peaks reached more than eighty thousand feet into the sky, higher than Everest on Earth, or Olympic Mons on Mars.

In fact they were so massive that they would sink through Terra's planetary crust. Except that Algeron was different from Earth. The centrifugal force created by the planet's short rotation had created a larger-than-normal bulge at the equator. A bulge so huge that it had turned into a mountain range, which due to the gravity differential that existed between the two poles, weighed only half what it would on Terra.

With the added altitude the air had grown steadily colder, and Booly, only half-warmed by his proximity to the Trooper II's body, wished he had thought to bring a parka. But the temperature, and the fact that his platoon was bone tired, was nothing compared to the worry. What was happening? And why hadn't he heard from Parker by now? He knew this trail, knew that it would lead him up through the same pass that had witnessed countless ambushes during the last five hundred years, and had no wish to add to the makeshift graveyard that had long been established there. Booly remembered the patches of snow that never melted, the green-yellow lichen that grew on the heavily weathered stones, and felt a shiver run down his spine. Should he continue? Or turn back? The wind whistled down off the glaciers and knifed through his clothes.

Thanks to the fact that the officer thought he was in pursuit of everyday bandits, and had no idea that he had been selected *the* target, his efforts to defend against a full-scale ambush would be wasted. All Nightkiller needed was one clean shot and the whole thing would be over. The officer would collapse, his platoon would fire in every direction, collect the body, and withdraw. Nice, clean, and straightforward. The way all murders *should* be handled but seldom were. Yes, the bandit thought to himself as he withdrew the specially crafted rifle from the carefully greased scabbard, brains over brawn. It works every time.

With his cohorts placed to provide supporting fire should it become necessary, Nightkiller placed the rifle across his back, and climbed up through the jumble of rocks. Once near the top, he slowed rather than break the skyline, moved sideways until he found a gap between two boulders, and pulled the weapon into position.

It was chambered for hand-loaded 7.62-millimeter ammunition. The clip held twenty rounds but one would be enough. The rifle had a custom-shaped butt, an adjustable trigger mechanism, and a high-quality 1.5 X 6 day/night scope.

The bandit snuggled against the cold brown wood, peered into the scope, found the point where the trail made a long, slanty line against the opposite slope, and traced it back to a stand of wind-twisted trees. A scout stepped out in front of Nightkiller's cross hairs, scanned the surrounding slopes through a pair of olive drab binoculars, and stopped.

The would-be assassin felt his heart skip a beat as the other Naa looked directly into his scope. Then, after ten or fifteen seconds, the scout turned away. What, if anything, had he seen? Nightkiller held his breath as the legionnaire said something into his boom mike and another figure appeared. The all-clear! Good. The waiting was nearly over. The bandit pulled the sling around his elbow for additional stability, locked his cross hairs onto a spot just beyond the trees, and settled down to wait. It wouldn't be long.

Parker, now known as *Gunnery Sergeant* Parker, leaned backwards to the point where the swivel chair threatened to topple over, smiled, and opened the com link. "Delta Base to Honcho One. Over." A bevy of technicians, all privy to what was going on, gathered behind him. They had worked hard to prepare a surprise party for the bandits and wanted to be there for the climax.

Booly, squinting up into momentary sunshine, answered. "Honcho One here . . . go."

Parker scanned the monitors in front of him. Only one of the images mattered and that was the one that showed Easytalk Nightkiller from behind. The minisat, on temporary loan from the Navy, would soon be out of position. Another tac-eye would be along in about five minutes, but a lot could happen in five minutes, and Parker wanted closure now.

"We have a hole in the cloud cover. The subjects are in sight. They are approximately one mile southeast of your position. One bandit appears ready to fire on your column. He has eight bio bods in reserve. Request permission to fire."

Booly frowned. One bandit positioned to fire? With eight in reserve? It didn't make sense. An ambush would require all eight of them, and more, if they hoped to win. So what was going on? A hunting party, perhaps? Traders crossing the pass? A mistake would be horrible. He imagined pencil-thin energy beams slicing down out of the sky, the smell of singed fur, and bodies burned beyond all recognition. Bodies like his mother's, his uncle's, or any number of other relatives'.

Booly knew that most if not all of his brother and sister officers would presume that the Naa were guilty, would give the order without hesitation, and shrug helplessly if they were wrong. Because in spite of their valor during the first war, and in spite of their acceptance into the Legion since that time, the vast majority of humans saw the Naa as geeks. Parker sounded tense. "Delta Base to Honcho One. Cloud cover closing. Request permission to fire."

Booly opened his mouth and found that the words came of their own volition. "Honcho One to Delta Base. Permission denied. Repeat . . . permission denied."

Parker pulled his hand away from a button and leaned back in his chair. His face was expressionless. A tech said, "Aw, shit. We had the geeks right where we wanted them and the captain lets them go! Maybe what I heard was right . . . maybe he takes after his mother."

The swivel chair squeaked as it turned. No one saw Parker pull the pistol, it just appeared in his hand. The tech looked down the barrel and straight into the jaws of hell.

The gunnery sergeant smiled. It was not a pretty sight. "Yes, as a matter of fact the captain *does* take after his mother. Have you got a problem with that?"

The sunlight disappeared as the clouds closed in. In spite the fact that the Naa *might* be innocent hunters Booly doubted that they were. There were too many of them, for one thing, especially since there was damned little game at these elevations. No, they were up to something, all right, and he wanted to know what it was. The exchange with Parker had taken place on the command channel, which meant that his scouts were unaware of the danger. He switched to the team frequency. The platoon had continued uphill and he adjusted the range accordingly. "Honcho One to Honcho team . . . We have what might be hostiles three-quarters of a mile southeast of our position. Trooper IIs close on me . . . we're going in.

"Squads Two and Three will take cover and fire on my command. Squad One will turn and guard our rear. Quad One will Support Squad One."

Booly heard three acknowledgments as the squad leaders checked in, saw three Trooper IIs close in around him, and pointed upwards. "The trail switchbacks up ahead and curves to the right. The hostiles are on the other side of the valley about halfway up. They'll have a clean shot at us the moment we clear those wind-bent trees. The faster we go the less bullets we take. Questions?"

There were no questions so Booly gave the order to move, and hung on for dear life. A Trooper II could achieve speeds of up to fifty miles per hour flat out, and even though she was moving uphill, Helmo was up to thirty-five miles per hour in no time at all. But the ride was far from smooth and it took strength, skill, and a harness to hang on.

Booly felt a strange sense of exhilaration as they left the shelter of the trees and broke into the open. Maybe this was the way ancient warriors had felt as they rode into battle. Their dooths thundering towards the enemy, their swords slicing through crisp mountain air, and their comrades to either side. Energy flowed through the legionnaire's body as he moved to the rhythms of his cybernetic mount and a long, echoing war cry flowed from his lips.

The sudden appearance of the Trooper IIs caught Nightkiller by surprise. He had served in the Legion himself so it took little more than a second for the bandit to realize that he was under surveillance by a tac-eye. Maybe the breed was smarter than he seemed.

The bandit resisted the temptation to look up into the sky and hunched his shoulders against the energy beam that might or might not come. All he needed to do was stay calm, lead the first cyborg like so, take a deep breath, release it ever so slowly, and squeeze the trigger. The report and resulting recoil seemed like an afterthought. Nightkiller watched and waited for the officer to slump against his harness.

Booly felt tiny bits of hot metal pepper his face, heard a clang, followed by the sound of a distant rifle shot. Helmo's brain case was dimpled where the slug had hit. He yelled into his mike. "Honcho One to Honcho team . . . We are taking fire from high to the right! Hose 'em down!"

Nightkiller threw himself backwards as the legionnaires opened fire. Their automatic weapons made a sound similar to ripping cloth, and rocket-propelled grenades thumped all around. The bandit abandoned all thoughts of completing his mission and concentrated on a successful escape instead. Speed was of the essence. A boot slipped on lichen-covered rock. He fell, landed wrong, and swore as pain lanced up through his leg, and called for help. "Rockthrow! Perkins! Give me a hand!"

Dooths grunted, gear clanked, and rocks flew away from hooves as his followers hauled themselves up onto their saddles and headed towards the pass. None would meet his eyes. Nightkiller hobbled after them. "Wait! Wait, damn it!"

Perkins, one of two humans in the band, rode the last dooth. He led Nightkiller's animal on a jury-rigged lead and clearly intended to steal it. The Naa limped along behind and called his dooth by name. It jerked against the lead and rolled its eyes. Perkins turned, looked annoyed, and leveled his rifle. Nightkiller saw a flash and felt his knee explode. The ground hit him hard. He wanted to die, wanted to kill himself, and was reaching for his handgun when darkness pulled him down.

Booly felt an odd sense of disappointment as Helmo arrived in front of the body. His knees hurt as he jumped down and felt for a pulse. It was thready but palpable. The officer called for a medic and tried to feel good about what they had managed to accomplish. All the effort, all the risk, just to capture a single bandit.

Yet both the Legion and the tribes had played this game for a long time now, so long that it had claimed a place in both of their cultures, and become self-perpetuating, because when there was no *real* enemy to fight, the Legion had traditionally attacked the Naa, who had responded by building combat into the rites of warriorhood, thereby promulgating a sort of ritual warfare. Until recent times, when the Hudatha had provided both parties with a common enemy.

Was this what he wanted to do with his life? Hunt bandits through the hills? Or provide similar services on other planets? The question followed the officer out of the mountains, onto the plains, and through the wire that surrounded Delta Base.

23

He who hunts shall also be hunted . . . for such is nature's way.

Naa proverb
Author unknown
Standard year circa 150 B.C.

Clone World Alpha-001, the Clone Hegemony

The com-ball had traveled a long, long way. The device had originated on Beta-001, clamped itself to the skin of an outbound robo-freighter, remained in place until the ship reached Alpha-001's gravity well, transferred itself to a surface-bound shuttle, slipped past customs, and hid until darkness fell.

Then, in accordance with the programming provided on Beta-001, and new information downloaded from an illegal micro-sat, the com-ball reactivated the expensive antigrav generator that kept it aloft, and used air jets to maneuver its way through Alpha-Prime's gridlike streets.

Expensive or not, the antigrav unit couldn't lift the device any higher than a few hundred feet, so it was forced to wend its way between rows of high-rise buildings, all of which looked the same, and were filled with equally identical people. Many of whom could be seen through brightly lit windows, sitting with mostly same-sex companions, or watching government-approved holos.

But none of that was of interest to the com-ball, which had been given a specific mission, and didn't care about anything else. The building it sought was located in the most run-down section of the city, the part that had been built around the first spaceport, and was therefore different from the rest. There was irony in that, since the quarry was different, too, but that particular nuance lay beyond the parameters of the machine's programming.

Having located what it believed to be the correct choice, the messenger verified the address using one of the government's global positioning satellites, circled the eleventh floor, found the room designated as 1106, hovered outside long enough to make sure the subject was home, and rose to survey the roof.

Protective mechanisms might have been placed around the building, the com-ball's programming was quite specific about that, which meant that the machine had to find and neutralize any such devices prior to entry. And sure enough, the messenger found six full-function detectors, a pre-provisioned escape route, and two carefully disguised hidey-holes, one of which contained a considerable quantity of illegal weapons and other equipment.

Having completed its survey, the com-ball activated certain subprograms and destroyed the sensors with carefully placed bursts of coherent energy. Then, satisfied that it could enter the structure unannounced, the device propelled itself towards the side of the building.

Fisk-Eight had been living in room 1106 for quite some time now. He looked up into Yee-Two's face and wondered what she actually felt. Her eyes were closed and her mouth was open. Was the appearance of pleasure real? Or just another aspect of what he had paid for? Ah well, no matter. She had a nice body and knew how to use it.

Yee's artificially enhanced breasts flopped up and down as she moved, and tiny beads of sweat had appeared on her upper lip. Fisk-Eight was extremely close to orgasm when the com-ball smashed through the window and sent shards of glass flying in every direction.

Yee was on a downstroke when the messenger put an energy beam through her head. It entered through the back of her skull, exited between her eyes, and burned a hole through the anarchist's pillow. The body had toppled sideways and was in the process of falling when Fisk-Eight went for his handgun. A red dot appeared in the middle of his chest and froze him in place. The voice was unexpectedly familiar. "Move and you will die."

Fisk-Eight thought the voice belonged to Alpha Clone Marcus at first, but realized his mistake as the com-ball projected beams of light into the room and a pair of images appeared. The first belonged to the Alpha Clone Pietro, and the second to his brother Antonio. Although he had never been in direct contact with them, Fisk-Eight was well aware of the fact that the Alpha clones had financed his cell, supported the assassination attempt, and if Pietro's expression was any guide, were far from happy.

Though programmed to accomplish certain things, the com-ball's artificial intelligence was free to tackle the job in any way that it saw fit, and used that freedom to weave the anarchist's surroundings into the message it had been ordered to deliver.

"So," the image named Pietro began, "you imagined that you could simply walk away from your failure, hole up here, and escape the consequences."

The com-ball remained where it was, but the red dot had started to drift a little, down off Fisk-Eight's chest, and over his lower torso. It takes a long time to die from an abdominal wound and the anarchist pulled his stomach in. "No, I did the best I could, but things went wrong."

"Yes, they certainly did," Pietro continued smoothly. "Marcus lives, the Legion whore shares his bed, and Alpha-001 functions as an undeclared ally of the Confederacy. All because of you."

"No," Fisk-Eight insisted desperately, unable to take his eyes off the slowly circling red dot, "it wasn't my fault!"

"Oh, but it was," the image of Pietro said calmly, as it paced back and forth. "Tell him, Antonio, tell him why it was his fault, and how the situation can be corrected."

Antonio smiled vacantly. His hair gleamed with pomade and his body was strangely transparent. "It might interest you to know that you are the *only* Fisk still alive. You encouraged Fisk-Three to sacrifice himself during the assassination attempt, and we terminated the rest, starting with the child called Twenty-seven, and working our way through two-hundred thirty-six more. Would you like to know why?"

Fisk watched the dot. It drifted downwards and lingered over his already shriveled penis. His throat was tight and he found that it was difficult to speak. "Yes, tell me why."

"Because," Antonio said, his eyes also on the dot, "you and those like you are an aberration, one of the few mistakes the Founder made. She feared that a society without anarchists might become *too* stable, might grow complacent, and fall of its own weight. So to keep my brothers and me on our toes, and create a counterbalancing effect, she commissioned the Fisk line, the Trotski line, and a couple more. The unintended effect was that by existing, by being *who* you are, you and your brothers had a tendency to destabilize those around you. So much so that you even undermined the effectiveness of your own cell, sacrificed a member of your own line, and went your own way."

"That's right," Pietro said brightly, his ghostlike eyes glowing from out of the gloom. "Tell him what he must do to survive."

The dot was stationary. It seemed to pulse slightly and Fisk-Eight felt a growing sense of warmth around his genitals. Sweat covered his forehead and he held on to the bedsheets with both hands. "Tell me, tell me what I can do. . . . "

Antonio nodded. "First, you must recognize that my brother and I rule by genetic right, and that you are descended from an inferior line."

Warmth had turned into real heat. His genitals felt as if they were on fire. Fisk-Eight felt his eyes start to bulge. "Yes! I'm inferior! I'll do whatever you say!"

"And then," the Alpha clone continued unemotionally, "you must find a way to get close to our brother Marcus and kill him."

Fisk-Eight fought against the pain. What was that smell anyway? Burned linen? Singed pubic hair? "Anything . . . I'll do anything you want."

The pain started to fade. "Excellent," Pietro said, pausing at the foot of the bed. "Do as we command, and life will be very pleasant for you."

Both images faded to nothingness, the dot disappeared, and the com-ball floated out through the broken window. The anarchist held his genitals with both hands, ignored the smell that emanated from the vicinity of Yee's body, and started to think. Marcus would have to die, that much was clear, the only question was how.

Mosby turned slowly, admiring herself in the full-length mirror. Her body had a tendency to gain weight and she had done battle with it through a regimen of dieting and exercise. But her breasts were visibly larger and the lower part of her abdomen more rounded than before, a fact that accounted for the increasing tightness of her uniforms. The changes in her body served to confirm what the self-administered test had already told her. She was pregnant.

The knowledge made Mosby happy, since she had wanted to have a baby for a long time, but her joy was clouded by the problems that faced her. Although she and Marcus had enjoyed an extremely active sex life, free of all contraceptive measures, they had never discussed what would almost surely happen as a result, and Mosby feared that the reality of her pregnancy might cause a crisis in their relationship.

Also, there was her career to think of, and her obligations to the Legion. There was absolutely no doubt that President Anguar knew of her affair, and had ordered her superiors to ignore the situation so long as it served the Confederacy's purposes, but what if Marcus denied her? She would miss him, but she would miss the information provided by his spy even more, as would the rest of the Confederacy.

It all served to make the next few days even more important. Marcus had invited her to his country estate. She hoped her stay would provide the perfect setting in which to tell the Alpha clone about her pregnancy and secure their relationship. A relationship that would meet her needs and the Legion's as well. Mosby padded out of the bathroom and into the bedroom. A rather generously cut summer-weight dress had been laid out on the bed and she looked forward to wearing it after a week of supertight uniforms.

Bio-storage Building 516 was just as unassuming as its name. What appeared to be a low-slung warehouse was actually just the topmost level of a multistoried building that reached down instead of up. But in spite of the precautions taken to protect it from aerial attack, the uppermost levels of the facility were relatively accessible and given over to various kinds of genetic research.

The levels below them were a good deal more secure, however, housing as they did the backup supplies of sperm and ovum necessary to ensure that the Founder's grand vision would be enacted, even if the primary and secondary storage facilities located thousands of miles away were somehow destroyed.

But it was the deepest levels, those to which only a trusted few had access, that Fisk-Eight wished to visit. But every lock has a key, and thanks to his training and will to survive, it took Fisk-Eight a surprisingly short time to find the one that he needed.

By activating his carefully nurtured network of contacts and informants, the anarchist discovered that a gentech named Crowley-Three had not only managed to avoid using the government-mandated contraceptives, but had also given birth to an unsanctioned free-breeder baby, and was necessarily raising the one-of-a-kind infant at home. Converting the unfortunate woman to his needs was almost too simple, since Crowley knew that the authorities would take her child off-planet should it be discovered, and leave her behind.

So Fisk met the gentech in the cafeteria, pretended to have a friendly conversation with her, and accepted the I.D. badge that she slipped under the table. It said "Visitor" across the front and Eight clipped it to his breast pocket while pretending to tie a shoe. From there they went to a bank of elevators, waited for one to arrive, and stepped aboard. The anarchist found himself in the presence of eight clones, including four additional Crowleys. All were female, had wide-set green eyes, and a scattering of freckles across their noses.

Three exchanged greetings with them, explained that Fisk had been ordered to run a storage audit, and would be accompanying them to the lowest level. A variety of genetic lines had been sent to carry out this task in the past so the Crowleys nodded, welcomed the anarchist to the facility, and entered into an animated discussion of the weather. The platform paused twice to let others get off. The anarchist felt his stomach muscles tighten as the elevator dropped to the lowest level. Crowley-Three swore she had taken care of the necessary clearances, but had she? The fact that she had given birth to an unsanctioned baby, and had managed to conceal it from the authorities, argued for her competence, but who could be sure?

The door swished open and he followed the Crowleys left, off the platform. A security guard got off his stool, gave the clones a cursory once-over, and checked Eight's pass. He frowned, ran a scanner over the bar code printed along the bottom edge of his card, and smiled when a green light came on. "Thank you, sir. You may proceed."

Fisk-Eight nodded agreeably, followed Crowley-Three down a side corridor, through some double doors, and into a white-walled room. Crowley pressed a hand against the wall, waited while her prints were scanned, and turned as a door opened. The anarchist followed her into a comfortably furnished apartment. An easel filled one corner, music floated on perfumed air, and plants thrived under fiber-optic-supplied sunlight. A far cry from the laboratorylike setting he had envisioned. A man sat gazing at a holo sculpture. He turned, stood, and smiled. "Crowley-Three, isn't it? I thought so. Your walk gives you away. And who might this be? I don't remember seeing your line before."

Fisk had fancied himself as immune to the effects of celebrity but found himself wanting to address the man as "sir." Because even though he had been through different experiences, and was therefore mentally and emotionally distinct from the Alpha clone Marcus, the backup *looked* exactly the same. It took an act of will to remember that this *wasn't* the same man, and was in fact little more than a living organ bank, on standby in case Marcus needed a new heart, liver, or kidney.

This was where things could get tricky. The anarchist had made certain assumptions about the backup's life experience, about his state of mind, and everything rode on his being right. Fisk-Eight cleared his throat and looked at Crowley. "Get the container we agreed on plus the auto cart. And remember, one word, and your secret will be out."

Crowley grew pale, nodded in a jerky manner, and backed out of the room. The backup observed all this with a slightly raised eyebrow and turned to Fisk. "This grows curiouser and curiouser. I have an implant. Tell me why I shouldn't use it to summon help."

Fisk-Eight spread empty hands. Everything depended on what he said. The words were chosen with care. "Because I can offer you the one thing you want most . . . freedom."

Although the villa suffered from the same lack of architectural flair common to most structures on Alpha-001, the site made up for it. Set into the side of a heavily forested slope, and located at the top of a sheer two-hundred-foot drop, the veranda looked out over the shimmering surface of a lake. The Founder's cartographers had blessed the body of water with the designator NE-47/65, but Mosby thought it deserved a name, and was in the process of picking one when Marcus sidled up behind her. His lips found an earlobe and his hands cupped her breasts. "And how is my favorite general this morning?"

"Fine," Mosby lied, remembering the morning sickness that had started her day. "And how is my favorite world leader?"

"He couldn't be better," Marcus said warmly, kissing her on the cheek, then moving away. "I have news. News your superiors will want to hear."

Mosby felt her heart beat just a little bit faster. "News? What kind of news?"

Marcus scanned the buffet table, selected some fruit, and forked it onto a plate. "The very *best* kind of news. The kind the enemy doesn't know you have."

"You're rotten to the core," Mosby said petulantly. "Tell or die."

Marcus shook his head in mock amazement. "Legionnaires are *so* violent. I'm surprised the Founder didn't use your particular genetic line to staff our officer corps."

Mosby grinned. "Sure, so you could ruin her plan by seducing thousands of women who look like me. Besides, my parents were ministers, so spill it."

Marcus grew serious. "My spy tells me that the Hudathans are preparing to attack a planet called Algeron. That's a military world, isn't it?"

Mosby nodded. "Yes, Algeron belongs to the Legion and represents an important strategic target. We didn't expect an attack quite so soon, but Poseen-Ka lost the first war there, and will be eager to secure it. May I share the news?"

The question was a mere formality, and both of them knew it, but Marcus waved a piece of fruit in her direction. "Of course. That's why I told you."

Mosby nodded and left the veranda. She had a secure porta-com in her luggage. The message would be on its way within a matter of minutes.

The guard, one of an entire company of Jonathan Alan Sebo's stationed in the vicinity of the villa, watched the limo approach, saw the insignia on the front bumper, and popped to attention. His salute was crisp and professional.

Fisk-Eight, dressed as a chauffeur, braked the car to a halt. He touched a button and waited while the driver's side window whirred out of the way. He searched for and found the knowing smile that one servant reserves for another. "Good morning, soldier . . . Alpha Clone Antonio to see Alpha Clone Marcus."

Stupid foot soldiers aren't half as valuable as intelligent

foot soldiers, so the original Sebo had been chosen as much for his I.Q. as his physical makeup and well-tested courage.

But soldiers grow used to orders, especially when they came from well-known authority figures, and Sebo-945 was momentarily confused. The sergeant of the guard, Sebo-612, had made no mention of a high-level visit, yet there was no denying the existence of the driver, the limo, and the bumper insignia.

Sebo-945 was about to call for assistance when another window whirred down. There was also no denying the identity of the head that poked out. Everyone knew Alpha Clone Antonio and his greasy hair. He looked annoyed. "Is there a problem?"

Sebo-945 popped another salute. Right or wrong, he would take the chance. "No, sir. Routine security check, sir. I'll call the villa and let them know that you arrived."

The Alpha clone smiled and motioned 945 closer. "Do me a favor, soldier, and *don't* notify the house. It's our decanting day, and I want to surprise brother Marcus." The leader followed his comment with a wink and Sebo found himself winking in return. "Yes, sir! It shall be as you say, sir. Congratulations, and many happy returns."

The Alpha clone nodded politely and disappeared behind polarized glass. The barrier swung up and out of the way, the limo whispered down the gently curving drive, and Sebo made the appropriate entry in the gate log. There was little doubt that 612 would approve of his actions and give him a well-deserved attaboy.

Sun streamed down through the trees that bordered the veranda and dappled the flagstones with branch-thinned light. Marcus sat gazing out over the lake as Mosby emerged from the villa and took an adjoining chair. He turned, smiled affectionately, and held out his hand. "I'm glad you're here."

Mosby felt his hand close around hers and knew that a better time would never come. She smiled in return. "You're not the only one with news. I hope you want me here once I tell you what it is."

Marcus frowned. Had she received orders? There was a war on, after all, and Mosby was one of the Confederacy's top generals. Yes, they had allowed her to stay as part of their plan to secure his assistance, but other needs might be greater. "Orders? Did they give you orders?"

Mosby shook her head. "No, nothing like that, although you may wish that they had. The news is that I'm pregnant."

Marcus had known that he'd hear those words one day and wondered how he'd receive them. Would he be shocked? Worried? Frightened? Any such emotions might be appropriate since there would be no hiding her pregnancy, and once delivered, the baby would change the future of his planet. The laws forbidding natural childbirth would have to be revoked, the ties that bound them to the rest of the Hegemony would be forever severed, and the changes that resulted would usher in a new, more democratic form of government. He would be unemployed.

All such thoughts should have left Marcus depressed, should have sent him searching for a way out, but they had no such effect. An expression of tremendous joy came over his face, he leaped to his feet, and pulled Mosby to hers. Her heart leaped as he danced her around the swimming pool. "That's wonderful, incredible, joyful news! Will it be a boy or a girl?"

Mosby laughed, held on for dear life, and felt her worries melt away. "I don't have the foggiest idea . . . that's part of the fun."

"Marvelous," Marcus said happily, pausing to catch his breath, "just marvelous. I can hardly wait. When? When will our little surprise be born?"

"Never," Fisk-Eight replied calmly, "since both of you are about to die."

Mosby spun, reaching for a side arm that wasn't there. The anarchist shook his head and waggled a handgun in her direction. "That'll be enough of that, General. Put your hands on the top of your head. And you can save your energy, Alpha Clone Marcus, I have a little black box that can and is jamming your implant's ability to send. It worked on your brother here . . . so it'll work on you."

Marcus continued his attempts to send on the chance that the man in front of him was lying and felt ice-cold fear trickle through his bloodstream as another Alpha clone stepped out onto the veranda. "Antonio? Is that you?"

The other man shook his head. "Nope, just one of your trusty backups, out for a little stroll. Nice place, by the way . . . I'll enjoy it."

Fisk-Eight saw a look of realization settle over the real Alpha clone's face and laughed. "That's right, Your Clone-ship, all he has to do is wash the grease out of his hair, and presto—a brand-new and considerably more loyal Marcus is born. Your brothers wanted you dead . . . but this will please them even more. Now walk over to the edge of the veranda and climb up on the wall. Let's see if you can fly."

The backup watched his brother back towards the rock wall and the abyss beyond. Here it was, just what he'd always dreamed of, the opportunity to be a *real* Alpha clone. He remembered the passage of the years, the seemingly endless parade of video clips of Alpha Clone Marcus as he cut ribbons, met with workers, toured factories, attended meetings, and reviewed troops.

And all he had to do to in order to take control was to assist in his brother's murder. Of course a *real* leader would tidy things up by getting rid of the free-breeder female, the anarchist named Fisk-Eight, the gentech called Crowley-Three, and two or three others, but that would be relatively easy. *If* he really wanted to rule, *if* power meant that much to him, *if* it was worth the price.

Mosby felt the wall touch the back of her calves. She had already decided that there was no damned way that she would jump off the cliff of her own volition. The baby would die, and so would she, but they'd go down fighting. She measured the distance between herself and the would-be assassin, shifted her weight to her right foot, and prepared to charge.

Marcus knew his lover would go for the gun and had decided to beat her to the punch. The gunman would kill him, there was little doubt about that, but it would be worth it if she lived. Especially since he had little doubt that once Mosby got her hands on the anarchist, his life would end shortly thereafter. He had already started into motion when the backup threw himself at Fisk's legs.

It was a clumsy move, and one from which there would have been little chance of recovery, had the clone been acting alone. But the *real* Marcus hit the anarchist after that, quickly followed by Mosby, who wasted little time in snapping Fisk-Eight's neck.

It took a few moments for the three of them to untangle themselves and stand. Marcus looked at his twin. "Why? It probably would have worked."

The backup shrugged. "No offense, brother, but when I thought about the way *you* live, compared to the way *I* live, I wasn't sure which was worse. Life in my apartment beats the hell out of your meetings. Of course there are my organs to consider, but what the hell, you look reasonably healthy. Let's make sure you stay that way."

Marcus laughed, slapped his brother on the back, and turned to Mosby. "Come here, honey . . . I want you to meet your future brother-in-law."

24

You can't say that civilization don't advance, for in every war they kill you in a new way.

Will Rogers
Standard year circa 1925

The Planet Adobe, the Confederacy of Sentient Beings

Drang was bad, but Adobe was even worse, O'Neal decided as she up-linked to a spy-eye and scanned the surrounding terrain. After the long, somewhat tedious journey from Drang, she had found herself in a new and largely untested body. It was sleek where Trooper IIs were chunky, 25 percent lighter than its predecessor, and 50 percent more lethal. All of which was nice if you cared, which O'Neal did not.

But if the body under her brain case had become smaller, her role had grown more complex, because in addition to her responsibilities as a squad leader the noncom had five analog bodies to keep track of. Each body, or extension of herself, had a different form and function. A pair of low ground-hugging weapons platforms guarded her flanks, two nearly invisible battle disks hovered overhead, and a serpent-shaped construct lay coiled twenty yards in front of her position. Thanks to new, interactive holo armor, all were nearly invisible from above.

O'Neal withdrew from the high-altitude spy-eye and looked through her own vid cams. Miles of iron oxide–rich hard pan stretched out towards the point where cliffs dropped into a chasm so deep it made Earth's Grand Canyon look like an irrigation ditch.

In spite of the fact that O'Neal and her squad had never been anywhere near the canyon, a great deal of information had been downloaded to her computer, and she had seen video of the river. It was brown with silt and leaped like a thing gone mad as it rushed towards lower ground. It would be five, maybe six days, before the water emptied into Big Salt Lake, from which a good deal of it would eventually evaporate, starting the whole cycle all over again.

But none of that mattered. What mattered was the fact that a platoon-sized force of killer robots had been programmed to eliminate her squad, and in spite of the high-flying spy-eye, hordes of robotic mini-scouts, and a shitload of fancy sensors, she didn't have the foggiest idea where they were. A significant problem since the androids had better-than-average AI units and were heavily armed.

But of even greater danger, to her squad at least, was the fact that O'Neal couldn't find a reason to care. She was currently rated among the top 5 percent of the noncoms on Drang, but hadn't made any effort to get there, and was operating more from habit than anything else. She was tired of being scared, tired of being a soldier, and tired of living on the inside of machines. Even new and improved ones. Death, and the ensuing peace, seemed ever more inviting. The only thing that had prevented her from calling for a fire mission on her own position was a sense of obligation to her team and a desire to punish the Hudathans for what they'd done. And the supersecret "Counter Blow" program had the potential to do that. Or so she told herself, but with less and less conviction all the time.

"Blow," or "the blow job" as the troops inevitably referred to it, was nothing less than an all-out effort to counter the threat from the Hudathan cyborgs who had done so much damage on planets like Jericho. So rather than strap even more hardware onto aging Trooper II bodies, the brass had decided to create a whole new generation of cyborgs. A "paradigm shift" as they liked to call it, designed to win the war and secure the peace.

"Which is where I come in," a voice said in her mind.

Try as she might, O'Neal had never been able to adjust to the fact that her "symbiotic co-warriors," as the training holos euphemistically called them, could access her thoughts anytime they wished, although the entity she called "Weasel" was the only one of them capable of articulated thought. She sent one in his direction. "You come when I *tell* you to come . . . so shut the hell up."

The being called Weasel sent a rude thought in her direction but lapsed into silence. Which was just as well, because just as DIs could "zap" cyborgs for disciplinary reasons, O'Neal could punish her mostly nonsentient analogs if they got too far out of line.

There were five analogs, counting Weasel, and with the possible exception of him, the rest fell into the category of what most sentient races considered to be animals, i.e., creatures more reliant on instinct than cognition. All were trainable, however, and like Terran dogs, preferred to hunt in groups, a trait that was supposed to make them more amenable to operating as part of a team, never mind the fact that "the team" had been jerked out of perfectly healthy bodies and dumped into cybernetic counterparts.

O'Neal's fire team consisted of Weasel, a near-sentient tunnel dweller from Zyra II, whose long snakelike body was coiled out in front of her position; Frim and Fram, ground-dwelling carnivores from Myro Major, both of whom had been installed in highly maneuverable tracked-weapons platforms; plus Drapa One and Drapa Two, better known as "One" and "Two," who were leather wings, had originated on Santos XI, and flew small disk-shaped battle disks.

Though not as articulate as Weasel, the other four members of the team communicated via unmitigated emotion, and though unable to understand the exact nature of the robotic threat, sensed O'Neal's general uneasiness, and were on edge. Knowing that her analogs had hair-trigger "fight or flight" reflexes, the human overcame her negative feelings to broadcast waves of "everything's all right" comfort. The tension eased a little and O'Neal uplinked to her battle disks.

The vast expanse of clear blue sky; the sweep of reddish, rock-strewn earth—everything was as it had been before. Or was it? Had those boulders been so close? Or had they been further away?

One of the things that O'Neal liked about her new body was the fact that everything she "saw" was stored in buffer memory for a period of six hours. The legionnaire made use of that feature by retrieving what she'd seen an hour before and superimposing it over what she saw now.

The comparison, and the fear the noncom experienced when she saw it, scared the analogs and caused them to gibber in the background. O'Neal sent a warning in their direction, opened the command channel, and zapped copies of what she'd observed to each member of her nine-borg squad.

"Baker Four to Baker Team . . . the boulders you're looking at have advanced ten yards during the last hour. I want condition-five readiness starting now."

The confirmations came on the team freq while O'Neal switched to the company push. "Baker Four to Charlie Six."

"Go, Baker Four."

"I have estimated two-four enemy units two hundred

yards forward of my position. They are in-creeping at a rate that should put them on the perimeter at sundown. Request permission to engage.''

Charlie Six, a DI who was playing the role of company commander, was ensconced in air-conditioned comfort about twenty miles away. He looked at the monitors and grinned. O'Neal was sharp, no doubt about that, but was she foolproof? Meaning, could she deal with a fool, and still do the right thing? He opened his mike. ''Permission denied.''

O'Neal could hardly believe her nonexistent ears. Permission denied? The sonofabitch must be out of his frigging mind! Assuming he had a mind. Was there a real honest-to-God reason for his refusal? Or was this a test of some sort?

The noncom smiled internally. Maybe Charlie Six had her confused with someone who cared. A plan came to mind. If it worked she'd be free to engage the enemy *before* they ended up in her lap . . . and Charlie Six could kiss her chrome-plated ass. She sent an image to Weasel.

It showed him crawling to within fifty feet of the still-creeping boulders. His reply was nearly instantaneous and incorporated some of the profanity he had learned since induction. ''Bullshit! The rocks will turn into killing machines and blow my pointy butt off!''

O'Neal sighed. It would be a long time, if ever, before the Legion got the same unquestioning obedience from Weasel that they expected from bio bods and cyborgs. ''Shut the hell up and get your tail out there before *I* blow it off.''

The analog obeyed but she could feel his resentment the whole way. The analog's snakelike body appeared as little more than a fifteen-foot-long heat differential, and even that would disappear as his temperature rose under the direct sunlight. The robots would detect him, of course, but that was the whole idea, and should serve to get things rolling.

The long armorflex body wasn't all that different from the one Weasel had been born to and provided him with a side-to-side snake's-eye view of the ground. He was smart enough to understand some of the dangers, and didn't like this particular errand. What was the human up to anyway? Charlie Six said, "No," and no meant no, didn't it? At least that's what she'd told him, not just once, but dozens of times. Not that humans were especially consistent, since they usually had one standard for themselves and another more stringent requirement for everyone else. The egg-sucking bastards.

Interactive camouflage, electronic countermeasures, and high-density shielding can work wonders, but there comes a point at which their effectiveness disappears and a robo-tank looks like a robo-tank. Unfortunately for Weasel, that point arrived at the exact same moment that an armorflex snake looked like an armorflex snake. The robots opened fire on him. He turned, made use of what little cover there was, and snake-slid towards home. The analog's report, made while bullets churned the dirt around him, was more than a little shrill.

"Damn it, Sarge! I'm taking fire from at least twenty, repeat two-zero armored vehicles. Tell one of those flap-assed leather wings to pull my butt outta here!"

O'Neal noted the breaks in both military and radio discipline but knew better than to comment on it. The fact that the analog had included the number of enemy vehicles was an improvement over the week before.

"Negative, Baker Nine . . . extraction denied. Find a hole and pull it in after you. The fire mission starts three-zero seconds from now."

The DI known as Charlie Six chuckled and made a no-tation on the portacomp strapped to his right thigh. Having discovered the robots, and having been denied permission to take what she knew to be the correct action, O'Neal had intentionally provoked an attack on one of her analogs, thereby gaining authorization to fire according to the rules of engagement, while still remaining inside the bounds of military discipline, and saving her squad from possible destruction.

It was the kind of gutsy, out-of-the-box call that a lot of noncoms are hesitant to make, which is why Charlie Six listed O'Neal as a potential PFR, or "promotion from the ranks." Given that many of the cyborgs were criminals, they had traditionally been ineligible for command. But, what with the famous Chien-Chu coming back from the dead, and an increasing number of "accidental" cyborgs like O'Neal, the policy had changed. Casualties had been heavy, and the brass needed officers.

In the meantime O'Neal had called on the tubes located five miles to her rear for an artillery mission. Within a matter of seconds 155-mike-mike rounds were screaming out of the sky and exploding among the tanks. Fire flickered around the massive machines as their twin gatling guns filled the sky with lead. Some of the shells exploded, hurled chunks of red-hot shrapnel in all directions, and spared the tanks below. Still, every third shell was steerable, and packed enough AI to dodge the worst of the defensive fire. O'Neal saw one of the tanks take a direct hit and explode into an orange-red fireball. She shuddered and gave thanks that no sentients had been aboard. It made her wonder, if this was a training exercise, what would the real thing be like? Mauled, and at risk of total destruction, the robots withdrew.

The next few hours were passed repositioning her squad in case one or more of the attack bots had managed to get a fix on them. Especially important in case the DIs declared an "intelligence failure" and provided the previously ground-only enemy with air cover.

But once they were dug in, with their positions separated by the standard fifty feet, and the parameters for interlocking fields of fire entered into their on-board computers, there wasn't much to do.

It was then that the usual tidal wave of depression rolled over O'Neal and pulled her down. Her analogs stirred uneasily, checked their sensors, and decided that all was well. After all, this wasn't the first time the human had felt this way, nor would it be the last. Besides, with the exception of the ground-dwelling carnivores from Myro Major, the rest of the analogs had been nocturnal, and were equipped with sensors so good that darkness held little fear for them.

Still, one can't be *too* careful when it comes to the safety of one's ass, so Weasel checked to make sure that the noncom was truly off-line, assumed her manner, and ordered Drapa One and Two out on a reconnaissance mission. Which was a lot like sending *himself* on a reconnaissance mission, since the roundabout electronic linkage allowed Weasel to "see" what the leather wings saw, "hear" what their pickups heard, and "feel" what they felt.

It was an exhilarating sensation, floating out over the plain, looking down on an ocean of light green blotches, each surrounded by successively darker rings, eventually fading to black. Most, if not all of the blotches were rocks, still in the process of releasing heat acquired during the day, laying where they had for hundreds of years. Still, the odds were good that at least *some* of the blotches belonged to robots, their infrared signatures doctored to look like those that emanated from the rocks.

Electronic prey was what One and Two were looking for, just as they had searched for the night-feeding xunus of their native steppes, plucking the fat little creatures from beside the safety of their burrows, and carrying them into the night.

Two noticed something and her excitement was immediately transmitted to Weasel through O'Neal. A blotch was moving, slowly to be sure, but in a determined zigzag course that would eventually carry it to the Legion's lines. The leather wing requested permission to destroy the robot and Weasel stalled. He used words to prod O'Neal. "Sarge! Come out of it! Something's coming our way!

O'Neal heard from a long ways off. They were bothering her, always bothering her, and for what? So they could live another day. Why the hell bother? What if the miserable little bastards had thoughts instead of instincts? They'd be as depressed as she was, that's what. The words formed and sent themselves back to Weasel. "So who cares? Let 'em come."

Weasel swore and felt his head hurt with the effort to think. What would O'Neal do in this situation? Not *this* O'Neal but the real one? The battle disks repeated their request and the analog was forced to continue his impersonation. "Permission denied. The target is a scout. Find the force that sent it."

Leather-wing resentment flooded back through the interface and Weasel fought to control his anger. He was doing the best he could, wasn't he? What did the fly-by-night assholes want anyway? Eggs in their beer? Not that he knew what beer was or would want any if he did.

The DI's attention had been elsewhere, throwing a frontal assault at another poor bastard, and watching him flunk. He turned his attention back to O'Neal. The training plan called for a frontal assault on her position as well, but the instructor felt that would be too easy for someone of O'Neal's obvious abilities, so he opted for something a little more challenging.

The Hudathans had used microbots on two different battlefields so far. The first use had taken place on Worber's World when they broke out. The second had occurred on

Diko II just weeks before where a half million tiny machines had come within half a pubic hair of defeating a battalion of marines.

But numbers aren't everything, and thanks to the fact that the geeks had demonstrated a marked aversion to loading their constructs with a sufficient amount of AI, it was possible to outthink them. So, given the fact that a full complement of training machines had arrived, and O'Neal didn't know about them, there was an opportunity to provide her squad with a valuable lesson. The challenge was to allow enough casualties so that it *felt* real without overdoing it. It would be damned tricky with all that live ordnance flying around. Charlie Six made a notation on his portacomp, issued a series of orders, and settled back to watch.

Weasel was startled when the first shell exploded over their position. Who the hell was firing on them, and where the hell were they? The battle disks hadn't reported jack shit yet all hell had broken loose. Frim and Fram started to back and fill, their tracks throwing up rooster tails of dirt, as their weapons searched the sky. Weasel took his fear, his desire to live, added it to similar emotions provided by the other analogs, and forced it through O'Neal's despair. ''*We need you!*''

The thought, powered by the strength of the emotions behind it, appeared in letters ten feet tall. O'Neal read them once, twice, then three times. Suddenly she had it, the thing she'd been searching for, and hadn't been able to find. The squad needed a leader, but it didn't need *her*. Any noncom would do as long as they were competent. But the analogs were different. They needed her the way a child needs a mother, to provide emotional support and guidance in a dangerous world.

The knowledge pulled her up out of the darkness and into the alien night. Shells exploded overhead, analogs gib-

bered, and the squad demanded orders. Weasel sensed her
return and provided a sitrep that was damned close to military. "The wings saw a scout but couldn't find the force
that sent it. The arty attack started about six-zero seconds
ago and consists of nonlethal air bursts."

The fact that someone had ordered the battle disks into
the air registered on O'Neal's mind along with the knowledge that there was no time to ask about it. She brought up
the list of offensive weaponry that the enemy was supposed
to have and verified that artillery was on it. Still, why now?
Especially since the live fire exercise was supposed to be
over in less than two hours?

But pondering whys and wherefores doesn't make much
sense when someone is determined to blow your ass off.
The noncom checked her battle comp.

Twenty or thirty air bursts had gone off with no effect.
Why? She should have casualties by now. The answer came
from another member of her squad. "Baker Six to Baker
Four."

"This is Baker Four . . . Go."

"I have artillery-delivered combat-equipped microbots in
the air over my position. Request permission to engage."

It took O'Neal three seconds to confirm the fact that
while microbots did not appear on the list of "enemy"
weaponry, they weren't proscribed, either, which left *her*
holding the bag. She made the call. "Permission granted.
Fire at will."

The night was split into hundreds of geometric shapes as
the cyborgs and their analogs opened fire on the incoming
machines. Many were destroyed but some survived. Most
were no more than a few inches across during the air-
dispersal stage, but combined on reaching the ground and
assembled themselves into a variety of self-directed weapons systems. The newly formed units included highly mobile gun platforms, self-propelled energy cannons, and a

variety of smaller but nonetheless effective attack units. Making a bad situation even worse was the fact that many of the devices had dropped inside the Legion's defensive perimeter.

Capable though it was, O'Neal discovered that it took her on-board computer way too long to find and destroy the tiny airborne targets, so she concentrated on the larger constructs instead. Her tool-hands moved in short, jerky arcs as the cyborg opened fire with her arm-mounted weapons.

A partially assembled weapons platform staggered under the assault, swiveled on newly built treads, and fired a half-charged energy cannon. O'Neal felt the heat but shrugged it off. Her shells found a still-unprotected ammo bay and detonated the missiles inside.

The explosion created a shockwave. It hit the battle disks, threw them out of position, and rolled away. The leather wings regrouped, linked their computers into a single fire-control center, and returned to work. Though difficult to hit from the ground, the microbots were vulnerable from the air. Hundreds of them exploded under the renewed assault.

The robots were far from defenseless, however, and O'Neal saw more than one battle disk explode at the center of their massed fire, or arc across the star-spattered sky to crash against the rock-hard ground. The despair felt by thirty-plus analogs threatened to pull O'Neal under, but she used a vision of badly mangled robots to rally them, and ordered a counterattack. The results exceeded both her and the DI's expectations.

Both afraid and angry, the squad's analogs lashed out with an intensity the humans had never seen before. Weasel wrapped himself around a self-propelled gatling gun that had pushed in from the north, crushed the firing mechanism, and fried the machine's fire-control processor with his eye lasers.

Frim and Fram ganged up on what amounted to a tank, moving in until their gun muzzles were only inches away from the robot's flanks and firing until their tubes glowed. One of the shells got through, found a subprocessor, and sent the machine into a tail-chasing spin. The leather wings finished it off.

More than satisfied with the result, and concerned lest he generate more casualties, the DI sent an electronic message. The robots that could backed away and disappeared into the night. Those that were unable to do so remained where they were. Monuments to what a combination of technology, fear, and hate can do.

The sight could have been depressing but O'Neal felt something different as she looked out over the battlefield. The analogs had proved their ability to operate as a team, most were still alive, and she had found a reason to exist. It wasn't much . . . but it would have to do.

25

In those days, however, it was quite common for sentries at Camp Amilakvari to throw coins into the barbed wire . . . wait for African children to scamper in to retrieve the money . . . then shoot them for trying to get into camp.

> *Ex-legionnaire Christian Jennings*
> Mouthful of Rocks
> *Standard year 1989*

Planet Algeron, the Confederacy of Sentient Beings

Most of Fort Camerone had been hardened and placed deep underground, where it was safe from anything short of a direct hit from a nuclear missile. So, with the exception of missile launchers, antenna arrays, and fly-form landing pads, the one-story surface structure looked similar to Legion citadels that dotted North Africa in the long-distant past.

And in spite of the fact that there was very little likelihood that legionnaires would ever return fire from the crenellated battlements, the likeness was far from accidental. The architectural details had been placed there to evoke the past, to remind those within that they were the latest links in a chain that had been forged in the heat of battle and tested by time.

The duffel bag contained enough gear to carry Chrobuck through a five-day pass and threatened to slide off her shoulder. She readjusted the strap, returned the sentry's salute, and stepped out through the main gate.

A half-track full of visor-faced bio bods rumbled by while a pair of patrol-worn Trooper IIs passed in the opposite direction. Their servos whined in unison and one of them had a pronounced limp. Chrobuck acknowledged their salutes and noticed that the air reeked of ozone. Voices shouted barely heard orders, music leaked out of a hover truck's cab, and rotors whapped as a cybernetic load-lifter dropped onto a nearby pad. The dust disturbed by its passage floated upwards to join the ever-present pall of smoke. The sun shimmered and climbed higher in the sky.

Further down slope, beyond the free-fire zone and the constantly shifting crab-mines, hundreds of randomly spaced domes could be seen. They were made of earth, reinforced with whatever the Naa could lay their hands on, including wood, plastic, and scraps of metal, many of which had been polished to reflect the light of the sun. But no matter how much they glittered, Naa Town was still made of mud.

Although most Naa lived in heavily fortified villages a long ways from the fort, some of the more marginal members of their society had been attracted to the relatively easy money that could be made working for the Legion during the day, and for the bored, entertainment-starved legionnaires at night, although the concepts of "day" and "night" had only limited meaning on Algeron, and commerce never really stopped.

Still, as Chrobuck made her way down the intentionally switchbacked road, through the heavily fortified checkpoint, and into the town beyond, she couldn't help but compare what she saw with her own youth, and conclude that mud huts were a step up from the overcrowded habitat on which she'd been raised.

Six square feet of worn metal deck, that's how much her mother, sister, and she had been able to rent each night, most of it paid for by recovering sludge from the holding tanks, running errands for drunk spacers, or stealing anything that wasn't nailed down. And maybe other things, too, things her mother refused to talk about, things that made her cry at night. Things that paid hard currency, which, when saved year after dreary year, piled up until there was enough to ship two girls off-hab, and pay for the schooling that enabled one to qualify as a med tech, and the other to gain admission to the academy. Yes, Chrobuck decided, there are worse things than mud huts and wide-open spaces.

The pungent odor of incense closed around her like a cloak. There wasn't a single legionnaire who didn't know what the incense was for, since it was common knowledge that the Naa had an acute sense of smell, and found many of the odors that emanated from the fort to be offensive. Which explained why a thousand tendrils of slowly burning incense trickled up to join the smoke generated by an equal number of cook fires and glaze the otherwise blue sky.

Chrobuck liked the smell, the exotic feel, and took pleasure in her surroundings. There was life here and it felt good after Jericho's dark and brooding ruins. An army of cubs swarmed out to meet her, each armed with something to sell, or the promise of something to sell.

They were all sizes and shapes and ranged in age from four or five to early adolescence. All had short, sleek fur that came in a highly individual assortment of colors and patterns. Clothing was minimal and tended towards sandals, shifts, and trousers. Their heads were strikingly human in shape and size, having similar ears, noses, and mouths, although their teeth lacked canines and had a more even appearance.

And in spite of the fact that they knew the Legion's chain of command backwards and forwards, every single one of them had promoted Chrobuck by one rank. "Over here, Captain! The finest wine on Algeron! Only five credits per gallon!"

"Welcome to Naa Town, Captain! Why wear plastic when my father makes holsters from hand-tooled dooth hide? Just fifty credits."

"Hey, Captain . . . you hungry? My momma makes the best chow you ever had. Come and see."

It reminded Chrobuck of the days when she had worked the corridors on Orhab II. She laughed and summoned a grubby little female to her side. "Tell me, little one . . . where would I find the male known as Sleepshort Warmhand?"

The cub's face lit up, and she took Chrobuck's hand and led her towards a hard-packed path. Some of the youngsters departed in search of other customers, but the rest tagged along, pelting each other with pebbles and laughing gaily.

Domes crowded in around the walkway. Some were very new, having been built on the rubble of their predecessors, but none were older than the previous war, when both the fortress and the town that had formed in front of it had been obliterated by the Hudathans. Adult faces appeared every now and then, gazing over low mud walls, peering out through open shuttered windows, or looking down from flimsy makeshift ladders. None were openly hostile, but all seemed cautious, as if unsure of what her presence might portend. That, plus the fact that nearly every single male went armed, caused Chrobuck to watch her step.

The sun had passed zenith and dropped into the western sky. Long, hard shadows reached for the east, darkened the streets between the nearly identical domes. Chrobuck lost her bearings. But the cub urged the legionnaire forward with cries of "This way, Captain!" and tugged on her fingertips. Finally, after what seemed like miles of walking, the child came to a stop, looked up, and held out her hand for payment.

The dome looked like all the others and Chrobuck was suspicious. "How do I know this is the one?"

The reply came from behind her. "Because Feetdance would never mislead a customer ... would you, Feetdance?"

The child shook her head solemnly and Chrobuck turned. This officer really *was* a captain and her salute was automatic. He was handsome in an exotic sort of way and Chrobuck realized that he was half-human, half-Naa, a supposed impossibility, except for the fact that he was there, watching her through half-amused eyes. "My name's Booly and you're Chrobuck. Welcome to Algeron, Lieutenant ... I'm sorry about what happened on Jericho."

Chrobuck nodded wordlessly and felt someone tug on her trousers. She turned, paid the child what she hoped was the right amount, and watched her skip away. Booly smiled. "So tell me, was it a long walk?"

Chrobuck shrugged. "It felt like a couple of miles."

Booly laughed. "It probably was ... in spite of the fact that the most direct route is half that distance. Come on, Sleepshort isn't here yet, but we can wait by the fire."

Chrobuck felt strangely awkward as she followed the other officer down a short flight of carefully excavated stairs and into a circular living area. The fire pit was raised above the floor and served as both furnace and stove. Coals glowed under a smoke-blackened pot and the smell of soup filled the air. Booly gestured Chrobuck towards a hide-covered couch and sat down beside her. "I wasn't sure you'd come. The supply convoy would have been more comfortable and a heck of a lot faster."

Chrobuck smiled. "The note said I'd see the way the Naa *really* live, not to mention the fact that it came from my commanding officer."

Booly had felt fortunate to get a platoon leader with combat experience but was concerned about what effect the battle of Jericho might have had on her. Everything seemed all right, however, and he was encouraged. "Yeah, that wasn't fair, was it? But so many legionnaires have a distorted impression of my mother's people that I couldn't resist the temptation to provide you with a guided tour. Plus, the more you see of the terrain the better."

Chrobuck was searching for an appropriate response when a Naa appeared carrying a load of what looked like carefully bound reeds. He was male, small by the standards of his race, had thick golden fur streaked with white, and spoke Naa with what Chrobuck had learned was a northern accent. "So there you are, right on time, just like the hairless ones you associate with."

Booly stood and Chrobuck followed his example. He cleared his throat. "Lieutenant Chrobuck, allow me to introduce Sleepshort Warmhand, a friend of my family's."

Chrobuck responded with stiff, somewhat formal Naa. "It's an honor to make your acquaintance, Warrior Warmhand, may I assist with your burden?"

Warmhand directed a scowl in Booly's direction and lay the reeds on a rough-hewn table. The palms of his hands felt rough where they touched hers. "My apologies, Lieutenant . . . I had no idea that my brother's nephew's friend would bring such a sweet-smelling warrior companion to my humble abode. Please forgive my comment."

"There is nothing to forgive," Chrobuck replied lightly. "The offense was ours since we were early."

Warmhand aimed a significant look in Booly's direction. "I like this one . . . you must keep her."

"Thanks for the advice," Booly said dryly, "but the

Legion has first call on the lieutenant's affections. You brought the reeds?''

Warmhand gestured towards the table. ''Are they not here? Right in front of your eyes? Of course I brought them.''

Booly smiled patiently. ''Thank you. My mother will be pleased. Your name will be honored.''

''As well it should be,'' Warmhand replied, turning his back on Booly. He produced a knife and sliced a one-inch section from one of the reeds. ''Reeds such as these are gathered from Great Circle Lake, two hundred miles to the west. The best ones grow furthest from the shore. To harvest them you must wade out, duck underwater, and cut them near the roots. Here, rub the end on your throat, and tell me if Windsweet will approve.''

Chrobuck did as instructed, felt a momentary wetness where the reed touched her skin, and was enveloped by the most wonderful scent. It smelled like peaches, only different somehow, and she had no difficulty understanding why any female would want it. ''It's wonderful . . . she'll love it.''

''Good,'' Warmhand said gruffly, wrapping the reeds in a piece of camouflaged fabric. ''You must protect them from the sun or they will dry out.''

''How much do I owe you?'' Booly asked, reaching for his wallet.

''Nothing,'' Warmhand said, waving the offer away. ''Give my best to your mother . . . and tell your father that his son spends too much time with off-worlders.''

Chrobuck smiled at the only slightly more diplomatic choice of words. Booly collected the reeds, tucked them under an arm, and grinned. ''You forget that my father is human, and that I too share their blood.''

The Naa paused for a moment, looked Booly in the eye, and shook his head. ''I forget nothing. This is the planet that birthed, suckled, and raised you up. Your future is here.''

The words reminded Booly of the unresolved questions that lay ahead. Should he stay in the Legion? Or would the Hudathans settle the question by leaving him dead on a battlefield somewhere?

The two legionnaires left shortly after that, wound their way between some domes, and emerged onto a street where a group of children stood guard over Booly's scout car. Fifteen minutes was sufficient to carry them away from the settlement and towards the north. The newly risen sun felt warm against their cheeks as Booly accelerated along the broad, flat road, aimed the vehicle at a distant peak, and allowed his cares to slip away. He looked at Chrobuck, caught her smile, and felt glad to be alive.

The Hudathan was huge. He grinned what seemed like a human grin and moved forward. The knife had a serrated edge and gleamed in the jungle-filtered light. Chrobuck tried to move, tried to reach for a weapon, but found her arms were made of lead. The trooper was closer now, his body blocking the trees above, as the knife went up and back. Chrobuck screamed, and woke to find herself standing upright in the back of the open scout car, with Legion-issue blankets puddled around her feet. It was night and Booly's face was lit from below. The flashlight wavered as he stood. He looked concerned. ''Are you all right? Can I help?''

Chrobuck shook her head and felt embarrassed as her entire body started to shake. His arms felt comforting at the same time that Chrobuck knew they shouldn't be there and allowed them to stay. Booly spoke in her ear. ''It was a dream, wasn't it? I have them all the time. They get better, though . . . and eventually go away.''

Chrobuck looked up and over his shoulder. The stars

twinkled through the crystal-clear atmosphere. A shudder ran the length of her body. "They're coming, aren't they? And when they get here there will be more killing, more dying, and more dreams."

Booly rested his chin on the soft stubble that covered the top of her head. She smelled of leather and his mother's perfume. "Yes, they will come and make more dreams."

"Then why?" Chrobuck asked. "Why bother?"

"Because of Feetdance," Booly answered softly, "and all those like her."

Chrobuck remembered two little girls, the sacrifices that their mother had made, and nodded against his chest. They would kill for Feetdance . . . so she would survive.

The road, which overlaid an ancient trail, had been widened and graded by the Legion's Pioneers but was still subject to washouts and landslides. It climbed and climbed and climbed some more, taking them farther and farther into territory that had once been categorized as "disputed," and still was according to the Naa. The views were spectacular, though, so in spite of the nonstop ear-popping, gear-shifting, engine-revving climb, Chrobuck enjoyed the ride.

It was easy to imagine what it had been like twenty or thirty years before, leading a patrol up along the constantly switchbacking trail, knowing you were under surveillance, waiting for the ambush that would almost certainly come. The steeply pitched slopes, rocky terrain, and hair-pin curves would be easy to defend and hell to conquer.

All of which raised the question of why? It wasn't as if the old empire needed more rocks. No, it was something more, and something less than that. The emperor had insisted that all of the sentient races within his sphere of influence acknowledge his rule. And of even more significance perhaps was the fact that the Legion and the Naa shared the same set of values. Values such as bravery, honor, and sacrifice. So, given the fact that both needed someone to fight, and took a sort of perverse pleasure in doing so, they had fought endless and mostly inconclusive duels along trails like this one.

As if to prove her point, Booly fought the vehicle around a pothole-defended corner, pointed to a pile of carefully stacked rocks, and yelled over the noise of the heavily strained engine. "Two cyborgs and four bio bods died there. It happened four years before I was born. My grandfather, Wayfar Hardman, led the war party that killed them. Eight of his best warriors died getting the job done."

Chrobuck noticed the pride in his voice and wondered how it was focused. On the legionnaires? Or the Naa? It was as if her commanding officer was the embodiment of the relationship between the Legion and the Naa. Was that why she found him so interesting? Or was it something more? Not that it mattered . . . since any relationship beyond the one defined by the chain of command could cause problems. Chrobuck turned her attention towards the scenery and away from her companion. The road climbed some more, rounded a series of blind curves, and emerged into a broad U-shaped valley. Part of the land was under cultivation. The rest was dotted with shaggy dooths, their coats ragged with newly grown wool, grazing on the last of the summer grass. Booly pulled over and paused. He produced a pair of binoculars, scanned the valley, and handed them to Chrobuck. He said two words and they meant more to Chrobuck than they did to him. "My home."

"Home." The word resonated as Chrobuck swept the binoculars over the meadow to the mountains beyond. A home was what she had always wanted and never had. Not on Orhab, not at boarding school, not at the academy. It was a powerful word, replete with images of security, permanence, and family. It was the essence of what non-nomadic sentients fought for, that and the freedom to be who they wanted to be, and worship whatever gods they chose. How good it would feel to utter that word! To know where home was, to be accepted there, to have a sense of place.

The rest of the journey was made at less than ten miles per hour as newly arrived warriors spurred their mounts alongside, yelled rapid-fire insults that Chrobuck couldn't understand. Cubs piled into the backseat, fought each other for space, and instructed Booly on how to negotiate the maze of obstacles that intentionally obstructed the road. For in spite of the fact that tribal warfare had decreased during the last twenty years or so, the embers of old rivalries burned on, and had been rekindled of late. Or so it seemed from the intelligence reports Chrobuck had read.

A V-shaped fissure split the high rock wall that lay ahead, creating a natural choke point through which attacking troops would be forced to come, making it easy to defend. A sort of parking lot had been established just outside the entrance and was presently populated by three rather ancient Legion surplus trucks, along with a spanking-new APC, which flew a Confederacy flag from a one-whip-style antenna, and a Unified Tribes pictograph from the other. Booly saw the direction of Chrobuck's gaze and yelled over the tumult. "It's my father's! He was named as ambassador to the Confederacy immediately after the first war and has held the post ever since."

Chrobuck nodded, grabbed her bag away from a curious cub, and followed the crowd towards the V-shaped passageway. While still some distance away, she noticed that the dooth droppings became thicker and thicker as they approached the opening, and that the Naa had solved this problem by supplementing a series of naturally placed stepping-stones with ones of their own. This allowed the dooths to pass back and forth between the valley and the village while their owners stayed four to five feet above the never-ending muck. Curiously enough, the smell that nearly gagged Chrobuck left the normally sensitive Naa completely unfazed. Had they grown used to it? Did they like it? There was no way to know.

Once they passed through the fissure, another, smaller valley was revealed. There was no sign of the adobe domes that Chrobuck had expected. In fact there was nothing much to see beyond some corrals, what appeared to be a ceremonial fire pit, and countless carefully maintained holes. Holes from which more Naa poured, laughing and shouting, grabbing Booly and lifting him up into the air. Cries of ''Neverstop Cragclimber'' reverberated between canyon walls and it took Chrobuck a moment to realize that Booly had a Naa name in addition to a human one, and had left it behind. A wise decision, knowing the bigots at the academy.

The noise dropped off as a Naa female emerged from one of the holes, followed quickly by a human male. The female was beautiful, with short, downy fur; charcoal gray eyes; and full, almost sensual lips. Her love was obvious as she wrapped the younger Booly in a warm embrace and kissed his cheek. Then, as the female released the young officer, his father stepped forward, greeted him with the adult hand-to-forearm grip, and smiled. His eyes were sky blue and twinkled with affection. ''Welcome home, son, it's good to see you.''

Having greeted their son, they turned to his guest and Chrobuck found herself embracing Windsweet, and the smell of her perfume. She offered the bundle of reeds. The syntax was formal but appropriate to the situation. ''Greetings, honored Mother, your son obtained these from a distant land, and brings them for your enjoyment.''

The moment seemed to stretch, to elongate, as they looked into each other's eyes. The intensity of the gray eyes was startling, and Chrobuck felt as if everything she had ever felt, thought or experienced had been laid bare for the other female to access, evaluate, and pass judgment on. But if such was the case, there was no denying the warmth of Windsweet's response, or the unexpected meaning of her words. "So, precious one, the seasons have passed, and you arrived as the Wula sticks said you would. Welcome home."

26

We were together since the war began. He was my servant—and the better man.

Rudyard Kipling
Epitaphs of the War
Standard year circa 1916

With the Hudathan Fleet, off the Planet Zynig-47, the Confederacy of Sentient Beings

The sun shone from a clear blue sky, the air smelled of decaying flesh, and the Hudathans didn't even notice. Shards of multicolored glass crunched under Sector Marshal Poseen-Ka's boots as he strode through the ruins of the Confederate city. The glass, and the city itself, had been extruded by an obscure race called N'awatha, who took the physical form of tentacle-headed worms, and had committed mass suicide soon after the Hudathan fleet dropped in-system. All of which had been part of a dramatic, but ineffectual attempt to convince the invaders that the entire race was dead, when the truth was that millions of well-fed larvae waited just below the planet's surface, and had genetically transmitted memories of everything their parents had known. Not that the officer cared, since he had other, more pressing problems on his mind.

The present situation had arisen when a Hudathan emissary had overtaken the fast-moving fleet, demanded that it assume an orbit around the sun, and ordered Poseen-Ka to land on Zynig-47 for what he referred to as "personal consultations." All at the expense of the Hudathan people, who had every right to expect that the fleet would follow up behind its hard-won advantage and deliver the *intaka*, or "blow of death" to the planet Algeron. But no, some jumped-up, half-brained nitwit who happened to be related to a member of the new Triad had decided that he knew better and brought everything to a halt.

Suddenly, approximately two land units in front of him, a multicolored glass high-rise, its carefully placed worm ramps visible through a nearly transparent exterior, cracked, shattered, and collapsed in an avalanche of glass. The noise was deafening. Poseen-Ka frowned and Nagwa Isaba-Ra appeared by his side. "Sir?"

"Who fired on that structure?"

"I believe it was Counselor Rewa-Ba, or a member of his party, Sector Marshal."

Poseen-Ka gestured disgust and stepped over the body of a dead and nearly desiccated worm. A beautifully wrought glass dagger protruded from the creature's side. The Hudathan was a soldier, and soldiers destroy things, but for a purpose. The wanton destruction of a building was as foreign to the Hudathan as the human concept of pity.

Kenor Rewa-Ba, Counselor to the Hudathan people and nephew of Triad member Selor Rewa-Ba, was a bit frightened. And with good reason, since he had acted without his uncle's knowledge, and contrary to expectations, in a society where expectations were synonymous with duty.

But the Triad was a long ways off, and sometimes weeks

behind the news, which meant that he must act on his own. Fortunately, after months of prolonged nagging, his uncle had released Rewa-Ba from the tedium of governmental affairs and permitted him to conduct a "fact-finding mission" out along the frontier, a wise investment, and one that was about to pay off.

Rewa-Ba aimed the vehicle-mounted recoiless rifle at another one of the fantastically shaped crystalline structures, sighted on its base, and fired. The muffled bang, followed by an equally muffled crash, and sheets of falling glass were most gratifying. No wonder so many of his peers had chosen the military. Destroying things was fun. The fact that his bodyguards thought he was an idiot, and gestured to each other behind his back, was lost on him.

Rewa-Ba had chosen another building, and was just about to bring it down as well, when Dagger Commander Molo-Sa touched his shoulder. "Sector Marshal Poseen-Ka has arrived."

"What? Who? Speak up, you idiot."

Molo-Sa's face was completely expressionless as he removed the protectors that covered the counselor's funnel-shaped ears. "Sector Marshal Poseen-Ka has arrived and is waiting to speak with you."

"Well of course he is," Rewa-Ba replied irritably, jumping to the ground. "He wouldn't want to speak with you . . . now would he?"

"No," Molo-Sa replied woodenly, "he wouldn't."

"Good," Rewa-Ba said importantly, "at least that's settled. Well, come on, the marshal is waiting."

Poseen-Ka *was* waiting, and judging from his expression, none too patiently. He was huge, somewhat grizzled, and very intimidating, as were the heavily armed troopers who stood around him. Rewa-Ba felt fear tickle the bottom of his belly, told himself that *he* was in charge, and assumed the same arrogant attitude that his uncle was famous for.

"Poseen-Ka . . . how nice to see you."

Poseen-Ka made note of the fact that the greeting was overly familiar, coming as it did from someone he had never met before, and intentionally rude, since his rank should have been included. He ran a critical eye over the short, pudgy figure in front of him and knew his initial impression had been correct. Rewa-Ba was a minor functionary who abused his authority, believed the lies fed him by subordinates, and couldn't find his posterior in broad daylight. He responded accordingly. "Please get to the point, Counselor . . . why have you seen fit to interfere with fleet operations? And why are you wasting my time with this meeting?"

The direct, clearly hostile approach took Rewa-Ba by surprise. He found himself on the defensive and the stutter that had plagued his younger days threatened to return. He managed to control it, but just barely. "I suggest you watch your tone, Sector Marshal . . . especially in light of the fact that I am the direct representative of the Hudathan people."

"More like the direct representative of your uncle's anus," Poseen-Ka replied contemptuously. "Answer my question or face charges in a military court."

Rewa-Ba's bodyguards exchanged amazed looks as their leader scrambled to recover some of his dignity. "I intercepted the fleet in order to provide you with critical information."

Rewa-Ba allowed the words to hang there, waiting for Poseen-Ka to ask the obvious question, but it never came. The soldier remained silent, certain that Rewa-Ba would crack, and unsurprised when he did. Having been unable to elicit the response he'd hoped for, the civilian tried the next best thing, a dramatic statement. "I have reason to believe that a spy has infiltrated your staff."

Poseen-Ka checked to make sure that Rewa-Ba was serious, turned, and looked at his bodyguards. He gestured towards Isaba-Ra. "Really? The Confederates have a spy on my staff? Is this the one? Or how about Kalo-Ka over there? . . . He's mean enough to be human. All right, Kalo-Ka, take off that mask, and show us your *real* face."

Everyone, including Kalo-Ka, laughed uproariously. The very notion of someone of another race passing as a Hudathan was absurd. Rewa-Ba felt his resolve start to melt away and knew that his only hope lay in being right. "Right makes its own rules," his uncle liked to say, and Rewa-Ba knew it was true. If he was right, and could prove that he was right, Poseen-Ka would have to eat his words. "Go ahead and make light of the situation if you wish, Sector Marshal Poseen-Ka, but remember this: if there *is* a spy on your staff, the Confederacy knows that you're coming, and is waiting for you."

Poseen-Ka gave it some thought. In spite of the fact that the Confederacy would be expecting an attack on Algeron, *expecting* and *knowing* were two different things, since the latter allowed for a concentration of forces that could overwhelm his fleet. So, annoying though the counselor might be, it seemed prudent to hear him out. "All right Rewa-Ba, where's your proof? Let's see it."

Rewa-Ba loved drama and this was the moment that he'd been waiting for. He gestured to his bodyguards and imitated the tone that his uncle used with underlings. "Bring the human and the holo player."

There was an uncomfortable pause while one of Rewa-Ba's functionaries made his way over to a carefully sealed command vehicle, ordered a guard to unlock the side hatch, and drew his side arm. The door slid open and a human stepped out.

The prisoner wore an olive drab flight suit and a red baseball cap. He hadn't shaved for three or four days and looked tired. The name tape over his left breast pocket read "Lt. Bruce Jensen" and he was scared. The same luck that had helped him out of a hundred jams, including the one on Jericho, had suddenly deserted him. He'd gone hyper to escape a Hudathan DE, exited on the edge of the Orlani System, and discovered that both of his normal drives had suffered battle damage. That's when he'd sent a distress call, finished a bottle of Old Hand, and drifted off to sleep. He'd been asleep—okay, passed out—when Rewa-Ba and his merry men had happened along, intercepted the distress signal, and tracked it to its source.

The aliens had already blown the outer hatch and were hard at work on the inner one when a cacaphony of alarms pulled Jensen out of a rather pleasant dream and into a real-world nightmare. He had barely managed to scramble into his space armor and was about to execute a random hyperspace jump when vacuum sucked the atmosphere out of his cabin and a Hudathan appeared. The good news was that he was alive, but at what cost? Highly classified information had fallen into the enemy's hands, and it was his fault.

A pair of troopers grabbed Jensen's elbows and half carried, half walked him to the place where their superiors stood. Jensen looked at the officers and hoped that the smaller, softer one was in charge. It quickly turned out that he wasn't.

"So," Poseen-Ka hissed, "who are you?"

Jensen was surprised by the Hudathan's command of Standard and swallowed to clear his throat. "First Lieutenant Bruce Jensen, sir."

"And your assignment?"

"Pilot of the *LRS-236.*"

"LRS stands for 'long range scout'? Sometimes used as couriers?"

Jensen shrugged.

"And you were captured without being able to destroy the dispatches you carried?"

Jensen stared straight ahead. Poseen-Ka signaled understanding and turned to Rewa-Ba. "So, Counselor, show me the information recovered from the human's ship."

The official gestured and some jury-rigged electronic components were brought forward. The markings and relatively small controls were clearly human in origin. A folding table was put in place, cables were connected to a power source, and switches were thrown. The relevant section of a much longer message was cued and ready to go. Rewa-Ba couldn't resist the temptation to introduce it. "My intelligence officer informs me that the speaker is General Marianne Mosby . . . and that her message is directed to General Ian St. James."

Poseen-Ka had heard of Mosby and met St. James immediately after the Battle of Algeron. A battle that he had lost and the human had won. Though still somewhat skeptical about the value of Rewa-Ba's intelligence, the sector marshal wanted to judge for himself. He signaled understanding and waited while the final button was pressed. The air shimmered and an image appeared. The human female wore Legion khaki and seemed to be on familiar terms with the person she was talking to. ". . . so, although it wouldn't be prudent to discuss *how* we know, suffice it to say that we have it on good authority that Poseen-Ka will attack Algeron, and soon. With that in mind we are sending additional naval units to your system along with two battalions of marines. Now, moving on to the question of supplies . . ."

Rewa-Ba gestured and the image disappeared. "There's more, but it's boring stuff, mostly, all about logistics."

Poseen-Ka could have told the civilian that logistics was the most important part of any war but saw no reason to waste his energy. "Thank you, Counselor, I retract my earlier comments, and indeed thank you for bringing this information to my attention. The Triad chose wisely when they sent you on your present mission.''

Rewa-Ba felt his heart swell with pride. The great Po-seen-Ka had praised him! Now, to make sure that word of his success found its way to the proper quarter . . . ''So, you will inform the high command? And take the fleet back towards Hudatha?''

Poseen-Ka registered surprise. ''Take the fleet back? Whatever for?''

Rewa-Ba felt confused. ''Why, to avoid the trap, of course. You have no choice.''

''Oh, but I do,'' the sector marshal replied confidently. ''Scouts will be sent to make contact with other elements of the fleet. They will head for Algeron and drop hyper at the same moment that we do. By destroying the Confed-eracy's fleet, we will chop months, perhaps years off the war.''

''But what about the spy?'' Rewa-Ba said desperately. ''Shouldn't you find him first? What if he reveals *this* plan as well? Besides, the message never got through, so there may be less of an opportunity than you suppose.''

Poseen-Ka struggled to control his growing impatience. ''Anything is possible, Counselor, but consider the facts: The human chose to omit *how* the information was ob-tained. We use couriers as well . . . some of them are miss-ing. Which is why we send important messages in a multiplicity of ways, as does the enemy. Why look for com-plex answers when the simple ones are more likely?''

Rewa-Ba was far from satisfied, but knew he couldn't win, and settled for what he already had: a success with no responsibility for whatever ensued. ''I bow to your exper-tise, Sector Marshal. I'm sure you know best. How would you like to dispose of the human?''

Poseen-Ka motioned to Isaba-Ra. ''The human is of no further value. Shoot him.''

Isaba-Ra drew his side arm, felt his stomach start to

churn, and wanted to scream. Jensen hadn't understood the words but the action was clear. He turned and started to run. Isaba-Ra led the pilot, knew he could drop him, and allowed the moment to pass. He jerked on the trigger, felt the recoil, and heard the bang. A glass sculpture exploded as Jensen sprinted for a building.

Isaba-Ra was about to fire again when the sound of an automatic weapon ripped the air, Jensen stumbled, and jerked as a hail of bullets hit him. Isaba-Ra holstered his weapon, turned, and saw that Poseen-Ka was amused. "You'd better spend some time on the range . . . even I shoot better than that."

More than three standard days had passed by the time that Isaba-Ra made his final decision, checked to make sure that the clues were as they should be, and left the small but comfortable cabin. His diary, created over the last couple of days, would document a severe case of depression, as would some unsent letters and the dark, somewhat morbid sketches that decorated the bulkheads. He hoped to escape but any number of things could and probably would go wrong.

The thing that worried him the most was the possibility that the Hudathans would discover what sort of creature had lived in their midst. He was worried not out of loyalty to the Hegemony, or the Confederacy of Sentient Beings, but to others like himself. Assuming that there were any.

There was the normal ebb and flow of foot traffic in the corridors. Isaba-Ra saw spear leaders flanked by their body-guards, ratings on errands, troopers headed to eat, and pilots just back from patrol. The same pilots who might be ordered to follow and kill him if he managed to clear the ship.

Clusters of internally lit pictograms hung over the center of each intersection, evenly spaced light strips passed overhead, identical junction boxes appeared every twenty feet or so, and gratings clanged under foot.

A pair of heavily armed troopers stood next to the command deck's lift tube. They gestured the respect due to a sector marshal's aide and allowed Isaba-Ra to enter. The platform carried him one level upwards, where more guards checked his identity and allowed him to pass. Poseen-Ka's quarters were less than fifty feet away and the spy felt his heart beat faster as he marched down the hall, turned into the cubicle that served as his office, and paused to make sure that no one had followed. The corridor was empty. Reassured, he closed the outer hatch, drew the energy pistol that officers were required to wear aboard ship, and checked to make sure that it was fully charged. A second weapon, hidden in the waistband of his trousers, doubled the firepower at his command.

The inner hatch provided access to the small galley in which the sector marshal's meals were prepared. First meal had been served and consumed. The cook was on his break and would return in fifteen minutes or so. Stepping inside, the spy tiptoed to the window through which food was passed, and inched the panel aside. His heart was in his mouth. What if Poseen-Ka had broken his routine? What if the sector marshal had chosen to sit on the *other* side of the table? And was staring at the panel?

But the Hudathan was where he was supposed to be, back to the opening, peering into his latest terrarium. To the best of Isaba-Ra's knowledge, tending the plastic bubble, and the miniaturized likeness of Hudathan countryside that lay within, was the only form of recreation that Poseen-Ka allowed himself. It seemed ironic that the aspect of Poseen-Ka's personality that most humans could understand was the one that left him vulnerable to assassination.

Careful to make no sound, he brought the energy pistol up, aimed it at the back of the Hudathan's head, and put his finger on the trigger. This was the moment that he'd planned for, when he would kill the enemy leader, weaken the fleet, and reduce the possibility of a Hudathan victory. Because while the fleet had plenty of capable officers, none of them was on a par with Poseen-Ka.

But the spy couldn't bring himself to pull the trigger. Because in spite of the fact that the sector marshal had the blood of countless innocent sentients on his hands, Isaba-Ra liked and respected him. The pistol wavered and was withdrawn. Isaba-Ra slid the panel closed, tiptoed out of the galley, and into his office. He was in the lift tube on his way to the flight deck three minutes later.

The process of signing out for a training mission, peeling away from the fleet, and running like hell turned out to be a lot easier than Isaba-Ra thought it would be. But the Hudathans were known for strict discipline, and when the prescribed number of interrogatories brought no response, fighters were dispatched to bring him back.

The spy thought about killing some of them, but knew that it wouldn't make any difference, since the fighter didn't have enough range to reach a Confederacy outpost. So he looked out through the canopy, took aim on a star, and ignored his pursuers.

Poseen-Ka was in the process of placing a tiny cabin next to a gunmetal gray lake when the news arrived. Nagwa Isaba-Ra, the best aide he'd ever had, was dead.

27

Victory at all costs, victory in spite of terror, victory however long and hard the road may be; for without victory there is no survival.

*Winston Churchill
To the House of Commons
Standard year 1940*

Planet Algeron, the Confederacy of Sentient Beings

Enormous though it was, the wardroom aboard the battleship *Invictor* was packed with officers. It was a long, narrow room filled with theater-style seating. Looped holos of famous naval battles, all against the Hudathans, graced the slightly curved bulkheads. Most of the audience were of human stock, but Sergi Chien-Chu saw others as well, including a contingent of hard-looking Ramanthians, and a scattering of Naa. They were the most visible evidence of his efforts to broaden membership in the Confederacy's armed forces but not the most important.

No, there were thousands of Trooper IIIs to consider, with their melding of sentient and near-sentient life-forms, the Say'lynt in their spacefaring swimming pool, and a host of races busily producing the ships, weapons, and materials required by those capable of physical combat. And, thanks to the Hudathans' ruthless extermination of even the most helpless civilizations, their suffering was widely known. As a result, the resentment Anguar feared failed to surface, all the races felt a sense of partnership, and the Confederacy had been strengthened rather than weakened.

As the senior officer of LEGCOM Algeron, General Ian St. James had accepted the role of moderator, and launched into the inevitable introduction. Chien-Chu heard his name surface in the ocean of words and forced his mind to the task at hand. He waited for the applause that nearly always followed the list of his accomplishments, stood, and made his way to the podium.

Although everyone present had seen him on countless news vids, many had never seen him in person, or in *this* person anyway, since his new, mostly cybernetic body was at odds with the rather portly version that had preceded it. He wore the uniform of a vice-admiral. The room hummed as the officers marveled, joked, and commented on his blond good looks. Chien-Chu understood and smiled from the podium. A sea of faces looked up at him. "Thank you, General St. James . . . and greetings, fellow sentients. We are gathered in the name of a great cause." The words hung in the air, conversation died away, and Chien-Chu took possession of the room.

"The cause I speak of is even greater than freedom, for without survival, freedom means nothing." There was scattered applause and Chien-Chu waited for it to die away.

"Many of you have heard rumors that the Hudathan fleet is headed this way, that they mean to crush Algeron, before taking the inner planets. I am here to tell you that those rumors are true, that we are gathered on the eve of a great battle, and that everything we care about is on the line."

Some of the officers nodded soberly, others exchanged glances, and the rest stared straight ahead. They knew many would die and wondered if they would survive. Chien-Chu knew what they were thinking and responded to it. "President Anguar wanted to be here, wanted to be at your side when the battle was joined, but was overruled by the joint chiefs. Even if we lose here—and I pray we won't—the battle must go on. But my staff and I *will* stay, and while most of us are better at firing off memos than rifles, we can sure as hell make coffee."

The laughter served to relieve the tension and Chien-Chu gave silent thanks as he used his highly enhanced vision to pan the forty-second row. Most of the officers were smiling or talking to their neighbors.

Someone shouted: "Let's hear it for the admiral!" Three huzzahs rang out, each louder than the last. Conscious of how critical morale would be in the coming battle, and cognizant of the fact that he wasn't likely to elicit a better response than the one he already had, Chien-Chu brought his speech to a close.

"Thank you, not only for the cheers, but for your courage. This is the last time we will be able to assemble like this. Take what you heard, what you felt, and what you know back to your units. Tell the sentients under your command what's at stake. They will carry us to victory."

The applause was thunderous and lasted a full three minutes. Finally, after it died down, the officers stood and shuffled towards the doors. Most were cheerful, or as cheerful as they could be given the circumstances, but there was at least one exception. Captain Cynthia Harmon, commanding officer of the warship *D'Nooni Dai,* had a frown on her face. Because while all the rah-rah stuff might be fine for the others, they had something to shoot with, and with the exception of six bolt-on energy weapons, her ship was unarmed. A problem she planned to remedy.

Harmon put on her most determined "don't mess with me" expression, plowed into the oncoming crowd, and fought her way towards the stage. A group of high-ranking officers had gathered around Chien-Chu and were trying to impose their individual agendas on him when the marine biologist shouldered her way through the outer circle. "Excuse me, General, sorry, ma'am, thank you, sir . . . I need a word with the admiral."

Seeing her, and glad of an excuse to escape the gold-braided trap that he found himself in, Chien-Chu produced his best plasti-flesh grin. "Captain Harmon! What a pleasant surprise! How fare the Say'lynt?"

"Very well, thank you," Harmon replied tartly, "assuming they aren't killed before they can accomplish their mission."

Chien-Chu sighed. He should've known. His selection had been the correct one, and while Harmon would no doubt deny it, she had turned into the very thing she had once despised. A military officer. He nodded patiently. "The *Nooni* is an old ship, as I recall . . . what would you suggest?"

A number of more senior officers frowned at Harmon's effrontery but she ignored them. They had careers to consider and she didn't give a damn. Not about rank anyway. "I want missile launchers, something with a little punch, in case the Hudathans penetrate the fighter screen."

Chien-Chu established an electronic link with the ship's master computer, made a lightning-fast query, and nodded his agreement. "It shall be as you say. Four launchers were stripped out of the *Spirit of Ramantha* the day before yesterday. They're on the way. Say hello to Rafts One and Two for me . . . they help just by being here."

Harmon nodded, realized that she should've said something military, but discovered that it was too late. Chien-Chu had disappeared behind a wall of blue and khaki.

It took three hours for Harmon's gig to land on the *Invictor*'s flight deck and another thirty minutes to get clear. Traffic was that bad. But she had what she needed and the effort had been worth it. Ensign Hajin saw Harmon's smile and felt his spirits rise. If the captain felt good, then he did, too.

Lieutenant Connie Chrobuck used her glasses to draw a line across the land. The valley, which she had come to think of as *her* valley, was a broad U-shaped affair that had been cut by a retreating glacier.

The surface-to-air missile battery, also known as Delta Base, was dug in about halfway down the valley's length, where it could command a large sector of sky. It was not located near the supply dump it was supposed to protect, nor did it need to be, since the missiles it fired could engage targets up to a hundred miles away. Although most of the complex was underground, four widely spaced launchers sat on the surface, waiting for targets. Carefully camouflaged radar arrays dotted the surrounding ridges. Some were real and some had been planted there as decoys. They, along with thousands of others spread out across the planet's surface, had been networked together by means of a vast ECM-proof subsurface fiber-optic communications network. That meant that what one installation could "see," the rest could see as well, vastly enlarging the extent to which the surface defenses could be dynamically linked together.

But powerful though the SAM batteries were, they were still vulnerable to both aerial and surface attack, which was where good old foot soldiers came in. Booly's company had been assigned to defend Delta Base and they were stretched damned thin. The combat company consisted of four platoons. Two were comprised of infantry, one contained a badly mismatched set of cyborgs, and the last had been split between weapons, communications, and support, including intelligence, medical, and some hard-pressed cooks.

Chrobuck had the second of the infantry platoons and was in the process of infiltrating her commanding officer's perimeter. Or so she hoped. Her mostly Naa troops were masters at moving through this kind of country unseen and had successfully brought her to within fifty yards of the outermost minefield. The explosives were on safety, or so the Pioneers had assured her, but the thought of losing people to an accident was repugnant. Especially after the three days she had spent in Booly's village, where she had met many of their relatives. Relatives who were counting on *her* to bring their sons home in one piece.

Though she was of another race, and should have felt awkward and strange, these days spent in the Naa village had been some of the happiest Chrobuck had ever experienced. Starting with Windsweet's unprecedented welcome, and continuing with the most open-handed hospitality the young human had ever experienced, she'd been pulled into the embrace of a large extended family, which, if it had ever been shy regarding humans, had changed over the last twenty years.

Not only that, but there had been moments with Booly as well, moments when glances said more than words, when hands touched more than they had to, and bodies made surreptitious contact. It hadn't come to anything and couldn't come to anything given the nature of their relationship. But it was there just the same, like money in the bank, waiting to be spent.

"Baldy Four to Baldy One."

Chrobuck allowed herself a frown. Her supershort hairstyle had been mysteriously transformed into her call sign. She didn't know if she liked it, but knew better than to make an issue of it, since that would reveal that she cared. "This is Baldy One . . . Go."

"We found the command frequency for the crab mines and ordered them to stand down. The next countersweep

will identify the glitch ten from now. Request permission
to enter. Over.''

Chrobuck absorbed this bit of playacting and made one
last sweep with her glasses. She saw nothing out of the
ordinary and gave the necessary order: ''Permission
granted. Over.''

The legionnaires advanced leapfrog style as one four-
person fire team dashed forward, dropped to their stomachs,
and waited for the next to pass them by. It took eight
minutes and thirty-three seconds to make their way through
the minefield, reactivate the self-propelled explosives, and
start work on the chain-link fence. A variety of detection
systems had been designed to protect it, but nothing's perfect, especially when you know how to maintain and repair
it. Which is why half the platoon was inside, and headed
for the launchers, when a sentry spotted them and opened
fire. The detuned energy cannon washed them with harmless blue light and a voice came over the command freq.
*''Cease fire. Cease fire. The infiltrators have been elimi-
nated. Med check. Med check. Secure from exercise.''*

The outcome was somewhat predictable given the fact
that everyone in the company knew that an exercise was
under way. Still, it served to keep the legionnaires on their
toes, which was especially important, given the fact that a
real attack was almost certain, with life-and-death consequences for everyone concerned. That's why Chrobuck
heard less complaining than usual as the troopers made
their way down into their underground quarters, racked
their weapons, and prepared for chow. Chow she couldn't
eat because of the knot that constricted her stomach. The
dreams returned when she hit the rack. They were worse
than usual and left her tired and nervous.

All of the company's cyborgs were housed in the same
bay. There were eight Trooper IIs, a pair of quads, and one

Trooper III, although O'Neal and her analogs occupied the same amount of space normally devoted to three T-2s, a fact that had attracted the not-so-desirable attention of a cyborg known as Cassidy. O'Neal and her analogs were still getting organized when he swaggered over. All the gloss had been sandblasted off his armor, there was a patch where a high-velocity slug had torn through his pelvic area, and he boasted four hand-lettered tattoos. One was located in the middle of his chest at what would be eye level for most bio bods. It read Machines Rule. Looking at the words, and realizing how much smaller her latest body was, O'Neal felt more than a little intimidated. His words didn't help.

''Well, look what we have here, a brand-new kind of freak, complete with assistant freaks. Animal warriors, I wonder what's next? Cybernetic fleas?''

Except for the quad on the perimeter, and a pair of Trooper IIs that were out on patrol, the rest of the cyborgs were present. They laughed, not out loud the way bio bods would, but on channel 3, the frequency where most off-duty conversations took place. O'Neal sighed. It was funny the way human nature worked, the way bullies still acted like bullies, no matter what happened to their physical bodies. The fact that Cassidy was something of a freak himself made the whole thing even more absurd. She looked up into the other cyborg's vid cams. ''Save the histrionics for newbies, Cassidy, I've been around too long to take shit off the likes of you.''

Cassidy turned to his left, and O'Neal thought he was about to walk away, when he whipped right again. The spin kick came with mind-numbing suddenness. It was much faster than specs called for, suggesting that Cassidy had paid for some of the highly non-regulation battle mods she'd heard about. It gave him an unexpected edge, the kind that might work fine for a while, but could fail as well, leaving the cyborg disabled and vulnerable to attack. Not that she was likely to experience that sort of luck.

One minute O'Neal was standing and next she was on the concrete, looking up into the other legionnaire's expression-free face. She had allowed him to close with her and paid the price. Satisfaction was apparent in his voice. ''Oh, my goodness . . . it appears the sergeant was wrong. Maybe she *does* have to take shit off the likes of me. Isn't that right, Sarge?''

O'Neal was still in the process of getting to her feet when the analogs attacked. Weasel had already wrapped himself around Cassidy's legs when the weapons platforms hit the Trooper II from both sides, and the leather wings attacked his head. Fortunately their weapons had been safed or they might have killed their leader's attacker outright. As it was, he required major repairs and was placed on report for assaulting a noncom, an outcome that caused the rest of the cyborgs to resent O'Neal and ostracize her.

So, rather than slide into the company the way she had hoped to do, the legionnaire found herself isolated and alone. Well, not quite alone, since her symbiotic co-warriors needed her more than ever. Having little or no choice, O'Neal turned inwards, worked to hold the analogs together, and focused on her job. It seemed as if some things would never change.

Rior Tollo-Sa was one of three surviving members of Dagger Commando Six, an elite unit equipped and trained to penetrate enemy defenses prior to a spaceborne attack. But Tollo-Sa might as well have been the *only* surviving member, since the others were not only spread out over five hundred square land units of Algeron's surface, but had strict orders to ignore each other.

The insertion pod had functioned perfectly, the ceramic skin had burned away as it was supposed to, and carefully placed explosives had blown the device apart inside the atmosphere. Free-fall came next, followed by a long drop, and the spine-jarring thump of the number one chute.

He had felt good at first, swinging over the hills, falling towards the surface. But something, he'd never know what, had gone terribly wrong. The fabric over his head had collapsed, causing him to plummet towards the ground. It had taken every bit of the trooper's courage, every bit of the discipline that had been hammered into his head during months of training, to release the main chute, and wait for it to clear, *before* pulling the reserve. He screamed as the ground rushed up to kill him, screamed as chemicals flooded his brain, and screamed as the wind sucked the sound out of his mouth.

But then the main was gone, a computer-generated tone sounded within his helmet, and Tolla-Sa was free to pull the reserve D-ring. What followed came so quickly he had trouble remembering it. There was a hard jerk as the number two chute popped open, followed by a briefly glimpsed military installation, and the impact of the rock-hard ground.

Everything had gone black for a moment until he awoke screaming in pain, realized what he was doing, and bit down on his tongue. The enemy could hear, he knew that, but never, ever, had he felt pain like he did now. It seemed as if someone had rammed red-hot pokers into his right leg. Tollo-Sa looked down, saw the bone white splinters, knew he was bleeding, and fumbled for his belt-mounted first-aid kit.

It took only moments to find the injector's distinctive shape, drag it out of the belt pack, and slap it against his left thigh. He winced as the device squirted a painkiller-stimulant combo in through the pores in his skin, concluded that this particular pain was absolutely nothing when compared to pain it was supposed to counter, and waited for the drugs to kick in. They didn't take long.

The absence of pain felt wonderful, as did the sudden euphoria that accompanied it, but the bleeding continued. Tolla-Sa slapped a self-sealing compress over the wound, waited for it to harden, and tried to stand. He found it was impossible, lowered himself to the ground, and cut his way out of the parachute harness. Once free, he took a look around.

With the exception of an airborne creature that made its way through the air in a series of awkward-looking spurts, and a tiny, nearly invisible animal that chittered from the top of a nearby rock, there was no one in sight. Which would have seemed strange if it weren't for the fact that he'd been well under the enemy's sensors by the time the reserve chute finally opened. It was ironic to think that the same chute that had threatened his life might have saved it as well.

So, what to do? There was no point in trying to contact his comrades since chances were that they were too far away to pick up his signal and wouldn't answer if they did. No, the only thing he could do was complete his mission.

Tolla-Sa rolled over and dragged himself upwards. Like most Hudathans, the commando had excellent upper body strength, and used it to pull himself up the slope. Rocks tugged at his webbing, thorns raked his arms, and gravel shredded the palms of his hands. It was stupid in a way, this self-imposed torture, because the find-me beacon in his pack would have been just as effective in the gully, but he wanted to *see* the base the landing force would destroy, and know that his efforts had been worthwhile.

The sun had risen and set twice before the Hudathan reached the place where boulders blocked his way. Gritting his teeth against the pain that came when he stood, Tolla-Sa hopped around the barrier, eased his way through a gap in the rocks, and edged his way out onto a windswept ledge.

The sun had just peeked over the ridge to the east and sent long slanting rays down towards the surface-to-air missile installation. Tolla-Sa felt a grim sense of satisfaction, leaned back against the still-cool rock, and allowed himself to slide downwards.

It took a moment for the pain to subside enough for him to find another injector, slap it against his flesh, and settle into place. Then, having squirmed out of his backpack, and opened it next to his lap, the Hudathan reached inside. The beacon was round and warm to the touch. He pulled it out, flipped a cover up and out of the way, and pressed the button within. Nothing happened. Nor would it until such time as the Hudathan fleet arrived and demanded a response. Then the signal would go out, then the avengers would fall out of the sky, then his sacrifice would be justified.

Rior Tolla-Sa peeled a ration bar, took a bite, and watched the alien sky. It was just a matter of time.

28

When fighting a duel, the provident warrior should take care to hide a backup weapon somewhere on his person, thereby providing himself with one last chance should his pistol misfire, or sword be knocked away. A dagger or similar blade is highly recommended.

Dalo Tukla-Ka
The Guiding Hand
Standard year 1312

Planet Algeron, the Confederacy of Sentient Beings

The command center was empty except for the brooding figure of Sector Marshal Niman Poseen-Ka. The wall niche was comforting but offered little protection against the dangers ahead. His mind was absorbed by the never-ending need to balance objectives with risk. And there were plenty of risks, not the least of which was the possibility that two or more of his ships would exit hyperspace at the same time and destroy each other.

Common sense argued that if vessels entered hyperspace separately they should emerge the same way, but this was not always the case, as one commander had learned eighty years earlier, when he ordered 106 vessels to make a simultaneous jump, and lost three to collisions, an outcome that put an end to more than 400 lives and an otherwise promising career.

So, given the fact that Poseen-Ka planned to emerge from hyperspace with *thousands* of warships, the chances that something would go wrong were fairly high. Still, the Hudathan was convinced that the loss of a dozen ships, or even twice that number, would be outweighed by the advantages gained. Experience had shown that the best way to defeat the mostly human enemy was to take them by surprise, carpet-bomb their civilian population centers, and engage their military after the most important part of the battle had already been won.

But Algeron was a special case. The enemy knew he was coming, there were no civilian targets to speak of, and the Confederacy had assembled a fleet only slightly smaller than his own. Which explained why he had decided to gamble on the vagaries of hyperspace. It was critical to emerge from hyperspace with overwhelming force, to subject the Confederate navy to an attack so violent that they would be forced onto the defensive, and to seize the psychological advantage.

The potential impact on his career didn't matter to Poseen-Ka, and the possibility that *his* ship might be destroyed hadn't even occurred to him. After all, he had survived twenty years on a prison planet, and had every right to die in bed. He checked the harness that held him in place, watched time tick away on the readout over his head, and gritted his teeth. Five . . . four . . . three . . . two . . .

The ship jerked as it made the transition from hyper to normal space, the holo display blossomed like a high-tech flower, and a steady stream of reports came in. The voices were anonymous and nearly empty of emotion.

"There are one thousand seven hundred and sixty-four Confederate ships in-system. Unit actions have begun."

"Seven ships were lost exiting hyperspace; they include

the *Highland Spear,* the *Arm of Hudatha,* the *Spirit of War,* the *One True Race,* the *Glorious Purpose,* the *Enemy Finder,* and the *Defender of Truth.*''

Poseen-Ka winced as the list was read, glad that no one could see his weakness, sickened by the waste. Thousands of Hudathans had died and the battle was barely under way. Still, he had more than two thousand ships left, and they deserved every bit of his attention. The voices droned on. ''Consistent with command directive three-four-two intelligence has identified the enemy vessel most likely to carry the Confederate command. Execute attack plan 342, or hold?''

''Execute,'' Poseen-Ka said grimly, his eyes playing over the holo display in front of him. After all, the best way to kill a monster is to chop off its head, and even more so with this particular beast. The human military included some excellent leaders, General Norwood being a prime example, and he wanted them eliminated as quickly as possible. Orders went out, were acknowledged, and acted upon. A force of 243 ships separated from the main formation and went after the battlewagon *Invictor.* The voices continued and so did the dying.

The bridge crew looked strange in their unsealed battle suits, ready in case the hull was breached, but clumsy in the meantime. Chien-Chu was impressed by their obvious professionalism but concerned by what he heard via his com set. ''Fire control to bridge. There are two hundred plus bogies coming this way . . . contact twenty-three from now.''

Naval Captain ''Bloody'' Mary McGuire frowned, looked down into the holo tank, and spotted the vessels in question. ''Confirm target.''

''Target confirmed. There are no other high-priority targets in our vicinity.''

McGuire nodded. "Make sure the escorts have them, too. Standard checks on all systems. Delegate secondary armament to local control. Stand by to engage."

The naval officer turned to Chien-Chu. "Well, Admiral, it looks like the Hudathans want you and anyone else that might be aboard this ship. Can't say as I blame 'em . . . we have a task force working on the same objective."

Chien-Chu tried to appear unconcerned. His plasti-flesh face made it easier. "I'm honored. Let's provide them with a warm reception."

McGuire smiled grimly and went about the business she'd been trained for. Her words were terse. "Launch fighters." The Hudathans were closer now, and she had waited as long as she dared. The trick was to launch the fighters early enough to intercept the enemy, but late enough so they had plenty of fuel. The fighters left the *Invictor*'s flight deck five at a time, accelerated away, and joined similar craft launched by the battleship's escorts. Chien-Chu felt a sense of pride as he watched them go. The Viper-class Interceptors had not only been manufactured by Chien-Chu Enterprises, the chances were good that he'd worked on some of them himself, a more significant contribution than any he was likely to make as a play-pretend admiral.

Both sides had opened fire with long-range missiles and torpedos. Most were intercepted and destroyed hundreds of miles away but a few got through. Chien-Chu felt the deck lurch under his boots as a missile blew a hole in the ship's screens and a torpedo exploded against the hull. The holo tank flickered and came back on. Damage reports filtered in.

"Engineering to bridge . . . the ship's AI reports a pressure loss in sections P-42 through P-46. The port power routers were destroyed, backups on-line."

"Medical to bridge . . . launcher complex six suffered

collateral damage. We have four confirmed KIAs, three missing, and six wounded.''

"Com center to bridge . . . the carrier *Confederate Victory* took a hit on the bridge. She's still operational and Lieutenant Nakamura has assumed command."

McGuire had counted on the carrier to screen the flagship from some of the incoming fighters and a friend of hers had been the ship's XO. She fought to maintain her composure. ''Acknowledge message . . . confirm command. Request status.''

"The *Victory* reports twenty-five-percent readiness . . . launching now.'' And so it went, in a long litany of damage reports, casualty lists, and lost ships, until even a civilian like Chien-Chu knew that the aliens were winning the battle, or battles, since there were at least five or six major conflicts taking place within the system as a whole, with lesser skirmishes being fought in and around the nearby asteroid belt.

Then the Hudathan task force broke through the fighter screen and forced their way in. The escort ships went out to meet them but were overwhelmed by thousands of enemy attack ships. Chien-Chu's highly augmented fingers made dents in the armrests of his chair as he watched live video supplied by the fighters.

A cruiser lost her screens, took a pair of missiles up her stern tubes, and exploded. The light challenged the sun before darkness consumed it.

A fighter ran through a cloud of metallic debris, staggered, and came apart.

Two Confederate destroyers, their fighters clustered around them, blasted up towards the incoming task force. They fired in concert. A cruiser replied. Chien-Chu saw the enemy's defensive screens flare and disappear. Explosions rippled the length of the long black hull as energy beams probed for a weak spot. The fighters went in, fired their torpedos, and strafed the enemy hull. The Hudathan ship absorbed hit after hit. Then, just when it seemed that the alien vessel was impervious to the human weapons, it split in two. There was no explosion, none that Chien-Chu could see anyway, just a parting of the ways as the bow separated from the stern, and drifted away. A cloud of debris appeared, including pieces of duct work, a power grid, and what might have been bodies.

The bridge crew cheered, but their happiness was short lived as the battlewagon took multiple hits. During the next thirty minutes the Hudathans destroyed the *Confederate Victory*, two cruisers, and a troop carrier packed with marines. Chien-Chu wished he could do something, anything, to make a difference.

The first tendrils of smoke found their way out of a vent and thickened the air. An ensign coughed and sealed her suit. McGuire issued an order to a rating and turned in Chien-Chu's direction. Her face was tight and drawn. Defeat was written in her eyes. ''It's time to shift your flag, sir . . . I have a scout on standby.''

''Tell the pilot to load some wounded and get them clear,'' Chien-Chu said grimly, ''my place is here.''

McGuire nodded soberly. ''Yes, sir . . . sorry, sir, but I have orders to the contrary. Sergeant . . . the admiral is under arrest. Take him to his shuttle. On the double.''

Vice Admiral Chien-Chu had no more than seen the marine, and formulated his reply, when the *Invictor* exploded.

Captain Cynthia Harmon had never heard Commander Tom Duncan swear . . . but she heard him now. ''The double-dipped, miserable slime-sucking sonsofbitches killed the *Invictor*! She exploded!''

Harmon looked into the *Nooni*'s holo tank and saw it was true. The double-dipped sonsofbitches *had* destroyed the *Invictor*. Which meant Chien-Chu was dead, along with

McGuire, and Lord knew how many other senior officers, all of whom were *real* warriors, and therefore critical to any sort of successful outcome. She thought about the Say'lynt, how helpless they were, and knew what Valerie would want her to do. "Secure for a hyperspace shift. Enter the coordinates for IH-47-whatever-the-hell-it-is and stand by to break formation."

The nearest members of the bridge crew looked surprised and Duncan turned in her direction. He cut himself out of the intercom and addressed Harmon directly. "Run in the face of the enemy? Have you lost your mind? You'll be shot . . . and rightly so."

Harmon had learned enough about the military to know that there should have been a "Captain" or a "ma'am" somewhere in the last paragraph but really didn't give a shit. She forced herself to display the same calm exterior that had sustained her in the Pacific. "No, I haven't lost my mind. Think about the Say'lynt, Tom, think about the fact that we have fifty percent of an entire species on board! What other race has invested half of its gene pool in a single battle? It isn't fair . . . and we're taking them home."

Duncan searched her eyes, saw the determination there, and shook his head sadly. "Sorry, Captain, but that amounts to an illegal order, and I refuse to follow it. The Say'lynt are members of the Confederate Armed Forces. We're staying and so are they."

Harmon had formed the words "we'll see about that," and was just about to say them, when an incredibly bright light exploded within her head. The scientist tried to move but found she couldn't. Raft One had entered her mind. His thoughts were clear and rather stern. "Commander Duncan is correct. It would be wrong to leave while other sentients fight on. Please do not presume to make decisions for our race, or make us party to a mutiny. Valerie would *not* want you to violate our sovereignty. Besides, as long as the Hudatha are free to roam the galaxy, there will be no safety for our planet, or yours for that matter.''

The *Nooni* shuddered as a flight of missiles exploded against her screens. A klaxon started to beep. The bridge crew looked from Duncan to Harmon and awaited orders. The light that had filled Harmon's head disappeared. She tried to move and discovered that she could. The biologist blushed and frowned at those around her. It had been a long time since anyone had taken her to task . . . but Raft One was correct and she knew it. "So what the hell are you waiting for? We have a battle to fight. Let's get on with it."

Duncan nodded, grinned, and turned his attention to damage control. It wasn't especially logical, but he respected Harmon, and was glad she had command.

Poseen-Ka was secretly pleased. So pleased that he had permitted his steward to bring a simple meal. He kept one eye on the ever-changing holo tank while he ate. The battle had gone better than what even his most optimistic scenarios had projected. His forces had scored more than three hundred confirmed kills while losing only half that number themselves.

And making a good situation even better was the fact that they had destroyed what had almost certainly been the human flagship, leaving the monster to flail about without benefit of its head. This accomplishment would have been even more notable had it not been for the fact that the humans seemed blessed, or cursed, depending on how you looked at it, with a never-ending supply of leaders. No sooner was one killed than another popped up to take his or her place. A norm that stood in marked contrast to his own culture, in which leaders protected their power, and did everything they could to eliminate potential rivals. A stupid and rather shortsighted tendency, but one he had grown used to. A voice that Poseen-Ka recognized as belonging to an intelligence officer sounded in his ear.

"The enemy's forces are fully engaged. The computer progs look good for Phase I of the ground assault."

Poseen-Ka felt the ship vibrate slightly as the starboard missile launchers were fired. Phase I of the ground assault plan called for an orbital bombardment of the primary ground targets. He gave the necessary order. "Permission granted. Implement Phase I."

Although Chien-Chu had never lost consciousness, the explosion, followed by the wild tumble through space, had left him dizzy and disoriented. He looked around. Algeron was a pale disk against which blast-torn hull plates, ruptured solar collectors, mangled consoles, and other, less identifiable debris were silhouetted, drifting in their own individual orbits. Hundreds of lesser items, including hand comps, coffee cups, fire extinguishers, and what looked like a severed hand were visible as well.

Something bumped Chien-Chu's shoulder and he turned to find himself peering through a blood-spattered face plate. The technician's suit had been holed, resulting in a violent decompression. What was left looked like something out of a nightmare. Chien-Chu screamed, heard no sound, and pushed the body away. Wait a minute . . . how could he push the body away? Or do anything else, for that matter? Especially since he was dead?

Space-suited hands came up, passed through the open face plate, and touched his plastiskin face. That's when Chien-Chu remembered: cyborgs need some air, but not very much. They can thrive in a vacuum. As he had proved time and time again while welding. In fact, the only reason he had agreed to wear space armor was to set a good example, and appear more human. An excellent decision, since the suit boasted a com set that was superior to the one in his head, and had an on-board propulsion system.

The industrialist checked the emergency freq, and discovered that hundreds of people were in the same fix that he was. Some of them had been drifting for quite a while, and were running out of air. They had priority for rescue and rightly so. It would be hours before his number came up, assuming the search and rescue crews lived long enough to find him, which looked less and less likely. Lights flared as a ship fired its energy cannons. Chien-Chu turned in that direction, called on the suit comp for instructions, and did what he was told. The result was clumsy but serviceable. He spurted forward. The ship, a huge, awkward-looking affair, grew larger.

Rebor Raksala-Ba had been dreading the moment when he and his comrades would be scattered over the planet below. The orbital bombardment had lasted for little more than a single planetary rotation before the Regiment of the Living Dead had been ordered into action. As they fell, their ball-bearing-shaped entry capsules glowed pink and the friction wore them thinner.

The cyborg heard a series of short beeps, followed by a steady tone . . . and knew that the humans had painted his capsule with radar. By now they were firing up into the sky, killing Hudathans as fast as they could, not knowing or caring about his particular fate. Raksala-Ba found the thought both comforting and disturbing as he confronted the fact that he, the most important person in the universe, had been reduced to little more than a blip on a screen. He prayed that the computers would select someone else, someone like Assistant Dagger Commander Gudar Kabla-Sa, who was a major pain in the ass and deserved to die.

The capsule rocked as an antiaircraft missile detonated nearby. Raksala-Ba's on-board computer informed him that the entry vehicle had started to disintegrate. The warning preceded the event by five seconds. The chute popped open, slowed the cyborg's fall, and provided sufficient stability for him to deploy his wings. The wings were a recent addition, thought up by some half-wit who would never have to use them, intended to provide the cyborgs with ''enhanced battlefield mobility,'' which translated to more hang time, and left them exposed to additional ground fire.

The regiment had experienced technical problems during training, so Raksala-Ba was grateful when the chute was released, and his wings were extended. He banked to the right, vectored onto one of the beacons the Pathfinders had planted, and swung into a ragged-looking formation. Other troopers, those who had survived the antiaircraft fire, did the same. Together they wobbled through the thin mountain air and dropped towards the valley below.

Raksala-Ba recognized their objective as a surface-to-air missile battery, one of many scattered across the planet, and saw the craters left by the orbital bombardment. The fact that many of the shell holes overlapped each other provided evidence as to the intensity of the attack. The humans would be eager for revenge, but the cyborg took comfort from the fact that ship-class missiles were expensive, and the enemy would be unlikely to spend one on him.

It didn't take very long for the thought to generate some bad luck. Four carefully camouflaged gatling guns opened fire along with computer-controlled energy cannons and crew-served automatic weapons. Cyborgs started to die. Kabla-Sa lost a wing, swore, and corkscrewed in. Others met similar fates. Raksala-Ba noticed that some fired all the way down while others screamed in fear. The Hudathan wondered which kind he was but didn't really want to know.

Ridges rose around them, Raksala-Ba saw a Pathfinder and wondered why he was sitting on a ledge. The bio bod gestured respect and vanished upwards. The ground rushed up to meet the cyborg, his wings fell away, and the real battle began.

Due to the fact that the *Nooni* was the only ship of her kind in-system, and didn't exhibit the physical or electronic characteristics necessary to generate a high threat index, she had been largely ignored. But with the battle under control, and a clear numerical advantage, the Hudathans were free to engage secondary and tertiary targets. Targets such as the big, slow Colony-class ship, which, after sustaining more battle damage, had only limited mobility.

A pair of fighters made a run down the port side and Harmon felt the command chair shudder in response to the torpedo hits. The hull was thick, thank God, thicker than those provided to newer vessels, but far from invulnerable. Due to the fact that the Say'lynt habitat took up nearly 86 percent of the *Nooni*'s mass, the ship had 70 percent fewer airtight compartments than most vessels her size, and could be destroyed with a single well-placed shot.

The missile launchers promised by Chien-Chu had failed to materialize, which left Harmon and her crew with little more than some overworked energy cannons and some jury-rigged slug throwers. Still, the gun crews had destroyed a fighter fifteen minutes earlier, and were doing the best they could. A chief petty officer touched her arm. "Captain?"

Harmon snapped at him and immediately regretted it. "Yes, Chief? What do you want?"

The CPO had been in the Navy a long time and wasn't about to be intimidated by a reservist. He had bushy eyebrows and peered out from under them. "An officer came in through the main airlock. He claims to be Vice Admiral Chien-Chu."

Harmon sat up in her seat. "What? That's impossible!

Chien-Chu died when the *Invictor* exploded. No one could have survived.''

"A cyborg could," the chief said evenly. "Although he had one helluva time catching up with us. The admiral requests permission to join you on the bridge."

The *Nooni* shook as she absorbed the brunt of another attack. Orders were given and a steering engine went off line. "Permission granted," Harmon said irritably. "Send a couple of marines. I know Chien-Chu personally, and if this jerk is an imposter, I'll throw him in the brig."

The *Nooni* didn't *have* a brig, not a proper one anyway, and the chief had seen Chien-Chu on video, but saw no reason to mention that. He left the bridge, found Chien-Chu, and snapped to attention. "Permission granted, sir. Through that hatch, and up the ladder."

The industrialist nodded and made his way to the bridge. Harmon recognized him and came to her feet. "Admiral Chien-Chu! It's *you!*"

"None other," Chien-Chu agreed calmly. "How are we doing? How many ships have the Say'lynt immobilized?"

Harmon shrugged helplessly. "None. I requested permission to launch a psychomotor attack on three different occasions and all of my requests were denied."

Chien-Chu felt his nonexistent stomach knot with anger. "*Who* denied your requests?"

"Overall command has changed hands three times since the *Invictor* was destroyed. The flag shifted to a captain named Zimmer."

Chien-Chu winced in response to the casualties and the person who had assumed command. Zimmer was elderly, ill, and by some accounts addicted to painkillers. In spite of the briefings he'd received regarding the Say'lynt and their capabilities, he had assumed they were useless. The decision was obvious. "I'm assuming command. Get Zimmer on-com and tell him that the reports of my death were somewhat premature. Pass the word to the fleet. Order the Say'lynt to take control of as many Hudathan ships as they can hold for a sustained period of time. Execute.''

There is, Poseen-Ka concluded, something especially satisfying about a pleasure long delayed. The vast majority of his adult life had been spent fighting the humans, and now, as he passed out of his prime and into his latter years, victory was finally at hand. It felt right somehow, like the end of a well-told story, when all the pieces fit together.

Yes, he decided, the years of hardship and privation had been worth it. The battle was his. Even now the *Death Dealer* was cruising through what remained of the human fleet, throwing her considerable weight behind lesser vessels, while administering the occasional coup de grâce. It was an excellent time to tour the ship and congratulate the crew.

The sector marshal released his harness, stood, and headed for the hatch. At that moment a powerful but invisible force took control of his body and froze it in place. He didn't know it . . . but the marines had landed.

The battle began in darkness, as ghostly green blobs appeared in night-vision goggles, computers fed firing coordinates to hard-wired brains, weapons cycled to ready, and fingers rested on triggers.

Many, perhaps most officers would have been satisfied to hunker down within the perimeter and wait for the enemy to attack, but Booly went out to meet them. He had a variety of reasons, not the least of which was the fact that the Hudathan bombardment had blown a hole in the northernmost section of the minefield, providing the enemy with access to the interior fence. Of course some self-deploying crab mines and computer-controlled automatic weapons could have been used to at least partially close the gap. No, the real reason Booly took his company out was because he thought he could win. And why not? His troops knew the terrain better than the enemy, were used to the never-ending shifts from daylight to darkness, and were well trained. All of which meant that it was worth a try.

The wing-equipped cyborgs had been a surprise, but not a disastrous one, since they made wonderful targets, especially after they landed on the flat ground towards the north end of the valley, and were bunched together.

Booly smiled grimly as explosions strobed the darkness and a line of 155-mike-mike artillery rounds walked their way through the enemy lines. The legionnaire thought about being scared but didn't have the time. There was too much to do. The first step was to have what remained of the minefield temporarily deactivated so that he and his company could pass through. Once outside he sent a second order and the explosives were rearmed.

All of the Trooper IIs were equipped to carry a bio bod on their backs, and Booly rode a Trooper II who insisted on the name Reaper, and seemed to enjoy his job. Not typical, but not uncommon, either, as there have always been those men and women who glory in the life-or-death nature of combat.

Gravel crunched under Reaper's steel pods as the cyborg carried Booly forward. Heat radiated away from Reaper's back and warmed the legionnaire's chest. He found his mouth was dry, his knees were weak, and he had a sudden desire to urinate. He needed something to do, something to take his mind off the very real possibility of his own death, so he jacked into the T-2's more powerful com system. The lack of unauthorized traffic pleased him. Radio discipline was important especially now. One of the SAM launchers had been destroyed during the orbital bombardment but three survived. They swiveled towards the east, steadied on a target, and fired together. He heard the whoosh of displaced air followed by a roar as twelve missiles accelerated away. The legionnaire resisted the temptation to look and thereby sacrifice his night vision. Booly blessed the artillery fire that passed overhead and dreaded the moment when it would end.

Raksala-Ba cursed the incoming artillery fire and prayed it would end soon. This was worse than training, worse than Jericho, and worse than his dreams. The ground shook under him, hot metal screamed through the air, and clods of dirt rained down on his back. Someone whimpered and a noncom took his name.

The *good* news, if the term had any real meaning in his present circumstances, was that the enemy had come out to meet them, and had little choice but to call off the fire mission or suffer the effects of it themselves. And while the humans were notoriously stupid, there was no reason to think they were *that* stupid, so the pounding would almost certainly end.

And end it did, so close to Raksala-Ba's thought that he wondered if the two were somehow connected, and dismissed the idea as superstitious nonsense. Orders entered his hard-wired brain. They were clear and concise. "The humans are approximately five hundred units forward of our position. The aggressor force consists of cyborgs reinforced with regular troops. We beat them before and we can do it again. Attack and show no mercy."

Raksala-Ba stood, looked left and right, and saw his comrades do likewise. The sun had risen. Water vapor drifted away from their backs and dirt fell to the ground. The cyborgs looked like an army of corpses rising from their graves. They looked, Raksala-Ba thought, like the name they'd been given. He felt a sense of pride. The Regiment of the Living Dead had never lost a battle and *would* never lose a battle. The thought filled him with confidence and he followed the others into still-steaming shell craters.

"Corporal Waterfind here, Lieutenant . . . we've got three-zero, repeat three-zero geeks inside the wire, and they're headed for—" A burst of machine-gun fire cut the legionnaire short and served to confirm his report.

Chrobuck wanted to scream "Where the hell did the sonsofbitches come from?" but managed to restrain herself. While Booly had led the rest of the company to meet the Hudathans she'd been left to defend the base, an assignment she had objected to and argued against. But there had been no escaping the calmly stated questions.

What if the counterattack failed? What if Booly was flanked? What if his force needed a line of retreat? Some sort of reserve was critical, and since Chrobuck was the only combat-experienced officer that he had, she was the obvious choice.

So it was Chrobuck, and not someone else, who had to cope with the fact that thirty Hudathan troopers had found their way in through the defenses and, based on information provided by multiple sensors, were busy attaching explosives to the number two launcher.

The temptation to focus on the *wrong* thing, i.e., how they had gotten through the bases's defenses, rather than the *right* thing, i.e., how to kill them as quickly and efficiently as possible, was nearly overwhelming, but Chrobuck forced herself to do it. She grabbed her assault rifle, barged out of the security center, and pounded downside hall. She shouted orders into the boom mike and dies hit-

"We have geeks inside the wire! I re̶ ̶ ̶endlies̶ the wire! Button up and watch your̶ ̶on Force One will ting the surface three from no̶ẋ . . . two will standby and assemble at the top of sh̶ ̶ await orders."

A substantial portion of the reaction force crammed themselves into the elevator with her and were still donning their body armor, checking weapons, and running com checks as the platform rose towards the surface. Chrobuck found herself squeezed into a corner as cyber techs, com operators, and cooks crowded in around her.

The elevator came to a stop, the troops located towards the front of the platform burst through the doors, and Chrobuck followed. There was no way to know if the Hudathans were any good at monitoring the Legion's communications, but they had tons of captured equipment, so it seemed safe to assume they knew how to use it. Chrobuck used hand signals to divide her troops into three fairly equal groups and sent them out towards launcher number two. She led the first squad herself and made contact within seconds.

Four Hudathans appeared from behind a sensor housing and opened fire. Slugs blew air into Chrobuck's face. The longer they delayed the humans, the more time the demolitions team would have to finish their work. Chrobuck fired from the hip and saw a Hudathan collapse. A legionnaire screamed, grabbed her knee, and fell.

The second squad arrived and opened fire. The Hudathans staggered under a hail of bullets. They fell over backwards and landed in the bomb crater behind them. More troopers rose to take their places and Chrobuck felt bullets thud against her armor. She fell, made it to her feet, and stumbled forward. She remembered Jericho, remembered how it felt to die, and screamed into her microphone. The ___ heard, joined the primal scream, and followed her ___ massed autom___ ___mans staggered under the impact of ___ Some made it to the ___ fire, and many of them died, but troops below.

___ ___m and fired down into the

This was something that only a handful of veterans had faced before, an in-your-face infantry assault at close quarters, by troops who kept on coming. The Hudathans reeled under the force of the assault, broke, and ran. They didn't get far. The legionnaires had no mercy for those who had sterilized entire planets. They fired until all of the enemy troopers were dead. Chrobuck had released an empty magazine, and was about to replace it when an explosion knocked her off her feet. Launcher number two was gone.

Sector Marshal Poseen-Ka struggled against the invisible bonds. They had held him captive for what? Two hours? Three? It seemed like an eternity. An eternity during which he'd seen the course of the battle change right in front of his eyes, because while the crew had been immobilized, the ship's AI had continued to function, as had the holo tank.

Having sprung their surprise and immobilized one-third of the Hudathan fleet, the humans had followed up in the same way that Poseen-Ka would have, with an all-out attack on the unaffected ships. And in spite of the casualties suffered earlier, the Confederate forces had proved themselves more than a match for what remained of the sector marshal's forces.

Slowly but surely, the humans had dissected his carriers and cauterized his cruisers, until that portion of the Hudathan navy held captive was stronger than the part that was free, an accomplishment enabled to some extent by Poseen-Ka's own subordinates, who, afraid that they might make a mistake, did nothing at all.

Through it all Poseen-Ka struggled against the force that held him in place, focused his considerable will on breaking free, and felt a series of small, almost imperceptible loosenings. Loosenings that he had stretched, and stretched again, until he regained partial use of his arms and legs.

The Hudathan had been mystified at first, terrified by the

new weapon the Confederacy had invented, until the truth had dawned. Back during the first war, as his fleet had swept across the mostly Human Empire, he had paused over a planet covered with water, occupied by creatures who used their minds to take control of a low-orbiting space ship.

General Norwood had been his prisoner then, and agreed to serve as a sort of go-between. And he, fool that he was, had spared the ocean-dwelling sentients, reasoning they could be killed later on, after the Academy of Scientists had studied them. But that, like all the mercies he had mistakenly indulged in over the years, had been an error. Some clever and resourceful mind had remembered the creatures, had seen their potential, and put them to use.

Poseen-Ka used his rage as a lever, applied it with all his might, and finally broke free. It still felt as though he was walking through gelatin, but he was free enough to move. It took every bit of strength he could muster to access the ship's AI, and having done so, to request the coordinates of all ships that were capable of carrying a large quantity of water.

The computer produced three possibilities, and the sector marshal chose a strange, one-of-a-kind vessel as the most likely candidate. His choice was confirmed when further analysis showed the ship in question had become the nexus of fleet-wide communications.

With that accomplished, Poseen-Ka used brute strength to force his way through corridors full of eye-bulging manikins, down an empty lift tube, and into the ready room, where his space armor was stored. Zippers, seals, and closures, which should have been easy to operate, had been transformed into monsters that had minds of their own. It was as if they *wanted* him to lose, *wanted* to drain him of energy, although he couldn't think why.

Finally, almost exhausted from the effort required to don

his suit, the sector marshal made his way out through the lock and onto the flight deck. A senior crew chief stared at him, fought to break the unseen bonds, and flapped his arms up and down. The Sector Marshall wanted to help but feared that an attempt to do so would be unsuccessful, and consume what little energy he had left.

Poseen-Ka ignored the pilots and technicians who tracked him with their eyes, placed one incredibly heavy foot in front of the other, and climbed the roll-away stairs. A pilot stood poised at the top and made grunting sounds. The sector marshal squeezed past. The trip from the lock to the control room lasted hours, or at least seemed to.

Then, having forced himself to remember controls he hadn't touched in years, Poseen-Ka fired the shuttle's engines, gave himself permission to launch, and blasted towards the steel-framed stars. The target lay somewhere up ahead. He would find the waterborne aliens and kill them.

Booly had assigned one Trooper II to supplement Chrobuck's security forces. That left seven T-2s, two quads, and the single T-3 to tackle the best that the Hudathan cyborg corps could throw their way. They approached the enemy in what academy textbooks called "an open-U formation," and the Naa referred to as "killer horns."

The idea was to make contact with the Hudathan flanks first, while directing a withering fire up the center. With that in mind, three T-2s had been assigned to the left side, four had taken positions on the right, with O'Neal and her analogs holding the center. A pair of quads, one located to O'Neal's right, and one to her left, completed the formation.

Booly, along with the company's bio bods, brought up the rear. They ran to keep up and paused every now and then to fire the shoulder-launched "borg killers" they'd been issued. The conflict was little more than a head-to-head winner-take-all display of brute strength with cyborgs on both sides playing key roles.

Raksala-Ba gave thanks that the artillery attack had stopped, zoomed through the smoke, and panned the advancing line. He felt a hollowness where his stomach had been. His legs whined rhythmically but seemed disconnected somehow.

The artillery barrage had created a moonscape of overlapping craters. They looked like an obstacle course. Raksala-Ba tried to decide which was worse, descending down into the holes where he had protection but couldn't see the enemy, or climbing up out of them, when the enemy was free to shoot at him, but he could see them and fire back. The fact that cybernetic body parts lay scattered around the shell holes didn't make his decision any easier.

He climbed to the lip of a large crater, cursed the soil that crumbled under his pods, and peered over the top. Cyborgs to the right and left of him did the same. An order was given and they scrambled over the top. Shapes appeared through the smoke, etched themselves across his targeting grid, and became steadily larger. Firing solutions appeared down the right-hand side of his vision and priority targets took on a ghostly glow.

Most of the targets were consistent with the cyborg's expectations, but some—six, in particular—didn't match anything in memory. Two hovered in midair, two advanced like miniature tanks, one slithered along the ground, while the last dodged this way and that, making good use of cover. The objects moved as if controlled by a single mind, and when they opened fire, the results were devastating.

O'Neal saw the enemy cyborgs climb up out of the shell hole, sent the appropriate thought to her analogs, and watched the Hudathans run into a hail of lead and coherent energy. Many were killed or severely damaged. The rest seemed to falter, gain courage, and move ahead.

The noncom glanced around, saw the quads lurch up out of the broken ground behind her, and open fire with their gatling guns. The slugs flew over her head but came within inches of the leather wings who hovered above. They directed screams of animal outrage through the interface and turned towards their attackers, a stupid thing to do since they were heavily outgunned. O'Neal fought to control them. "No! Do not fire! They didn't mean to hit you. . . ."

Raksala-Ba gave thanks for whatever it was that had distracted the enemy. He fired and experienced a powerful orgasm as a Trooper II exploded.

Dirt fountained around O'Neal as the enemy opened fire. Something hammered against her legs, knocked them out from under her torso, and left the legionnaire staring at the sky. The microprocessors that controlled the lower part of her body sent pain through her feedback systems and were suppressed by her battle comp. The noncom projected herself up to the battle disks, saw what lay ahead through their vid cams, and ordered the analogs forward. The quads, gatling guns still firing, lumbered by, their footsteps shaking the ground.

The enemy cyborgs were in the open now. They fired as they came. Still linked with the leather wings, O'Neal saw the borg known as Reaper fall, saw Booly jump clear, and urged her analogs to fire. They did, and the effect of their combined weaponry, along with their maneuverability, made the necessary difference. The enemy line paused, wavered, and fell apart.

Raksala-Ba couldn't believe the way his arm flew off, the way something smashed through his torso, the way that his head flew through the air, landed, and bounced towards the enemy. Darkness came and was supplanted by primitive black-and-white vision as the emergency power supply located at the base of his heavily armored brain box kicked in. So he lived long enough to see the sun, the quad that made it disappear, and the disk-shaped foot that descended towards his face. It was then, in the split second before he died, that Raksala-Ba remembered the first time he'd been killed, and wished it had been the last.

Captain Cynthia Harmon didn't take the threat seriously at first, not after surviving countless fighter attacks, and the missiles fired by larger ships, the most recent of which had holed the engineering spaces, just missed the habitat, and left the *Nooni* hanging motionless in space. But Duncan was insistent and she gave in. "All right, Tom, a Hudathan shuttle is headed this way, so what's the big deal?"

Duncan was used to Harmon's sarcasm by now and ignored it. He issued an order to the ship's AI and pointed towards the holo tank. "Watch this."

Harmon watched as every object represented in the holo tank went into reverse. It seemed silly at first, and the scientist was about to ask Duncan what he was doing, when she saw the shuttle back its way into a Hudathan ship, and not just *any* ship, but what had previously served as their command vessel, until the Say'lynt seized control. She was shocked. "But that's impossible!"

"Tell the pilot that," Duncan said grimly, "because he thinks he can do it. The AI projects impact seven from now."

Harmon watched the holo fast-forward and drop to normal speed. The shuttle was represented by a small red delta and it looked closer than before. "Impact? He plans to ram us?"

"I think that's a distinct possibility," Duncan said dryly. "I advise that you notify the admiral, call for help, and put every weapon you can on the shuttle. The pilot knows about the Say'lynt and is willing to die."

Harmon glanced at Chien-Chu. The industrialist cum

military leader had taken the third officer's chair and was locked in a discussion with senior members of the fleet. She released her harness and got to her feet. "No, *you* tell the admiral. I have a Hudathan to kill."

Poseen-Ka stared straight ahead, partly because that was his direction of flight, and partly because it required effort to turn his head. The force was growing stronger all the time. Because the sea creatures were closer? Perhaps, but it didn't matter, because knowing wouldn't make any difference. That, when he thought about it, had been the purpose of his life. To destroy those who could bring harm to his race, to impose order on chaos, to make a difference. And this, his final blow, would free the fleet to complete that work.

Poseen-Ka watched as a spark of light grew into a large globe-shaped ship. Sunlight played across the surface of its hull and stabbed the darkness around him. The Hudathan wanted to jink from side to side, wanted to take evasive action, but couldn't find the energy. The shuttle bored in.

The turret had suffered a hit but the AI claimed it was operable. Harmon worked her way inside, freed a dead marine from the control chair, and took his place. The body drifted out through the shattered canopy and kept pace with the ship. Harmon adjusted the harness to fit her smaller body and wondered why her breathing sounded so loud. Then, secured to the chair, she took control of the weapon.

The sight swung down in front of her helmet. It took a moment to find the enemy vessel and lock on. The shuttle was steady, which was good, but the nose-on approach made for a small target, and would require some skill.

Harmon stomped on the right foot pedal, felt the cannon swivel in the direction, and swore when the grid stopped six inches short of the target. Something, a piece of metal or plastic, had jammed the track. Two extremely precious minutes were consumed freeing herself from the harness, finding the chunk of debris, and pulling it free.

Other weapons were firing by now, crisscrossing the area around the shuttle, but to no effect. Harmon swore, clipped the harness into place, and stomped on the right-hand pedal. The cannon obeyed this time, stopped where she wanted it to, and spit bolts of coherent light.

The energy bolts looked like blobs from Poseen-Ka's perspective, and came his way with what would have been mind-numbing speed, had his mind been free to do as it wished. But it was elsewhere when the shuttle exploded, elsewhere when the body it had occupied was vaporized, safe within the memories Raft One had called forth.

Poseen-Ka looked, concluded that the village looked no different than it had during his childhood, and ran down the cobbled street. It felt good to be home.

Harmon felt a sense of exultation as she watched the enemy shuttle explode, quickly followed by a stab of fear, as large chunks of alien metal tumbled in her direction. The scientist's eyes widened as her fingers fumbled with the harness release. It worked, but too late, as a large chunk of black fuselage hit the weapons emplacement and smashed the biologist's body.

Harmon had expected pain, darkness, or nothingness, anything but a warm sandy beach and softly surging surf. The voice came from somewhere in front of her. ''Come on! Hurry up!''

The voice belonged to Valerie, *her* Valerie, and Harmon's heart leaped with joy. She ran into the water, felt it close around her, and swam towards her friend. The sun was warm and there was no darkness.

29

... And so, having committed grave crimes against sentient life, the Hudathan people are hereby sentenced to imprisonment within their own system, until such time as they are judged fit for admittance to interstellar society.

*The Confederacy of Sentient Beings
Resolution 2596/1089.8
Standard year 2596*

Planet Earth, the Confederacy of Sentient Beings

Moolu Rasha Anguar checked to make sure that the exo-skeleton was operating properly, forced his facial muscles into the semblance of a human smile, and stepped out into bright sunshine. The day was beautiful by human standards but warmer than he liked. The president looked out onto thousands of upturned faces, a scattering of tall, skinny trees, and a circular lagoon. A breeze swept in from the ocean, roughed the surface of the water, and sent wavelets lapping at the beach.

A battalion of Trooper IIIs, their analogs arrayed around them, crashed to attention. Platoon Leader Lieutenant O'Neal frowned as Frim and Fram sent waves of boredom her way, bullied them into submission, and scanned the ranks before her. They were perfect. Life was tolerable.

The applause built and continued as cameras swooped in to capture the president's image and send it out to the billions who watched from their homes. Anguar had appeared on twenty-seven planets, dispensed thousands of medals, and the victory tour was only half over. And while he hated the endless speeches, tributes, ceremonies, and monuments, he loved the wild diversity of the citizens who came to see him, resplendent in their multicolored skin, fur, feathers, and scales, noble behind their beaks, noses, and antennas, strong on the legs, arms, tentacles, and wings that had won the war.

Anguar gloried in the fact that all of them were obnoxiously alive, scheming and conniving to get whatever they could, eternally at each other's throats, whining about the things they lacked, already forgetful of the foe they had so recently vanquished. The truth was that they were nothing less than marvelous, and if holding the Confederacy together meant dragging his skinny ass all over the universe, then that's what he'd do. The president held up his hands and waited for the applause to die down.

General Marianne Mosby and President Marcus were seated a dozen yards away. They smiled at each other and looked down at their baby. She didn't look like either one of them—not yet, anyway—and it didn't matter in the least. The baby yawned, blissfully unaware of the scandal her birth had caused, the resulting upheaval, or the somewhat tenuous nature of the relationship between her parents. She felt warm, full, and just a little bit sleepy. There was nothing else that mattered.

A little further out, under the awning rigged to protect ambassadors from the sun, the honorable William Booly, Sr., sat with his wife Windsweet, their son Major William Booly, Jr., and his fiancée, Captain Connie Chrobuck. Both wore newly purchased civilian clothes and looked slightly out of place. It would have taken experts to tell the difference between the woman's natural leg and the one grown in the lab, or the man's biological eye and the electronic prosthesis that filled one socket. But there was no mistaking the love between them or the determination to build a common future.

Behind them, shoulder to shoulder with the Naa bodyguard named Knifecut Easykill, stood a tall, somewhat gaunt-looking human, with a face like death. He'd been a soldier once, that much could be seen from his carriage, but he looked comfortable in his civilian clothes. As others watched the president . . . he watched them.

But it was beyond the last fringes of the crowd where the most exotic spectators lay, a small portion of their snow white fibers floating just under the lagoon's surface, while the rest of their bodies extended far out to the sea. In spite of the fact that the Say'lynt were among the most decorated soldiers in the Confederacy, and the most loved, they were eager to return home. Home, where Rafts Three and Four waited, where Harmon would be buried next to her friend, and where a bugle would play taps for another unlikely hero. Anguar smiled and the ceremony began.

Many, many thousands of miles away, in a village not far from the Mongol city of Hatga, a middle-aged blacksmith lit his welding torch and adjusted the resulting flame. The man, along with his distinguished-looking wife, had moved to the area only months before. First they built a home on a parcel of land that had been owned by the blacksmith's grandfather. Then they opened a smithy. Not because they *had* to, but because they had worked all their lives, and thought of work as a privilege.

A group of children watched in wide-eyed wonder as the man applied the blue-white flame to a shattered truck axle and began the time-honored process of joining metal with metal. The blacksmith remembered his grandfather, the extent of the old man's expectations, and wondered how he'd done. Had he lived up to at least some of the old man's standards? He hoped so.

Both pieces of steel turned white hot and came together. The addition of filler metal from a welding rod completed the seam. A little boy sat back on his haunches, wiped his forehead with the back of a grubby hand, and nodded approvingly. "It will hold. You did a good job."

The blacksmith examined his work, smiled, and got to his feet. "You know what? I think you're right."

ROBERT A. HEINLEIN
THE MODERN MASTER OF SCIENCE FICTION

❑ **TRAMP ROYALE**   0-441-00409-1/$12.00

A never-before-published, firsthand account of Robert A. Heinlein's travels around the world. Heinlein takes us on a fascinating and unforgettable journey of our own planet Earth.

❑ EXPANDED UNIVERSE   0-441-21891-1/$7.50

❑ I WILL FEAR NO EVIL   0-441-35917-5/$6.99

❑ STARSHIP TROOPERS   0-441-78358-9/$6.50

❑ STRANGER IN A STRANGE LAND

0-441-79034-8/$7.99

❑ TIME ENOUGH FOR LOVE   0-441-81076-4/$7.50

❑ THE CAT WHO WALKS THROUGH WALLS
0-441-09499-6/$7.50

❑ TO SAIL BEYOND THE SUNSET
0-441-74860-0/$7.50